From Heartaches to Happiness

By
Bobbie Burgett

PublishAmerica
Baltimore

PublishAmerica has allowed this work to remain exactly as the author intended, verbatim, without editorial input.

ISBN: 978-1-61582-424-3 (softcover)
ISBN: 978-1-4489-7833-5 (hardcover)
PUBLISHED BY PUBLISHAMERICA, LLLP
www.publishamerica.com
Baltimore

Printed in the United States of America

DEDICATION

I would like to dedicate this book to all my family, beginning with my husband, Wayne, my son, Steve, and my daughter, Dina. Each of them has been my encouragement during the entire writing of this book. My sisters, Mildred Osborn, and Jackie Fritz who always said I would be published. My family is precious to me and this is my way to say thanks and I love you for your support.

From Heartaches
to Happiness

Prologue

B.J. and her brother Grady had been walking for hours and were still about six miles from their house. Both were tired and night had brought an unexpected chill in the air. B.J. was fourteen and Grady was only eight.

"How much further, B.J.?" Grady softly asked as he desperately tried to keep up with his sister.

"We should be able to see the lights from the house in about two hours. Mama promised she would leave us a lantern burning outside the barn. I know you're tired and cold, and I am too, but we have to keep going."

B.J. stopped instantly and held out her arm to stop Grady.

"Shhhh!"

Both froze in their tracks, because in the trees ahead they could see the moonlight glistening off the baronets of the Union soldier's rifles. The soldiers on patrol, like most nights, were hoping to steal the local farmer's livestock. B.J. and Grady squatted down in the tall Kentucky grass and stayed as quiet as they could. B.J. grabbed her brother, and hugged him to her. She knew Grady was scared she was too. Their daddy, John Hall was off fighting the war like all able-bodied men, and B.J. had to take on responsibility that most men would have shied away from.

Time seem to stop as the soldiers got closer and closer to them. They hugged the ground and all but held their breath. The Yankees soldiers slowly went pass. Now B.J. was glad that she listened to their hired man

Joshua. Joshua had suggested they take their remaining livestock to the cave to hide them.

Joshua had been with the Hall family a long time. Joshua was a half-breed, but he was good with horses. The Halls had raised thoroughbred horses for years, even before the war began. B.J. made sure the soldiers didn't confiscate their registered stallion. Every time the soldiers came collecting for the Union cause, as they put it, Dude, the Hall's registered stallion was hid. B.J. and Grady were on their way back that night from hiding the last five horses they had managed to keep from the army.

Joshua had stayed behind, scared that the army would find him and he would end up in a Yankee uniform like so many blacks that were told they were free from slavery. Kentucky was north of the Mason-Dixon Line. The town of Bowling Green was in the southwest corner of Kentucky, but this did not keep a large percentage of the farmers and horse breeders, from being sympathizers with the South. The very cause of this war was slavery, but the Halls didn't believe in slaves. They had Joshua, but Joshua was like part of their family. John Hall had built a cabin for him to live in and he was fed and clothed for his work on the farm.

After what seemed safe, B.J. said, "I think it's safe to go now."

She and Grady started again in the direction of their home.

Back at the Hall farm, Ida Hall had been pacing the floor for hours, wondering if her children were safe. It was late, later than they planned the trip would take. Ida continued to look out first one window and then another—no sign of her children. "Lord, please keep them in Your care and bring them home safe." Ida prayed aloud.

Light from the barn could be seen by B.J. and Grady as they stumbled toward the house. B.J. almost had to carry her brother. Thank God they had made it home without being caught by the soldiers. Now B.J.'s prayers would be for God to take care of Joshua and their horses. The cave was huge and there was plenty of water in the bottom stream.

B.J. and Grady tapped lightly on the front door and waited for their Mama to open it. When Ida Hall opened the door she had a rifle in one hand. This was the only gun left in the house and it too had been hid from the soldiers.

"Come in, hurry. I know you are both wore out, cold and hungry. I've

8

got some hot stew waiting for you," Ida said as she leaned the rifle against the wall and went to the stove to dish up food for her brave children.

B.J. and Grady took off their coats, washed up and dropped in their chairs to eat. Grady was so tired B.J. hoped he would be able to stay awake to eat.

After several mouthfuls—swallowed down by hot-milked laced coffee, Ida sat down with her children.

"How did it go? Was there any trouble finding the cave Joshua told us about?"

"No Mama, we didn't have any trouble going, but we did run into a troop of soldiers coming back. We saw them in time to hide till they passed us. Did they come here tonight?" B.J. asked her.

"No, it's been quiet tonight. I've prayed for ya'll safety. I felt I should have gone with you. This war has got families separated and even fighting each other. Lord, I hope it don't go on much longer. God has made it possible for us to at least have food on our plates. Want some more stew?"

B.J. could see tears welling in her Mama's eyes and knew her Mama was worried about more than just for food. Ida Hall took her apron and wiped her eyes with one corner.

"No ma'am," Both replied knowing their food had to be rationed in order for it to last.

"Then let's get you two into bed, it's been a long hard day. Your Dad will sure be proud of you for saving our horses from the soldiers. Remember him and all the others in your prayers tonight."

B.J. nudged Grady and both got up to go to the attic to their beds. Their heads barely touched their pillows and both were asleep for the night.

Word came that the war was over at last. General Robert E. Lee had surrendered to General Ulysses S. Grant—the south had lost.

John Hall was one of the men that came home from the war less of a man than when he left. John's lower left leg had been blown off by cannon fire in one of the battles. He now walked with a peg leg, but he could walk. Some of the men John served with had to be carried on stretchers, and they would be of no good to their families in the future.

When Ida, B.J. and Grady heard the war was over they shouted, hugged each other and danced in a circle. Now came the waiting. The family prayed their daddy would soon be coming down their road home.

Joshua got word the war was over. Joshua knew crops had to be planted for the next winter, so he brought the horses and came down from the cave. Joshua plowed the fields and planted corn and oats for the horses feed. There was a garden plowed and planted. The family would have food and Joshua knew he could not wait for Mr. Hall. No telling when he would return, if ever.

Everyone was working the garden that warm June day when a shout came from someone coming down the road. Ida was the first to stand up and shade her eyes from the sun to see. Ida couldn't recognize John at first because of his limp, but she stood straining her eyes and as he came closer Ida threw down her hoe and ran to him. B.J., Grady, and Joshua followed. John Hall stopped and waited for them to get to him. With opened arms he hugged each of them. Thank God the war was finally over for this family, their loved one was home.

"This war is over and behind us; there is no need to mention what took place because of the war ever again." John told his family.

John held no ill feelings for any of his friends or neighbors, but some of them didn't see things as John did, and the war stilled lived among them in the form of hatred that festered like an open wound. John understood—lives had been sacrificed in some families, property destroyed, slaves taken from them and devastation caused by invading troops—they had cause to hate.

"Ida things will never be the same around here again. There is no money for people to buy horses and that's what we do—raise and sell horses. Let's take the children and what little we have left and go west and claim the free land the government is offering settlers."

That night at supper John and Ida told the children about his plan. The sell of their farm was completed, except for their horses, and the Halls packed what meager belongings they could carry aboard the train they would take to St. Joseph, Missouri.

Chapter 1

The Halls finally reached their first destination, St. Joseph, Missouri. The horses and trunk and what few boxes were unloaded. John Hall and B.J. walked their horses to the livery stable for boarding. Ida and Grady stayed with the household goods that were unloaded on the train platform. The new and larger city brought new and different problems. Since they didn't know anyone, they didn't dare trust leaving anything unprotected from strangers and thieves. Missouri was a northern state and there were carpetbaggers and sympathizers from both the north and south and ill feeling still existed over the war.

"Listen to me now because this is important—keep your opinions quiet about the war. People will kill people over which side they fought with and believed in." John Hall warned his family. "Anyway, we're not making Missouri our home; it was just a passing thru place until we can get set up with a wagon train going west."

After checking his family into a hotel room, John and his son went in search of information on the wagon train. They found the Wagon Master and were given a list of necessary supplies. The first and most important on the list was their wagon. After buying the wagon and harness, John and Grady went to the livery stable and bought their four wagon horses. They drove the wagon back to the hotel where Ida, B.J. and their belongings were loaded

There was a group already gathered at the outskirts of town and John was told to pull his wagon in line and remain there until their departure.

"Ida, you and B.J. will sleep in the wagon and Grady and I will sleep under it. We have got to get use to living in this small space; it will be out home for many months." John told his wife.

B.J. helped her mother with the cooking and keeping their small area clean, but it wasn't because she wanted too. B.J. would rather be seeing after her horse at the livery than cooking and cleaning.

Grady was more content during their stay in St. Joseph, there were boys his age to run and play with, but B.J. was too old to play with the smaller children and too young to sit and talk with the older ladies. B.J. was lonely and wandered further from the train than her father allowed. Her parents were not aware of the time she spent away from them. Her daily walks soon took her as far as the livery stable, where one person in particular caught her attention.

Wayne Thompson worked at the livery stable and took special interest in the Hall's horses. Wayne was older than B.J., but that didn't stop B.J. from being physically attracted to him. B.J. studied the strength of his jaw line, the chiseled cheekbone and nose, passed over the faint cleft in his jutting chin, hesitated a second on the sensual line of his mouth before lifting her gaze to his eyes. His deep blue eyes and big smile made B.J. notice him even more. Wayne knew horses and the first morning B.J. went to the stable to check on Dude, and Wayne came over to her and pretended to be interested in Dude just to get acquainted with her.

"That stallion is a lot of horseflesh for a pretty young girl like you to own," Wayne said as he swaggered up to the stall where Dude was being held.

"Yes he's a lot of horseflesh, but nothing I can't handle. I raised him from a foal and we know each other real well." B.J. answered without looking back at Wayne.

"What breed is he? I know enough about horses to know he's different from our quarter horses. He has a small head, long, slick neck, and well filled-out withers, with strong hindquarters. I know he is at least sixteen hands high and I bet he is long winded."

"So far you've described Dude perfectly. He's bred for speed and endurance. Dude is a mix of Kentucky thoroughbred and Morgan breed.

Dude is one of the best-gaited horses you will ever ride and is gentle as a lamb." B.J. bragged as she rubbed her stallion's neck.

"None of our mustangs or quarter horses comes close in comparison. Would your dad want to sell him?"

"Dude is my horse, and he is not for sell. We're taking him with us to breed and raise more like him. Dad has a mare that is full-blooded Morgan breed, and we hope from the two of them to come up with a good western horse, one that has speed as well as endurance."

B.J. left the stables proud that through Dude; she was able to get acquainted with Wayne. Now B.J. wasn't quiet so eager to leave St. Joseph.

The next day found B.J. wandering off to the livery under the pretense of checking on Dude. When she walked in Wayne only rose up from shoeing a horse and muttered, "Good morning, little lady."

"Good morning," B.J. replied, and about that time her father walked up behind her.

"B.J., don't you think you should be back at the wagon helping your mother? The stables are no place for a young girl."

"Yes sir." B.J. answered and as she left she smiled at Wayne.

Wayne returned the smile. He knew her plans had been foiled. On her way back to their wagon, Wayne was on her mind. That smile, those sparkling blue eyes and his strong arms as he lifted the horse's leg to check his shoe. The rebuttal by her dad was worth getting just to see him. Afterwards, B.J. had Wayne on her mind constantly.

That night, lying in bed she heard her parent's talking. B.J. wasn't eavesdropping, but the canvas walls of the wagon bed weren't soundproof.

"Don't let B.J. go to the stables alone. It's no place for a young girl and besides I think she has eyes for that young man, Wayne Thompson." John Hall said.

"Well, B.J. is definitely growing up, and we can't stop what is normal. B.J. will most certainly find a young man, and we will have to be prepared for it. The time is closer than you are willing to admit, John."

B.J. smiled in the darkness of the wagon bed and turned over and dreamed of Wayne that night.

Time was running out for Wayne and B.J., the train was almost ready to pull out of St. Joseph, and Wayne would be left behind. As badly as Wayne wanted to go west with the train, he couldn't. Wayne had no money for the trip, and no one could afford to take him with them. The other people, like the Halls, didn't have extra provisions; they had spent everything they managed to save just to buy the wagon and horses.

Wayne came to their camp several times during their stay to talk to John Hall about his horses and to ask about their destination. During these visits, Ida would deliberately find something for B.J. to do in order to keep her away from Wayne and the conversation. B.J. would be helping with the cooking, or schooling her brother Grady in his studies. Most young ladies B.J.'s age were married or engaged to someone. Until now B.J.'s love for horses seemed more important than young men, at least until she met Wayne. There were ways to slip from the camp without her mother knowledge and B.J. would work her way to the livery stable so she and Wayne could be alone.

Mr. Palmer, the owner was wise to her. He would watch her, smile and say, "Here to check on your horse again. Don't you trust him in our care?"

B.J.'s main reason was to seek out Wayne so they could have time together before her family left St. Joseph. Missouri.

The day the wagon train left, Wayne came to see the family off. He make a special effort to get B.J. aside to tell her that as soon as he could work and save enough money, he would be coming west to find her. B.J.'s promise to Wayne was to write him a letter as soon as their home was found and their lives were settled. B.J. told Wayne their destination was near Casper, Wyoming and North Platt River was also a possible choice.

"Watch out for all those rough cowboys in Cheyenne, I don't want any of them stealing my girl away from me."

Being called, "Wayne's girl" thrilled B.J. so she told him, "No cowboy will take me from you."

Wayne looked around and then pulled B.J. to him. His hand closed over her chin, lifting it to receive his kiss. This kiss would remain with B.J. forever. B.J. felt he had burned his brand into the softness of her lips. All she needed to do was close her eyes and she could feel his lips on hers.

The wagon-master rode down the line telling everyone it was time to move out. B.J. climbed in the back of the wagon and waved to Wayne as they began rolling out of St. Joseph. Wayne stood waving back to her for as long as he could see their wagon.

When the last wagon was way down the trail, Wayne slowly walked back to the livery stable. It would be lonesome for him now with B. J., and her family gone. Wayne made up his mind to save every penny he could earn and join them as soon as he could. Wayne had been born in St. Joseph, Missouri, but he had often wondered what it was like to live elsewhere. Wayne was the only child of Charles and Marilyn Thompson, and he lived with them until four years ago. Both his parents died of cholera. Wayne survived the disease and lived to bury his parents. Charles Thompson, his dad, was a lawyer and made good money in the booming town of St. Joseph. The railroad ended here and most everyone heading west stopped for several days to make connections with a wagon train.

Wayne grew up in this town and received as much education as the school could provide, but chose not to go back east to further his education. Wayne loved being around horses and he hung around the livery stable purposely to be close to them. There was a time when his dad and he came to a bad disagreement because of Wayne's love for horses. Mr. Thompson wanted Wayne to work in his law office as his assistant, but that was not what Wayne wanted.

When Ol' man Palmer, the owner of the stable, saw how good Wayne was with animals, he knew he had an apprentice. With a little instruction and encouragement, Wayne soon became a pretty good blacksmith.

One day a foul-mouth, dirty, near drunken cowboy came to the stable wanting his horse kept for the night. The poor horse had been ridden into the ground, it was all lathered up and limping on one of its hind legs.

"Do you want me to check that limp, he might have a loose shoe?" Wayne asked out of pity for the horse.

"Hell no, leave my horse alone. Always trying to get more money from people."

The cowboy shoved Wayne backwards and against the watering trough, causing Wayne to lose his balance and fall into the water.

Wayne climbed out ready to fight the cowboy and would have, except ol'Man Palmer came between them. Palmer took the horse's reins in one hand and Wayne by the shoulder and led them both into the barn.

"Boy, didn't you see how that hombre was wearing them guns, all tied down and slick hammered? You don't go up against someone as mean and cantankerous as that cowboy, without asking to get shot."

"He shouldn't have pushed me into that trough of water all I asked him was if he wanted his horse shod."

"You're right. He shouldn't have. He shouldn't have ridden this old horse near to death either. He shouldn't be drinking and using foul language, but he is, and it's because he's a no account who don't give a diddly damm about his animal or for any man. It's best you get a little wet than have a hole blown through you. Next time—look a man over first—if a man cares for himself then more than likely he will care for his horse. It might save your life."

Wayne never forgot that advice. Wayne cared for all horses and thought all people should too, but he had learned differently. Wayne stayed on with Mr. Palmer, shoeing horses, learning to make harnesses, mending wagon wheels, and almost anything that a smitty needed to know.

After the cholera took the lives of Wayne's parents, he had to have a place to live. The banker informed Wayne that the house they had lived in for years still had a mortgage against it and Wayne didn't make enough money to pay the notes. Mr. Palmer let Wayne live in a room at the back of the livery for free. Palmer's wife would send a hot meal each day for him and with what little money he was paid, Wayne managed to buy his clothes and boots.

Two years had passed since Wayne's parents died, and one day a big, mountain-looking man rode up to the livery, asking for Wayne. Palmer came out back to get Wayne, telling him that someone was asking for him. Wayne had no idea who it could be, but followed Mr. Palmer to the front.

When Wayne walked out, the big grizzly looking man, dressed in buckskins, held out his hand and said.

"Howdy, I'm your uncle Webster Thompson, your dad's brother. I came as soon as I heard about your folks dying. I'm sorry I didn't get here sooner. Is there anything I can do for you boy?"

"No sir, I'm fine. I live at the back if the livery and I'm working for Mr. Palmer the owner. I couldn't stay in our house; the payments were more than I could make."

"How old are you boy?" Webster asked.

"I'm almost twenty. I've trained under Mr. Palmer to be a blacksmith. One day I hope to have my own business."

Webster had a funny feeling that the old smitty was taking advantage of Wayne's predicament and was getting him some cheap labor in the deal.

"Wayne, why don't you leave this and come trapping with me? I'll buy you a good horse, and we can replenish our supplies and traps and head for the mountains. Just the two of us."

"I'd better decline, Uncle Webster. I don't know anything about trapping and anyway I love being here helping with the horses.

"Well, if I can't change your mind, how about having supper with me tonight. I'll be riding out in the morning. I can't stay in towns for long; I've slept under the stars too long."

"Supper will be great. Where shall I meet you?"

"I'll come here and you show me the best eating place in town. How about six, will you be through work then?"

After eating, Webster walked Wayne back to the livery and ended up staying the night, sleeping in one of the stalls on some clean hay. The next morning Webster nudged Wayne foot. When Wayne looked up, the big man he was fully dressed. Webster had already saddled his horse and tied on his bed-role, ready to leave.

"You take care now, and the next time I'm in St. Joseph I'll look you up." Webster said as he gave Wayne a big bear hug.

Webster didn't wait for Wayne to reply; he turned, climbed on his horse and rode out like he rode in, very unnoticeable.

Wayne realized he was in front of the livery; he had been lost in his thoughts. Wayne changed his clothes and got back to work. He already missed the Halls, especially B.J. Wayne wondered how long it would be till he was financially able to go west to her. His days would be filled with getting all the extra work he could muster up because now he needed it more than ever. Wayne had to purchase a good horse and supplies before he could head west so every penny he made he would save.

Chapter 2

The morning was beautiful, a little cool, but just right for April. B.J. found her father harnessing up their teams.

"Dad, can I take Dude for a ride this morning? He needs some real exercise and I need to get away from this train for a while."

John Hall looked up at the clear sky, felt the warm sun on his back and agreed to let B.J. go. He knew B.J. wasn't a child anymore, even though he wanted to keep her one as long as possible. As B.J. rode away, John Hall felt pride in his heart for his beautiful young daughter. Barbara Jean, or B.J., as everyone chose to call her, was tall, but well developed for a girl only sixteen. B.J. had a small waistline, nicely rounded hips, and bust that were already full and shapely. She had long auburn-brown hair, big brown eyes, and a smile that caught everyone's eye. Everyone who met B.J. remembered her smile. They liked B.J. instantly because she made others as happy as she was. Her happiness came from within her heart, and her beauty was natural and refreshing.

John Hall watched as B.J. and Dude rode away that morning, knowing in his heart that she would be fine. John had practically raised B.J. on the back of a horse, so he knew B.J. could handle Dude. This had been proven time and again on their farm in Kentucky. B.J. had raised Dude from a colt to be her own.

The Halls had been traveling by wagon train for months, and Dude and B.J. needed some time to stretch their legs—to be alone. Actually B.J. needed it worse than Dude. For days, B.J. had followed the wagon on foot or rode in it, both had her bored to death. As many people as there were in the train, B.J. was the only sixteen-year-old girl. The other children were much younger like Grady her brother and seemed too young to talk to, or be around. There was no one B.J.'s age, boy or girl, to whom she could relate, so she spent most of her time helping her mother or baby-sitting some of the other folk's smaller children. Everyone was either older and married or much younger; anyway, they had nothing in common with B.J.

B.J. had Dude in a full, stretched-out run. The wind whistled in her ears and it felt good on her face that beautiful April morning. B.J. began to slow down Dude; she wanted to have a better look at this big open country. This part of the country fascinated B.J. What the family had been told when they left their home in Bowling Green, Kentucky was true. Before B.J. was a great plateau broken by a number of huge mountain ranges. The pine forests merged with the grasslands of the rolling plains, and at the base of the mountains was the brightly colored layers of rock formation. Some of the ranges were breathtaking; they shot from the floor of a valley nearly one and a half miles seemingly straight up into the sky.

B.J. walked Dude now, cooling him and patting him on his neck to relax him from their run.

"This country is beautiful, Dude. I think I'm gonna like it here, in fact I know I am."

As though Dude understood her every word, he tossed his head up and down, and B.J. couldn't help but laugh out loud. B.J. nudged Dude sides again and he quickly went to a canter. The ride was so smooth that B.J. felt as though she was floating along lost in the serenity and vastness of the new country. B.J. thoughts went back to the day the train pulled out and the goodbye kiss that Wayne gave her. B.J. was lost in daydreaming, but was quickly brought back to the present by a strange noise. The noise startled B.J. and she pulled Dude to a complete stop, and listened harder.

What was that noise? B.J.'s memory went into overdrive trying to ascertain what the noise was and where it had come from. Sitting atop Dude and looking around, B.J. realized her foolish thoughts had carried her farther from the wagon train than she meant to go. The beautiful hills and deep canyons that she had been focused on before now separated her from her family.

Turning Dude in the direction of a slight rise, B.J. nudged him to the top. From the knoll B.J. could see in all directions. Standing in her stirrups and looking as far as she could, there was no wagon train to be seen. Sound carries in the open country. The sound B.J. heard for only an instant, sounded as though it was coming from the east of her. Slowly B.J. rode Dude down the knoll and when they reached flat ground B.J. heeled Dude to a full run, thinking she was going east toward their train.

After a long hard run, B.J. couldn't understand why the wagon train was not in sight. How far had she ridden? B.J. stopped completely trying to spot a familiar scene or something in the surroundings to assure her that she had came from this direction. Nothing looked familiar and it was impossible to get her bearings.

"Where am I? How far have I come?" B.J. asked herself.

Once confusion takes hold, fear is right on its tail, and then panic settles in, and B.J. was fighting all three now. A feeling of desperation, was telling B.J. she needed to get back as soon as she could. B.J.'s dad would surely be furious with her for being out this long. Maybe the noise was her dad signaling her to return to camp. B.J. thought she was headed to the train, but evidently she had got turned around in her excitement.

Again she reined Dude, but in the opposite direction, and heeled him again to a full run. After several miles of hard out running, there still was no train in sight. Dude was breathing hard and B.J. knew she needed to walk him to cool him. They rode in circles right there on that spot, giving B.J. needed time to think and Dude time to get his wind. At last B.J. concluded she must go back to the knoll and get her bearings from there, so she started off again, riding at a slower trot, hoping this time not to miss any land markings from before.

The further B.J. rode, the stranger the terrain became. Where was that knoll? Most of all, where was her dad, mom and brother? Panic had B.J. in its grip now and she felt like a small child, almost ready to cry. The vast land kept stretching out before her—never-ending—just going and going, but where? How could their wagon train disappear? Where had B.J. gone wrong?

Looking around, the realization that it was only she and Dude, made B.J. tremble with fear. The day was almost gone and night would soon be on her. B.J. had to find her family before darkness settled, so she began riding again, but to where she did not know.

Chapter 3

The day had been long and tiring, so when the Wagon Master sent word down the train that they would soon be ready for night camp, it didn't disappoint John and Ida Hall. John was exhausted wrestling the team of horses and keeping the wagon out of the rough ruts in the trail. Very seldom did John Hall voice complaints about anything, but today was an exception. Little things had irritated John, and Ida had sensed it in his actions. Ida offered to relieve him, but John would not hear of it.

Grady was riding Lady, his mare and had enjoyed the day. B.J. had left early on Dude and frankly John had looked for her back much sooner. John and Ida Hall usually kept a closer rein on their only two children, but on this trip it didn't seem necessary. John knew he would see B.J. ride up almost any time now. The word came back to circle the wagons just ahead at the trees, and John sighed deeply, glad the day was over.

The wagons were circled each night because there was no way of knowing when trouble of any kind might approach. Tonight was no exception. John unhitched the two teams and took off their harness just as Grady rode up.

"Well, your timing is just right. Here, take these teams to the little branch and water them, then stake them out for some grass." John told his son.

"Ah-h-h, Pa. I always have to water the horses. When is B.J. coming back, anyhow?"

"Stop you complaining!"

Before John Hall could say anymore to his son, they heard shouts and turned to see what the commotion was. The scout who rode out ahead to more or less check the trail and also to look for impending trouble the train might encounter came riding at a full gallop, shouting at the top of his lungs.

"Indians! Indians!"

He had put spurs to his lathered horse and barely made it back to the train, because the Indians were right behind him, coming fast.

"Take those horses and get to that strand of trees. Hide them and yourself and stay there till it all this is over." John told Grady.

John turned to Ida; she was already getting his rifles and ammo out of the wagon. Together they pulled out their big trunk to use as shelter. Ida didn't appear frightened, but even if she were, John would be the last one to know.

Until now, there had been no time to think; you could only react, no time to wonder, just prepare, so the two of them did what they thought best. Ida and John ducked behind the big trunk, as the charging Indians came into view.

John turned, looking in the direction he sent Grady with their horses, but saw nothing.

"Good, Grady will be safe."

Before John could turn back, action erupted in front of them. For a stunned instant, they both looked at the painted faces of the Indians charging at them on galloping horses all spotted and painted too.

There was no time to take aim; everyone fired as rapidly and accurately as possible. Their targets were moving and a hit was accidental. The sound of guns firing was loud and nerve jolting. Ida kept John's guns loaded as fast as he fired and handed them to her. Ida rose up, reaching for another box of shells, and as she stretched out her arm, she felt the arrow hit her in the back with a sharp pain. The arrow was noiseless, but deadly. Ida slumped over the top of their trunk, trying to get up, but the arrow had done its intended damage. Ida knew she was drawing her last breath, and she wanted to say something, but her words wouldn't come.

John continued to shoot at the advancing painted-faced, whooping Indians. John extended the empty rifle, expecting Ida to have a loaded one waiting for him, but this time Ida didn't take the rifle from John's hand. John looked in Ida's direction and time stopped for him. Another arrow found its way home. John was hit center of his chest and instantly felt his life draining from him. John's last thoughts were of his two children. "Thank God they were safe."

The battle continued until the overpowering Indians claimed a victory. The Indians rode in, jumping the barricades into the inner circle, shooting their arrows and guns faster than the settlers could possible reload. Once inside the circle, the Indians really finished the settlers. It wasn't a long battle, the settlers, even though warned, was not prepared for the terrible onslaught of savages that rode into their lives.

The loud gunfire that roared in the silent wilderness so suddenly, stopped. Everybody was dead or so near dead, it was only a matter of time. The Indians rode through stripping the dead of their weapons, outer coats, boots, and hats. After plundering the dead bodies, the Indians climbed into the wagons, and with loud whoops and breathtaking yells, tore into all the supplies. Food was thrown everywhere. Once the Indians had what satisfied them, the raid was over and they swung onto their horses and took the settlers horses with them and left as fast as they had come.

The silence was deafening. Grady sat hidden in his safe place, holding as tight as he could to the last two horses. The horses had struggled, scared by the gunfire and Grady was unable to hold all five of them. There had not been enough time to tie them before the raid begin. Grady foremost thought was to keep them quiet and still like his dad had told him. Now the silence filled the air and the sun was nearly behind the overhanging rock formation he chose for a shelter. The horses stopped their struggling, and Grady realized he was shaking all over. Grady knew it was fear, even his teeth chattered so he clamped them together listening, hoping to hear his dad call him. No sound, no call for him, just eerie silence.

Grady's arm ached from tugging so hard on the reins to keep the horses in tow. He relaxed, letting them go slack. The horses dropped their heads to eat the grass under their feet. They had to be tied before it got so dark he couldn't see, but Grady was afraid to move. Grady listened intently, but heard only the loud beat of his heart and the horses crunching grass. His shaking begins to subside, so Grady eased up and tied the horses for the night. For some reason, Grady couldn't muster up the nerve to walk to the edge of the clearing to check on his parents, so he hide again, curled himself into a small knot and closed his eyes. Grady's hope was to sleep, but sleep was a long time coming.

Every noise, every chirp of an insect, every move from his horses seemed amplified in the darkness. But he was alive. Tears burned at the back of his big brown eyes, but so far he had managed to keep them there. As Grady lay curled into a ball of scared flesh, the noises of the night all around him, and wishing his dad would come for him, he finally fell asleep.

B.J. was determined to find the wagon train. Dude was tired and so was she, but B.J. kept riding, knowing she had to find the train soon. B.J. realized that she had been in the saddle all day, and she was hungry and thirsty and knew Dude had to be too. Darkness was fast approaching and B.J. had to find a place for her and Dude to stay the night. After taking a good look around, B.J. decided this was where they would stay the night. There was a cleared strand of grass just beyond the stream, so B.J. tied Dude so he could eat. Now that her mind was made up, B.J. began to unsaddle Dude. Dude's blanket would be her cover for the night, because the coolness of the night was gradually being felt. B.J. took her saddle and laid it on the leaves. The rumbling noise in the pit of her stomach reminding her she was hungry. She felt in her saddlebags for a biscuit that she had taken from the table that morning. The biscuit was hard and cold, but it tasted mighty good. B.J. saved half of it, just in case it was needed later.

The light jacket that she took from the saddlebags seemed thin, and she knew she had to make a fire. B.J. hugged herself for warmth thinking that a fire might attract wild animals or was it the opposite?

She found some matches in a tin, and picking up dry leaves and small twigs she lit one of the matches and the fire started. B.J. added larger dry limbs and after a short time had a good warm fire. B.J. walked around and gathered as much dry, dead wood as she could find for the night. Then she made several trips to the stream for rocks to form a circle for safety.

B.J. settled down to warm her hands at the fire. The fire crackling and the weird shadows it cast on the trees around her, made B.J. listen. The noise of the wind rustling the tree branches above and the insects chirping caused her heart to pump harder.

B.J. was scared. This vast, unsettled country made her seem small and insignificant. Suddenly B.J. felt a need to cover up, to become as small as possible. She pulled the saddle as close as she could to the fire, and then turned the saddle over and curled up in the bend, and with the blanket over her, she felt secure.

Each night sound grew louder and louder until B.J. finally pulled the blanket up around her ears, hoping to muffle the noises. Suddenly a howling noise pierced the night, making B.J. jump from fear. Her knees were shaking and she couldn't stop them.

"It was probably a coyote." B.J. assured herself. "But it was too close for comfort." B.J. added a little wood to the fire hoping to discourage the coyote or whatever. Afterwards she went back to her makeshift bed and tried again to stay warm and get to sleep. Eventually B.J. succeeded, because when B.J. awoke it was morning and the birds were singing.

B.J. got up cold and stiff. She started the fire at once and sat hugging the blanket around her till she warmed. B.J. knew she was still lost, and she was still scared, even if it was daylight.

B.J. sat with her knees drawn up under her chin and holding herself tightly and soon warmed up. She thought about the mornings in camp, when her mom would have hot steaming coffee laced with milk and sweetened with sugar, waiting for her and Grady. Next came a bowl of hot oats, steaming with brown sugar, and big hot buttered biscuits. Thinking of food made B.J.'s stomach start rumbling again, so she took out her hard, cold biscuit and finished it off. The rumbling stopped.

B.J. was warm and her appetite satisfied, so she got up and stretched, trying to get the kinks worked out. She walked to the stream and bent over to wash her face of the night's sleep. The reflection in the water revealed her long auburn hair needed combing.

Dude began to stir. Looking up, B.J. saw that Dude had eaten all the grass he could reach. B.J. led Dude to the stream to drink, and then saddled him. After B.J. finished, she went back to the stream and took her hat and filled it with water to put out her fire. Dude was ready to go as B.J. led him through the underbrush to the clearing. Putting her foot in the stirrup, B.J. swung herself into the saddle. Dude pranced around. The morning made him frisky and he was ready for whatever this day might bring. B.J. silently prayed that it would be a good day.

Dude chooses the gait he wanted to travel that morning, as B.J sat in the saddle thinking of their life in Kentucky, the good and the bad times. The Good Lord saw fit to watch over their family, and every time they had their blessing at meals, her dad thanked God for sparing them through those times brought on by the war.

B.J. never realized that Dude was going the direction he wanted to go, and she was just riding on his back, until Dude began acting strangely. Dude was tossing his head from side to side and then up and down. Dude sidestepped and changed his gait.

"What's wrong, Dude?" B.J. stopped and looked down to see if her horse had picked up a stone in one of his hooves. No, Dude's hooves were fine; he wasn't limping. B.J. stroked his neck, trying to settle him down, but Dude continued to act up, and B.J. wondered is something or someone was nearby. B.J. looked at their surroundings and vaguely things became familiar. This was Dude's way of telling B.J. that the sky was almost black with buzzards.

What was drawing so many of them? The buzzards were several miles away, but they were circling around one specific area. B.J. tried to calm Dude and they went in the direction of the swarm of buzzards.

"Something has to be dead or either in trouble to draw these creatures." B.J. said out loud

B.J. proceeded at a slower pace. Dude seemed to know what direction to go in and B.J. kept a tight rein on him and let him go at his pace.

The closer to the darkened sky, the more anxious B.J. became, imagining all sorts of things she would find.

"Settle down, now. I won't let anything happen to you." B.J. assured her horse. "It's probably another animal injured or dead."

Then a thought occurred to B.J. What if it was another person injured or dead? Would she be able to do anything for them? Her heart beat faster and the anxiety she felt was transferred to Dude. Slowly, ever so slowly, B.J. walked Dude closer to whatever caused the swarm overhead.

Topping the knoll, B.J.'s eyes widen in disbelief, and her mouth opened to scream, but no scream came. A hard kick of emotion hit her in the stomach and if she had eaten a big breakfast, she would have lost it "Oh God, how did this happen? I can't believe what I'm seeing." B.J. half cried.

Before her was the terrible scene of their wagon train. Some of the wagons were turned over and others were burned. People's belongings were scattered everywhere. Trunks pulled out and everything in them turned topsy-turvy, and dead bodies lay all around with flies buzzing overhead.

"Oh Lord, where are my Dad, Mom, and brother?"

B.J. got off her horse and slowly led him into all this death and destruction. Dude didn't want to go and frankly neither did B.J., but she had to find her family; maybe, just maybe, they had survived. The further B.J. went the more aware she was that this was not the case. There were dead bodies everywhere she looked. The ground was covered with men, women, and little children with arrows sticking from them. There was one woman killed holding her baby—both dead. Men killed still holding their guns. Why did this happen?

B.J. eased her way through the rubble of clothes, broken furniture, opened food, and dead bodies, so many dead bodies. She had never seen anything like this in her life and she hoped and prayed she never would again.

Where was their wagon? All the wagons looked alike to B.J., at least what was left of them. B.J. buried her teeth in her lower lip to hold back the sobs that was filling her chest and causing her to breathe rapidly. The guilt of not being there was eating at her. The tears broke loose and B.J. walked and cried, moving this way and that, trying to find anything she recognized of her family.

Finally, she found them. B.J.'s Dad and Mom lay half hidden by their overturned wagon. B.J. stood frozen and cried out loud. She had wanted to find them, but she wanted to find them alive. B.J. wanted the opportunity to explain to her dad where she had been and why it had taken her so long to find her way back. Only now she couldn't. They lay over the old trunk; her dad's arm half shielding her mother's body—arrows protruding from both.

B.J. reached down and stroked her mom's hair; it was tangled and needed combing. Her mom's body was cold and it broke B.J.'s heart. B.J. sat down and held her mom's head in her lap and clutched her dad's hand and cried for a long time.

"What am I to do? I can't exist without you two. You have been my life and I didn't get to tell you goodbye." B.J. cried aloud.

B.J. sat holding her parents until the tears stopped. She became aware of the silence around her. Suddenly B.J. thought about the possible danger she might be in. Were Indians still lurking about? Had they seen her and Dude come in? The destruction and death was foremost in her mind till now. B.J. began crying again, and her heart ached inside her chest, as she reached down and kissed them both and told them she loved them.

B.J. got up and looked around her in disbelief at the dead. The only sound was of paper rustling and the canvas whipping in the wind. B.J. heard the buzz of insects that the dead bodies were attracting, the breathing of Dude. Then, it occurred to B.J. that Grady, her brother, was not with her parents. Where could he be? B.J.'s mind was going crazy with thoughts like, what if the Indians took him with them? Why would they take Grady and kill all the over children? Then where is he?

B.J. got Dude out of sight and to safety. Since she had no way of knowing if the Indians would come back, she took no unnecessary chances. B.J. told herself that she could blend in with the other if she had too, but Dude could not, so she took Dude to a strand of trees about fifty feet off to her right and hid him. B.J. walked back among the dead bodies with the gall burning in her throat. She fought to keep it down. There she searched for Grady's body, but did not find him.

"Maybe he was in the back of the wagon." B.J. thought as she quickened her steps. B.J. opened the canvas back real careful and looked in. There was nothing but their clothes tossed in every direction. There was nothing to indicate Grady had been there. Where could Grady be? Getting out, B.J. let her eyes roam over the dead bodies lying all around.

They all looked alike, especially the children. Some were laying face down, and many were frozen in motion, like running to get away.

B.J. knew she must walk through the dead bodies again, and turn over the children who were face down. One by one B.J. turned each over enough to see their face, nausea was boiling in her stomach, but she knew she must go on. As B.J. looked she wondered again how such a catastrophe could happen. The wagons were circled; this was their protection, a type of fort for the people. The animals were to be brought into the center to keep them from running away. From the looks of things, B.J. could tell that everyone had done as they were trained.

"Why did everyone end up dead? There must have been a lot of Indians to do all this destruction." B.J. said aloud as she walked on lifting the bodies of the boys that halfway resembled Grady. She still had not found Grady and this brought mixed feelings. B.J. didn't know whether to be glad or whether to worry for Grady's safety.

B.J. went back to her Dad and Mom. With each step, her heart grew heavier and heavier. She had to get her parents buried; and then she would look for Grady again. B.J. reached down and kissed her parents again and said her goodbyes, remembering she would be with them in Eternity one day. B.J.'s tears started again as she wrapped each one in a sheet and looked around for a place to dig their graves.

Under the big cottonwood tree would be a good resting place for both of them, so she begin dragging their bodies in that direction. Now B.J. had to find a shovel from one of the wagons to dig their graves.

After what seemed forever, B.J. had a hole wide enough and deep enough for both her parents. She straightened up, she was exhausted and her arms felt as though they would drop off. B.J.'s back ached like never before, but she was almost finished.

B.J. rolled the two people she loved the most, into that hole, and cried as she lifted each shovel of dirt to cover them. Covering them didn't take as long as digging the empty hole, but it was harder. When B.J. finished, she slowly walked to the stream and carried rocks to cover the dirt and to make them a head stone. B.J. was exhausted, but in her heart she knew that compared to the fourteen years they had given her, it was very little.

Going back to the stream for the last few stones, B.J. saw something move further back in the brush. B.J. stood as still as possible, listening. She couldn't hear anything, and thought it probably a small animal. Carrying the last stones back to the grave, she saw something from the corner of her eye. Was someone back in the trees? B.J. listened but only heard her heart pounding in her chest. Then Dude neighed and B.J. knew this was his signal that he saw something too. B.J. didn't know if she should speak up or just walk back with her stones and see what would happen.

B.J. turned going back to the grave, and a familiar voice asked, "B.J. can I help you do that?"

B.J. froze in her tracks for a moment, and then turned and what she saw made her cry, except this time it was happy tears she was shedding. There stood Grady. Grady was dirty and his face was streaked by tears. His clothes were all torn and B.J. could tell Grady was still scared to death.

B.J. dropped the stones and ran toward him as fast as her two feet would carry her. They grabbed each other and hugged so tight, and held each other for the longest. Grady cried and B.J. cried. The relief of knowing the other was alive was almost more than either could handle. Both started speaking at the same time, asking, "Where have you been?"

After blurting out their answers, they grabbed each other and hugged again. Nothing mattered except that Grady was alive and with her now. Together the two picked up the stones and walked back to their parent's grave.

"I've been watching you." Grady said. "I have been so scared since all this happened that I couldn't say anything at first."

Grady tears streamed down his face and he hung his head in guilt. B.J. knew he was in shock and it was understandable after seeing all this destruction and death. When they finished placing the stones, Grady said.

"We should read from Dad's Bible."

B.J. left Grady at the grave and went to the wagon to find their Bible— the precious book her Dad had read to them from. B.J. hugged to it to her chest and walked back. B.J. had no idea what to read, but then as if God knew her need, the wind blew the pages of the open Bible and when B.J. looked down there was Psalm 121. B.J. began: "I will lift up mine eyes unto the hills. From whence cometh my help. My help cometh from the

Lord, who made heaven and earth, He will not suffer thy foot to be moved; he who keepeth thee will not slumber. Behold, He who keepeth Israel shall neither slumber or sleep. The Lord is thy keeper; the Lord is thy shade upon thy right hand. The sun shall not smite thee by day, or the moon by night. The Lord shall preserve thee from all evil, he shall preserve thy soul. The Lord shall preserve thy going out and thy coming in from this time forth, and forevermore. Amen." (KJV) B.J. closed the Bible and they stood silent for a long time.

Afterwards, they turned and walked away from the grave, not saying anything, just holding each other's hand. B.J. and Grady were sad, but each felt more secure. There were just the two of them now, and holding on was important. After a while Grady looked up at B.J.

"I wanted to stay with Dad and Mom, but Dad made me take the horses and hide with them."

"I understand." B.J. said as she squeezed Grady's hand. B.J. knew the guilt he felt firsthand because she felt it too.

A time to talk would come later, now B.J. must decide how the two of them were going to survive the night. They walked back to the wagon. There were things they would need. B.J. didn't want to scare Grady, but she was not sure they were as safe as the stillness of death presented. B.J. started gathering up quilts and blankets. Grady read her thoughts and collected some pots and pans. The two hurriedly got what they felt they would need for the night and put it in a big cotton sack. After they gathered food and put it in, B.J. tied the sack and started for Dude, Grady followed.

B.J. tightened Dude cinch strap thinking her and Grady would have to share Dude, she climbed on and reached her hand down to give Grady a lift up on back.

"You take our supplies and go on ahead. I'll get the other horses. My camp is on the backside of this strand of cottonwoods. The horses are tied there." Grady told B.J.

B. J. tied the sack to the saddle horn and eased Dude through the trees to where Grady had the other two horses tied. There was a small cave in the side of the hill.

"This is a good camp site Grady."

"The day of the Indian raid I found this cave and tied the horses here to wait for Dad to come and get me. Two of our horses were so spooked by all the yelling and shooting that I couldn't hold them and they got away from me. I was too scared to follow, so I came back here and kept these two quiet."

"We'll be safe for tonight anyway." B.J. assured Grady. She had heard that Indians never attacked at night, she hoped it was true.

B.J. handed down their sack of supplies to Grady and then she got down. She unsaddled Dude and tied him away from the other two horses. Grady began pulling grass and bringing it to the horses he had saved.

With the horses taken care of, now it was time to think about feeding themselves.

"Have you eaten anything since all this happened?" B.J. asked.

Grady shook his head no.

"Let's see if we can't get something fixed for us. I haven't had anything but a cold biscuit myself."

They gathered dry leaves and got a small fire started. After the fire was going good, B.J. filled the coffee pot and sat it on the ring of rocks around the fire. Before long they could smell the coffee, and it smelled good. The dry bread and beef jerky was taken out of their sack and they each took a piece. B.J. poured their coffee to wash it down. B.J. put down a quilt as close to the fire as she could and motioned for Grady to come and lay down. She covered him with another one and Grady looked up and asked,

"You're not going to leave me, are you?"

"No way little brother. I've found you and you're stuck with me from now on. Get some sleep, I'll get a few more limbs for the fire and I'll come and join you."

B.J. collected as many limbs as she could find in the dark and then she climbed under the quilt next to Grady. They both slept like babies that night.

Chapter 4

B.J. awoke to the singing of the birds and sunlight flickering through the trees into her eyes. She was cold and stiff, and as she slipped from their bed, she noticed that Grady had all the covers. B.J. got a fire started from the remains of the old fire. Taking the coffee pot with her, B.J. went to the stream to wash her face and hands and refill the pot. When the coffee began to boil, the aroma caused Grady to stir.

"Good morning brother, did you sleep well?"

"I sure did. I was warm."

"I know you had all the quilt. I almost froze." B.J. teased him.

Grady smiled, and sat up. He moved closer to the fire and hugged his knees up close to his body. The coffee was ready, so B.J. poured both of them a cup. They sat sipping the coffee and began to warm inside. The silence was broken by Grady. He looked up from his cup and asked.

"What are we gonna do now, B.J.?"

The answers B.J. gave had to be the right ones or she knew Grady could be easily discouraged and scared more than he had been. B.J. was the oldest, and had to portray an air of confidence, even when hers was low. Grady needed to feel B.J. was competent, so she replied with authority.

"First, we'll get some breakfast and then we'll see how this beautiful morning goes."

B.J. fixed a meal of hot oats, bread, and more hot coffee. Afterwards, Grady took the bowls and coffee pot to the stream and cleaned them. B.J.

went to check on their horses. All three were fine, but needed water, so B.J. led them to the stream and let them drink.

The two of them packed what few provisions they had left and tied the sack to the extra mare. They took one last look around; making sure the fire was out and then walked their horses from the trees. As they passed their parent's grave, they stopped for a moment, and then walked on. B.J. and Grady were trying extra hard to be strong because leaving their parents was hard.

As B.J. and Grady neared the circle of wagons, the buzzards were flying down to the dead bodies now, and making a terrible squawking noise. Grady stopped along the way and picked up a rifle, cocked it, and fired to scare them away.

"Don't fire again; we don't want to let anyone know we're here."

Grady nodded, knowing he had made a mistake, but it was sickening to see these creatures feast from their friends.

When B.J. and Grady got to their wagon, they began gathering things they would need to take with them. Together they picked up things and laid them on a piece of canvas, knowing that later they would have to eliminate some things. The bare necessities were all the extra mare could carry.

As they were going through their parent's trunk, B.J. found the papers her dad had tucked away on the free land the government was offering. There was also some money stashed in the box. B.J. took all this, knowing she would need the papers and money for their use when they got to their new home. The pictures her mom had brought B.J. took them also. She and Grady would treasure these from now on.

After finding money in their wagon, it occurred to Grady and B.J. that other wagons possibly had money and names of family they could contact about the tragedy. Grady went one way and B.J. went the other, until all the wagons had been searched and money and names written down to turn over to the proper authorities. The money totaled five thousand dollars, and that seemed like a lot to Grady and B.J., but actually each family just had a little over two hundred dollars. There were twenty-five families wiped out by the Indians with the exception of her and Grady.

B.J. took the lists of names and the money and put them in her mom's scarf and tied it under her shirt around her waist. They sorted through what they had collected, wrapped the provisions in the piece of canvas and put it on a packsaddle on the mare's back. Grady saddled Lady, his mare and found his dad's hat, pistol, and rifle. B.J. had picked up a pistol and tucked it into her belt. She put several boxes of ammunition in her saddlebags, slid a rifle into her saddle boot, put her hat on, took one last look around, and then mounted Dude.

"Grady, I wish we were able to bury these people, but we can't. I almost didn't get dad and mom buried, there are just too many of them."

"I know B.J. I hate to leave them lying here for the buzzards, but what else can we do."

They rode off. It was hard to do, but it was the only thing to do. When they got to the outer edge of the wagon circle, B.J. spotted the body of the wagon master. B.J. stepped down, walked to his body and took a map from his vest pocket.

"What are you doing?" Asked Grady.

"I'm getting the map he's been using." B.J. answered as she folded it and put it in her saddlebags.

B.J. mounted Dude again and they finally rode away leaving all the death and destruction behind them. They also left the two people they loved the most in the world. B.J. had no idea what lay ahead for either of them. Nevertheless, both knew they could not stay. There was no one to guide or tell them when they went wrong except the Good Lord. B.J. knew they would learn many things as they went along, things they probably would never need to know otherwise.

The day began well, they accomplished what was needed for now and she hoped it ended as good for them.

"Lord, guide us and keep us safe." B.J. silently prayed as she kicked Dude to a trot. Grady was right behind her.

John Hall had taught his children the importance of knowing the sun rose in the east and set in the west. They rode the rest of that day, letting the sun be their guide. B.J. and Grady kept to as much tree-covered land as possible, hoping not to be seen. The Indian raid on the train made them very aware of another attack by Indians. Water was also a primary consideration.

B.J. knew Grady was tired; he kept shifting in his saddle. B.J. was tired too, but she knew they needed to cover as much territory as possible. Once out of this section, maybe they could breathe easier. B.J. kept the horses at a pace that would not wear then out too soon. These horses were their future and she certainly didn't want anything to happen to them.

"B.J., when are we gonna stop, I'm tired?" Grady asked.

B.J. could see how the sky was turning a dusty lavender hue, so she began looking around for a place to stop for the night. There was a strand of trees ahead and it would be good cover if water were close. B.J. pointed to the trees and led Grady in their direction. Grady didn't object; he was too tired. Neither of them was used to being in a saddle all day. They both looked forward to getting off the horses, if only for a night.

There was a pool of water caught between two rocks; it was feed by an underground spring. Good enough. There was cover from the trees, fresh water, and plenty of dead firewood to last the night. Dude stopped, B.J. stepped down and Grady followed suit. Grady unloaded the pack from the mare and laid it under the trees. They unsaddled their horses and found a grassy spot, and hobbled them for the night. Grady rubbed them down to dry them off, and then carried their saddles to the trees.

The day was ending, and bringing with it the coolness of the evening. Grady took his heavy coat and put it on. The fire felt good as they sat eating their supper of beans, bacon, and bread. They had their coffee to warm them too. They were getting the knack of making camp because it took less time than before. The food was good or either they were awfully hungry. When they finished eating, B.J. poured Grady and herself another cup of coffee. They sat sipping it.

"How far do you think we came today, B.J.?"

"It's hard to tell till we see some kind of road marker. Then I can look on the map and see the mileage."

Grady gathered up the dirty dishes and took them in a pan to the pool of water to wash.

B.J. let him, after all she cooks the meal and he needed a share of the work. While Grady washed the dishes, she put down the bedrolls, and then gathered enough wood to keep the fire going through the night.

B.J. got the map from her saddlebag and took it back to the fire. It was hard to read by the light of the fire, but her eyes began to adjust. According to what the Wagon Master had marked, the train had left the Nebraska Territory, crossed the North Platt River and was nearing the settlement of Medicine Bow, where the train was when the Indians attacked. If Grady and she were heading in the right direction, they should be just about to Medicine Bow.

That next morning, B.J. and Grady had been riding for at least two hours when B.J. brought up the subject of going into Medicine Bow.

"We'll be coming to the turn off to Medicine Bow soon." B.J. said.

"Good. At least we'll be seeing other people for a change." Grady said excitedly.

"Now wait a minute, I heard Dad and Mom talking the last night we were all in camp about the dangers the Wagon Master explained could happen if the train went into Medicine Bow."

"What danger is there in going to a town?"

"Dad told Mom there were all kinds of misfits that hung out there, like robbers—men wanted by the law. There is no law there to protect innocent people. The Wagon Master planned to send a couple of men into town to get supplies and mail, and keep the train on the trail." B.J. explained to Grady.

B.J. could see the disappointment in Grady's eyes.

"Listen Grady, I'd like to go into town too, but just the two of us and as young as we are, well, it presents problem. What if we were robbed or beat up? Who would protect us?"

After thinking for a few minutes, Grady agreed with B.J.

"You know, Sis, I guess we had better keep on going. Forget this town, we have enough supplies and there will be another one and it will be safer."

B.J. was glad they agreed. They rode on and as they passed the wooden sign, "Medicine Bow," with an arrow pointing in the direction of the town. Grady said.

"Well, Medicine Bow, your loss, our gain."

Meanwhile in the town of Medicine Bow, Webster Thompson stood looking east into the rising sun. The red-orange ball crept slowly upward. Webster leaned against the porch post, sipping his cup of coffee and letting his thoughts wander.

"How beautiful the sky is this morning." Webster said aloud.

Every since Webster came to the town of Medicine Bow, six months ago, he got up every morning wishing he was out there in the wilderness again. Webster was an outdoor man who lived in the wild for three years by himself. He came into town to sell the furs he had trapped and to get supplies. The owner of the general store saw a small wooden box that Webster had made, and he liked it. The storeowner purchased it from Webster for his wife to put her jewelry and trinkets in. Once his wife laid hands on it, the whole town knew of the box, and Webster had been busy since making boxes for all the women in town.

Webster loved working with pretty wood. His boxes were made from cedar. Webster was gifted with a special talent for carving. He carved designs on the outside lid and down the sides. The people in town paid him well and kept finding other things for Webster to make.

Webster Thompson was a bachelor and his only family tie, a nephew named Wayne Thompson, lived in St. Joseph, Missouri, so there had been no need for Webster to hurry out of Medicine Bow. The people treated Webster with kindness, even giving him a small shop to do his wood working from. He slept in the small room at the back and no one bothered him. One of the town ladies delivered a hot meal to him each day, but in spite of all this, every morning that same old feeling of leaving came on Webster really strong. He didn't know how much longer he could restrain himself. The mountains in the distance seemed to be calling to him.

Webster stretched his big frame and went back inside to fill his coffee cup again. He buttered a slice of bread, thinking this would serve as breakfast for now, and went to the bed headboard that he had been working on for several days. When this piece was finished, Webster decided he would leave this town and go back to his dearly beloved wilderness. He had been cooped up too long; he needed fresh mountain air to breathe.

Webster did his best thinking when he was carving. Feeling the wood as he carved the curly cues and whirls into the beautiful wood, Webster thought, "Here I am fifty-five years old and don't even own a bed, or have a home to put one in."

Several years ago things could have been different. Webster had fallen in love with a beautiful young lady, but her father didn't thing a wood carver was suitable for his daughter, so he sent her back east to college. It was there she found an educated man, stayed and married him. Never had Webster let himself get close to another woman. Now when he needed female companionship, he knew where to go to get it, and he wasn't hurt afterwards. Yes, his mind was definitely made up; it was time for him to pack up and leave this shop and head back to his wilderness.

When Webster completed the bed, he took it to the storeowner. The owner was well pleased and already had another project for Webster to start on. Before the owner could tell Webster what he wanted, Webster spoke up.

"This is my last job. I've got to be moving on. If you will figure my wages, I'll give you my order for my supplies and we'll be settled up."

"Oh surely you're not leaving us. I've got orders for more of your carved furniture. Is it more money you want? We'll be happy to pay you more if you will only stay." The storeowner pleaded.

"Nope, don't need any more money, just need to leave, so let's get this order filled and I'll be on my way." Webster was determined that he would not be talked out of his decision.

Webster packed his provisions onto his packhorse, tying them down real tight. He climbed on his horse and took the lead rope to the pack horse in one hand and his reins in the other and turned them west going out of town. Webster sighed as he settled into his saddle, he felt good sitting there; it had been empty too long.

Webster and the packhorse rode out just as they came in, six months earlier. He had money in his pocket for a change and food on his packhorse. Life was good. Webster rode out of Medicine Bow leaving the town a little better, at least some of the ladies thought so. Now they had new furniture without having to pay a fortune to have it shipped to them from back east. Webster wondered if the day would ever come when people out here would have all the nice furnishings they had back east. That day would come because everything was changing. Take for instance, the land the government was giving to people to get them to settle out here. It was at that moment that the idea struck Webster. "Why not go and claim me a piece of land and build me a home and settle down on it?"

That's what Webster would do. He headed west knowing the free land was in the Wyoming territory. After being on the trail for a while, Webster noticed dust rising behind him. There were Indians to consider in this country, so Webster kept to the trees for cover. On the same trail ahead of Webster, B.J. and Grady were traveling. B.J. had noticed the dust trails, but didn't say anything for fear of scaring Grady. But she did keep her eye peeled as they rode on.

B.J. and Grady rode in silence. B.J. realized how alone, how young, and how vulnerable they were to the outside world. Now that their parents were gone, they would have to grow up fast and it wasn't easy to toss aside your youthful desires and think like an adult. But now everything had to be thought out very carefully.

The days were long, so to pass time, B.J. began pointing out different signs in the landscape to Grady. This was beautiful country if only their Dad and Mom could be here with them to see it. There were rock formations that were just breath taking. "The Lord really knew what He was doing when He made this country," was the very line John Hall had used trying to convince her Mom into coming west.

There were rocks with red, yellow, and gray color formations running through them. When the sun shone on these, they were awe-inspiring. Only the Lord could put such beauty together. The grass in the meadows was greening and so were the trees as they took on new leaves all different shades of green. An artist would have a field day in this country.

B.J. was brought back to the present in a hurry, because ahead, off in the distance, she saw black smoke. Anyone that ever lived on a farm knew the sign of smoke usually meant bad trouble. B.J. looked at Grady, he had seen it too.

"What should we do, B.J.? Do we ride on and try to help, or do you think we should ride around it? We don't want any trouble."

B.J. could hear the fear in Grady's voice and she understood after what he went through at the raid on the wagon train. It was times like this that her dad always made the decision, now it must be her.

"We need to see if we can help."

Grady nodded and they both kicked their horses to a full gallop. They headed in the direction of the smoke, knowing eventually they would see what caused the fire. The closer they came, the more nervous both became. They were close enough now that they could hear gunfire. B.J. reined Dude to a stop and Grady did the same. Grady knew rifle fire even better than B.J.

At first, B.J. and Grady kept their distance. They didn't know what was happening and they were really too scared to find out. They found cover in some trees and dismounted. Grady tied the horses. B.J. knew they couldn't defend themselves, so they sat and waited till the shooting stopped and then they would see if there was anyone left to help. B.J. wished she had been a man. Some help, riding in like Sherman's Army, and then realizing how little they could do to help. If she were a man she wouldn't be afraid to ride out and help those folks. Her intentions were good, but that's as far as it went for now. There was Grady, and she was responsible for him now, so she knew she had made the right choice.

The gunfire finally stopped, and then B.J. and Grady heard loud laughing and shouting. B.J. didn't think it was Indians. They didn't sound right to her. There were no yelps and whoops the usually came from Indians when they attacked. Grady got as close to B.J. as he could, and she put her arm around his shoulders and pulled him closer. The two remained silent hoping this would soon be over.

The noise stopped. They heard the thunder of many horses fade into the distance, going away from them. Thank God. B.J. had been afraid they would come in their direction and see them and their horses. B.J. and Grady waited at least another thirty minutes, and then they mounted and rode slowly to the foot of a knoll they had been on. B.J. reached over and stopped Grady and handed him Dude's reins. B.J. got down and slowly crept forward until she was in view of the burning ranch. B.J. counted at least three buildings, and one was burning, it was the barn. The hay was on fire. B.J. couldn't see everything because of the trees and the obscuring brush, but she saw enough to make her blood run cold and to bring back the memory of the wagon train.

The house was still standing and a shed and the corrals, but all the horses were gone. There was one old milk cow, her calf, a few chickens pecking around, and a dog lying dead in the front yard. There was no movement except the chickens, and they continued to eat as thought nothing had happened. No sign of human life anywhere. Maybe they had taken the people who lived there as prisoners.

B.J. stood and motioned for Grady to bring the horses up. She stepped up on Dude and they started slowly making their way down to the farm. When they reached the front of the house, they got off and tied their horses to the rail. The horses were nervous because they smelled the smoke from the barn.

"Tie them good." B.J. told Grady as she slowly walked up on the porch.

"Hello-o-o, anybody here?"

There was no reply. B.J. knocked softly on the half-opened door and the door squeaked, as it swung open. She couldn't believe her eyes. Behind her, she heard Grady inhale deeply. Neither of them said anything, instead they stood froze to the spot.

On the floor lay a man that had been shot at least four times. Blood was running from the spot where he lay. B.J. walked over and checked his breathing. There wasn't any; he was dead. Grady began crying so she put her arm around him and hugged Grady to her. They eased on through the house, not turning loose of each other. When they got to a room in the back, probably used for the bedroom, something told B.J. not to let Grady enter.

"You wait here." B.J. said as she opened the door just enough to look in.

B. J. went on in. Lying in a pool of blood, among the rubble of bedclothes, and with her clothes all in disarray, was a beautiful young woman. Her blonde hair was all tangled and twisted. Her eyes showed the terror from the torture she had received.

B.J. wondered how many of those men had his way with her before one or more of them shot her. B.J. straightened her dress before Grady came in the room. Grady was too young to see this

"Is she alive?" Grady asked, wiping tears from his eyes.

"I'm afraid not." B.J. replied as she led him from the room back to where the man's body laid.

After a close look B.J. and Grady agreed the Indians or whoever they were, only wanted whatever valuables the couple might have and their horses. It was evident that they were just plain hard-working folks, trying to make a go on a little piece of land. The horses would sell and bring someone a little money, but such a waste of lives for so little in return. Why did this sort of thing have to happen? It was just a few hours ago that B.J. and Grady was enjoying the beauty of this country, now it seemed so cruel, hard, and frightening.

"Let's get the horses out of sight."

"We're not going to stay here, are we?" Grady asked.

B.J. didn't answer, just walked pass Grady and began untying Dude. Grady tugged on her sleeve.

"Sis, don't you think we should leave here as soon as possible? Those men might return and find us here."

"I don't think they will come back; they got everything they wanted or they never would have left."

Grady shrugged his shoulders and untied his mares and together they led them to the shed in the back where the horses would be out of sight. Someone might decide to check out the fire as they had done. B.J. and Grady left the horses saddled just loosened their cinch straps. This way if they had to leave in a hurry, this would be the fastest way.

"Get some of that hay that isn't burned and give it to them." B.J. said.

B.J. went in search of a shovel; there were two graves to dig, two more innocent people who had gone on to be with their maker. As B.J. dug, she silently prayed.

"Lord, I know You are watching over Grady and me. You kept us from riding right into the middle of this mess and You kept us safe till it was over. Now, I'm asking You to keep us in Your care till we do the only thing left to do for these two."

After a while Grady came with another shovel and began to help her dig. Finally the hole was long enough and wide enough for both the man and woman. B.J. went back to the house to get their bodies. She took a quilt and wrapped the man in it and then dragged him across the yard to the grave they had dug. Grady helped her roll him into the grave.

B.J. went back for the woman. She found a clean sheet and rolled her off the bed onto it. B.J. closed her eyes and tried to straighten her beautiful hair, and then wrapped the sheet around her. The woman was so small that B.J. threw her over her shoulder and carried her to the grave. Laying the woman beside her husband, B.J. and Grady began shoveling dirt over them. When they finished Grady said.

"We don't even know their names."

"Wait, there is a Bible inside on one of the tables, maybe their names are written in it."

B.J. went in the house and came out with the Bible in her hand. "His name was Gene and hers was Frieda, Gene and Frieda Tucker."

"Are you going to read over them?"

B.J. turned to the 23rd. Psalm and together they repeated the whole Psalm. Afterwards they gathered rocks and made a marker for them.

"They need a marker with their names on it." Grady said.

"I don't think we're going to be here that long."

B.J. knew Grady was right; all graves needed a marker. What was making her so hard-hearted, this country or burying people? Right now she needed something to lift her spirits, and a good cup of hot coffee would do the trick. There was some serious thinking that she needed to do, so B.J. headed towards the house.

Grady was right on her heels. He was still scared at being here and B.J. knew this was why he didn't let her get to far from him. B.J. was glad she was there to comfort him, he was just a little boy and had already seen and been through too much.

When B.J. entered the empty house it gave her an eerie feeling. The house was empty and silent, and B.J. knew she had to keep these feelings hidden, so she headed for the stove.

"Do you think we should start a fire?" Asked Grady.

"I don't think those men will return this late. Anyway, like I said before, they got what they came for or they never would have left."

B.J. stirred the ashes and got the coals glowing red and then added some small pieces of kindling. Soon they had a fire going. Next B.J. found the fixing for a pot of coffee and sat it on the stove to brew.

"Go unsaddle our horses. We're staying here tonight."

Grady was out the door before she could finish what she was saying.

The coffee began to boil and B.J. slid the pot over so it would not boil out. She got two cups from the cupboard, found the sugar, and a pitcher of cream.

"Smells good, is it ready?" Grady asked as he burst in the room.

"I hope it taste good."

After they finished their cup of coffee, B.J. fried some bacon and told Grady to see if the chickens had laid any eggs. Grady came in with both hands full of eggs and they had bacon and eggs for supper that night.

"We will stay till morning, and then we will move on."

B.J. cleaned up the table and then went to change the linens on the bed. Grady went to the shed to bring in their supplies. He didn't want any critters to get into them during the night.

When time came to go to bed, B.J. could tell Grady was still uneasy about being there. He was afraid the men would return, so B.J. suggested they sleep with their clothes on and in the same bed. Grady seemed satisfied then. B.J. got their pistols and put them nearby. Grady was as tired as she and he didn't hesitate to climb in the bed. B.J. locked the front door, and then put a chair in front of it. She didn't sleep that sound, but taking precautions didn't hurt. B.J. climbed into the bed next to Grady. He was already snoring and soon she was asleep too.

Chapter 5

That next morning B.J. was suddenly awakening by a rooster crowing. Since Grady and she had been on the road, usually birds singing and sunlit peeping through the trees awakened her. It took her a moment to recall where they were and what had happened.

The soft bed felt good and B.J. thought how easy it would be to get spoiled to this sort of living. Grady was still sleeping so soundly, as B.J. eased from the bed trying not to wake him. B.J. put her boots on and went to the kitchen to restart the fires. The mornings were cool, but in the cabin was nothing to compare with the wide open they had been sleeping in. B.J. had the fire going in the fireplace and soon the room was nice and warm.

First came their pot of coffee, and then B.J. decided to make a batch of fresh bread. What they had been eating was stale and almost gone. When she put the bread in the oven, B.J. started a pan of bacon frying. B.J. heard Grady stirring in the bedroom and in a few moments he came into the kitchen rubbing his eyes and looking confused as she had been earlier.

"Good morning, sleepy head."

"Boy, does something smell good. Is that fresh bread I smell?"

"I'll be ready in a few minutes; go and wash up."

Without hesitating Grady started for the door. B.J. took some of the eggs and scrambled them, and then she put it all on the table and they sat down to hot breakfast at a table. It sure tasted good. After eating all they wanted, B.J. put the leftovers on the back of the stove for lunch. She filled the kettle with water from the bucket and sat it on the stove to heat. There were dirty dishes to wash.

"While we're here, I think I'll wash up our dirty clothes. We need to wash our bodies too. Neither of us has bathed since we started this trip."

"I've got to check on the horses, feed them and turn them into the back corral." Grady wasn't as eager for a bath as B.J. seemed to be, so he took his hat and headed for the door.

When B.J. finished cleaning the kitchen, she called for Grady to come and bathe. Grady came in smiling, something B.J. hadn't seen in a while.

"Why are you smiling?"

"This wouldn't be a bad place to stay for awhile." Grady said, scratching his head.

B.J. left Grady to his bath and she went about gathering up their dirty clothes to wash. She had those same thoughts while she was making bread that morning. Just having a real stove to cook on instead of a campfire was a delight to her, but she hadn't said anything.

After Grady bathed and dressed, B.J. took her bath. The warm water felt good, so she washed her hair too. B.J. got out and dried off and put on clean clothes. She felt good being clean in and out for a change. She combed her hair dry in front of the fireplace and was just about to pull her boots on when Grady came running into the house all red-faced and out of breath. Grady was so excited he nearly ran over her.

"What is wrong with you?"

"I saw something in the woods behind the house." Grady said after he caught his breath.

B.J. walked to the back of the house with Grady. "Where? What did you see?"

Grady just pointed in the direction of the woods.

"Was it an animal?"

"No!" Grady was actually shaking with fear.

"What did it look like?"

"It was something shiny, like the sun reflecting off a piece of metal." Grady said, pointing where he saw it.

B.J. stood looking, shading her eyes from the sun, trying to see what Grady was describing, but she never saw anything. She wondered if it was

Grady's imagination, or if he really had seen something. Whatever, it wasn't there now, so she turned going back into the house.

B.J. poured them another cup of coffee hoping to settle Grady's nerves. They had settled back enjoying being full, clean and warm, when suddenly there was a strange noise, making both of them look up at the same time.

"What was that?" B.J. asked.

Did Grady have her spooked too? B.J. got up and went to the bedroom where she left the pistols the night before and got both of them. She handed one to Grady. They went to the front door and opened it to look out. B.J. and Grady half expected whatever had caused the noise to be in the front yard, but when they opened the door, there was nothing. They stepped out on the porch to have a better look around, when suddenly, "Yee—haaa", came echoing through the air. The loud yell came down the road from the west of them.

"Yee—haaa! Yee—haa! The yell came again. B.J. and Grady could see a stagecoach coming toward the cabin and it was the driver yelling as he urged the horses on. The stage rattling and the thunder of the horse's hooves was the noise they heard earlier.

B.J. looked at Grady and he looked at her. There they stood, like they had been caught at something they were not supposed to be doing.

"What are we going to do?" Grady asked, half scared and half ashamed.

"We can't do anything but explain why we're here."

So they stood waiting for the stage to get to the cabin. When the fast moving stage pulled to a stop, the trail of dust following caught up to it. B.J. thought about her laundry she had just hung out to dry. Oh, well!

A dirty old loudmouth driver was the first to speak. "Where'd you kids come from? Is Gene and his misses in the house?"

B.J. hesitated and so the driver bellowed, "Hey, Gene!"

The driver jumped down from the driver's seat and started towards the house.

B.J. stepped off the porch to meet him. "There're both dead. We buried them yesterday." She told the driver and pointed in the direction of their graves at the edge of the yard.

"Oh no!" Came from inside the stage and B.J. looked and saw a lady and two other men.

The old driver heard it also, so he turned to the people inside and said. "Ya'll might as well get out; we're here even if Gene and his wife ain't."

The stage door opened and all three climbed out. The lady was nicely dressed in spite of the dust that had settled on her clothes. Her husband helped her down. The other man stood brushing the dust from his suit.

B.J. backed up. She was half afraid of the old driver, and half ashamed of being where she wasn't supposed to be. Grady kept quiet the whole time and remained on the porch, like it was a safe haven for him. Grady was afraid of the driver too.

"Well, where are all the stage horses?"

"They took all the horses with them after they killed the Tuckers." B.J. explained.

"Horse thieves too. Well, they'll get what's coming to them when they try to sell those horses. The stage line has a special brand, and no thief can sell them without getting a noose around his neck and being hanged on the spot."

Hearing the driver gave B.J. goose bumps and evidently the lady felt the same because she came to B.J. and put her arm around her and hugged B.J. close. The lady arms felt good, kinda reminded B.J. of how her mother hugged her.

"Don't pay any attention to that driver. He isn't near as mean as he lets folks believe he is." She turned, still hugging B.J. and started toward the cabin.

"Boy, come help me unhitch these horses, they've got to be fed and watered and let rest some, since there is none here to take their place."

Grady looked at B.J. first, and she nodded her approval. Grady, then went to the stage and began helping the driver with the stage horses.

"I'm Mildred Brasher and this is my husband Sid. We're on our way to St. Louis to visit my ailing mother."

"I'm B.J. Hall and that was my brother Grady helping the driver." B.J. held out her hand to shake there during the introduction. The second man introduced himself as Charles Whitehead.

"How long have you children been here, and where are your parents? Mildred Brasher asked.

B.J. knew they had been riding for a long time so she offered them a fresh cup of coffee. The driver and Grady came in the cabin.

"Sit down Sid, B.J. was just beginning to tell us how they came to be here." Mildred Brasher said.

Sid didn't look so happy, but he pulled up a chair, took a cup of coffee, and listened as B.J. told them about Grady and her sad experience. When B.J. finished, everyone at the table had a sad look on their face. Ed was the first to speak.

"You kids have had it pretty rough, haven't you?"

Neither of them spoke, then B.J. said, "It could have been a lot worse; I suppose, we could have been killed with our parents and the rest of the train."

Sid nodded his way of agreeing.

"Well, it's almost lunch. Let's see if we can't get something fixed for these men. B.J. can you help me in the kitchen and the rest of you men, which means you too Grady, get outside till we call you to eat."

Again Grady looked at B.J. for approval. She nodded, and Grady went with the men to the porch.

Mildred Brasher took two buckets to the porch and told the men that one was for water and the other was for milk. The men could decide who filled each. The meal was prepared by her and B.J. and put on the table where B.J. already had the dishes, silverware. They fixed canned beans, potatoes, ham and the fresh bread left from breakfast. The men were told to wash up and come eat. As Sid came in he had his bucket running over with milk.

"Pardon me, ladies, whose stallion is that out back?" Ed asked.

"He belongs to me." B.J. answered.

"Well, he sure is having himself a good old time with one of your mares."

B.J. turned red in the face and looked at Grady. "I told you to keep Dude separated from those mares."

Grady just hung his head, and B.J. felt bad for jumping on him; after all he was just a kid.

Ed broke the silence, "There's one way to look at this situation. You'll have the beginning of your herd in eleven or twelve months." Then Ed threw back his head and laughed and everyone began laughing too.

Grady broke into a smile and B.J. felt better too.

After finishing the meal, the men pushed back their chairs to smoke, and Mildred and B.J. removed the dishes to clean up. The conversation the men were having was about the stage going back since they now knew about the Indians attacking the wagon train. Mr. Whitehead recommended the stage continue on since they were not going the same route of the wagon train, he felt they would be safe, Sid and Mildred agreed. B.J. was glad she wasn't in on the decision-making. So Ed finally said they would go on to Medicine Bow and stay the night there. Ed would telegraph the stage line to get further instructions, and he could get fresh horses in Medicine Bow too.

"Don't you and Grady want to come with us instead of trying this trip on your own?" Ed asked B.J.

"Let me talk to Grady and see how he feels and I'll get back to you." B.J. motioned for Grady to follow her outside.

Before B.J. could ask Grady, he said, "I don't want to go back sis. This is what Dad and Mom wanted for us, and anyway we don't have anything to go back to."

B.J. instantly thought about Wayne in St. Joseph, but knew that was being unfair to Grady. Wayne would have to be another time and place, right now it was what Grady and she wanted. Grady was right. Their dad had worked hard to come west. B.J. knew in her heart it was meant to be this way. Having made up their minds, B.J. and Grady went in and thanked Ed and the others for the invitation, but told then their decision was to go on.

"Ya'll are welcome to stay right here and run this relay station. The stage line will hire you both. You will have a ready built home and all you will have to do is care for the stock and feed the passengers." Ed said with a worried look of concern on his face.

They shook their heads no.

"Thank you for the generous offer, but our future isn't here. We'll have to go on." B.J. said to Ed.

Ed hesitated, dropped his head and left the room, under all that dirt and that loud mouth and rough exterior, was a softhearted, kind natured man. He simple was afraid of showing his feelings to two lonely kids. Ed tried to keep his feelings hidden, but B.J. knew differently and so did Mildred.

"I told you Ed wasn't so bad, didn't I?"

In just a few minutes Ed came back into the cabin. "How much do you two know about shooting a pistol or rifle?"

They explained they knew very little.

"Get your firearms and follow me."

B.J. and Grady went with Ed and he gave them a quick lesson in loading and firing their pistols and rifles. The guns were so loud it made both of them nervous.

"This might mean life or death for ya'll, now pay attention to what I tell you."

Grady was the better of the two. He had been hunting with their dad. Ed took their holsters and adjusted them to fit their hips, and made them promise to wear them when they left the relay station. Ed was beginning to frighten B.J. by telling them all the things they might encounter. Grady seem to hone in on his every word.

B.J. remembered a saying her dad often used, "An ounce of prevention was worth a pound of cure." Well, Ed was giving her and Grady several ounces. Ed cared, even though his rough exterior still prevailed, his warmth came through to them. Ed may be big, rough, and loud outside, but inside he was tenderhearted and it showed.

"Now listen kids, there is a Fort not too far from here. If you keep to the trail on your map, you might see some troopers along the way. They patrol about three days out from the fort, only thing, you are about six days away, so for three days or so, you're gonna have to be mighty careful. I don't think you will run into any trouble. We just came from the direction you are going and everything was fine when we came through."

Ed, B.J. and Grady went back to the cabin and Ed told his passengers they would be leaving in a few hours.

"I've got one more important job to do." Ed told them, and then he went back out. They had no idea what Ed was going to do.

Everyone was enjoying the quiet and peaceful afternoon when Grady suddenly burst into the room. "Come quickly, B.J."

B.J. got up and followed and so did everyone else.

"Look!" Grady said as he pointed to the two graves where they had buried the Tuckers.

Ed had made a wooden marker with their names on it and the year they died, and had put it in the ground at the head of the graves. All of them walked to the grave and stood silently.

"I knew these folks a long time. This is the least I could do for all the good meals and coffee I got from them." Ed explained.

Not wanting anyone to think he was an old softie, Ed said in his grumpy voice, "Boy, come help me hitch up these teams, we're burning daylight." Then Ed walked off toward the corral with Grady right on his heels.

B.J. knew the stage passengers would need fresh water for their canteens, so she went to the well and filled them. B.J. also wrapped some food left from lunch for them. The teams were hitched to the stage and everyone hugged her and Grady before they got in, even Ed. He gave them last minute advice, naturally, and then climbed up to the driver's seat.

"You can stay here at long as you want and eat as much food as you need, and take as many of the supplies as you need when you leave." Ed said again.

Taking the reins in his big rough hands, Ed let out that loud "yee— haa", slapped the backs of the horses with his reins, and off the stage went.

B.J. and Grady stood looking until the stage was out of sight. Suddenly it seemed awfully quiet. They went back into the house and sat down at the table. The silence was overbearing. Why had they come, if leaving was going to be so sad?

"Do you want anything to eat before bedtime?" B.J. asked.

"No, my appetite is gone." Grady answered.

"Go make sure the horses are secure for the night and I will warm us a cup of coffee."

Grady left and when he returned he had a shirttail full of eggs.

"I thought we could eat these for breakfast."

B.J. took the eggs, and as she was putting them in the basket she thought, fresh eggs, milk, a real stove, and a warm bed with a roof over our heads at night, were going to be hard to ride away from come morning.

"Grady how much longer do you want to stay here?"

Grady hesitated.

"Well, we've got to make up our mind or we will never get back on the road."

"Let's sleep on it and maybe in the morning we can decide."

They got ready for bed. The day had been long, but exciting. Maybe tomorrow would bring another good one.

Chapter 6

Webster Thompson, after leaving Medicine Bow, had been on the road and in the saddle for several days. Webster decided to camp for the night. He was weary to the bone from being in the saddle so long. Webster had become soft living in Medicine Bow all those months, and he would have to acclimatize his body to riding great distances again.

The road had been lonely and Webster was barely out two days when he saw smoke billowing in the distance. The first thought that came to Webster was an Indian attack. He prayed he was wrong, but nonetheless he rode toward the smoke, but didn't show himself, for fear he was right. Webster circled and went south staying to the shelter of the trees where he felt safe. After tying his horse, he went on foot to a spot in the bushes where he could see what was happening.

Webster had his long glass from his saddlebag and as he crawled the last few feet up a small rise, he extended the glass and focused it toward a house and barn where the smoke was coming from. There they were, outlaws with a band of renegade Indians. They were the sorriest of men that breathed. The band was riding roughshod on two innocent people, burning their hay and barn. Webster saw the man trying to defend his farm, but he was outnumbered. It galled Webster to admit to himself that he couldn't be of any help, even if he went to them. There were so many that all he could do was lay in the grass and watch.

The fight was over soon because one of them shot the man, and afterwards they busted through the door of the cabin and found his woman. Webster heard her scream. He knew what the outlaws were doing to her. If ever Webster felt sick to his stomach, it was then. After a few minutes her screaming stopped and Webster dropped his head and thanked God. The woman was dead and her torture was over.

The outlaws celebrated their victory with a jug of whiskey they found. The whooping and hollering went on for a long time, and then they got really mean. One of them shot the dog in the yard and some of the others began fighting amongst themselves. The leader got their attention by firing a shot in the air and waving his arm for them to follow his lead. The corral gate was opened and the horses run out. By then, they had satisfied their evil needs, so they each climbed on their horse and followed the small herd of horses. They left firing in the air and hollering as they left.

Webster lay back in the cool grass wishing he had at least offered to help the victims. He would have to live with his guilt now. Webster took his glass to take one last look before he moved on and this time he saw two mounted horses riding in the direction of the cabin. Focusing his long glass he could see they were only kids.

"Wonder if they lived there?" Webster asked aloud. He watched as the two rode slowly in and got off and tied up their horses. One was a girl and the other rider was a little boy.

Webster saw they had a packhorse with them and knew they were just passing and saw the smoke like he did, and came to help. Again Webster felt shame and more guilt and it bothered him so that he decided not to face the two young riders. Webster just watched from his distance. He saw the two children dig the graves and bury the man and woman. He waited longer and though about going to the cabin, but knew it would scare them, so he rode off.

Riding away, with the incident still fresh in his mind, Webster wondered why those two kids were out in this country alone. Neither looked old enough to take care of the other, even though they were doing a pretty good job of taking charge at that house back there. Webster made up his mind right then to keep track of those two kids and if he could help them out, he would. Those two kids had enough spunk to go to the rescue of the farmer and his wife, the least Webster could do was to trail close enough to help them, if the time came.

The day was coming to a quick close, so Webster found him a suitable place to camp for the night. He chooses carefully, knowing there was a possibility the outlaws and renegade Indians could return. Webster didn't want to wake up in the middle of the night with a knife at his throat. He doused his fire as soon as he finished cooking his food, and hobbled his horse nearby. The horse would warn him if anyone approached.

Webster curled up in his blanket, but he had a hard time sleeping. The thoughts of what happened earlier, or the two kids back at the cabin, would not leave his mind. Webster pulled his blanket closer around him and tried harder to shut all the happenings of the day out and finally dropped off to sleep.

The dawn broke to a chill and overcast sky. Webster threw back the blanket and immediately got a fire going to warm his aching bones.

"I'm getting too old for this kind of living." He said as he walked to the stream to fill his coffee pot. A hot cup of coffee would get him going in no time. As he warmed and waited for the coffee to brew, he marveled at the surrounding country. The weather made you think rain was coming each day, but it seldom did. This country took its time waking each morning.

After pouring a cup of coffee and sipping the hot liquid, Webster begins warming from the inside out. He decided to stay there a day or two to watch the house and the kids. This way he would know which direction they would be traveling and he could dog their trail until the right time, and then let himself be known without scaring them to death. Webster had made up his mind to see those two safely to their destination. One good turn deserved another.

Meanwhile, back at the cabin the morning was a repeat of the one before. The sun was shining, the birds were in their usual cheerful mood and the rooster crowed to awake B.J. She got the fire going and warmed herself, and then went to the bucket of water and washed the sleep from her eyes. B.J. started their breakfast cooking.

Grady woke and saw after the horses and then returned to eat. When they finished eating and enjoying a second cup of coffee, B.J. asked.

"Have you given any more though to leaving?"

Grady hesitated, and then said. "Well, I thought about it. I think it's time we moved on. We got to get back on the trail again, or we will never get to where we're going that's for sure."

"This place is tempting, but it's not ours, and we really have no choice. I'm thankful we could stay awhile, but unless we intend to take Ed up on his offer to run the relay station, then we must move on. I, personally, don't want the job. I'd rather have our own place like Dad and Mom wanted and died for, than stay here." B.J. stated most definitely.

"I agree with you wholeheartedly, and like Ed said 'Lets get this day started, we're burning daylight'" Grady laughed.

They both laughed and got up ready to get going now that their decision was made. B.J. cleaned up the dishes and packed a few things for them to carry. Grady went to saddle the horses and put the packsaddle on the extra mare. B.J. gathered up their clothes and put the comb and brush that had belonged to the dead woman in with them, and carried the bag out to Grady to tie on.

B.J. went back inside to double check everything. The fires were going out and they had not left anything behind. She felt almost sad leaving. The little cabin had been home to them for several days and she was going to miss it for sure. Taking their pistols and her hat and coat from the wall peg, she closed the door behind her, and walked over and handed Grady his gun. B.J. checked Dude's cinch strap, and the ropes on the packsaddle, looked up at Grady, who was already mounted, and then climbed up on Dude.

"Are you ready?" Grady asked.

B.J. nodded, kicked Dude and they were off. The horses seemed eager to be on the move again. Dude was really frisky, but B.J. managed to hold him back, despite the fact he wanted to run. She knew they had a long way to ride that day and there was a pack mare to think about also. Well rested, well fed, and clean, made them ready for what lie ahead.

The morning warmed, and turned into a beautiful spring day. B.J. and Grady soon shed their jackets finding the temperature just right for shirtsleeves. It was May and everything was waking from the long winter.

"You know Grady, Dad knew what he was doing when he picked this time of year to come West. I just wished he was here to enjoy it." B.J. said as she looked about her and enjoyed the warm sunshine.

"We'll enjoy it for him and Mom."

B.J. couldn't help but notice the maturity in Grady's voice since he had been around Ed and the other men. She was proud that Grady had managed to overcome his fear from the attack on the train.

B.J. took out her money and checked it.

"We've got a long ride, and the next big town we come to will be Fort Laramie. It's a hard six day ride, but our horses are rested and in fine shape, and we shouldn't have any trouble."

"Don't forget, Ed said we would probably see some Calvary Troops in about three days." Grady reminded her.

The stagecoach had left ruts in the sandy soil and all they had to do was follow them. They had been in the saddle about four hours, riding in silence, and just enjoying the fine spring morning, when B.J. noticed Grady shifting back and forth in his saddle.

"Hey Sis, lets take a break. I've gotten soft, sitting around; I'm gonna have to condition myself to riding again."

B.J. smiled and headed them to a strand of trees. She stopped and stepped down. They tied Dude and the mares so they could eat a little grass, and then the two of them walked around, stretching their legs trying to loosen up.

Grady's stomach growled and B.J. realized it was lunchtime so she got out a snack for them to eat while they rested. Afterwards, Grady lay back on the grass and looked up.

"Have you ever noticed how big the sky seems in this part of the country?"

B.J. looked up too. "I think I'm really going to like our new home."

The two of them rested a while longer and then knew it was time to go. They went back to the trail and gave the horses their lead. After riding a couple of hours, Grady reached over and tugged B.J.'s sleeve. She turned to him as he pointed in the direction of a low rise of mountains just to the north of them. B.J. thought Grady wanted her to see how breathtaking the mountains were, so she just nodded. Grady pulled her sleeve again.

"What is it Grady?"

Didn't you see that?" Grady said as he pointed in the same direction.

B.J. looked again, but didn't see anything except the mountains. She shook her head no and they rode on. B.J. though to herself, "I hope Grady isn't seeing things again." She was remembering the day at the cabin just before the stage pulled in when Grady though he saw something in the woods.

The day was drawing to a close and she needed to look for a good place to camp for the night. Their first day out had been a long one. But it had been a good one too. They came to the foot of the mountains that before seemed so far away.

"Grady, it will be dark soon, so we will camp here tonight."

B.J. rode Dude under the trees, got off, and began to unpack their supplies. Taking the horses Grady led them to then nearby stream to water, and then he hobbled them to graze for the night. B.J. gathered firewood and got a fire going. She went to the stream and washed her face and hands and then filled their coffee pot. As soon as the coffee brewed, she got out the food that was already cooked so they could eat. Grady brought the saddles and laid them down next to the trees and rolled out their bedrolls.

"Come on, it's ready, if your ready." B.J. called.

"I'm ready." Grady replied and took the plate of food that B.J. offered. They sit down and began eating.

B.J. sensed that something was bothering Grady, but she knew him well enough to know that he would eventually bring it up.

"Wish I had some of that fresh milk to put in this coffee." Grady said.

"We'll have fresh milk again one of these days, in fact, you will get tired of milking, I bet."

The night came upon them fast and before they knew it, the sky was pitch black. Having a fire for light was okay, but outside the realm of firelight, they couldn't see anything. When they finished eating, Grady took the plates to go and wash them at the stream. Grady took one step in that direction when both of them heard a sharp cracking noise, like someone or something had stepped on a dry limb and broke it.

Grady froze in his tracks, and B.J. got up slowly. She looked all around trying to see what made the noise.

"Maybe it was just an animal."

About that time the horses begin shifting around. They were nervous, and this was their way of telling B.J. and Grady that there was definitely something out there, but what?

B.J. and Grady stood right where they were, and then B.J. eased down and picked up her pistol. B.J. remembered what Ed had told them about pulling the hammer back, so she took her thumb and pulled it back. The gun was cocked and ready to fire, all B.J. needed was a target. Nothing moved in the darkness around them. Grady half-turned and saw B.J. had her pistol ready, and he sighed a breath of relief.

Time seemed eternal in the darkness of the night, and both thought whatever it was had left, but then they heard the noise again. B.J. and Grady still couldn't see anything it was too dark. Then from the pitch black of the still night came a voice that made them shake in their boots.

"Hello the camp."

Neither knew whether to answer or just stand still, hoping and praying whoever it was would go away.

"Hello the camp." This time louder than before indicating whoever it was had come closer.

Grady stepped back and closer to B.J., and she could see he was as scared as she was. Ed had neglected to tell them what to do in this situation. They both stood there, afraid to answer or move. Whoever was out there was coming into their camp, whether they answered or not. B.J. and Grady could hear the dry limbs snapping and the leaves crunching as the night visitor approached. The sounds told them someone was coming and coming fast.

B.J. held the pistol with both hands and prayed she would be able to use it, but frankly she had her doubts. She prayed silently, "Lord, please don't let them hurt us." Grady was standing next to her and she couldn't let him down. B.J. was shaking in her boots, in the darkness, but she kept her pistol pointed in the direction of the voice. Who that voice belonged to, they didn't know, all they knew was it was terrifying, but they bravely stood waiting.

All they could see was a gigantic outline of a man in the shadow of their fire. They stood frozen to the ground, not moving or saying a word. The man could only see their outline.

"Stop right there; don't come a step closer. I've got a pistol, cocked and aimed right at your heart and I intend to use it." B.J. bravely said, hoping the man couldn't see how bad she was shaking. Grady kept quiet, still in the same spot.

"Listen, little lady, I don't mean you no harm. I saw your campfire and smelled your coffee and it was more than I could resist."

He cautiously moved forward a few steps, but B.J. and Grady held their ground, too scared to move, but he would never know this. He could see the pistol now and it was aimed at him, so he didn't want to scare her into shooting him. He extended his hands hoping both could see he was not armed or dangerous. Still no response, so he took another approach.

"If I had intended to harm either of you, I never would have called out first. I could have waited till you were asleep."

B.J. thought about this a minute. What he said was true, but there was still something about a stranger coming out of the night that made a person leery of them.

"What do you want?" B.J. asked, sounding as tough as she could.

The man stepped forward into the light of the fire and B.J. and Grady could see his face. He was in his late forties, not too rough looking, but still B.J kept her pistol aimed at him and he saw it.

"Look, little lady, I could talk much better if that pistol wasn't pointed at me." He half-smiled at her.

"First tell us what you want, and then I'll decide whether to put down my pistol or not."

"My name is Webster Thompson. I've been watching you two since the fire at the cabin. When the outlaws left and you two rode up, I realized you were just kids and I stayed in the woods behind the cabin for fear of scaring you even more."

"You were in the woods at the back of the cabin. I saw the sun reflecting off your rifle barrel." Grady said, and then turned to B.J. and said, "See, I told you I saw something."

"Why were you watching us?" Demanded B.J., still holding her gun on him.

"Could we sit down and have a cup of that coffee while we talk?" He asked.

B.J. motioned for him to sit down, and she eased the hammer down on her pistol. Grady poured him a cup of coffee and he took a long swallow of the hot coffee.

"Man, this is good. I've been without coffee for two days."

B.J. had noticed this big hulk of a man didn't wear a gun, but he did carry a rifle on his saddle. After swallowing another long sip, he began his tale.

"I'm Webster Thompson. I've been a prospector, fur trapper, and a mountain man as some like to call me. I got tired of living in the wilderness alone, and frankly I wasn't having any luck trapping or prospecting, so I sold my furs and most of my traps and lived in the town of Medicine Bow for a spell. I made furniture for the general store for a living, until I got the yearning for the wilderness again. City living is okay for a while, but too many people and too close quarters begin to get on my nerves. I packed up and took to the trail. I'm on my way to claim some of that free land the government is giving to settlers. I've decided it's time I settled down and made something for myself."

B.J. no longer saw the man as a threat to them, so she begins to relax a little and so had Grady.

"We're headed for the free land also." Grady stated.

""How come you two are traveling alone?" Webster asked.

B.J. kept quiet, but Grady started again.

"Our parents were killed by Indians; in fact our whole train was wiped out. My sister and I were the only survivors. My name is Grady Hall and this is my sister B.J. Hall."

Grady reached over to shake the man's hand. Webster shook his hand and reached to shake B.J. B.J. was a little hesitant at first, and then she extended her hand to him.

"You still a little bothered about me being here, Missy?"

"My name is B.J., and I'm not nervous. Let's just say I'm cautious of strangers at night."

"Would you rather I leave?"

Before B.J. could answer Grady blurted out.

"No!"

Then Grady turned and looked at B.J. with pleading eyes.

"It's okay, you can stay."

"No harm will come to either of you from me. I'd find it a privilege if you will let me ride along with you come morning."

"Let's see what morning brings and discuss it more then." B.J. said as she put her pistol back in her holster.

Grady went on to the stream to wash the dishes from their supper.

B.J. noticed Webster looking at the empty plates. Webster never asked for any of their food, but it was evident to her that he was hungry.

"Have you had any supper?"

"No ma'am, but don't worry about me, I'll be fine now that I've had my coffee."

"Our parents taught us to share what we have with others." B.J. said as she fixes Webster a plate of food.

"You kids had good folks and it shows." Webster eagerly took the food and he didn't waste any time eating it.

Grady was back from the stream and laid their clean plates by the fire. When Webster finished, he took his plate to the spring and washed it and put it with the others.

B.J. was thinking here was another mouth to feed and their supplies would not last long, but she never said a word, instead she put the thought out of her mind, knowing he was there and they would have to make the best of it.

After hobbling his horse for the night, Webster brought his bedroll to the opposite side of the fire for the night.

"Good night Missy. You do not need to fear me being here, so sleep sound."

B.J. didn't answer, just snuggled up and closed her eyes. She prayed silently that the Lord would keep them safe through the night. This big man, who walked out of the darkness into their lives, seemed trustworthy, but B.J. knew the Lord would protect them, even from him if necessary. So she closed her eyes and was asleep in no time.

Chapter 7

When morning came, B.J.'s brain was telling her it wasn't time to get up. She had a hard time sleeping, so she pulled the blanket closer around her neck and turned over. Even with her eyes closed, her nostrils were getting the most delicious aroma and soon her stomach was growling, telling her she was hungry. B.J. knew it was time to be up and fixing breakfast.

Webster had beaten her to the chore. He had managed to trap some animal and had it cleaned and cooking on the fire. B.J. sat up and looked around, and then threw her blanket aside and crawled from her bedroll. She stretched and started to the stream to wash the night's sleep from her face and hands.

Webster met her with a coffee pot filled and ready to put on the fire.

"Good morning." Webster greeted.

"Good morning. I see you've been up for some time. Whatever that is cooking sure smells good."

"Its rabbit and it will be ready soon. I trapped it in one of my snares last night. I'll have some coffee shortly."

"You don't need to cook for us. I can take care of the cooking." B.J. told Webster.

"I've done it for myself for so long, I guess it just comes natural. I hope you don't mind me getting into your supplies for the coffee?"

"No. We've nothing to hide. In fact we've very little in there." B.J. said and then wished she hadn't.

"I'll do my share of finding what food I can for us. I don't want to mooch off you kids."

That was the first of many mornings for Webster, B.J. and Grady. Each morning was different because Webster was determined to be the first up and have something trapped, cleaned and cooking. Some mornings it was rabbit, turkey, or pheasant, but whatever it was, it was good. He knew how to season food with wild herbs and made the wild animals taste delicious.

B.J. didn't trust him at first, but after two or three days on the trail, she could see he meant them no harm. Webster needed their company as much as they needed him, and he had been good to them, and right away showed he would do his share and more.

Today was the day they hoped to arrive at Fort Laramie. The five days went by fast since leaving the relay station, partly because of Webster joining up with them. Webster kept them entertained most of the way by telling them about things that had happened in his life.

B.J. knew her dad would have approved of Webster. It was as if the Good Lord had sent Webster to them and B.J. never seized to thank Him in her prayers. There had been times when Grady and she were faced with fear that both felt they could cope with, and then God would send them angels in human form. There was Mildred and Ed at the relay station, and now Webster. All these people came along and gave Grady and her assurance and comfort and B.J. concluded that the Lord definitely was watching over them.

"Tonight we should be at the Fort's gate, and if that's the case, our trip is almost over." Webster said.

"Have you ever been to Fort Laramie?"

"Can't say I have." Replied Webster.

Ed had told them it was a medium size fort, not too many civilians' just military families. B.J. was eager to see other folks. There was also the matter of turning in the names of the dead on the train and giving up the burden of the money she had been carrying all this time.

The day wore on and after stopping for a noon snack, the three started again but didn't get far till they saw a cloud of dust in the distance.

"That'll be the troopers from the fort. They are headed in our direction."

Distance fooled you in this new country, because they rode a while before they met the troopers and when they did, the dust from all the troopers' horses nearly choked them.

"Troops halt." Roared the Lieutenant as he held up his arm.

They stopped, but only the lieutenant rode forward to meet and to speak to them.

"I'm Lieutenant Jeremy Swan, Fort Laramie."

After offering his services to them, he wanted to know where they were going and where they came from. Since he was directing all his questions to Webster, B.J. remained quiet and let Webster do all the talking.

After Webster finished, the lieutenant pointed in the direction they were to go and said, "I hope you have a good stay and it's a pleasant one."

The troopers saw the lieutenant raise his arm and they left just as fast as they had come. The troopers left in columns of two and B.J., Grady, and Webster were standing eating the dust they left behind.

"What was their hurry?" Asked B.J.

"All soldiers are like that. They are given a certain amount of time to go somewhere and to get a job done, and these are no different."

"Did he say how far the fort was?"

Webster shook his head and they rode on hoping it was just a short distance, but they ended up riding the rest of the day. They finally saw the fort looming in the distance just as the sun began to go down. The fort had a big gate with high walls made from huge logs. There were soldiers walking around the top of the walls and they could see Webster. B.J. and Grady when they came into view.

"Three civilian's riders approaching." Came the call from one of them.

"Open the gates." Came an answer.

The big gate swung open allowing Webster, B.J. and Grady to enter. Once inside they could tell there wasn't much activity this time of day. One soldier was visible on the ground and he came straight to them.

"I'm the Officer on Duty. Please state your business."

Again it was Webster they addressed, so Webster answered, "We're here to see your Commander or someone in charge. We've got information about a wagon train that was destroyed by Indians."

"Come right this way, sir." The officer started across the compound and they followed. He showed them where to tie their horses. They followed him up the stairs to a door with a sign that read, Headquarters Company B, Commanding Officer: Captain John Naples.

The officer on duty knocked on the door and they heard a voice say, "Enter."

They went in and B.J. wondered if the others were as nervous as her. Everything had been so formal, so official. Dealing with the authorities in this part of the country meant you had to deal with the Army, and this was what you got

The Captain was donning his coat, like he was meeting someone important, or either they had interrupted him after hours. Maybe his day was over and he was trying to relax.

Webster apologized for disturbing him at such a late hour, but he said, "Nonsense, how can I help you folks?"

The Captain motioned for them to sit down across from his desk. In spite of the formality his position projected, he appeared to be a kind man, full of concern.

"Well, what can I do for ya'll?"

Webster then looked at B.J. and the Captain turned his attention to her also.

"I'm B.J. Hall and this is my brother Grady. Our friend and traveling companion is Webster Thompson."

The captain stretched out his hand and greeted all three of them.

"I'm Captain John Naples, Commander of this fort. Please to meet ya'll."

B.J. told the captain how their wagon train was destroyed and she and Grady were the only survivors, and then she told him about the relay station and the deaths of the Tuckers.

"Where do you fit into this picture?" The captain asked Webster.

"I came upon them about three days out of Medicine Bow and have been with them since. I'm headed for the free government land that is offered to settlers."

The captain rubbed his chin and said, "A destroyed wagon train, dead parents, and a burnt out relay station, what else have you youngsters had to endure?"

Both of them nodded nothing.

"Who were the people killed at the relay station?"

"Gene and Frieda Tucker. We buried them and while we were there a stage came in and the driver Ed told us how to get to this Fort."

The Captain knew Ed. He turned to ask his officer if he was taking all the information down for the record.

"Yes sir." Came the reply.

B.J. took out the list of names and the money she and Grady had collected at the wagon train and laid it on the captain's desk.

The captain sat there looking at the list. "You two have had a rough trip. What I'm going to do for now is let you get a good hot meal, and a hot bath and a good night's rest; we'll complete this report in the morning. Sound good to you?"

All three agreed. They had a long day and they were hungry and they definitely needed a hot bath.

"Take these children to our guest quarters and make arrangements for them a meal and a bath. You can quarter Mr. Thompson with the enlisted men and make arrangements for him also."

"Yes sir." The officer said and motioned them to follow him.

They left Captain Naples office and went down the galleried walk to a door that was opened to Grady and B.J.

"I need to see to our horses." B.J. said.

"I'll have your belongings brought to you and your horses will be taken care of also. No need to worry, they will be in good hands."

B.J. entered the room they had been assigned, only to find a woman there. The woman was elderly but fully in control. She was directing the soldiers about where to put the tubs for their baths. The tubs were put in separate rooms and filled with plenty of hot water. Then the woman turned to B.J. and Grady and introduced herself.

"I'm Mrs. Naples, the Captain's wife. You children must be worn out from that terrible trip. How long have you been on the road?"

"It's been seven days since we left the relay station and last had baths."

Mrs. Naples nodded like she believed every word. B.J. realized Grady and she were getting rank. She wondered what Mrs. Naples would think of Webster and found it hard to hide her smile.

B.J. and Grady had their hot baths and hot meal just as the Captain promised.

"Grady, what do you suppose Webster is doing right about now?"

"I hope they aren't helping him with his bath." They both laughed, visualizing it.

"He is probably telling all the men one of his big tales right about now."

"We better get some sleep; we still have to see the Captain in the morning."

It was comforting to sleep in a warm, clean bed and feel safe at the same time. B.J. lay thinking how strange it was not seeing stars overhead, but she finally closed her eyes and was fast asleep.

They had a rude awakening the next morning; it was the sound of reveille coming from a bugle. B.J. was confused, but soon realized where she was. Grady came rushing into her room, rubbing his eyes.

"What is happening?"

"We're in the army now, and it's time to get up."

"Do they have to be so loud?"

"Well, it worked; we're awake like everyone else."

They dressed and hurried to the door. There stood Webster, clean-shaven, clean clothes, and almost unrecognizable.

"Why are you starring? Haven't you ever seen a clean shaven man before?"

"Yes, but not you. You clean up pretty good." Grady teased.

"Come on, it's breakfast time and in the army if you snooze, you get left out."

The three of then ate their food and enjoyed it until the bugle sounded again. B.J. looked at Webster and he volunteered, "Muster."

"Muster, what is muster?" Grady asked.

"Same as roll call in school. They have to account for everyone."

"Do we muster too?"

Webster laughed at Grady and shook his head. They followed the soldiers outside and watched as they formed a line and stood at attention while the bugler blew again and the flag was raised to the top of the flagpole. Then each trooper answered the roll call and they were dismissed to do their duties for the day.

"Uncle Webster," Grady had started calling Webster uncle for several days now. "Do I need to check on our horses?"

"No son, those horses are in good hands. These troopers depend on their horses for everything out here, and they know how to take care of them, ours included."

As Webster, Grady, and B.J. stood enjoying the morning and looking over the fort, the officer from the night before approached them.

"Good morning. I trust everyone had a good night sleep and a hearty breakfast?"

"Yes we did, thank you." B.J. answered.

"The Captain would like to see all of you in his office."

They followed the officer back to the Captain's office and were escorted into the room they were in the night before.

"Good morning. It's time we decided what needs to be done about your problem." The Captain had the list of names and the money that B.J. had left with him on his desk. He read the list of names and afterwards shook his head, like it was inconceivable.

"So many deaths and all unnecessary, and you say all that was taken were the horses and livestock?"

"They went through some of our food and supplies, but not knowing what everyone had, I couldn't tell what all they did take." B.J. explained.

"Were any of the folks scalped?"

B.J. looked at the captain in total confusion, so the captain rephrased his question.

"Did any of the bodies have their heads cut or part of their hair removed?"

B.J. thought back to the morning she walked through all the death and destruction looking for Grady. She had lifted their heads; there were no cuts or scalps removed. She remembered how unpleasant it was so she told the captain and this answered his question.

"This was not a war party, just hungry Indians wanting food. They have had a rough winter and it's too soon for crops, so they raid and kill to get food to stay alive till spring. I'm not excusing what was done here; just trying to explain what I think happened. I'm terrible sorry about your parents. I can get word to the families on this list, but I have no way of wiring money to them. I suggest you two keep the money. The money would have decayed with time if you had left it, and maybe you can find some use for it. I assure you it's legal. You will need a stake when you get to the free land and maybe this will compensate for the loss of your parents." Finished, the Captain stood.

"Thank you, sir." B.J. said.

"Feel free to wander around the fort and to stay as long as you need, just don't get in my men's way. There is a commissary if you need to replenish your supplies before you leave."

The Captain walked to the door with them, and turned to Webster. "You take care of these children Webster. They have experienced enough sorrow in their short lives, than most of us men do in a lifetime."

"Don't you worry sir, as long as they will put up with me, I'll be there for them."

The Captain smiled and returned to his office. The young officer asked, "How long will you folks be staying with us?"

"We'd like to give our horses a couple days rest and pick up some supplies before we leave, if that's okay?" Webster told him.

"Sure, sure, we'll have a detail of men returning tomorrow and they will have the latest report of any trouble. You might want to hear it before you leave. Check in with me and I'll tell you the latest so you will know what you will encounter along the way."

Webster, B.J. and Grady left the young officer and rambled toward the commissary. B.J. felt a big burden lifted from her. There was the money the Captain gave her still in the scarf and Webster eased over to her and suggested she keep her mouth closed about it while they were here. B.J. nodded and they walked on. She had taken a little of the money out before she replaced it.

"How about us going to the commissary and checking out what they have?" B.J. noticed Grady face perked up. Talking about their parents had saddened him, but now he was back on track.

"Yeah!" Grady happily replied.

The commissary was big and had about everything you could possible want or need. The stop was what all three needed. Webster came out with a new hat and Grady with a sack of candy that he had craved for a long time. B.J. purchased a new dress. Where or when she would wear it, she had no idea, but just being able to shop made the future look brighter.

When the three came from the commissary and was slowly walking around the fort, Webster noticed a shady-looking character standing against one of the buildings. This man had his hat pulled low on his head as though to hide as much of his face as he could. At first Webster tried to pass the man's being there off as normal. Maybe he was there to sell horses to the Army, or even a drummer, selling goods to the commissary. But after looking him over more carefully, Webster knew that neither fit his character.

The man had the look of a no-account that indicated he would as soon take from his own mother as anyone else. His clothes were nasty and unkempt, his boots worn and dirty and his face unshaven. He had a head of long straggly hair hanging from under his hat. On his hip was a gun wore low and tied down for a faster draw. No, he wasn't there for any good; goodness never entered this man's mind. Webster knew this type. There was one like him in almost every town, waiting to take from someone rather than earn his own living. Webster would have to keep a close eye on this character while they were here and especially after they left the fort.

Their stay at the fort lasted two more days. After the detail arrived and they got the latest scouting report, Webster, B.J. and Grady made their plans to leave. They went back to the commissary to purchase what supplies they would need to complete their trip. Webster made sure they had a good stock of coffee. Their horses were in good shape. The horses were rested and well fed and even had new shoes, thanks to one of the troopers. The trooper also informed Webster that one of their mares was with foal. B.J. suspected this from the relay station incident. They thanked him for the information and for the good care that had been given to their horses.

Webster paid a visit to the Captain before they left and was told it would take at least three, maybe four days before they got to Casper. Webster intentions were to inquire about the man who had been watching them at a distance. But according to one of the troopers at the stables, the man had left the night before, so Webster didn't mention the man. He didn't mention him, but Webster had not forgotten about him. There would be trouble from this character; Webster could almost feel it in his bones. There was no need to upset B.J. or Grady, so Webster made up his mind to be observant to everything around them as they traveled.

The next morning Webster, B.J. and Grady, all packed and saddled, stopped to thank the captain for his hospitality.

"I wish the best for all of you. My troopers can accompany you so far, if you want."

"That won't be necessary since there was no trouble reported from your detail, but thank you anyway." Webster said as he extended his hand to the Captain.

"Good luck B.J. and Grady. I hope your new home will bring you many years of happiness."

"Thank you sir." Both replied.

They turned their horses towards the big gates, and they saw them swing open to let them go through. The visit to Fort Laramie would hold good memories for them, like the relay station. B.J. and Grady had made more friends. Friends that would not be forgotten, because of the kindness they had shown to Grady and her.

They felt good being in the saddle and on the way again. Time was drawing nearer to reaching the land office and signing their names to land that would belong to them from now on. B.J. rode, lost in her thoughts about their future home, finding it almost impossible to believe in only four days the dream her dad and mom had for them, would become a reality.

The passing countryside was beautiful. The day passed quickly because B.J. was taking in all the breath-taking scenery surrounding them, thinking their property would be similar to this. Webster was taking in all the surroundings also, but for a different reason. Webster still had that uneasy feeling in the pit of his stomach. After hours of riding, Grady was the first of the three to speak.

"Am I the only one who is hungry?"

"Boy, all you think about is food." Webster answered.

"Give me a little time and my thoughts will be about other things. Right now I'm a growing boy and I need my food."

Webster looked at B.J. and asked, "Do you want to stop for the night? It is getting late."

"Yea, we'll look for a campsite."

A strand of trees was spotted up ahead, so they rode in that direction. When they arrived, Webster took a good look around. This site would provide them with terrain that would protect their backs during the night. They had water from a spring coming out of the mountainside and grass nearby for the horses. Camp was made for the night.

After cleaning up the dishes from supper, B.J. and Grady climbed into their bedrolls, and was asleep in a matter of minutes. Webster fixed his bedroll to look as though he was in it asleep, but instead Webster sat propped against a big tree in the shadows. Across his arm lay his rifle, loaded and ready. Tonight Webster would sleep with one eye opened and both ears tuned to any unusual sound.

The night sounds were soon accounted for in Webster memory. The crackling of the logs burning in the fire, the insects singing their nightly songs, the small creatures that prowled at night, and the horses shifting from one foot to the other to allow them sleep while standing. Webster knew each of these sounds as the night grew later and later, and soon they lulled him asleep.

The man that Webster had noticed at the fort had been tailing them all day, even though he left the fort a night earlier. He hid out purposely waiting for them. When he first saw the stallion that belonged to the girl, he made up his mind to get that horse. He knew good horseflesh and that stallion was some of the best he had ever seen. Asking around, he found out from the troopers that the party of three was headed to Casper, Wyoming to register for free government land. He also found out that stallion was a registered Kentucky thoroughbred and that no horseflesh this far west could begin to compare with him.

Standing in the distance bushes, the man watched as the camp settled down for the night. He could see the three bedrolls and most of all; he could see their horses tethered on a rope close-by. The campfire was burning low and soon he would have his chance to ease in and take that stallion right from under their noses. Waiting and watching, the man all but slivered as a snake would to get closer and closer. Extra precaution was taken to watch where he stepped and what he would brush against as he neared the horses. Finally, he was in touching distance of them, but the stallion was the fartherest from him. Dude got scent of the stranger and began shifting about trying to see where this scent was coming from. Once Dude pulled on his rope it jerked the rope that had the other horses tethered and caused them to begin moving around in fright also.

Webster was awake when Dude first snorted and jerked his head. After a few moments, Webster's eyes adjusted to the darkness and he could see a darker form than that of the horses easing closer and closer. Webster sat perfectly still, he knew whoever it was, and he was almost certain it would be the man at the fort, was trying to steal their horses, or at least Dude. The man had not seen Webster because he thought he was in his bedroll at the edge of the remaining fire, but Webster could see him real clear now.

Dude knew he was there also, because he was determined the stranger was not going to get any closer to him. The man eased up to the side of Dude and gently laid his hand on Dude's right hind leg. Webster could hear the shadow in the darkness whispering to Dude, trying to settle him down enough to untie him from the rope. Dude got quiet, so the man thought he had succeeded and eased himself around to the back of Dude. Webster purposely moved, making the man jerk his hand from Dude's withers and when he did, Dude took his cue and kicked out with his hind legs, knocking the man flat on the ground.

Dude was letting everyone know that something was wrong. He was whinnying and snorting, pawing the ground, and jerking his head up causing the other horses to do the same. Webster jumped to his feet and with his rifle cocked and ready, stood over the man waiting for him to get up. B.J. and Grady was right by Webster's side holding their pistols in their hands and trying to calm the horses down.

Webster took his rifle barrel and jabbed at the body of the man, but he never moved. Webster took his foot and turned him over. They could plainly see why the man didn't get up, his head was bashed in and part of his face and brain was missing. Blood was running down his neck onto the ground.

Grady gasped and turned from the bloody scene. He hid his face in B.J.'s side. B.J. felt nauseated, but stood holding on to Dude's halter and calming him as best she could.

"Go back to the fire; I'll take care of him." Webster told them.

"I've got to check Dude to make sure he isn't hurt first. Grady you go back to bed." B.J. told him.

"No sir. I'll help too. This involves all of us and we can't run from these sorts of things."

Webster covered the man head with a handful of dry leaves. Once that was done the rest wasn't so hard to stomach.

"Who was he and how did he get here?" Grady asked.

"He was watching us at the fort. I saw him there, but he left a night before we did, so I thought or hoped we wouldn't have any trouble from him. I was wrong, but I was ready just in case."

"Dude, was ready too." B.J. said as she finished feeling all over Dude.

"Was he going to steal Dude, Uncle Webster?" Grady asked.

"I'm almost sure he was giving it his best effort. He just didn't know how smart Dude is."

Webster went through his pockets and all he found was a twenty dollar gold piece. There was nothing to identify the man, or where his family might live. Webster stripped the man of his side arm and belt and handed them and his rifle to Grady to take back to the campfire. After Grady walked off, Webster took a piece of tarp and rolled the man up in it, and then carried his body away from their camp till daylight. Webster would bury him.

B.J. watched Webster as she stroked Dude, thinking what a close call all of them just had. What ever would they do if anything happened to Dude? He was to be their stud for their horse ranch. From now on Dude would be tied closer to them than the other horses.

When Webster and she returned to the camp, Grady had put more wood on the fire and they had good light and a good source of heat. Even though the nights were warming some, the after effects of the scare they experienced had chilled all of them to the bone.

"Let's try and get a little sleep. I don't think there is anything left to worry about. He was a loner and in the morning I will bury him and we'll search for his horse and provisions before we leave here." Webster said to B.J. and Grady.

B.J. woke the next morning to find Uncle Webster gone. At first she was puzzled and then she remembered the happenings of the night. The fire was going and a pot of coffee was brewing, but there was nothing cooking. Webster had spoiled her to getting up to a breakfast fixed and ready. B.J. knew where Webster was. He had saddled his horse and carried the dead man off to bury. She would have him breakfast waiting this morning.

B.J. went to the spring and washed off the night's sleep and returned to start their food. She was in the midst of frying ham when Webster rode in leading the extra horse. B.J. sat the skillet to the side and went to meet him.

"Why didn't you wake me and I would have helped you?"

"No one needs to start at day like I just did, especially a pretty young lady like you. You have had enough burying for one so young."

"I see you found his horse. Was there anything in his saddlebags to indicate who he was and where he is from?"

"No. Just a change of clothes and the usual things a man carries. He sure knew good horseflesh though. Take a look at this gelding he was riding. There's not a brand on him, so I thought we'd keep him rather than turn him loose. This saddle not in too good shape, but it would do in a tight. What do you think?"

B.J. walked around the gelding and felt his legs and looked at his teeth. "This horse is well taken care of and he isn't that old. Make a good saddle horse for anyone. Sure we'll keep him and that extra saddle. How about some breakfast? Are you hungry?"

"I found a nest of pheasant eggs that we could scramble with that ham." Webster began unwrapping eggs from his kerchief he had hidden inside his shirt and handed them to B.J.

B.J. took the eggs and finished cooking the ham and scrambled them in the same pan. The coffee was ready so Webster kicked Grady awake and sat down to enjoy a cup. Grady washed and came back to eat.

Afterwards they packed up their provisions and without saying anything more about the dead man, they started another day that would bring them closer to their destination.

Three days in the saddle passed and they were on the outskirts of Casper, Wyoming. During the three days they passed through some beautiful country. When they left Fort Laramie, they had headed north and the scenery changed entirely. Before Laramie they had seen mostly semi-desert country, dry and dusty, very few hill and no mountains. Now they were near the foothills of the Rocky Mountains. The grass in the lowlands was more abundant here. They could see a lot of ponderosa pines and what Webster called lodge pole pines.

B.J. noticed the difference in the climate. In Kentucky, the climate was hot and humid; here the air was dry and cool. It was the beginning of June and in Kentucky it would have been skinny dipping weather, but here a person still needed a light jacket, especially early in the mornings.

There were a lot of deer. Everywhere they looked would be little groups standing around, eating. The deer would look at them and raise their ears, and then go back to eating grass. Man had not spoiled this country, thus far. Webster would have a time with his traps here. They saw a grizzly bear, but tried hard to avoid him. Those fellows mean trouble and they knew it. As they went further into the foothills of the mountains, they began to see mountain goats.

"Wow! Have you ever seen so many different animals and so many of them?" Grady asked.

"I have, but not as close together as these are." Webster answered.

There was one section they passed through that really caught B.J.'s eye. There was a beautiful lake, like a natural reservoir, at least five miles wide. A strand of trees on one side made it perfect for a home site. B.J. looked this spot over real good, thinking there would be plenty of water all year, and the mountains in the background would protect anyone from the cold winter wind. After seeing this particular place, B.J. hoped and prayed it had not been claimed by anyone else. This was the section she wanted for her and Grady and Webster.

Chapter 8

The outline of the town of Casper could be seen in the distance. B.J. and Grady was excited to be this close to claiming the land their parents had died for. They wanted to kick their horses to a full run and get into town as fast as they could, but they knew the animals were tired, so they let the horses take their time.

"Now remember, B.J., you keep quiet about that money when we get into town. You never know who to trust in a strange town." Webster warned her.

"Yes, sir."

When they got to Casper, all three were surprised at how busy and crowded the town was. Compared to Fort Laramie, Casper was a large, booming town, almost as large as St. Joseph, Missouri. They rode down the main street and saw the many different shops and businesses. They saw some men sitting on the porch of a barbershop and Webster reined his horse in their direction.

"Good afternoon, gentlemen. Could one of you tell me where I might find the Government Land Office?"

One of the men stood up.

"Strangers, huh? Well, you see the general store sign just down the street a ways? The land office is just two doors down from there."

"Thank you kindly, sir." Webster said and turned his horse in the direction of the store and B.J. and Grady followed.

When they got to the land office, they tied their horses and went inside. The man behind the counter asked. "May I help you folks?"

B.J. took out the paper from her dad's box and laid it on the counter in front of the man. He picked the paper up and read it. "What name is the claim filed in?"

"The claim has not been filed yet; we are here to file it."

"But, you're just children. How are you going to homestead a place? You understand the government expects improvements within a year or the land reverts back to the government, don't you?"

"I'm their uncle, Webster Thompson, and I'll be helping them."

"Yes sir, I understand that. How old are you little lady?"

"I'm almost seventeen and my brother is almost thirteen."

"You two will be eligible for two sections. That's 1280 acres. Your uncle is eligible for one section. Do you want this land adjacent to each other?"

"Yes," they said in unison.

The land office manager went to a large map on the wall. "All the land marked by red has been claimed. Do you know where you want to settle?"

B.J. described to him the land they had traveled through that she like so much.

"So, you folks want south of Casper? That section is called the Deer Creek Range?" he pointed to it on the map. "Did you pass a lake about five miles in size?"

"Yes, yes that's the place. Has anyone claimed that section?"

"Nope, it seems everyone wanted to settle right around town and to the north, so if you want that section it's still up for grabs."

"Good, we'll take all our land right their." B.J. confirmed.

The man went back to the counter and began filling out the papers. Webster, Grady, and B.J. were all three beaming with happiness.

"That's a mighty good section of land you've chosen. You will be about a days ride from town if you folks need anything." He was writing all the time he was talking and when he finished the paper work, he went back to the map and filled in the section they had claimed with red. On the big wall map the land looked small; but B.J. knew that nearly three thousand acres was anything but small. That was more land than her Dad ever owned in Kentucky.

When the paper work was completed and signed and they had their copies, B.J. and Webster and Grady thanked the man and started for the door.

"Would you like to know the name of your nearest neighbor?" The land office man asked.

"Sure we would. We believe in being neighborly."

"The Brook family. They are fine Christian folks with three boys to keep Grady company and they live about halfway between here and where ya'll will be settling. Their ranch is just to the East of your section. Next time I see them in town I'll tell them they have new neighbors."

They thanked the man, shook his hand and left. Once outside all three embraced each other and danced for joy right there on the street front. Everyone in town knew their happiness because everyone who came by smiled and patted them on the back and welcomed them to Casper.

"What'll we do now?" Grady asked.

B.J. looked to Webster for suggestions.

"We need to find a hotel room, and sit down and talk about what we will need to take back to the land with us. We will have to make a list of supplies, buy a wagon, so much is needed, and we don't want to forget anything. Let's go rent a room and plan to stay the night and by morning we will be loaded and ready to head for home. How does that sound?" Webster was already untying his horse and B.J. and Grady followed his every move.

After finding a hotel and getting settled in, with the promise from the owner that hot tubs of water would be sent up for them to bathe, they climbed the steps to the two rooms they had rented for the night. B.J. took her key and Webster and Grady would share the second room. The three sat down and tried to remember what all was needed to begin their new home. Their list was made and it was a long one, but everything on it was necessary. Webster and Grady left going to their room.

B.J. had never stayed at a hotel before and she marveled at how nice the rooms were. B.J. had a fear that all their money would be gone much too soon, if they wasn't careful how they spent it. She wanted so much to have enough to buy the supplies to get their new house started and finished before cold weather. It was spring now and it would probably take them that long to get a decent house built and livable. The Lord had brought them this far and she knew He would provide for them, she would have to have stronger faith in Him.

B.J. finished bathing and dressing and went down stairs to find Webster and Grady ready and waiting.

"Did you get our horses taken care of?" B.J. asked.

"They are all fine. They will be fed and watered and all rested by the time we leave in the morning."

"Are we going to eat tonight?" Grady asked.

"Yes, we're going to find a place to eat a bite of supper."

"A bite. I want a whole meal." Grady said.

The three left the hotel laughing, in search of a restaurant. This had been a happy day for them and it was because the Lord was in control. Once they eat, they went down the street to the general store to purchase the items they had listed. Webster went to the livery stable to talk to the owner about wagon. He knew all the supplies could not be carried on the horses. When he came back, the storeowner was still filling their order and B.J. stood looking hungrily at a new black wood-burning cook stove. Webster walked up to her and she ran her hand over the top of the slick surface and he knew right then that B.J. would have to have that stove.

"Do you think we could afford this stove? It will cast $25.00."

"Get the stove, if you want it. I've got some money put back if we run short." Webster patted her on the shoulder and walked over to see what else the storeowner had put in their pile of supplies. "We will load this order early in the morning. I've got a wagon bought and a team to pull it, so if you can meet us here early, we'll get it loaded and out of your way."

"That will be fine sir, but you folks know that I don't do first business on credit. Since your strangers, I'll have to be cash or nothing. Sorry, but I've been burned too many times by folks that tried to make a homestead and ended up leaving and owing me money to boot."

"We understand. You will be paid in cash for everything we purchase. Include that stove over there with our order. If you will tell me how much the total sum is, I'll bring you cash in the morning." B.J. told the owner.

The storeowner did his adding and told B.J. the total of all the supplies and the stove was $150.00. B. J. would take the money from her scarf and have it ready come morning. That was a lot of money. If Grady and see were using what their parents had brought, nearly all of the two hundred would be gone. Thank God the Captain at the Fort had given them the other money too.

All three of them was satisfied and felt the money was well spent, so they left the store going to the hotel to get a good nights sleep.

B.J. found it hard to sleep that night. She had so many thoughts running through her head at once. The excitement of getting their land and buying their supplies was keeping her awake. B.J. finally had to force herself to think about the beauty of their land and to remember the lake and the trees, the quiet, peaceful surrounding and with those thoughts in mind B.J. drifted off and didn't wake till the next morning.

Their work was cut out for them without a doubt. There was so much that had to be done before winter settled in and B.J. knew they wouldn't have time for much else, but right then, before she left her warm bed, she took the time to thank the Lord again. B.J. thanked Him for his watch care over them and for bringing them to this beautiful country that was now their earthly home. She thanked the Lord for her parents who thought ahead to Grady and her future. They left what they had and lost their lives to show them their love. B.J. wished her parents could be there to see how beautiful their home would one day be, but inside her heart, she knew they knew.

There was a tapping on her door and she asked who it was.

"It's us, me and Uncle Webster. Open the door, we're ready to eat and get going." Grady answered.

B.J. smiled. "I'll be dressed in just a minute—keep your shirt on."

When B.J. opened the door, Webster and Grady were ready for breakfast and to begin their day.

B.J. had taken the money out of the scarf and tied it back around her waist and they went back to the restaurant where they had eaten the night before for breakfast. When breakfast was finished, they went to the livery stables for the horses and wagon that Webster had bought.

"Are you planning on pulling this wagon with those two extra horses you have?" The liveryman asked Webster.

"Well, yes, I had. Don't you think they can?"

"That's a heavy wagon, empty. When you get it loaded, it will take a team of good wagon horses to pull it any distance and to hold out. I've got a team of draft horses out back, with harness, which would pull a loaded wagon and anything else you will need to pull. Come on, I'll show you."

The three followed the man to the back corral and looked over his fence at the matched team of draft horses. The horses were huge. Their hooves were so large, that it would take two of Dude's hooves to be the size of one of theirs. Webster walked around them feeling them over real good and then looked at their teeth. They were a young team and very gentle.

"How much?"

"Well, as you can see this is prime horse flesh. I need to get my price and since I'm throwing in the harness, I would have to have at least $50.00."

Webster looked towards B.J. and she nodded. They were worth every penny. So Webster took the money out of his shirt and handed it to the liveryman.

"Here is your set of harness and I'll show you my heart's in the right place by helping you and that boy harness and hitch then to your wagon."

The liveryman brought the big draft horses around for Webster and Grady to harness. Then they walked the horses out back to the wagon Webster had bought. The wheels were tight and well greased. B.J. had saddled the other horses and had them out front of the barn when Webster drove the wagon around. Two horses were tied to the back and B.J. and Grady mounted and followed the wagon to the general store. Grady still led their one packhorse.

When they got to the store, Webster pulled the team to a stop, got down and tied them to the rail and Grady and B.J. did the same. They would all work at loading the supplies and then tying it down. Everything had to be stacked just right. Webster warned them that he didn't want to get home and half of it be missing or broken, especially the stove.

When they finished the storeowner asked, "Will you need anything else, miss?"

"Yes, fix up a sack of mixed hard candy, please."

B.J. had the money in her pocket and counted it out to the storeowner. Webster came in, Grady and he had tied a tarp over the supplies just in case of rain.

"Will we need anything else?" B.J. asked Webster.

After rubbing his chin for a minute and thinking, Webster asked the storeowner if he had two empty barrels. The man went to the back and came rolling one after the other to the wagon and Webster tied them to each side and put the lids on them.

"I forgot about water barrels. What do I owe you for them?"

"No charge. You folks just come back to see me when you need more supplies."

They thanked him and Webster climbed on the wagon. B.J. and Grady mounted and they left Casper going home.

"We're headed home." B.J. said and all of them smiled. Home—no sweeter sound—their stay in the big city of Casper had been good, but going home was better.

Chapter 9

After leaving Casper, the trail back to the land they claimed was a different one. The loaded wagon had to travel on a road, and because of this the trip home would take longer. The big draft horses pulled the wagon with little effort even after lumber was added. Before long they were out of sight of the town of Casper and well on their way.

Webster kept the team moving at a fairly good pace because they were anxious to get to their land. "We'll get to see where our neighbors live. We go right pass their place to ours."

"How much farther is it to their place?" B.J. asked.

"I figure we'll be getting there before dinner."

B.J. looked across to Grady, he was beaming. All anyone had to do was mention food and Grady was the happiest person on earth.

Webster noticed too and decided to have some fun with Grady. "Can't you just taste good old homemade vittles that may be offered to us, Grady?"

Grady smiled even bigger and kicked his horse as to hurry them on. Sure enough, after about an hour they saw signs of a ranch. The cattle were grazing all around as they entered a little valley. The road seemed to go right to the ranch house, and then continued on from there. They saw the big barn first, and then the house came into view. There were a lot of chickens in the yard and a big dog came running to the wagon, barking. The front door opened and a woman came out on the porch wiping her hands on her apron.

"Howdy folks! I'm Earline Brooks, welcome to our home. Won't you get down and stay while?" She asked as she walked out to the wagon and extended her hand to Webster.

Webster pulled the team to a stop, tied the reins around the brake handle, and stepped down.

"Afternoon Ma'am. I'm Webster Thompson and this is B.J. and Grady Hall." Webster removed his hat and continued, "Appears we'll be your new neighbors."

"I'm right pleased to make you folk's acquaintance, and pleased to know we'll have nearby neighbors, too. My husband, Ralph and our three boys are up the valley seeing to our cows. They'll be in for dinner shortly. Ya'll just come on in and make yourselves at home. We don't get many visitors around here and I'm starved for news. Where is it you folks hail from?"

B.J. and Grady stepped down and Grady asked if he could water their horses.

"Certainly, Son, help yourself."

Webster and Grady led the horse to the water trough, but B.J. followed Mrs. Brooks into the house. B.J. was impressed at how nice everything was. The house wasn't what you would call fancy, but it was clean and homely. She could tell working folks lived here. The smell coming from the kitchen caused her stomach to growl in hunger.

"I need to see to my dinner, B.J. Come on in, won't you? I hope you folks will stay and share our meal with us?"

"Thank you ma'am, but we don't want to be any trouble for you. We mainly wanted to get acquainted with our new neighbors on our way to our new land."

"Trouble? It's never trouble to welcome newcomers with a little meal. It's nothing fancy, mind you, and we love to share what we've been blessed with. Please say you will stay."

How could anyone in his or her right mind refuse an offer like that, B.J. thought? "We will stay on the condition that you will let me help you finish the meal."

Earline handed B.J. an apron and put her to work peeling potatoes. On the stove was chicken frying and in the oven were apple pies baking. B.J.

89

finished peeling the potatoes and Earline put them on to cook and her and B.J. started setting the table. It was a big table, but they finally got all the plates and silverware placed.

"How many boys do you have, Mrs. Brooks?"

"Three and they can eat as much as their dad."

"I know about boys appetites. Grady can't be filled."

"Growing boys need to be fed good; it helps them grow into big, strong men."

"Is Webster kin to your Dad or Mom?"

"Neither, we met him on the trail and realized we were headed in the same direction and for the same purpose, so we just joined up. You could say Grady and I, sorta adopted him, and he adopted us."

"He does seem like a good man, so maybe he was a God sent for you youngsters. I guess everything is ready, so I'll call my troops." Earline walked to the porch and rang the steel triangle hanging there. Webster and Grady knew what that sound meant too, so they finished up in a hurry.

Webster and Grady had finished washing, when the old dog jumped up and starting down the road, barking. They could see four riders coming as hard as they could.

The man and boys were surprised to find them there. Earline introduced Webster, B.J. and Grady to her husband Ralph, and her three boys, Norman, Dale, and Greg. Everyone shook hands all around and after washing they went into the big kitchen and seated themselves around the table. Everyone bowed their heads and Ralph Brooks asked the blessing. The food started around; it did look and smell good and it sure taste good.

What a wonderful meal! The food, the conversation, and the friendly atmosphere told B.J. that yes, these were good people to have as neighbors. They had been made even welcomer by an invitation to stay the night.

"We've got to be on our way. Leaving good company like ya'll is hard, but getting to our own land is something we've been a long time trying to accomplish." B.J. explained. She helped clean up the dishes and Webster and Ralph Brooks walked out to their wagon. When Earline and B.J. finished the dishes, Earline wrapped up all the food left for them to take.

"You will need supper when you do get there, and here is enough for ya'll."

"Thank you for everything." B.J. reached up and hugged her neck.

When they went outside, B.J. noticed two of the boys giving Dude a good looking over.

"Is this your stallion, B.J.?" Norman asked.

"Yea, he's mine."

"He sure is a fine horse. I've never seen one quite like him before. What breed is he?"

"Dude is part Kentucky thoroughbred and part Morgan, one of the best horses you could have."

Ralph Brooks had noticed the stallion too. "Are you gonna breed him. B.J.?"

"That's our plan. We hope to improve our stock with these two mares. One is already with foal. We might try breeding Dude with a quarter horses, like ya'll have."

Ralph nodded his head in approval of her plans.

After thanking the Brook's again for their hospitality, they said goodbye and started down the road. The visit had been really nice, the meal delicious, and it was assuring to know they would have fine neighbors, but now it was time to go home. Not knowing the road, they would have to go as far as daylight would let them. Then camp and get an early start the next morning. The important thing was this was the last leg of their long trip.

Webster, Grady and B.J had been riding at least three hours and they were coming into more of the mountain ranges now. This country was beautiful. There was plenty of grass and game of all kinds. Coming over a little rise that opened into another valley, B.J. noticed Dude acting up. B.J. couldn't figure what was wrong with him, but Webster pointed to a meadow just ahead, where there were other horses.

B.J. had never seen so many horses in one place, just grazing. Dude neighed, and was answered by several mares. B.J. held him tight because Dude wanted to go to the mares.

"Keep a tight rein on him, he smells those mares." Webster shouted to her.

About that time a big stallion started in their direction. Dude was fast becoming a handful. The stallion was beautiful. His black coat was as shiny as silk and his tail was so long it dragged the ground. The black stallion reared on his hind legs, pawing the air.

"He's telling Dude those are his ladies and to steer clear."

"That stallion doesn't have a thing to worry about from Dude or me."

Taking his rifle, Webster fired a shot into the air and scared off the stallion and his mares followed. B.J. finally got Dude calmed down.

"I sure would like to have that big black." Said Grady.

"That would be asking for trouble. That black was born free and he will always be free. It's possible to take a wild horse and tame him, but when they are mean, and that black looked about as mean as they come, then all you've got is trouble."

B.J. didn't want anything to happen to Dude. To them, Dude was their bread and butter of the future. Dust caught up with them and Webster, Grady and B.J. were forced to find a camp spot for the night. Webster decided they would hobble the horses tonight, but would picket them close to their camp. After eating a little supper, they settled down to sleep. In the morning they would continue on home.

Early the next morning found the three eager to get to their land. When they came within sight of the lake, they really did get anxious. B.J. rode on ahead, followed by Grady and the extra horses. Webster had to take it slower because he didn't want to turn the wagon over with all their belongings and supplies on board.

B.J. got off Dude and walked around the spot she imagined the house should be built. She looked all around and the beauty of the unspoiled surroundings was breath taking. This was a special place and now it belonged to them. B.J. could visualize how it would look when the house, barn and corral was finished. Her train of thought was interrupted by Grady.

"Is this where we will camp till we get a house built?"

"I like this spot, do you?"

"Yea, but we better wait for Uncle Webster and see what he thinks."

Webster pulled the wagon in about that time and stopped the team.

"Is this where you want to set up camp, B.J.?"

"What do you think about it?" B.J. asked Webster.

The two of them walked around looking for a better camp spot, but there was none to be found. Webster stretched to get the kinks out.

"This spot looks fine to me. We'll be far enough from the lake that we won't have to worry about snakes and close enough for plenty of water. The trees behind are mostly pines, just what we need to build our cabin. The land is gently sloped toward the lake for good drainage; I think its ideal."

Looking further they saw that a mile or so behind where the cabin was planned to be, the hills began to gradually get higher. This was good because the mountains would cut most of the northern wind in cold weather. All in all, it was a perfect spot to put their cabin, so with all the pros and cons discussed, they began unloading the wagon on that spot. The supplies came off first and then it took all three of them to unload the stove.

Webster cut some poles and then took the tarp, and he and Grady had a tent up in no time. They stored their supplies in it, hoping no bears would be tempted. The bears were near because they had seen them on the trail. The tent would also serve as a place to sleep till it warmed a bit more at night.

B.J. began gathering firewood and Grady helped Webster unhitch the draft horses from the wagon. After the horses was taken care of, Grady came back to help B.J. with the wood. She got a fire started in the new cook stove and found their coffee pot and got it brewing. Seeing a brand new cook stove sitting out in the middle of nowhere with smoke coming out of the pipe, seemed funny. Funny or not, B.J. knew she had to get something cooked for them to eat. They had not eaten since early that morning.

"What're we having for supper?" Grady inquired.

"Whatever is the easiest to fix."

Webster walked up and added, "Cook a lot of that "whatever", and make a big pot of coffee to go with it."

Everyone was in a good mood. It was fun for a change to get pot and pans out to cook in. While B.J. was cooking, she noticed that Webster walked down to the lake and stayed for quite a long time. B.J. called to him and Grady when she got the food ready. When she looked at Webster approaching them, he had a string of fresh fish in his hands.

"Where did those come from?"

"Right out of our lake, and there's plenty more. If Grady will help me clean them after we eat, we'll have them for breakfast."

After supper, B.J. cleaned up the dishes and Webster and Grady cleaned fish. Webster put the fish in a pan of cold water with a tight lid. He didn't want the night critters to steal them. Webster poured himself another cup of hot coffee and stretched out on his blanket. It was already dark by now, so they stayed close to the fire.

"In the morning Grady and I will begin cutting some of the pines and dragging them up to start our cabin. B.J., you will need to make the mud to go between the logs in order to make them air tight. The work is gonna be hard, but I'm sure we can do it. We will built one large room, and then add to it."

After talking more about the cabin, Grady decided to check on the horses again. He wanted to make sure all were well tied for the night. B.J. gathered more wood and put it by the stove and Webster rolled out their bedrolls in the tent. The last chore that B.J. did was to fill the coffee pot and set it off the stove for morning.

The three of them climbed into their beds and Webster asked if they had their pistols nearby?

"Yes sir, are you expecting trouble?" B.J. asked.

"No, just being cautious." Webster answered as he removed his boots and threw his blanket over him.

They were all tired but glad to finally be home. B.J. closed her eyes, but instead of sleep, a vision of the black stallion came to her. That stallion was fantastic, so sleek, big and coal black, but not as grand as her horse, Dude. There would never be another stallion as beautiful as Dude. B.J. thought about the black's mares too. What a nice price they would bring if they could be caught. Would it be possible to catch all those horses and where would we keep them? All these thoughts going through B.J. mind kept her from falling asleep. Thinking about all the work that lay ahead for them, made B.J. realize too, that another man around to help, would cut the time in half. B.J. knew what she had to do, and it was something she had wanted to do for a long time. Now her mind was satisfied and she slept.

The birds cheerfully singing and a delicious aroma of food drifting through the air awakened B.J. Sitting up, she sniffed and knew immediately it was the fresh fish that Webster had caught. He had breakfast going for them. B.J. climbed out of her blanket and took a pan of water from the water barrel and washed the night's sleep away. She walked over to the stove and saw that Webster almost had the fish finished. B.J. gave him a big hug.

"You should have waked me. This is my job; you will have enough work to do today without doing the cooking too."

"Good morning, B.J., are you hungry?"

"I sure am; it was the smell of those fish that woke me. How long have you been up?"

"Well, I've fed the horses, made biscuits and coffee and have the fish almost ready to eat."

"Did you leave anything for Grady and me to do?

B.J. walked over to Grady and threw back his blanket. "Time to roll out, brother."

Grady stretched and pulled on his boots and then went and washed his face and hands. Webster handed them a plate filled with fresh fried fish and good hot biscuits. Then he went back for the coffee pot and cups, filling one for each of them. They asked the blessing and started their morning off right.

When they finished, Webster went to the team of draft horses and Grady jumped up to help harness them. B.J. put the dishes in a pan of water and set them on the stove to heat. By this time, Webster and Grady were back with the team.

"Are you taking the wagon with you?" B.J. asked.

"No, we'll just need the horses today. We'll cut and drag the logs up until we have enough to build one wall, or until we give out."

Webster climbed on one of the draft horses and B.J. gave Grady a foot up to get on the other one.

"Hand up the saw and axe to us." B.J. handed one to each.

"How do I mix the mud? How much will we need?"

"Go down to the lake to the cleanest spot and take the shovel and fill that box with the stickiest mud you can find, and then add dry straw grass to it. Mix them together and drag the box back here, using one of the mares. Be careful. Keep your eyes peeled for snakes and everything else going on around you. Grady and I will be within hearing, so if you get into trouble, fire two shots and we'll come a' running."

Webster and Grady rode the draft horses off. B.J. was left alone, but that was okay; she had plenty of work to do. B.J. cleaned up the dishes first and then rolled up their blankets. Before starting with the mud, she sat down and wrote a letter. B.J. had promised Wayne that she would let him know where they settled. Now it was time to send it to him. She didn't know if Wayne would reply, but she had to try. This was what she had wanted for a long time, in fact since they left St. Joseph, Missouri.

When the letter was finished, B.J. hid it in the tent till she could mail it. The next time they went into town she would post it at the post office, but until then she would not tell Webster and Grady. B.J. didn't want to hear their teasing. She put on her pistol and found the shovel she would need and headed for the lake, dragging the wooden box Webster had made that morning.

The box was heavy, but B.J. managed to get it to a cleared spot on the bank of the lake. Afterwards B.J. went back and harnessed one of the mares and took her to the spot and tied her nearby. She began shoveling. The mud was thick and heavy and required all the muscle she had to get the job done. B.J. found that if she only filled the shovel half full, she could work faster. Before B.J. knew it, she had the first box full so she began pulling dry straw grass and mixing it with the mud. After awhile B.J. decided to take off her boots and socks and get in the box and walk around to mix the mud and straw. This was much easier and kinda fun, like something she would have done when she was a little child.

B.J. tied the harness to the box and walked along the side as the mare dragged the box up to where their cabin was to be built. She shoveled out her first box of many that she would mix that day. B.J. was determined to have a good size pile of mud waiting when Webster and Grady returned. This procedure went on for several hours, filling the box, mixing and emptying it. B.J. went down to the lake and filled a bucket of water and poured it over her pile to keep it wet enough to spread. She heard Webster and Grady coming back with the logs.

Each had three big logs tied together and chained to the horses. The horses dragged the logs as Webster and Grady walked along each side. When they got to the cabin site, they pulled the horses to a stop and unchained the logs. The logs were big around, long and straight, and looked as though they would go a long way at building the cabin.

After several hours of hard work, everyone was ready for a lunch break. Grady already had a built-in appetite, but hard work only made it bigger. After eating they went right back doing what they had done before. The three of them kept up this pace for several more days, and the walls of the new cabin began to take shape. The work was the hardiest B.J. and Grady had ever done, but Webster knew what he was doing and between supervising and doing over half the work, he ended up working the hardest. Grady tried, but he wasn't a full-grown man and he could only do so much.

When darkness came all of them was ready for bed. They ached from swinging axes, digging in the mud and plastering it between the logs as they were stacked one on the other. When morning arrived, it was a repeat of what had been done the day before. B.J. was getting good at making mud and packing it between the logs.

The cabin was now taking shape. Once the four walls was up next came the cutting of the doors and windows. The roof was last and took longer because they needed smaller trees for rafters and beams. Webster had to scout the land to find the smaller trees, so B.J. took this time to wash up their clothes and cook a much-needed meal for them.

That morning as B.J. was washing clothes, she saw a cloud of dust off in the distance. She was alone and concerned enough to think of signaling for Webster and Grady, but decided to wait to see who the rider might be. B.J. was glad she waited because it was Norman Brooks, their neighbor.

Norman rode in stopped his horse and B.J. invited him to get down and stay a while. Norman looked around, amazed at the work they had been able to complete.

"Ya'll have really been working."

"Yea, we've been staying at it. We really don't have much choice; we want a roof over our heads before winter sets in."

"Around here we can have some pretty rough winters."

B.J. noticed Norman seemed a little awkward and kept looking for Webster and Grady.

"Uncle Webster and Grady have gone scouting for smaller trees for the roof. They should be back shortly. Would you like a cup of coffee? It's all I can offer you. I got a meal on cooking, but it isn't ready just yet. Uncle Webster has had me doing the mudding."

"Oh that reminds me, Ma sent you folks some vittles." Norman went to his horse and untied a covered basket. He handed it to B.J. dropping his head, in a shy way.

"I'm sorry B.J., I'd forget my head if it wasn't attached to my shoulders."

"Norman have you eaten today, it's a long ride from your house?"

"No ma'am, but I can wait till the others get here." He smiled.

"Well, make yourself at home. I've got to finish this wash or we are gonna be without clean clothes."

B.J. finished the washing and then put on a pot of coffee. She knew it would not be long before Webster and Grady returned and she wanted a fresh pot to go with what she had cooked and with the delicious food Mrs. Brooks had been so thoughtful to send.

"I wish I had a table to put all this good food on, but you understand Norman it takes time for these things."

"Yes ma'am, I do. It was the longest before we had a table and chairs to eat from. Ma got so tired of holding her plate in her lap every meal. Us men never pay it any mind, but I know it's those kind of things that bother a woman."

"You'll make some woman a good husband one day. Come on, I'll show you what we have done so far on our cabin."

Norman and B.J. were just coming out of the cabin as Webster and Grady rode up. They got down off the horses and shook hands with Norman and Webster asked.

"What brings you down our way, Norman?"

Before Norman could answer, Grady spotted the basket of food.

"This is what brought him down. Mrs. Earline knew we were all starving for good food."

Norman grinned and shook his head. B.J. spread a blanket and put the food on it. Grady got the plates, silverware, and cups and they all sat around the blanket, like it was a table. Uncle Webster gave thanks mentioning the generosity of the Brook's family and how blessed they were to have such fine neighbors. When he finished they enjoyed a good meal and apple pie for desert.

There was a lot of talking during their meal, catching up on all the latest since they left the Brook's ranch. Norman told Webster that he could stay a couple of days to help, if he wanted him. The news brought a smile to all their faces. They needed all the help they could get and appreciated his offer. Norman could do a man's work and this would help Webster immensely.

When the pie was finished and all the coffee drank, they went back to work, cutting trees. B.J. cleaned up the dishes and saved the food that was left for their supper. B.J.'s thoughts were not on her work, they were more on the day she would have a proper kitchen. A table and chairs for people to sit in and all the nice things like Mrs. Brooks. B.J. knew this all took time and getting the house finished first was the beginning. She continued to straighten up their campsite. Norman was company and she wanted him to at least have a clean place to enjoy while staying with them. After folding the blanket that served as their table and putting it back in the tent, she straightened the woodpile by the stove, and took her straw broom and swept the area.

B.J. took a towel and a bar of soap and headed for the lake. She should be able to get her bath before the men returned. She realized how bad she looked the minute Norman rode up. After today she would take more notice of her appearance. When B.J. got to the lake she undressed and waded in. The water had warmed and she found an ideal spot in which to bath. The bottom was clean but there were some bushes and limbs for privacy too. The deeper the water, the cooler it was, but B.J.'s body adjusted. She washed her hair and ducked under to rinse, and then soaped herself all over. The bath made B.J. feel so good that she hated to come out, but she had too. If she didn't get dressed before all the men folks returned, they might see her. Before she started for the bank, B.J. looked around the camp and knew it was safe for her to come out.

B.J. had just got dressed when she heard Grady call.

"B.J., where are you?"

B.J. came walking up from the lake with her hair tied up in a towel, just before Grady got panicky.

"We were worried something had happened to you."

"I just went to the lake to wash a little dirt off. A bath would help the two of you."

Norman laughed, "Wow, B.J. you sound just like my Ma."

"Why do women folks always want a fellow to bath?" Grady asked looking at Norman and Webster.

"Maybe because they know what they are talking about." Webster said as he reached for a towel and a bar of soap and then headed for the lake.

"Well, come on Grady."

Grady didn't like the idea at all, but followed Webster and Norman anyway. After awhile all B.J. could here were a lot of yelling, laughing, and splashing coming from the direction of the lake. B.J. was glad she thought of this; it gave them all a break from their work and a little time for some pleasure. People need time to enjoy themselves.

Webster, Grady, and Norman came back all clean and smiling. After bathing, naturally meant the work had stopped for the day. They built up the campfire and took the opportunity to sit and talk. Webster excused himself and rode off on his horse. None of them knew where he was going, but they felt assured he could take care of himself. The day was getting late and the fire felt good and warm after cooling off in the lake.

"B.J., have you decided on a brand for your horses?" Asked Norman.

B.J. looked puzzled.

"In the west all animals are branded, horses and cows. This is so people can tell who the rightful owner is if the animal strays from your land." Norman added.

"I haven't thought about it Norman. What do you think a good brand would be?"

"You could go with several brands. You could use a Double-H, or B-G brand. You might like the Rocking H or B.G. Bar."

Norman explained they had to register the brand they chose in their name. B.J. told him that Grady and Webster and she would have to think about it. She honestly didn't like the idea of sticking a hot iron to Dude's hip anyway. It seemed so cruel.

They heard a horse approaching and looked; it was Webster with two wild turkeys tied to his saddle. Grady got up to help Webster clean them and before long they were on a spit roasting for supper. While they waited for the turkeys to cook, B.J. told Webster what Norman suggested about the brand. Webster favored the Rocking H, so their decision was unanimous. Norman would get his dad to make it for them since he was a blacksmith.

B.J. put on a pot of coffee and took out the food that was left from lunch to go with the turkeys. She spread the blanket and they shared another good meal before bedtime. Norman had come prepared, so he spread his bedroll beside the fire with Webster and Grady.

"Webster the next thing you need to build is your corral. The horses need a place to walk around and it would be a lot safer, especially at night. There are a lot of wild animals coming around at night. There is a black stallion that runs free and he tries to steal every mare within a hundred miles."

"We saw him on our way in. That stallion is a beautiful animal and he had a brood of mares with him." Webster said.

"I thought he and Dude were going to fight right on the spot." Uncle Webster had to scare the stallion away by shooting in the air." B.J. said.

"I'd love to own him." Grady said.

"That black is a long way from here." B.J. said, trying to convince her as well as the others. B.J. couldn't stand the though of anything happening to Dude or their mares. She had raised Dude from a colt and it would break her heart if Dude got hurt.

"Dude might surprise us when it comes to that black. Dude is a lot stouter and taller and I believe he could hold his own against the black." Webster said. He saw the look of concern on B.J.'s face.

"Your right. I know I'd love to have a colt from Dude. I think he is one of the finest horses I've seen. We've got a beautiful bay mare, with four white stockings, but no blaze face like Dude's. Anyway, I think a colt from the two of them would be a winner." Norman said.

They talked horses a little longer and B.J. could see Grady was on the edge of sleep and Webster had gotten quiet, so B.J. said her goodnights and went to the tent. Norman put more wood on the fire. Any one could tell he wasn't use to sleeping outdoors like they were. Norman climbed into his bedroll. Another day had come to an end. B.J. lay thinking what the Lord had helped them accomplish. She looked at the outline of their cabin against the black night, she was proud of it even though it didn't have a roof. Patience, she reminded herself, and then said her prayers thanking the Lord for sending Norman to help them.

The Lord knew their needs in advance and He supplied them. Every since the death of her parents, when it seemed Grady and she would get bogged down and weary, along came someone to help them, to lift their spirits. First there was the stage people, Ed, Mildred and her husband, and then Uncle Webster and now Norman. B.J. closed her eyes and could see in her mind what their place would look like one day. There would be a nice house, with a front porch, flowerbeds, barn, and corrals. Lord, she prayed, please let it happen if it's Your will. B.J. fell asleep then and slept like a baby for a while.

Still half asleep, B.J. heard voices', they sounded far off. First, the thought something was wrong and she sat straight up in bed. Then she realized she had simple overslept. Webster, Norman and Grady were talking and sipping coffee. B.J. climbed out and hurriedly pulled on her boots, and brushed her hair back and tied it with her ribbon.

"Why didn't you wake me?" B.J. asked. "I'll get breakfast as fast as I can."

"Take your time; we're going after the logs we cut yesterday. We can eat when we return." Webster said as he sat his cup down. B.J. nodded in relief. This way she could fix a decent breakfast, she didn't want Norman thinking she was lazy.

The men were gone long enough for B.J. to cook biscuits and bacon and scramble eggs. The coffee was fresh and when they returned they ate heartily and returned to their work. They wanted to get the roof on the cabin if possible. The rafters were first and then came the gables. It was amazing how much bigger this made the cabin look. Webster got the doors and windows framed and afterwards realized they had not purchased enough lumber for the roofing. There was enough to make a table and two benches though, so that evening they had supper on the new table.

B.J. proudly served rabbit stew and eating it from their table instead of their laps, made it taste better. After supper they discussed the trip into town for the rest of the needed lumber and roofing. Now B.J. knew she would get to mail her letter. Since sunrise came early, B.J. knew she couldn't go to town with bathing. She had finished the mudding on the walls and around the door and windows. She had to get this mud off before dark, so B.J. told Webster that she was going to the lake to bath.

Webster, Norman and Grady went back to working on the corral since the work on the cabin had come to a halt. B.J. took her towel, soap, and a change of clothes and headed to the spot where she last bathed. She eased into the water and began soaping her hair. B.J. ducked under to rinse the soap out and when she came up, she couldn't believe her eyes.

On the lake bank in front of B.J. stood one of the biggest grizzly bears she had ever seen. The bear had not noticed her, but smelled her clothes. B.J. sand as deep into the water as she could and began easing along the bottom away from the bear and around the bend of the lakeshore. B.J. wanted to get Webster's attention without telling the bear she was in the water. B.J. knew that bears could swim and would not hesitate to come into the water after her.

B.J. could see Webster now, but he could not see her. If she stood up, well she would expose herself to the bear and the men. She began waving her arms in hope of getting Webster's attention. B.J. succeeded. Webster saw her and waved back but continued with his work on the corral. B.J. tried again. This time Webster had his back to her, but Norman saw her and waved back. She wondered if they thought she was playing around. What was she to do? Next she tried softly calling to Webster and waving at the same time. This was a mistake. The bear heard her, but Webster didn't.

Into the water the bear came. B.J. had no choice now but to scream her head off and swim as fast as she could away from the bear. Webster turned and when he saw the bear he reached down for his rifle and fired a shot into the air. The shot didn't phase the bear; he just kept going after B.J. The water slowed the bear a little, but it did not stop him. B.J. glanced at the men, but didn't take her eyes off that bear. The bear was gaining on her. Webster came running down to the lake and was taking good aim at the bear which was within feet of B.J. now. B.J. kept swimming, and Webster stopped, took his time, and fired. The shot hit where it counted and the bear let out a loud roar and fell back into the water. B.J. was so relieved that she almost forgot and stood up naked in front them.

"Why didn't you call me earlier?"

"I couldn't stand up, I'm naked, so I waved at you and all you did was wave back." B.J. said.

All three of the men stood on the bank looking at her and the dead bear and laughed.

"If ya'll will get out of here, I'll get out and put on my clothes." B.J. was mad and embarrassed as she swam back to the shore where her clothes were. She got dressed in a hurry and walked back to Webster, Norman and Grady. They were trying to get the bear out of the lake onto the shore. They ended up getting one of the horses to drag the wet bear he was so big. After seeing the bear up close, B.J. knew the bear was bigger than she thought, in fact, the biggest bear she had ever seen.

"You're lucky we happened to be close B.J. That bear could have killed you."

"Grady, why do you think I was waving and shouting my head off?"

B.J. learned a good lesson. She would never again bath without watching the shore at all times.

They tied the bear to a big tree and skinned and dressed him out.

"Well thanks to B.J., we'll have some bear meat for awhile. I'll cure out the skin and you can use it for a rug in our cabin. It will be warm this winter." Webster said.

B.J. was clean for the trip to town but she was exhausted too. She would have no trouble sleeping tonight. The day had been long, exciting, and tiring for everyone, so they crawled into their beds for a good night's sleep—they thought.

Sometime in the middle of the night, Dude's neighing and kicking the corral fence woke everybody. Jumping up to see what was wrong; they soon discovered it was the black stallion visiting. The black wanted their mares. Dude was trying to discourage him as best he could. The black rose high above the fence and pawed the air, his ears flat against his head, and his eyes rolled in a wild frenzy. The black flared his nostrils and screamed again toward the darkened sky. Dude was doing all this from inside the corral. The noise was deafening in the middle of the otherwise silent night. Webster and Norman grabbed their rifles and started toward the corral.

The black stallion dropped on all fours and pawed the ground.

"Don't kill him." Grady shouted.

"We're trying to discourage him." Norman answered.

Webster and Norman fired into the air, the shots settled the black some, but he stood his ground. He ran back and forth and stopped and pawed the ground, along the sides of the corral, as though he was doing a dance for the mares. Dude moved the mares one way and the black moved with them. The black was cleverly positioning to jump the fence, until he saw B.J. slowly easing herself toward the corral.

Webster fired again, this time at the ground in front of the black's feet. The black froze, and then every muscle in his body tensed and twitched. The black stallion came at B.J. like a fast freight train. He reared up, pawed the air with his front legs and then brought his hooves down to the ground right in front of B.J. B.J. never backed away, and as they looked face to face at each other, she showed no fear of the black, and he showed no fear of her. The black stallion was telling B.J., in the only way he could, that they had not won this victory; he would definitely return. The Black shot pass them so fast that they felt just the air on their faces. Everyone stood frozen to their spots and watched the black until he was out of sight.

"Do you suppose he will return tonight?" B.J. asked as she rubbed Dude nose.

"It's doubtful. He tries one time, hoping to get the mares, but seeing how Dude turned on him, I doubt the black will be back." Norman said.

"We won't see or hear anymore from him tonight, let's get some sleep." Webster said.

B.J. stood rubbing Dude's neck and talking softly to him. Webster walked up to her and hugged her real tight.

"Your world revolves around this horse, doesn't it? Don't ever put yourself into danger by trying to come between two stallions when they are fighting. I know you worry about Dude's safety, but you saw he was able to take care of himself and the mares. He can't take care of you thought."

Webster rubbed Dude's neck and then B.J. and he walked back to their beds. Norman and Grady were already sound asleep and so B.J. went back to her tent and before she closed her eyes to sleep, she took one last look at Dude.

Chapter 10

The incident the night before with the black stallion left everyone a little nervous, but the trip into Casper was without trouble. There were signs of the black stallion and his herd of mares, but they were nowhere in sight. B.J. hoped it remained that way; she didn't want a fight between him and Dude. B.J. was confidant that Dude would be the victor; but she just didn't want to see it happen.

The group had been on the road for several hours now with Grady and Norman riding on one side of the wagon and B.J. on the other. The spring morning was beautiful and everyone was enjoying the fact that winter was gone for now. The trees were budding and the birds singing, but best of all was the grass was greening. To a rancher, this meant no more breaking ice in the water trough and hauling hay to the animals for feed.

Webster and Norman decided to go by the Brooks ranch and ask for the loan of Mr. Brook's wagon and team. Two loads of lumber would save time and energy. Norman had spent two days with B.J. and them and there might be chores that his dad needed for him to catch up. If not, it would be worth a try. They would get to see their neighbors again and thank Norman's mom for the delicious food.

Before they knew it the outline of the ranch came into view. Ralph Brooks, Dale, and Greg were out riding herd on their cows and saw the wagon approaching. As they neared the ranch, Earline came out of the house and greeted them. She was wiping her hands on her apron, without a doubt she had been cooking. "You folks get down and rest awhile. I've just finished churning and have plenty of cool buttermilk. You're welcome to a glass and some hot biscuits I've just taken from the oven."

Naturally, this was not something Grady could refuse, so he was the first off his horse and had him tied when Ralph and the other boys rode up to join them. Webster and Ralph talked about all they had been able to accomplish with the much-needed help from Norman. Webster thanked Ralph for letting Norman come over and stay. As they enjoyed the milk and biscuits, Norman told about the episode with the bear and B.J. in the lake. Then Grady shared with them about the visit from the black stallion during the night.

"My goodness, you've had a lot of excitement." Ralph said.

"Dad, Webster and I talked about using our wagon and team to haul the rest of the lumber they will need. Are you going to need it for a couple of days? I'll drive one wagon and it will save them having to make a trip into town for another load."

"That's a good idea, Norman. The wagon is just sitting out back. Dale, you and Greg go harness up the team and hitch them to our wagon."

"I'll help." Grady volunteered.

Webster knew they couldn't stay any longer if they were to get to town and get loaded today, so they said their goodbyes and climbed on their wagons and horses. Earline came with a basket of food and handed it up to Webster. Webster, B.J. and Grady tried to refuse, but she wouldn't hear of it. They thanked her and headed out.

"Son, you behave yourself now." Earline shouted to Norman.

Norman looked embarrassed and said, "Aw Ma, I'm not a little kid anymore."

"I'll watch out for him." Webster promised.

Since the group had milk and biscuits there was no need to stop till they got to town. Casper was busy as usual. People were everywhere and traffic was heavy. Webster went to the lumberyard first and got as much lumber as the two wagons would carry. While the lumber was being loaded, B.J. and Grady went to the general store for their supplies. B.J. decided this trip to get ten hens for fresh eggs. The storekeeper suggested she also purchase a rooster, so she took him too. She got seed for the garden she planned to plant. B.J. was waiting for the order to be filled when Grady came running into the store.

"B.J., come quick. I want to show you something."

"I'll be there in a few minutes, Grady."

Grady went back outside and the storekeeper finished her order. B.J. paid her bill, but noticed an awful commotion outside. The storekeeper went out with her to see what it was all about. They found a large gathering of spectators from the town and as B.J. milled through them to find Grady, the sneering and yelling grew louder and louder. Forcing her way into the ring of spectators, B.J. found Grady wrestling with two bigger boys in the dirty street. B.J. tried to separate the three of them, but got shoved out of the way. They were rolling around in the dirt and hitting on Grady. Grady's bloody nose indicated he was receiving the worse of the fight.

The storekeeper yanked one up by the collar and threatened if he moved form the spot, but the boy jerked away and returned to the fight. B.J. had tried again to separate them, but the heavier of the two had her down in the dirt hitting on her, while the other one went back to beating Grady. B.J. was kicking and pulling his hair, anything to get the fat, nasty, mean boy off her so she could help Grady. With all the screaming, yelling from the spectators, the kicking up dust by the fighters, they failed to see Webster and Norman ride up.

Webster saw that B.J. and Grady were involved so he shouted for the boys to stop, but neither could hear him over the yells of the on-lookers. This angered Webster. How could grown men and women stand around and cheer on a fight between youngsters, especially when a bigger boy was fighting a smaller one and the other fighting a girl. Webster knew how to stop this fight. He reached down and got his rifle, levered a cartridge into the chamber, stood and fired into the sky. The shot fired quieted the mob completely, but the four who were fighting, kept fighting.

Everyone turned to see Webster's big rough, masculine form looming above them, and kept silent. The mob didn't know what to expect because of the look on Webster's face. The look told them how distasteful he found this whole situation. Webster jumped down from his wagon and Norman followed suit. They reached into the heap of flying arms and kicking legs to separate the four.

"What the devil is going on here B.J.?"

B.J. straightened up and brushed the dirt from her clothes and hair. She was red as a beet in the face and Webster could tell she was still mad.

"Ask those two. They were on Grady like bees on honey when I came out of the store." B.J. pointed to the two troublemakers and then walked over to Grady to check on his bleeding nose and lip.

Grady was wiping the blood on his shirtsleeve till Norman handed him his handkerchief. B.J. had some bad bruises and her hair was full of dirt and all tangled from being twisted and pulled.

"What did you two boy have in mind jumping this boy younger and smaller than you? Webster was starring right in their faces now. "When did boys start fighting girls?" Neither answered, just looked at him with a smirk on their face.

"Why didn't some of you adults stop all this?" Webster asked as he looked about. No one answered; instead they all dropped their eyes to the ground, knowing they had been wrong.

"Mr. Thompson, these two are troublemakers and have caused the town much embarrassment for some time. Would you like me to get the sheriff so you can press charges against them?" The storekeeper seemed eager to see the two boys behind bars, but the thought of two kids, even bad kids, being jailed didn't set well with Webster, so he shook his head no.

"I'm doing you a favor, more than you did for this girl and her brother. I'm letting you go this time, but if you ever cause trouble for my family again, I'll personally turn you over my lap and tan both of your backsides. Do you understand what I'm saying?"

The two boys nodded yes, pulled away from Norman and the storekeeper and headed down the street. After they were far enough away, the oldest and heaviest boy turned and yelled. "I'll get you good the next chance I get." Then both ran as fast as they could, laughing as they went.

B.J. started after them, but Webster caught her by the shirtsleeve and held her back.

"They're all talk; forget them. We've got more important things to do."

Webster felt something rubbing his legs and looked down to find a little black fuzzy puppy. The puppy had come out from under the store porch and stood whining, waiting for someone to pet him. Grady ran over and scooped him into his arms, talking gently to him. B.J. walked over to pet him too.

"Is this what you wanted me to come see?"

"The man said I could have him if you didn't care."

"Is he what the fight was all about?"

"Yea, they tried to take him from me."

B.J. could see that Grady had already struck up a friendship with the puppy. "What kind of dog is he?"

"Part shepherd and part chow is what the barber said."

"Will he be mean or will he be a good watch dog?"

"Both."

B.J. knew that no matter the breed or what kind of dog he turned out to be, there were no separating Grady and the puppy now. After all the whole family had fought for him, so B.J. told Grady it was okay.

Webster said he wanted to stop at the stockyard at the edge of town to see about a milk cow and a calf. They headed in that direction. When they got to the Post Office B.J. stopped.

"I'll catch up to you later." She told them. B.J. climbed down and tied Dude and went in with her letter in her hand.

"Yes Miss, may I help you?" The Postmaster asked.

"I want to mail this please." B.J. laid her letter on the counter and paid the postage required. "How long does it take a letter to get to St. Joseph, Missouri?"

"About a week to ten days. Will you be expecting a reply?"

"Maybe. I'll check next time I'm in town." B.J. said as she left the post office. She climbed on Dude and started in the direction of the stockyards, but saw the others coming back in her direction, so she waited. B.J. noticed they had no cow tied behind the wagon. "Didn't you get us a caw?"

"Nope. Norman said his dad has one he will sell us." Grady told her.

All their shopping was done and loaded on the wagons, so they started down the road toward home just as the pink purplish dust started covering the evening sky. It wouldn't be long before all the days light were gone, but they would go as far as light would allow them, and then stop and camp.

When time to stop came, the group pulled over under the protection of some trees. The horses were taken care of and a fire started and coffee made. The basket of food from Webster's wagon was brought out and they enjoyed their supper. Grady ended up feeding most of his to the puppy.

"You're going to make that puppy sick. Puppies don't have an appetite as big as yours." Webster laughed. He was proud of how Grady had stood his ground against the ruffians in town that day.

Grady continued offering the puppy bread.

"By the way B.J., what was the trip to the post office for?" Webster asked.

"I wrote a friend of mine in St. Joseph to let him know where we settled." B.J. knew it was a mistake the minute she told it, because Grady immediately jumped on the chance to tease her.

"B.J.'s got a boyfriend and his name is Wayne Thompson." Grady said in a sing-song way.

"Did he say Wayne Thompson? Did this Wayne work at the livery stables in St. Joseph?" Webster asked her.

"Yes sir, he did. Why, do you know him?"

"Know him, heck he's my nephew. I guess I do know him."

B.J. told Webster how Wayne and she met and how badly Wayne wanted to come with their train, but didn't have the money saved. She even told Webster how he and she felt about each other. "I promised him I'd contact him as soon as we got settled."

"What a small world. When I left St. Joseph, I promised Wayne I would also contact him, if I ever settled down."

They both smiled. "I guess it was meant that Wayne didn't come with the train considering what happened. Uncle Webster, sometimes we fail to see how the Lord controls our lives. Here we've been with you for months and never known Wayne was your nephew. I always felt the Lord sent you to Grady and me and now to find that your nephew may be sent too."

"The Lord looks out for and helps them that help themselves. He took you and Grady under His wing long before I came alone. When He called your Pa and Ma to heaven, he substituted me for them. If it is His will then Wayne will find a way to get to you. I would certainly like to see him again. Wayne is a good man and a hard worker. We could use him for sure. Now lets you and me get us a good night's sleep." Webster laid his arm on B.J. shoulder and walked her over to her blanket. He gave her a big hug and noticed she was sore from the fight in town today. Webster was proud of her for jumping in to protect her little brother.

B.J. crawled under her blanket and noticed that Norman and Grady were already fast asleep. The puppy was curled up in Grady's blanket with him. Webster threw several logs on the fire and set the coffee pot off and went to his blanket and climbed in. B.J's thoughts that night were not on how sore she was, but were on Wayne and her hopes of getting to see him again. Grady's puppy whined a little as Grady hugged him closer and the night overtook them.

The cold gray dawn brought the group close to the fire. After eating their breakfast and having plenty of hot coffee they were ready to pack up. The sun rose in a cloudless sky and they headed the two wagon toward home. The going was slow, but before long they could recognize the territory closest to their cabin. They didn't stop at the Brooks ranch going back. There was a lot of work to be done and they knew they couldn't spend their days visiting. Norman had been a lot of help to Webster and Grady, but after they got the roof on the cabin, he would have to go back home to help with the cows.

The next days for all of them begin at sunrise and didn't end till sunset, stopping only to eat and sleep. The roof was finished and Norman loaded up his things and climbed up on the wagon to leave them. Webster, B.J. and Grady thanked him for all his help and told him how much they had enjoyed his company. They would miss him and it would be slower finishing up, but he was much appreciated. After he drove the wagon from sight, Webster and Grady continued to work around the place till sundown.

Webster was a carpenter and he knew how to make just about everything, from cabinets to beds, to rockers. He started first with the beds. All the feathers from the wild turkeys and prairie hens had been saved for stuffing mattresses. Webster made B.J. a dry sink next and shelves to store their supplies. The stove had been brought in to the kitchen and with the new table and benches the cabin was beginning to look more like a home. They had shutters for the windows, but Webster promised the next time they went to town, glass would be bought for the windows.

The stove heated the cabin. The only thing Webster couldn't do was lay brick for a chimney. He said he would hire someone to build them a fireplace before cold weather got there. B.J. was so happy with how everything looked. She wondered if Grady and she alone would have accomplished all this. Deep in her heart she knew that Webster was God sent, and she thanked God each night for him.

The months passed quickly now they had the work on the cabin finished. One morning B.J. was out hoeing her little vegetable garden. Webster and Grady had left to get more logs. They were now in the middle of building a shed for the horses before cold weather began. Grady's pup, now nearly grown, stayed behind with B.J. The pup starting barking and B.J. stopped hoeing and looked up to see why. She couldn't see anything or anyone, so she went back to her gardening. The pup barked again and this time ran down the road leading to town. B.J. called him back, but he kept up the barking. B.J. looked again. She was alone and wanted to be sure another bear didn't slip up on her. There was still nothing out of the ordinary, so she scolded the pup.

"Tuffy, hush. Are you just barking to hear yourself bark?"

Tuffy was the name Grady had given to him, saying he was a tough little pup. Tuffy would not leave the spot where he stopped, but still continued to bark. Straightening up, to rest her back, B.J. now noticed dust rising in the distance. Tuffy still barked and had now added a growl to it. Now B.J. understood what was wrong with the pup. Someone was coming down the road to the cabin. After looking longer, B.J. realized it would take a lot of horses to stir up that much dust.

"Tuffy, I bet the Brooks family is coming for a visit. This is a busy time for them, so it's likely not them."

B.J. looked again. Holding her hand to shade the sun from her eyes, she saw a wagon loaded with people.

"Oh my, I'm all dirty. The house is in a mess and I'll have to hurry to get things straightened up before whoever it is gets here."

B.J. dropped her hoe and ran to the cabin. She began wiping off the table and putting the dirty dishes from breakfast in a pan of water. B.J. grabbed a comb and gave her hair a lick or two and pulled it back and tied it with a ribbon, and then went back outside to wait for whoever was coming for a visit.

By now B.J. could see there was more than one wagon. There was a long line of wagon in fact.

"Tuffy, what is going on? Has something happened in town?"

From the look of all the wagons, everybody in town was coming to visit. About that time Webster and Grady pulled in the yard with their wagon loaded with poles. They too had seen the dust and decided to return to the cabin to see if there was trouble in town. Webster and Grady got down and stood next to B.J. waiting until all the wagons got close enough to find out what was happening. Grady tied Tuffy; he didn't want the pup scaring anyone's horses.

The first wagon was the Brooks family and they had others riding with them. They pulled their team to a stop and Webster invited them to get down.

"Ralph, what is this all about? I've never seen so many people before." Webster asked.

"All our neighbors have come to help get ya'll a barn raised, and today is the day it's gonna happen." Ralph Brooks told Webster.

Webster, B.J. and Grady just looked at each other in surprise.

Each wagon came up, stopped, and families began unloading. They introduced themselves to Webster, B.J. and Grady. B.J. knew she would never be able to remember all their names. Each family had a wagonload of different things. B.J. couldn't remember ever seeing this much stuff. There was hay, grain, and pieces of furniture, dishes, and silverware. Some brought quilts and pillows, almost everything and anything Webster, B.J. and Grady would need. Some of the wagons were loaded with lumber, saws, and nails. The land office manager had told everyone their situation and the neighbors decided to give B.J. and them a proper welcome with a housewarming and barn rising combined.

Everything began buzzing. Some of the men began cutting and hauling trees for the new barn. Everybody was busy doing something and no one was telling him or her what needed to be done. Some of the other men took some logs and before B.J. knew what was happening, they had added two more rooms to their one room cabin. They had the roof on and next a fireplace went up. B.J. couldn't believe her eyes, everything was happening so fast. It had taken Webster, Grady, and her three days to get one wall up. There were about forty men working compared to the three of them, and these men knew what they were doing too. A porch went on next and the one room cabin became a house. The look changed before B.J. eyes, like a caterpillar emerging into a butterfly.

B.J. was overcome with pride and joy, and she knew in her heart that she must find some way to show these fine neighbors how much she appreciated them. She went looking for Earline Brooks, the only one of the ladies that she really knew.

"Mrs. Earline, what can I do to show my appreciation? Let me at least fix food for everyone."

"The food came with the help. We want you to just get acquainted with the other young people and let us ladies handle preparing the food." Earline told B.J.

B.J. stayed and helped the women anyway. She would feel strange with youngsters Grady's age. B.J. wanted to contribute something, so she went to her garden and picked all the lettuce that was growing and made a green salad. B.J. proudly put it on the table with all the dozens of other bowls of prepared food that was brought.

Someone brought a whole pig and it was roasting on a spit. Grady was given the job of turning the pig so it would not burn and it smelled delicious. The storeowner's daughter was keeping Grady company, so B.J. went back to help the ladies.

B.J. looked in the direction where the barn was to be built and to her surprise the men had the tall middle section finished. Webster was right in the middle of all of it. They worked hard and fast as a team. As B.J. climbed the steps of the new front porch she noticed the windows now had glass panes in them. This was more than her heart could hold. B.J. was overcome with emotion and tender love for these good people who cared enough to come and even supply the needed material. Tears of joy rolled from her eyes and down her cheeks and B.J. walked away to keep anyone from seeing her cry.

What would her neighbors think if they saw her crying at a happy time like this? B.J. couldn't help it; she sat down on the bank of the lake and let the tears flow. They were happy tears for B.J. and also tears from the memories of her parents. She thought how pleased her parents would be just knowing her and Grady had such good thoughtful neighbors.

Someone touched B.J. on the shoulder. B.J. turned to see Earline Brooks.

"Is anything wrong, B.J.?"

Just asking was all it took to really start B.J. to crying. She felt so foolish, but she couldn't help crying.

"I know how you feel; the same thing happened to us right after we moved out here. These same good folks helped us to get started." Earline said as she hugged B.J. to her.

B.J. wiped her eyes dry and nodded, and the two walked back to the house.

The men were all starved and needed food for energy to finish, so they took a break to eat. All the food was uncovered and placed on make shift tables. The pig was ready and sliced and bar-be-cue sauce added. Everyone came and joined hands and Ralph Brooks gave thanks for the wonderful day of friendship and fellowship. He asked God to bless the food and the hands that prepared it.

Everyone took a plate and circled the tables, filling them as they went. It was impossible to get all the food on a single plate. B.J. couldn't remember when she enjoyed herself so much. She naturally went to the table where the Brooks family was sitting and joined them along with Webster and Grady. Everyone was eating and talking and enjoying themselves. The time went by fast and the men knew they had to finish before dark, so they went back to work. The women put the food away and cleared the tables of dirty dishes. The young men had brought their musical instruments, so they got them out and before long there was music to enjoy as they worked. Some of the youngsters danced while the women clapped their hands to the music. When the men finished the barn some of them took their wives and danced to several tunes.

B.J. hated to see the day end, but it did end. Everyone knew they had no choice but to call it a day or the neighbors would be the middle of the night getting home. First they loaded their tools, and then their wives and children. They lit their lanterns, turned their wagons around and left one by one; going down the same road they had come on. Webster, B.J. and Grady stood saying goodbye and thanks until the last wagon was out of sight.

Webster was in the middle with his arms resting on B.J.'s and Grady's shoulders. When the last wagon left, the three of them turned to look at what had been accomplished that day, it was a miracle. There was a lantern lit inside the house outlining the new size it now was. The cabin looked huge, especially with a porch and the big chimney sticking up. There was a new barn, three times larger than the house, but the room would be needed for all the horses they would have someday. Hay was already in the loft and stalls for Dude and the other horses at night. Webster, B.J. and Grady felt it a blessing to have such good neighbors.

Once inside they felt even better. No one spoke, just looked about at the changes. Now they definitely had a home, a home that anyone would be proud of. B.J. was almost to the point of crying again, she was so proud. Someone had built a fire in the new fireplace and there was a rocker sitting in front of the fire along with two other big stuffed chairs. The women had sewed and hung curtains on the windows. Now they had three big rooms, a bedroom for Webster and Grady, and one for B.J. The original room was now the parlor and kitchen combined. B.J. knew her dad and mom would be so happy for them. The three of them vowed that night that if any of their neighbors needed them, they would be there.

Chapter 11

Several weeks had passed since the barn rising, and Webster, B.J., and Grady were trying to get several little things finished. B.J. had not taken her horse, Dude for a ride in all this time. There never seemed to be enough hours in each day to get a ride in. Dude was becoming frisky because of lack of exercise.

Every night Grady put Dude in his stall, but Dude managed to get the stall door opened to have a little romp one night. B.J. just happened to come out the next morning as Dude came running up in the yard. That's when B.J. discovered Dude's nightly escapades. She walked over to Dude and could tell from the way he was lathered up that he had gone some distance. B.J. took Dude by the halter and led him into the barn to cool him down and to feed him, and then she put him in the corral.

B.J. had no idea where Dude had wandered off too, so she put it out of her mind thinking he just wanted a chance to run off some of his energy. Anyway B.J. disregarded the happening. But a couple of nights later, the same thing occurred. This time B.J. questioned Grady.

"Did you put Dude in his stall last night when you put the other horses up?"

"I sure did. Dude went right in, and I closed the gate and fastened it, just like I do each night."

"Somehow Dude is getting out and staying gone all night. This is the second time Dude has come home early in the morning all lathered up.

Wherever he is going, it's a long way. I'm afraid Dude might not come back one morning."

B.J. made up her mind to talk to Webster. Maybe he might shed some light on how Dude was getting out at night.

"I wouldn't worry myself with Dude's adventure as long as he came back each morning," Webster told her.

This didn't quiet satisfy B.J.'s concern. Dude was their income—when they began using him for stud—and she decided to devise a plan. One night B.J. watched Dude and discovered how he was getting out. B.J. had Lady saddled and waiting once she saw Dude take his nose and lift the gate latch, she jumped on Lady and followed. The big barn doors were left opened because it was cooler on the animals, so after Dude left B.J. was right behind him. She trailed far enough behind that he would not know she was there.

Dude seemed to know right where he was going. B.J. had Lady in a slow run at times just to keep up with Dude. B.J. had told Webster her plans, and he cautioned her about being out at night alone, so she wore her pistol. The darkness and the distance made it hard for B.J. to know where they were going. She depended on Dude as the guide, and then when he began to slow, she realized he was close to his stopping point. B.J.'s eyes adjusted to the darkness and she could see where they were. Dude had brought her right to the valley where the black stallion and his mares stayed. Dude was visiting the stallion's mares while the stallion was gone.

"You rascal! What am I supposed to do with you?" B.J. said quietly.

B.J. knew she couldn't go riding in there without upsetting the mares, causing them to maybe stampede, and if they stampeded, Dude would follow. B.J. sat on Lady's back and watched as Dude sniffed out each one of the mares until he found one that was in season. Then Dude worked with her until he got her away from the herd and to himself. B.J. thought she would just let Dude have his fling and then follow him back to the ranch, but it didn't work that way. Out of the corner of her eye, she saw the black stallion coming back and he was furious because he could smell Dude. B.J. didn't know what to do, her heart raced as she watched the black paw the air as he raised high on his hind legs. The black stallion neighed a scream that penetrated the stillness of the night and that was when Dude saw him.

Dude left the mare and went in the direction of the black stallion. Dude had been challenged and he accepted. B.J. sat frozen. She wanted to stop what would definitely be a fight between the two great stallions, but she knew she couldn't. B.J. remembered how scared she was the night at the corral when the black warned her, so she kept Lady still and quiet, hoping he would not see them. Never in her wildest dreams had she thought Dude was visiting the Black's mares and now here they were face to face in what was to be the showdown. The fight would just have to take place.

The mares were circling around the two stallions, stirring up a lot of dust. Squeals and neighing could be heard from both the stallions, and they bit and kicked each other around the neck and on their rear shanks. Both stallions had their ears flat back, their nostrils flared, indicating how mad they were. B.J. wanted to stop it—she was afraid Dude would really get hurt—but what she saw was Dude holding his own with the black. Each time the black reared to paw the air and come down on Dude, B.J. held her breath. Dude seemed to know just which way to turn to avoid being hurt by the black's hooves. The fight continued for a long time and Dude was getting the best of the black. Dude bit him several times and the black screamed from pain. There were several kicks from Dude that actually caused bleeding and B.J. could tell the black was weak and slowing down. The black stallion began running away from Dude, but Dude went after him again and again, until finally the black ran off.

Watching astraddle Lady, B.J. exhaled, glad that neither fought to the death. She knew it came to that sometimes. The champion, Dude, was strutting his stuff. Dude walked around the herd of mares tossing his head and neighing a victory neigh. Searching the surroundings, B.J. could plainly see the black was not gone. He stood at a distance looking back and calling, wanting his mares to come to him. When Dude heard the black, he pawed the air and neighed. Dude had won and the mares were his, so the black disappeared from the scene.

B.J. felt relief because it was over, but she wondered what Dude would do now. Would Dude stay there with his mares, or would he leave them?

After fighting to get them, it seemed very unlikely that Dude would abandon them now, so B.J. waited and watched as Dude circled the herd of mares. Horses talk to each other by neighing and Dude was telling each one his plan. After completing the circle, Dude started running in the direction of the ranch. B.J. couldn't believe what she was seeing. Dude was taking the mare's home. B.J. nudged Lady to follow behind the herd all the way to the ranch.

"Wait till Grady and Webster sees what Dude has brought home. Boy, will they be surprised." B.J. said aloud.

When the herd of horses and Dude reached the ranch, Dude began neighing, louder than he did when he fought the black. B.J. had never hard Dude scream like he was tonight. Dude knew what he was doing, because Webster and Grady came running out of the house carrying their guns. Neither knew what was happening in the middle of the night. But as the herd of mares began coming into the ranch yard, they found out. Dude had come home with at least fifty mares. He was proud of his accomplishment, and he wanted everyone to know.

"Open the corral gate." B.J. shouted to Webster and Grady.

The poles were let down and slid back and Dude led the mares into the corral. The mares begin to settle down as Dude worked his way back to the gate and Webster let him out. B.J. was off Lady and by Dude side now. Dude was pretty banged up and definitely needed some doctoring. She led Dude into the barn and stood waiting for Webster and Grady to come and check his cuts and scratches.

A lantern was lit so they could get a better look at Dude's injuries. None of the cuts were deep enough to require stitches, and most would heal within days. The hair would grow over them and not even leave a scar. Webster took some antiseptic salve and applied it to each cut and scrap. This was to prevent the flies from pestering Dude and infecting the raw places with larva. B.J. applied liniment to a cloth and gave Dude a good rub down. She knew Dude was exhausted from the fight, and afterwards she dried him off and put a blanket over him for the night. Dude would be sore, but this would help some.

Then Webster took a lock and locked Dude stall door. He was making sure Dude didn't get back out in the cool night air. They blew out the lantern and the three of them walked out to look over Dude's mares. Even in the dark they were a pretty sight, but morning would show them more, so all three went in to bed. B.J. could rest good knowing Dude was safe at home where a champion should be.

B.J. jumped out of bed the next morning, thinking she was the first up, got dressed and headed straight for the barn. When she opened the barn door, she found out differently; there was Webster and Grady looking after Dude.

"Is he alright?" B.J. anxiously asked.

"Yes, he is fine," answered Webster.

When B.J. got closer she could see Dude's scratches were still red. The bites were a little swollen, but Webster was putting more medicine on them. Dude turned and faced B.J. and she began patting him on the neck and rubbing the side of his face. B.J. was so thankful that Dude wasn't hurt any worse and wasn't killed. Webster left the blanket off so the scratches and bites could get air and heal.

"You will need to take him out and walk him around later today or he will be sore." Webster said to B.J.

"Have ya'll eat breakfast?"

"Nope, we were just as anxious as you to make sure Dude was okay." Webster said.

"Grady, you get the bucket and milk the cow and I'll gather the eggs on my way back to the house." B.J. suggested, as she left to get their breakfast.

After breakfast the three took their coffee cups and went to the corral to get a closer look at their new mares. In the morning light the mares were beautiful. There were so many the corral almost couldn't hold the lot. After looking closer they found that several of the mares were ready to foal. B.J. and Webster knew that before winter they would have at least five more than they had now.

One mare in particular caught B.J's eye. The mare was a beautiful dark roan, chestnut brown with black stockings, mane, and tail. The mare had a white star on her face.

"If the black's the father to her colt, it will be a beauty." Webster said.

"I bet it will be black and it'll be a stallion." Said Grady.

"If it is, you can have him to keep, since you didn't get the big black." This roan mare would be the first to foal and it wouldn't be long.

"There is something we're forgetting." Said Webster as he rubbed his chin. "How are we going to feed all these horses through the winter?"

B.J. had been so busy enjoying the new herd that the thought of feeding them never entered her mind.

"Do you suppose Mr. Brooks would have any hay he could sell us?"

"Why don't we ride over and see? We need to get the new branding iron he is making for us."

"Okay, I'll go with you. Remember, you said you would teach me to drive our wagon and team, well this would be the time to do it." Grady told Webster.

B.J. nodded okay and they hitched up to leave for the Brooks ranch. B.J. fixed them a box lunch and told them she wanted them back by dark. She handed the lunch up along with a canteen of water and reminded them to be careful. Webster patted the rifle between him and Grady.

"Don't worry about us, we'll be fine. Just don't forget to walk Dude today or he'll be so stove-up he can't move tomorrow."

"I won't forget. Tell everyone at the Brooks ranch hello for me."

B.J. watched till the wagon was out of sight and then she went in to clean the house. She washed dishes and make up all the beds and even sweep the floors. When she got to the front porch B.J. noticed a chill in the air, so she put several small logs on the fire. Fall was in the air and B.J. knew that winter wasn't far behind. Now that B.J. had finished her chores, she went to the barn to take Dude out for his walk.

B.J. had a jacket on, but the overcast sky made the day have an eerie look to it; and it gave B.J. a feeling that something was going to happen. She took the lead rope and went to Dude's stall for him. Dude was anxious to get out of his stall so B.J. walked him right by the corral full of mares. Dude perked up, wanting to put on a good show for the mares. They walked around the yard for at least forty-five minutes, and then she noticed how cloudy it was becoming.

"I better get you back inside. You don't need to get wet while you're still so sore from your fight." B.J. said taking Dude back into the barn. She brushed Dude really well and gave him a little feed and some extra hay and decided to call it a day.

B.J. noticed as she walked Dude the horses were cutting up some. The herd was circling the corral acting awfully nervous. At first B.J. thought it was because Dude was out, but now that she had put him back in the barn, the horse continued to act up. B.J. looked around wondering if the black was near, but she didn't see any sign of him; maybe it was the changing weather. Sometimes storms cause horses to be nervous, but there had been no lightening, so B.J. walked over to the corral and Tuffy, their dog, followed her.

The mares were milling around and some were even pawing the dirt, acting terrible confused, so B.J. climbed the corral fence to get a better look. B.J. found the problem; one of the mares was down on the other side of the corral. She walked around the corral to where the mare lay. The beautiful roan they had discussed that morning was lying on her side and rolling about. Tuffy begin barking.

"Tuffy, hush, she might be sick."

B.J. stood looking down at the mare and then it occurred to her that the mare was trying to foal. How stupid could she be? She had seen horses foal before on their farm in Kentucky. This mare was definitely getting ready to have her baby. About that time a loud clap of thunder shook the sky and it started raining. B.J. knew she needed to get the mare inside, if at all possible. She climbed down and started under the bottom rail, but realized she didn't have a lead rope with her. B.J. slid back out and ran to the barn for a rope.

This time, while inside the barn, she unlatched the side doors coming out into the corral. When B.J. came out she was right in the middle of the herd of wild mares. The lightening and thunder had then upset and now they were really milling around so badly that B.J. lost her direction to the mare that was down. B.J. took it slow as she eased herself through the group of horses. She knew she could be knocked down and trampled easily, but she kept on course. Tuffy begin barking as if directing her, so she followed the sound of his bark. The rain was coming down in sheets now and it was hard for B.J. to see where she was going and watch the moving horses too. Finally, with Tuffy's help, she found the mare.

B.J. very slowly and gently talked to the mare and got the rope around her neck, hoping it wouldn't make bad matters worse. She pulled on the rope and to her surprise, the mare got up on her feet. The mare let B.J. lead her to the barn door, but danced around when B.J. opened it. The mare was very nervous and her eyes widened as she looked from side to side at the strange surroundings. B.J. soothed her fears by gently talking and tugging on the lead rope. The mare went in the barn and then B.J. talked her into one of the stalls. B.J. had timed it perfectly, because the storm outside had worsened.

B.J. took her rope off and left the stall. The mare immediately began turning and circling the stall, trying to find a place to lie down. The mare lay down and began rolling from side to side in the fresh hay. B.J. knew it reasonably took thirty minutes or longer for most mares to foal. Her clothes were soaked from the rain and she was chilled, so she headed to the house to change. The sky overhead was darkening by the minute, and she couldn't help but worry about Uncle Webster and Grady. She hoped they were nearing home.

B.J. found dry clothes and changed, this time making sure she had her poncho. Before leaving the house she lit two lanterns, one to leave in the house and one to take to the barn with her. The lightening and thunder continued, but with more intensity now and B.J. hated to go back out, but she knew she needed to know how the mare was doing. B.J. ran to the barn and after hanging the lantern up, she walked over to the mare's stall. The mare was lying there, on her side and was breathing extra hard. Something was wrong. The mare should be forcing the foal out, but instead she rolled her head from side to side, snorted, and blew through her nostrils real hard. B.J. knew the mare was in trouble, so she went to her head and gently rubbed her face and talked to her. B.J. felt the mare's stomach; it was hard as a rock. The foal was knotted up inside her. No wonder the mare was laboring so the foal was turned wrong. The foal's feet were coming first and it was kicking the mare to death. The mare would never be able to have this foal unless it was turned. There was no way it could be born. B.J. knew she was the one who would have to turn it. She thought back remembering watching her Dad do this and she hoped she was strong enough to turn this one.

B.J. rolled up her shirtsleeve and went to the mare's tail. It was necessary to get both hands inside the mare and turn the foal around. The head should come out first. B.J. hoped the mare would cooperate, as she slid one hand into her. There, she felt the foal; it's legs, and as she reached a little further, B.J. felt the neck and head. She also felt the contractions tightening against her arm. B.J stuck her other hand into the mare and reaching as far as her arms would let her reach, she started turning the foal. B.J. was actually shoulder deep into this mare's behind, trying to gently work the foal around, when from the darkness, she heard a man's voice say, "Looks like you could use some help."

B.J. was so involved in turning the foal that when she heard the man's voice, she was scared half to death, so she naturally jerked her arms out and this scared the mare too. B.J. had no idea who this was. She had not heard anyone come in the barn. B.J. was squinting her eyes in the semi-darkness of the lantern light trying to see who offered help. At first all she saw was the dark outline of a man. His face was shaded and his wet poncho and hat didn't help either. The startled look on B.J. face told him he better explain himself in a hurry. He could tell B.J. was scared, so he removed his hat and poncho and then he moved closer to the lantern. The light caught his face and B.J. could see who he was but was having a hard time believing what she saw.

It was Wayne Thompson, as big as day, right there in their barn, and in the middle of a storm, with B.J. shoulder deep in a mare's behind.

"Well, how about the help, do you need it or not?" Wayne asked again.

B.J. was so flabbergasted she couldn't answer. She sat and stared at him with her mouth wide open. Wayne climbed into the stall, handed B.J. a dry empty feed sack to wipe her hands on and said, "Let me do that. I think my arms are a little longer than yours. You go to her head and hold her still."

B.J. took the feed sack and dried her hands, and then moved to the mare's head so Wayne could take her place. Wayne slipped his arms into the mare and gentle worked, turning the foal, and in a few minutes the mare began pushing with each contraction. Out came the head, and then the front legs, body and last the hind legs and tail. The mare snorted a sigh of relief and Wayne moved back for her to pass the afterbirth. Wayne took the dry sack from B.J. and begins wiping the foal off. It was a beauty, solid black, just like its father.

"Is it a filly or a stallion?" B.J. asked.

"You got yourself a black stallion."

The mare got to her feet and turned to look for her baby. She called him to her and when he saw his mother, he slowly, but wobbly got to his feet and made his way to her and to his supper. The foal sucked and the mare let him take his time.

B.J. and Wayne were so engrossed in watching the mother and baby that neither had said anything. B.J. was the first to speak, "Did you get my letter?"

"I guess I missed it. I've been on the road two months."

"How did you know where to find me?"

"I followed the same trail your wagon train came on until I got to Fort Laramie. The Captain explained about the death of your parents and all the others. The Captain said you were coming to Casper to claim your land, so when I got to Casper I asked and got directions to your place. Here I am."

B.J. looked and listened to Wayne, but found it hard to believe he was actually standing right there beside her after all this time. She had looked forward to the day of Wayne's arrival, but now she found herself embarrassed because she knew she must look awful. Suddenly, B.J. got real shy.

"Well, it looks like everything here is going to be fine for the night. What say we go wash up?" Wayne said, breaking the silence.

"Oh sure, forgive me, this has been one more week. I seemed to have forgotten my manners."

As B.J. and Wayne walked to the house, she told him about Dude's fight with the black and all the new mares they had acquired from the victory.

"Where is Grady?" Wayne inquired.

Then it occurred to B.J. that Wayne didn't know about Webster because he had not received her letter.

"I've got a lot more to tell you, but lets get washed up and have a cup of coffee while we talk. I'm chilled to the bone from being wet and in that barn."

Afterwards, she poured them cups of coffee and fix both of them a bowl of stew, because neither had eaten. As they eat, B.J. told Wayne about meeting up with Webster on the trail and how he had stayed with them and helped them build the house and all. This time Wayne was at a lost for words. Finally, he said, "I'm happy to know Uncle Webster is here. We lost contact about two years ago. It's a small world, isn't it B.J.? I just couldn't visualize how you and Grady could have accomplished all this in such a short time, and I certainly would not have believed Uncle Webster was a part of it."

"Well, we had even more help from our neighbors. Everyone came and helped us get our barn and corral built and even added to our cabin. This is a good place to live. All the neighbors are special people and willing to help any time."

"This sure is a nice house and you have it nicely furnished."

"Uncle Webster made most of the furniture. There isn't anything that man can't do."

"The last time I saw him he was a mountain man. Living in the mountains and trapping furs. He wanted me to come along with him, but I declined. I like people too much."

"I'm glad you declined or I wouldn't have met you otherwise." B.J. realized she had let her emotions show and she grew red in the face.

"I'm glad I did too. I haven't been able to get you off my mind since you'll left St. Joseph. Every day, after ya'll left I regretted not going with your family. But after the Captain told me about the tragedy, I'm glad I didn't go with you. I'm glad you and Grady were saved and I'm especially glad I finally caught up with you."

Wayne stood and started around the table towards B.J. He wanted to take her in his arms and hold her close, making his dream complete. Wayne wanted to flourish her with kisses, waking up the buried love they had shared in such an innocent way. But before he reached B.J. Tuffy, the dog, begin barking and Wayne froze in his tracks.

B.J. could see the look of desire in Wayne's eyes as he approached her chair and she responded by rising to meet him and enjoy his embrace. But the dog barking stopped both of them for the time.

"That must be Uncle Webster and Grady back with the load of hay. Let's go and surprise them with your being here and with the new foal."

They grabbed their jackets and were out the front door. Tuffy was still barking from the porch. They went to the barn and swung open the big barn doors just as the wagon pulled in the yard. Webster and Grady was wet, but the tarp had the hay protected. Webster pulled the reins and called, "Whoa there!"

Webster and Grady climbed down and shook water from their hats. B.J. brought the lantern into the barn and in the light they started unhitching the horses and putting them into their stalls for the night. Grady took a sack and dried the team off and gave them hay and feed.

Wayne stood in the shadows and kept quiet during all this. B.J. took Webster by the hand and walked to the stall where the mare and her new foal were. She held the lantern up so the light shined on both of them and a big smile crept across Webster's face.

"When was it born?"

"Tonight, right in the middle of the storm and it's a he. We got us a black stallion. The foal was breach and I had to help the mare or she would never have survived."

"B.J. had a little help." Wayne said as he walked into the light. He removed his hat and when Webster saw his face, there was another big smile.

"Boy, wonders never cease. When did you get here?"

"Tonight, right in the middle of two storms, one brought on by nature and the other by your mare. I found B.J. shoulder deep in that mares behind, trying to help her have that stallion."

Webster and Grady stood looking at the both of them in amazement.

"I could have turned that foal if you hadn't scared me so. Wayne crept in on me and asked if I could use a little help. He was all wet, poncho and hat, and I couldn't tell by the light, who it was. I jerked my arms out and that made the mare even more nervous."

"You could have turned that little stallion, I'm sure."

"Stallion? Did someone say it was a stallion? Is he black? Grady asked.

"Yes, he is black, and yes you can have him like we promised." B.J. told Grady.

"Every time we leave B.J. alone, she gets into trouble."

"I wasn't in trouble; the mare was. I got her into the barn and thought she could foal by herself, but she couldn't, so I was in the process of doing what had to be done when Wayne came in."

"B.J. did have everything under control. If her arms had been a little longer, she turned that foal for sure." Wayne said in B.J. defense.

"I'm proud of you, but you shouldn't be fooling around those wild horses. You could have got your head kicked off." Webster said.

They took the lantern and headed for the house. B.J. washed her hands and put Webster and Grady stew on the table with cups of hot coffee. Webster and Grady changed into dry clothes and sat down to eat. Wayne and B.J. sat at the table to hear about the trip to the Brooks ranch. They got a load of hay and tomorrow Ralph Brooks and the boys were coming over to help brand the mares and maybe even break some of them. Ralph had told Webster that the Army would buy the horses if they were saddle broke.

"Tonight, when I put a lead rope on the mare, she wasn't afraid. We might find more of them will be that tame."

"Tomorrow, we'll have us a rodeo," said Grady.

"Grady, what're you going to name your stallion?" B.J. asked.

"Well, since he was born in the middle of a storm, I'll call him stormy."

"I think that's a perfect name, only I hope he is stormy in name only."

Chapter 12

Ralph Brooks and his three sons begin gathering what they would need to take with them to the Rocking H. The Brooks family had been ranchers for a long time, but their specialty was cattle, not horses. Ralph was one of the original cowboys who had lived in the Wyoming territory all his life. After years of fighting Indians and outlaws, he chose to remain here, even though his family never owned a place of their own. Ralph's dad had always worked someone else's ranch, but Ralph intended to leave his children a legacy. When the government began issuing free land grants, he took advantage and claimed all the land the law allowed for his family. Times had been hard for his family at first, but as time passed, good fortune came their way and soon they had enough cattle to sell. Things were much better for them now.

Norman, the first son of Ralph and Earline was a good son, eager to learn all about ranching. Ralph remembered how happy he was twenty years ago when Earline told him she was expecting. Naturally he wanted a son, but he would have loved a daughter just as much. Childbirth wasn't easy for Earline and if the storekeeper's wife hadn't been there, she might have lost the baby and died herself. After seeing what a hard time Earline had, Ralph was afraid for her to have more children, but Earline assured him the Lord would take care of her.

Ralph's next son was Dale; he was born four years later. Earline nearly died again, but kept her faith that the Good Lord was taking care of her. Four years after Dale's birth, Craig was born. Three boys and it had to be the last born to them because Earline's health wouldn't let her survive having any more.

Their house was as large as needed, and their ranch was prospering well enough to afford them a good living. They counted this a blessing from the Lord.

Norman brought Ralph back to the present by asking, "Dad, how many horses did Webster say they had?"

"I think Dude brought in about fifty mares."

"Are we gonna break all of them tomorrow?"

Ralph knew this wasn't possible. "We'll break as many as we can. I promised Webster our help and we'll do our best."

Ralph and his boys had all they needed tied to their saddles along with their chaps. The supper bell rang and they left for the house. Ralph noticed how much colder the weather was getting, so he told the boys to gather an armful of wood and bring it with them to the house. Earline had a delicious supper waiting for all of them. She was concerned about all of them going to help break the wild horses.

"Tomorrow, I want all of you to be extra careful. Wild horses are dangerous. Those mares are probably as dangerous as that black stallion. I don't want any one coming back with a cracked head or a broken arm or leg."

"Yes, Ma'am," all three answered in unison.

Ralph laughed and Earline started in on him.

"I want you to look out for these boys and for yourself as well. I can't run this big ranch by myself, so ya'll better come home in one piece."

"Yes, Ma'am." Ralph smiled. Aggravating her even more.

The next morning was beautiful, but cooler. The storm had brought the cool weather with it. When the rooster crowed, B.J. jumped up and dressed. She combed her hair and pulled it back with a ribbon. She had to get an early start this morning; they had four coming to help them, and she needed to have a good breakfast waiting. There was already a fire in the stove and one going in the fireplace too, so B.J. knew Webster had beat her up.

B.J. thought Webster had gone to the barn to feed and milk and gather eggs, so B.J. started making her bread. She make extra and put it in the oven and then started a pot of coffee. Webster entered the kitchen with a shoulder of fresh meat.

"Where did you get this?"

"I lucked up and shot a young deer, got it skinned and here is a shoulder to cut meat for breakfast." He laid the meat on the side table and took the egg basket and milk bucket and left again. When he opened the door she felt the cold air. It was only September, but she was in Wyoming now, not Kentucky.

B.J. started the meat frying on the stove and then peeled some potatoes to go with it and the eggs. The men would need a hearty breakfast for the work that lay ahead of them today. She was trying to impress Wayne too.

"Good morning, B.J. Something sure does smell good." Wayne remarked as he entered the room.

"I'll have breakfast in just a minute, but the coffee is ready now if you want a cup."

Wayne got a cup from the cupboard and filled it. He stood watching B.J. cook. Wayne being that close made B.J. nervous and she was glad when Webster came in with the milk and eggs. Webster sat the milk and eggs down and nodded to Wayne.

"Sleep good? I know you were all tired out from riding all day."

"I slept like a rock. It was a while before I got used to Grady's snoring, but then I turned over and sawed a few logs myself."

Webster headed for the bedroom and they could hear him telling Grady, "Time all rodeo folks were up and at it."

"Are they here yet?" Grady asked as he climbed out of his bed and began dressing.

"Not yet, but it won't be long. They will be riding up and we want to be ready. Wayne, you broke any horses lately?"

"No, but you know what they say. Once you break one you don't forget how."

"Well today, we've got quiet a few to break and brand."

"Have you checked on stormy this morning?" Grady asked Webster.

"Yes, he's up and running all around the stall. Dude seems in good spirits this morning too."

B.J. had the table set and breakfast finished just as Tuffy started barking. They knew it had to be the Brooks, so everyone headed for the front door. Ralph and his boys rode up to the hitching rail in front of the house and climbed down from their horses.

"Good morning, neighbors." Webster greeted as he shook hands with all four of the men.

"Come on in. B.J. has just put breakfast on the table and we've plenty for everyone. Hot coffee waiting to warm your innards." Webster laughed.

Wayne was introduced to all the Brooks and everyone sat down to eat.

B.J. was hurrying to clean up the breakfast dishes so she could go and watch the horses as they sorted them out. Some they would keep and others they would turn loose. The horses that were kept would be the ones they branded. B.J. dried the dishes and put a big venison roast on the stove with potatoes and carrots around it. This would be their lunch. She made three apple pies and put them in the oven.

When B.J. got outside, the men were all sitting on the corral fence looking at the horses.

"When does the rodeo start?" she asked.

"You've got some good looking brood mares here, B.J. What we need to do is decide which one you want to keep and which you want to sell." Ralph told her.

B.J. climbed up so she could see and they started dividing the horses. They called them "keepers" and the number of keepers was more than the number of sellers.

"Lets get this group branded and separated from the others and then we can come back and sort them a second time." Ralph suggested.

The boys started a fire and put the branding iron in to get red-hot. Each got his rope and picked out a horse and swung his rope over its head. Once the horse was eased to the rail, they let the poles down and took him or her out. They discovered they had several young stallions that would end up gelded, if they kept them. With the horse outside, another rope was swung from Norman's horse to tie his back legs, so the roped horse would lie down. Then the hot branding iron was applied to his hind shank and he was branded. When all were branded, then came the time to brand the ones they had brought from Kentucky. This meant Dude as well.

135

B.J. left for the house, she could not bear watching them stick that hot iron to Dude. She pretended she needed to check on lunch. B.J. watched from the kitchen window and almost caught herself running out to stop the branding, but knew it was necessary, so she turned away so as not to watch. The branding was finished, and then the work of breaking the horses began. Wayne helped with this part as well. He had worked the livery stable in St. Joseph, and he knew how to handle horses. Some of the horses were all but saddle broke and ready to ride off, so it made it go fast and easy. Others were as wild as the black stallion and presented a problem for a while. The Brooks boys knew how to handle most of them.

There was a total of forty-five, twenty-six of the horses were mares. Out of the twenty-six, four were to foal before bad winter came. Thanks to Dude, B.J. and them were off to a good start. While he was there Ralph looked at Dude's cuts and said they were healing fine. He also looked at little Stormy and remarked how much like his daddy, the black, he was.

"You've got yourself two good stallions now, and maybe even more on the way. I would like to bring my mare, when she comes in season, and breed her with Dude. How much would you charge me?"

B.J. looked at Webster and then it occurred to her all the work the Brooks had helped them with.

"For you, the first one is free."

Webster smiled to show he was satisfied with her decision. They stopped for lunch and as they ate they talked about the horses. Afterwards the men went right back to breaking the horses that were to be sold.

The day came to an end. The men stood in the front yard, a tired and weary bunch. The Brooks still had their trip home ahead of them. Ralph told Webster that he was going to town one day this week and if he wanted him too, he would send a telegram to Fort Laramie informing them of the horses B.J. had to sell. He also would register their brand.

"You need to get rid of as many horses as you can before winter get here. There will be no grass for them and it will cost you to keep them."

"Please send the telegram and let us know what the army says as soon as you hear." Webster told him.

Ralph and his boys saddled up to leave. Thanking them for all their help and for making the branding iron didn't seem enough, but they would not take any pay. B.J., Webster, Wayne, and Grady stood watching as the four rode away. Afterwards they walked back to the corral and looked at all their horses wearing the Rocking H brand. B.J. felt proud and she noticed the horses didn't act like the branding hurt one bit.

This had been a good day, but they were all tired. The night was cool, so they went inside to the fire. They sat talking and drinking coffee and finishing up the last of the apple pies.

"As soon as Dude is well, you ought to turn the horses out onto the grass to graze. Dude will keep them around. They will fatten up on the grass too and as soon as the Army wants them they will be ready." Wayne suggested.

"I think it's a good idea." Webster said.

"You're sure Dude can keep them around?" B.J. questioned. She remembered the black and wondered if he dared come back.

"Those are tame horses now. We took the wild out of them today, by breaking them. They know Dude's their leader and they will stay right with him."

The subject changed from horses to building a bunkhouse. Webster and Grady would get on it in the morning and Wayne would start building a blacksmiths shop. There were plenty of horses that needed shoeing.

"I've got to catch up on my canning. My garden is coming in and we will need the vegetables for this winter." B.J. told them.

It seemed that everything that needed to be done focused on the coming winter. The coolness in the air told them it was coming for sure and winter would not be far off. Winter was exciting, but B.J. dreaded this first one. Everyone who lived in this part of the country said it snowed as deep as your rooftop. Winters like that gave people cabin fever.

Webster threw another log on the fire and got Wayne to tell them everything he had seen on his trip out and everything that had happened before he left St. Joseph. They were starved to hear from the outside world. B.J. thought of all that had happened since they rode away from the destroyed wagon train and it seemed like a century ago, but it wasn't. She knew that with each passing day their lives had improved and that none of it would have been possible without the Good Lord taking care of them.

With each passing day, the weather got colder, and this was one of those mornings that made you wish you could just stay in bed. The sky outside was overcast with purplish-gray clouds hanging low and you could feel the dampness in the air. B.J. heard the rooster crow and wished that she had never brought the thing; all the rooster did was remind her it was time to crawl out of her warm bed and get the day started. B.J. dressed and combed her hair and went to the kitchen only to find Webster had the stove hot and the fireplace going. He stood in front of it sipping on a cup of coffee.

"I see your up before the rooster again this morning."

Webster nodded, "There's coffee on the stove, get you a cup and join me."

B.J. washed her hand and face and got her a cup of coffee and sat down on the hearth so the fire would warm her as she drank it.

"What are you and Wayne planning on doing today?"

"I guess we'll try to finish the bunkhouse and cut another load of firewood."

Firewood was necessary for the coming cold months ahead. Each day there was always work of one kind or another. Webster and Wayne had been cutting firewood and Grady was feeding the stock and milking and feeding the cow and her calf. B.J. fed the chickens and gathered the eggs. Grady constantly complained, saying the cow didn't like him; she was always kicking at him. Webster told Grady to warm his hands before he started milking her and she would like him better. Grady didn't consider these chores manly, but he did them while he complained.

This morning was no different than the other mornings when Webster roused him out of bed; Grady came into the kitchen stretching and yawning. He asked.

"Have you milked, Uncle Webster?"

"Nope, that is your permanent job from now on. You drink the milk, and you are gonna have to get it out of the cow."

"Do I have to milk before breakfast is ready?"

"You have plenty of time." B.J. answered.

Grady grabbed his heavy jacket and hat and started to the barn. In just a minute or two he was back in the house. "The cow got out somehow. I'm going to saddle Lady and try to find her."

B.J. nodded, thinking he wouldn't be gone long and continued cooking breakfast.

Webster. Wayne and her sat down and ate, taking their time, and having another cup of coffee. They thought Grady would come barging in any minute. But Grady didn't, so Webster and Wayne got up to begin their day's work. B.J. started cleaning up the dishes and put Grady's breakfast on the back of the stove to stay warm. B.J. got busy canning and totally forgot about Grady.

When Grady left on Lady searching for the cow and her calf, he had no idea which direction she had gone. He rode out looking for their tracks in the softened, rain-soaked dirt. There were none to be found, or either Grady didn't have the tracking savvy to know them when he saw them. But he rode on till he came to a cow pile and this he did recognize. Grady thought he was headed in the right direction and hoped to spot the cow grazing somewhere nearby. The further he rode the more convinced he became that she had not come this way, so he backtracked to the cow pile and went in the opposite direction. Grady did this three times before he got down and took a closer look at the pile. It was an old one and this frustrated him all the more.

Grady's empty stomach was making his patience run short, so he climbed back on Lady and rode on. He came to a trail some animal had traveled enough to leave, so he followed it. Grady was cold, damp, and extremely hungry, and becoming more irritable. His irritability was what caused him to be unaware of how narrow the trail was becoming, and of the fact that Lady didn't like the going one bit. Grady kept kicking Lady on and the horse, feeling the uncertainty of her footing, began balking. He kicked her again and this time she obeyed, but after taking the first step, Lady began slipping in the loose stones on the narrow trail.

Grady tried to compensate by pulling Lady back, but it was too late. Lady was so confused and scared now that she reared up, and began falling. This caught Grady off balance; he slid off her back and rolled over to get out from under her. The mare scrambled to her feet, but all Grady heard was the clatter of her hooves on the stones and the rockslide as he went over the side of a small cliff. Grady had rolled in the wrong direction and down the cliff he went until he landed on a small ledge just big enough for him to grab hold of. Grady lay holding his breath, thinking he was headed for the bottom.

When the rocks stopped coming pass him, he looked at the root growing out the side of the bank that he had grabbed hold of. He knew he couldn't hang here for long. Grady slowly mustered enough strength to ease himself back up to the flat part of the small ledge. There was just enough room for him to lie on it. He tried to stand up but the loose stone began giving away, causing him to almost go over the edge. Grady lay there listening to Lady above him. The mare shook herself like a wet dog shaking off water. He heard Lady pawing the ground and her hooves scraping the rocks to get her footing. Grady knew she was trying to find her way along the side of the narrow path.

Rocks and dirt were raining down on Grady from all the loose ground the mare was struggling in.

"Oh God, don't let her drop over the side." He prayed out loud.

Grady knew if Lady fell, it would probably kill him and her. After what seemed forever, Lady got her footing and was able to get across the narrow pass on the cliff's edge. Once across, Lady stood snorting with relief. Grady took a long breath and hoped she had ended up on the side of the path that led home. All he could do now was wait till Lady got hungry enough to go back to the barn, and then the others would know he was in trouble and come looking for him.

Grady eased himself into an upright position by holding on to another root. He looked down and then he got scared. The bottom looked endless. All Grady could see were treetops waiting to grab him when or if he went over. Grady warily drew his knees tight against his chest. He noticed his sleeve was torn in the tumble over the edge. His elbow was scrapped and bleeding. Grady took a piece of torn sleeve and blotted at the blood, trying to stop the bleeding. He was chilled to the bone. The jacket he was wearing was fine for running to the barn to milk, but he knew now that he needed something much warmer to be out in this weather.

Listening, Grady could hear Lady munching grass, if only Lady would go home. He thought of talking to her, but decided differently. He didn't want her to stay around, so he kept quiet. B.J. would wonder why he hadn't brought in the milk and come looking for him, so all he had to do was to wait, stay still and try to keep warm.

B.J. finished her canning and as she cleaned up she noticed Grady's breakfast plate still on the stove. This was when she realized that he had not come back. Grady never missed a meal. B.J. looked out the window hoping to see Grady coming across the yard with a bucket of milk, but instead she saw the cow and her calf standing in front of the barn door bawling to get in to eat. She grabbed her coat and hat and went to the barn to see if Grady was there.

"Grady, what are you doing?" she asked angrily as she pulled the barn door opened. The cow and calf entered right behind her. Looking around B.J. could see that Grady wasn't there and neither was Lady. She tied the cow, got a milk pail and began milking so the cow would stop her bawling. B.J. was furious at Grady for not doing his job. When she finished, she fed the chickens and gathered the eggs and headed back to the house.

"I don't know what he is off doing, but when he does get back, I'm going to give him a good talking too." B.J. said aloud.

B.J. started their lunch, and then got on with the cleaning. She made beds, picked up dirty clothes and had the house swept almost to the front door when she heard Tuffy barking. "That must be Grady." B.J. was all set to chew him out, but saw when she opened the door that Tuffy was barking at Lady. Lady was standing outside the barn door, but Grady was nowhere in sight. She had come home without him.

B.J. dropped her broom, grabbed her coat and hat and ran to the barn. Webster and Wayne had also seen the horse without Grady, and they came running. They all looked Lady over to see if there were any signs of trouble, but there was nothing to indicate anything was wrong.

"What do you supposed happened to make Lady throw Grady and then get away from him?" B.J. asked.

"It could have been a number of things." Webster answered as he and Wayne went into the barn to saddle their horses. B.J. followed and saddled Dude too. Before they rode out she went in to get their ponchos because it had started raining and she wanted to set the beans off the stove. Wayne handed her Dude's reins and Webster had Lady with him, and they rode out. Webster and Wayne were just as anxious as B.J. was to find Grady.

It was high noon and Grady had been gone since before breakfast. Grady was afoot and the weather was worsening. Webster, Wayne and B.J. headed out to search for Grady, but none of them knew the direction he had gone. They hoped they would run upon him soon.

"Did you see which way he went this morning?" Webster asked B.J.

"No. I figured he would be right back."

The rain was coming down harder now and to talk was difficult, so they decided to divide up and signal if anyone found his trail. They were to fire two shots if they saw any sign of Grady. B.J. rode, looking at the ground as she went for tracks of the cow or of Lady. The grass was tall enough to show signs easily, but she saw nothing. About that time she heard two shots, so she turned Dude and kicked him into a run until she came to Webster and Wayne. One of them had found the cow pile and this one was fresh, so they knew the cow came this way, but there were no signs of horse hoofs anywhere.

B.J., Wayne, and Webster separated again, riding in three directions hoping for more signs. The sky began darkening and thunderclouds began to form in a hurry. A bright bolt of lightening streaked the darkened sky and brought a loud clap of thunder. They continued searching even in these conditions. They had to find Grady more than ever now. No one needed to be in this cold thunderstorm.

Sitting curled in a knot, trying to stay warm, Grady prayed silently that he would soon be found. His stomach growled from emptiness and he was scared, especially since the thundering and lightening began. Grady tried to keep back the tears, but it was impossible. He kept thinking grown men didn't cry, but it didn't help because he wasn't grown. Grady was only thirteen, and even though he had seen death, he was still young and frightened. He sat hugging himself with one arm and holding to the snarled root with the other. The thunder roared and the sky was lit up by streaks of bluish-white lightening bolts. Grady drew into as small a knot as he could, and hoped help was on the way.

All that day Webster, B.J., and Wayne rode in the cold rain, going in every direction they thought Grady could possible go in, but there was still no sign of him. It was as if the earth had swallowed him up. How could anyone simple disappear like Grady had? B.J. knew it was getting late, her stomach was telling her and the sky was darkening with every minute. She did not want to end the search especially with night falling, and neither did Webster or Wayne, but they pull their horses to a stop and called B.J. over. It was raining so hard now they had to shout just to hear each other.

"Let's call it a day and go back to the house. We can start afresh in the morning. We will go in a different direction and with good light we will find him." Webster suggested. Webster could see from B.J.'s expression that she didn't want to stop the search, so he suggested they take a different route going home. That little thread of hope was the only reason B.J. agreed to leaving the search. She was determined to find Grady.

The three headed towards the ranch still looking as they went, but the weather now lessened their chances of finding signs, and none of them had the slightest idea of what happened to Grady. They knew the cow was okay; she was home in the barn. They knew Lady was okay, but what they didn't know was where Grady was and if he was okay?

The sight of the ranch house made them know they had been unsuccessful. Wayne took the horses to the barn to dry and feed them. Webster followed B.J. into the house. He lit the lanterns and put several logs on the fire. B.J. went to her room to change to dry clothes she was soaked. Webster had the stove going and the coffee boiling when B.J. came out, so she put the beans back on and began frying some meat to go with them. Her heart wasn't in eating and it was all she could do to concentrate on cooking supper. Wayne came in from the barn after kicking mud from his boots. No one was talking. B.J. told Webster and Wayne to get out of their wet clothes before they caught pneumonia. She was thinking mostly about Grady out in the cold rain.

They left to change and B.J. tears started. She cried while she set the table for supper. B.J. dried her eyes just before they came into the room. The three sat down to eat, but no one had an appetite. They went through the motions of moving their food around, not talking, just thinking. B.J. sipped the hot coffee and it warmed her enough to make her want to go back and hunt for Grady again. Without saying anything, B.J. pushed her chair back and started for her coat. She had one arm in the sleeve when a hand grabbed her and jerked her around. B.J. thought it was Webster, but when she turned she saw it was Wayne.

"There is nothing you can do out there tonight but make yourself sick trying."

B.J. ignored Wayne and pulled loose of his hand and continued to put her coat on. Wayne grabbed her by the shoulders, turned her around to face him this time. She could see the intensity in his eyes when she looked up at him.

"Now listen to me. We will find Grady, but we'll have to wait for first light to do it. If you go out there tonight in this storm, all you are doing is searching in vain."

This time Wayne eyes were softer and were more convincing. B.J. stood there looking at his blue eyes all but begging her not to go.

"Honey, we wanted to find Grady as badly as you. We're just as disappointed that we didn't, but it is useless to go back out in that storm tonight. Anyway, Grady has sense enough to find shelter and hold up where it is dry till we get to him."

B.J. thought for a minute on what Webster said. He was right; he did want to find Grady. The tenderness that both had shown was more than B.J. could take; she broke down and cried like a baby. Wayne took her in his arms and she leaned against his big chest. He hugged her to him until she stopped crying. B.J. could feel strength from being in his arms and warmth flowing from him. Leaning back, she looked up into his eyes and said, "Thank you. Thank you both."

"Are you all right?" Wayne gently asked.

B.J. nodded as she backed away from Wayne. She didn't want to leave the warmth of his arms, but she knew she must. "I'm going to bed. I'll clean up the dishes in the morning."

When she closed her bedroom door, she fell across the bed and her tears began again. The only one to ask for help was God, so she closed her eyes and prayed for God to keep Grady safe and well through the night. B.J. fell asleep before she finished.

B.J. could feel Wayne holding her in his arms and talking softly to her.

She awoke and found it was a dream; instead he was standing over her bed and calling her name to wake her. B.J. smiled up at him and he smiled back.

"Are you ready for some breakfast? Uncle Webster has it ready and waiting. We though you needed your rest, so we let you sleep in."

"I'll be right out." B.J. answered, feeling guilty.

When Wayne left, she tossed the quilts back and it occurred to her that someone had undressed her last night. B.J. pulled on her jeans and tucked in her shirt, grabbed her boots and started for the door. Before she could ask, Webster spoke.

"I was the one who undressed you and put you to bed last night, so don't go getting your dandruff up about it. Someone has to look after you. You could have caught your death of cold just lying on top of the covers like that."

B.J. walked over and gave Webster a big kiss on the cheek and thanked him for taking care of her. They sat down and ate a big breakfast, and talked about how they were going to begin their search.

Wayne had the horses saddled and waiting out front and had Grady's mare tied with them. They got into their coats, gloves, and hats and took some food that Webster had packed knowing Grady would be famished. The rain had stopped during the night and the sun was shining, so it made the day seem hopeful. They mounted their horses and rode out. They stated in a different direction. The three headed towards the foothills instead of going back to the valley where the cow usually grazed. The morning was cold and B.J. couldn't help but think about Grady being out in the storm all night.

Webster, Wayne, and B.J. rode on with Wayne in the lead. The trail they followed seemed to be one that something or someone had made before, but it became narrower as they went along. The shelly rock on the trail was loose despite the rain the night before, so the horses had to feel their way. On one side was a drop-off and not only was the trail narrow, it was also dangerous. Lady, Grady's mare, began to act up. Webster was trying to keep her calm and watch his horse's footing at the same time. Webster got down off his horse and handed B.J. his reins. He went back to Lady to calm her and led her across the narrow ledge of a trail. Lady continued to prance around, slipping and loosing her footing. Wayne saw the problem and came back to help Webster with the mare. The two of them got her settled down, but Webster told B.J. to get off Dude and walk him across the ledge. B.J. climbed down and was leading Dude when Webster said, "Quiet, did ya'll here that?"

Nobody heard anything and started with the horses again.

"Wait a minute, I heard something."

B.J. and Wayne listened. They all stood perfectly still.

"There it is again. Down there, it's coming from down there."

This time they all heard the sound and smiled at each other.

"Take the horses on up ahead and tie them." Webster said.

Wayne took the reins and walked the horses away from them.

"Grady, Grady." Called B.J.

An answer came back. "Down here, I'm down here."

They begin looking off the steep side of the trail expecting to find him at the bottom of the ravine. They still could not see him. They could hear him faintly calling to them.

Wayne went back to get a rope from his horse. He tied it around his waist and told Webster to lower him over the side real slow. B.J. helped Webster with his end of the rope, and Wayne started over the edge. They eased him down real slow and then he yelled for them to stop.

"What is it, is he there?" asked B.J.

"I've found him. He's on a ledge just big enough for him, but he seems okay,"

Now they had to find a way to get Grady up.

"Get another rope and lower it for Grady to tie onto."

B.J. did as she was told and when she came back, they lowered the second rope down the cliff. It seemed an eternity before Wayne called for them to pull Grady up. Then Webster realized they had to do something about Wayne's rope. They couldn't turn Wayne's rope loose or he would go over.

"Wayne, can you get a foothold in something while we turn your rope loose to pull Grady up?"

"I already have, so pull away; I'll be fine."

Webster and B.J. let go of Wayne's rope and concentrated on getting

Grady up the cliff. They found it wasn't easy, but before long they could see Grady's head. B.J. was so relieved now that she knew he was alive and not hurt too bad. They got Grady to level ground and went back to haul Wayne up the cliff. It was harder because Wayne was heavier than Grady, but they finally made it.

Grady lay on the ground and when they got closer, they could see he was shivering all over. Wayne focused on getting a fire started and Uncle Webster and B.J. began taking off Grady's wet clothes and putting on the dry ones that B.J. had packed. Webster brought out the medicine and food and was rubbing his legs and arms trying to warm him. Finally Grady began to thaw and he was more than ready to eat. They kept him close to the fire and talked.

Grady explained about Lady slipping as they came over the trail and when she reared it threw Grady off balance and he went over the side of the cliff. He caught himself on the ledge and held on all night. He was afraid to try climbing back up because the rain had the dirt wet and slippery. He feared ending up going all the way to the bottom, so he just lay there and held on through the storm all night.

"My hands got so cold I was afraid I would accidentally turn loose during the night and fall."

B.J. knew he was being brave for their sakes, but she could hear the fear in his voice as he spoke. She hugged him and told him that everything was okay now.

"Will you be able to ride back or do you want to double up with one of us?" Webster asked.

"I'm not going to ride Lady back over that narrow trail again."

Neither were any of them, but they couldn't help but laugh. Leave it to Grady to be the one to make a joke of something that had worried all of them to death.

Chapter 13

Several weeks passed since the scare with Grady and things settled back to normal. B.J., Grady, Webster, and Wayne were busy getting ready for the first winter in their new home when Ralph Brooks and his son, Norman visited. The visit was a surprise. The morning the two rode up, Webster greeted them and invited them in for a warming cup of coffee by the fire.

"What brings you two out on such a bitter cold day? How is all your family?"

"Everyone is fine, trying to get ready for these cold months ahead."

Grady had to tell them about his little mishap and they listened. Finally, Ralph went to his coat and took out a telegram and handed it to B.J. She took the telegram, but hesitated about opening it. Telegrams always made her nervous, maybe because they might be bringing bad news, so she looked first to Webster and then to Wayne. B.J. wanted them to give the go ahead to open it. They both nodded their heads indicating for her to go ahead and open it.

B.J. gently opened the envelope and began reading, and then she looked up smiling. Well her smile told them it wasn't bad news, but they waited till she told them what it was about.

"The army wants our horses." B.J. said gleefully.

B.J. went around the table showing the telegram first to Webster, and then to Grady and Wayne. They were all smiling and patting each other on the back.

"When do we have to have the horses at Fort Laramie?" Webster asked.

"They want them within three weeks at the most." B.J. answered.

"That doesn't give us much time." Webster added.

"You should be on the way as soon as you can because winter is nearly on us and the going will be slow. You'll wake up one morning and find snow on the ground." Ralph promised.

Norman agreed with his dad and told them he would help if they needed him.

"Thanks, Norman. We'll need all the help we can get." Webster replied.

B.J. excused herself to start lunch for everyone. She felt like celebrating. The Army was going to buy thirty of their horses, and this would be enough money to see them into spring.

While they were eating, the decision was made to leave in three days. This would be time enough to pack provisions and pick out the thirty horses they were going to take. That would leave them with fifteen plus the horses they started with. Most of the fifteen were mares and some with foals. Ralph Brooks had also brought their registration showing their brand was legal. Norman and he mounted up and told them that Norman would be back in two days to help with the packing and all.

"Tell Mrs. Earline hello for me," B.J. called, "and thanks again for all you've done for us." The Rocking H group stood watching as the two men rode off.

There was nothing better than getting good news to brighten everyone's spirits.

"Uncle Webster, do we have enough provisions to make that trip?" B.J. asked.

"Wayne and I can go hunting in the morning for a couple young deer. We have enough beans, potatoes and flour for bread and we have plenty of coffee. I believe we can make it without stopping in Casper."

"We'll have to stop coming back and replenish our supplies for several months. Once the snow falls, our trips to town will be limited." Wayne volunteered.

They next assigned chores for the trip. B.J. wanted to go but after talking it over, they decided she would stay there to care for the other stock and see to their cow.

"Yeah, you can milk her for a change; we men have more important things to do." Grady said.

B.J. started baking several batches of bread and made a big pan of gingerbread and some sugar cookies for their trip. She knew it would be lonesome on the ranch without the others, but there would be plenty for her to do. She then made the list of supplies they would need to bring back. Wayne stuck his head in the kitchen while she was baking.

"Something sure does smell good."

B.J. offered Wayne a sugar cookie and when he reached for it their hands touched for just a second. She felt a strong sensation of something pass through her. Wayne stood eating his cookie and looking at her with a longing in his eyes. He too, had felt the same sensation. To break the silence, B.J. asked, "Is it sweet enough?"

"Not near as sweet as you," Wayne answered as he leaned down and kissed her on the cheek, and then headed for the door.

B.J. was glad he went outside because she was red-hot from blushing. She reached up and touched her cheek; it was still hot where he kissed her. B.J. stood there thinking about the kiss and almost let the other pan of cookies burn.

The two days passed quickly and Norman was back on their doorstep like he promised. His mom had sent B.J. a sack of dried apples and one of sweet potatoes. There were also several pumpkins for the Thanksgiving holidays.

"Thank you Norman. We will never be able to repay your family for you generosity." B.J. told him.

"We don't want pay; the day might come when we are on the receiving end."

The plan was to leave at daybreak the next morning. They would take the wagon for their supplies and it was estimated they would be gone at least two weeks barring bad weather.

"B.J. if you happen to need anyone, you ride to the Brooks ranch as quickly as you can. Norman said his mom and dad would try to check on you while we're gone." Webster told her.

"I'll be fine. Don't you go off worrying about me. Those horses will be enough worry for all of you."

"Just don't go getting into any trouble. You know how you do when we leave you alone." Grady told his sister.

"Just listen to who's talking. Can't even keep up with a little ole cow and you think I get into trouble." B.J. kidded him.

Grady was to be their driver this time. He had enough experience now to handle the team without any trouble. Daybreak came and everyone was up without having to be called. After a big breakfast, they let the poles down on the corral and herded the thirty horses out the gate. Grady hugged B.J. and climbed aboard the wagon, reminding her to milk the cow every morning. Webster handed her pistol to her, and told her to keep it handy. He hugged her and climbed on his horse. The last one was Wayne, he came to B.J. and gave her a big hug that lasted longer then the others and then kissed her on the lips.

"See you when we get back. Take care."

"I will." B.J. promised.

"Awe, come on Wayne. Who needs all that mushy stuff anyway?" Grady said.

"One day you will think differently about that mushy stuff," Wayne answered as he climbed on his horse.

B.J. waved goodbye until they were out of sight. Tuffy was pulling at his rope; he wanted to follow after them.

"Come on boy; let's get out of this cold." B.J. said as she opened the door and turned Tuffy loose in the warm house. Once inside, B.J. realized how empty and quiet it was with everyone gone. She got busy cleaning. This would be a great opportunity while the men weren't under foot. B.J. kept so busy that the first day passed before she realized it. Her stomach growling made her aware of the time. She knew she had to feed all the stock and get them ready for night before she could eat herself.

Grabbing her coat, B.J. headed for the barn with Tuffy right on her heels. The men felt Tuffy would be a good watchdog for her. Dude was the first one B.J. fed, and then Lady. She noticed how big Lady was getting with her foal. B.J. gave both grain and hay and then went down to the other stall to feed little Stormy and his mother. Next the cow and her calf, which was almost as big as his mother. After feeding and watering all the stock outside, her chores were finished so B.J. blew out the lantern and started for the door. Tuffy stayed right with her the whole time, but he was sniffing the air and nervously looking around. B.J. reached down and patted him as they walked to the house.

Just as B.J. got to the porch, Tuffy started acting crazy again. She wondered what was bothering the dog. Was it a wild animal getting too close to the house? B.J. remembered the bear and looked around, but it was already too late and almost dark, so all she could see was the outline of the terrain. She patted the dog's head again and let him in the house. Tuffy would sleep in side with her tonight, or else he would be barking his head off.

B.J. fixed her a bowl of hot soup and bread and a cup of hot coffee. She sat down to eat when Tuffy jumped up and ran to the door and started growling. The hair on the nape of his neck was standing straight up, indicating he was mad at something or someone who was not suppose to be around there.

"Come here, boy," B.J. called to him, but Tuffy wasn't leaving the door. He growled again and began scratching on the bottom of the door. This was making B.J. mighty nervous. She sat wondering if she should open the door and look out. B.J. knew from his actions, that the minute she opened the door, Tuffy would shoot out pass her and if it was a wild animal it could kill him and her.

"Why do these things always happen to me?" B.J. asked aloud.

B.J. sat and finished her soup, hoping whatever it was would just go away. No such luck. Tuffy knew it wasn't gone, because he continued to scratch on the door wanting to get to it. B.J. offered Tuffy a bowl of soup and he did come over and lap it up, but went right back to the door afterwards.

B.J. tied a rope to Tuffy's collar so he couldn't run after whatever it was. She slowly opened the door and immediately Tuffy began pulling, but B.J. held him close. B.J. had her pistol in one had and the dog in the other as she stood on the porch trying to see what was upsetting him. Quickly, B.J. pulled Tuffy into the house and locked the door. She leaned against the door wondering had she really seen something, or was it just her imagination. No, it wasn't in her mind. She saw a shadow of someone on horseback. Now she must decide what to do. Should she just ignore this or should she take her pistol and go check for certain? B.J. knew she would not be able to sleep without knowing for sure, so she put on her coat and grabbed a lantern and her pistol and this time out she would turn Tuffy loose to run off whatever it was she saw. She couldn't just sit back and let someone steal their horses, so she opened the door and her and Tuffy started towards the barn.

Tuffy didn't run ahead of her, he stayed right on her heels, but still growled and had his bristles up. Slowly B.J. went to the barn, straining her eyes against the darkness to see past the glow of the lantern. When she got to the barn she saw the door was still latched, so she hung the lantern outside and began walking in the direction of where she saw the shadowed figure on horseback. After a while her eyes grew accustomed to the darkness, but she saw nothing. Holding her pistol in front of her, B.J. looked closer as Tuffy sniffed the ground at her feet; so she stooped down and found hoof prints in the dirt.

At first B.J. thoughts were the prints were from some of their horses, but upon looking closer she could tell the horse that left these prints didn't wear shoes. There was only one set of prints and they led away from the barn. B.J. went back to get the lantern but then decided to leave it for the night. This way she could see from the house if anyone came around again tonight. She and Tuffy went back to the house. B.J. locked the doors and hung up her coat. Tuffy was already resting in front of the fireplace. She added two more logs and warmed herself.

"Whoever is out there is gonna get mighty cold tonight." B.J. said to Tuffy. As thought he understood her, the dog whined. B.J. got her a cup of hot coffee and brought it back to her favorite rocker in front of the fireplace. She was convinced that the visitor had left or Tuffy would still be acting up and right now the dog was sleeping by the fire. B.J. pulled a blanket around her. Her intentions were to get good and warm before going to bed, but before she knew it she fell fast asleep in the rocker.

When the rooster crowed, B.J. knew she had slept in the rocker all night. She threw the blanket back and stood, as she stretched she realized how sore and stiff she was. B.J. stretched and reached for the poker to get the fireplace fire going again. Tuffy had moved to the door wanting out and when he whined she remembered the night before. B.J. got the fire going in the stove and put on a pot of coffee and then she put on her coat and hat and headed for the barn to check on the horses.

The lantern outside was still burning, so B.J. blew it out as she went by. The barn door was latched—a good sign—so she went in and everything seemed okay. The cow was ready to be milked and all the horses were blowing and snorting, ready to be fed. B.J. took care of all her chores and headed back to the house with her bucket of milk. She fed Tuffy and let him stay inside with her.

The sun was up and it would warm the day, so B.J. thought she would take Dude for a ride. Dude hadn't been run in several days. B.J. poured her a cup of coffee and went back to the fireplace to enjoy it with a slice of buttered bread. With all the men gone to deliver the horses, her work was really very little. She sat thinking about the hoof-prints she had seen in the dirt last night and was determined to check them out further this morning.

B.J. got her coat and hat and went back to where she saw the prints the night before. She looked around again and sure enough it was an unshod horse. Who would ride horses with no shoes? Then it came to her—Indians. Indians rode unshod horses. She remembered hearing the Captain at the Fort talking to Webster about this. Naturally her thoughts went back to the destroyed wagon train and how the Indians had killed everyone for the livestock and food. The Captain said the Indians wanted the livestock to eat. The weather was cold then, and it was cold now.

B.J. saddled Dude to have a better look around the ranch. She had on her pistol but it wasn't much comfort to her. She guessed she would have to wear the pistol till the men returned, now that the fear of Indians had come. B.J. rode away from the house looking for more of the unshod prints. She knew not to go too far, so she circled the place and kept looking. Out back of the barn she found more of the same tracks. B.J. stepped down from Dude and tried to figure out just how many of them had visited last night. She wasn't a tracker so she climbed back on Dude and headed back to the barn. The run Dude needed would have to wait; it was just too risky to leave the house and livestock right now. She put

Dude back in his stall and she went back in the house. B.J. hated to be cooped up all day, but she felt it was safer until the Indians showed their hand.

B.J. leaned against the windowsill looking out. She had no idea that Indians were looking back at her that very minute. Tuffy was gone. He had left while she was riding. No telling when he would return, some days he stayed gone all day chasing rabbits. Even if B.J. whistled it wouldn't bring him back to the house. Normally B.J. wouldn't pay this any mind, but now she wished she had tied Tuffy so he couldn't wander off. When he got tired he would come home, then she would tie him.

B.J. caught a glimmer of something out of the corner of her eye. She thought maybe it was Tuffy, so she looked again. Whatever it was wasn't there now. B.J. felt a chill go over her and wonder if it was her nerves or the weather. She went to the fire to warm and noticed her woodpile was low. The men usually took care of keeping the wood box filled, but the men weren't here so she would have to fill it herself. She may as well do it now; she didn't want to run completely out of wood for the fire.

B.J. donned her coat and hat again and headed for the wood shed. She knew it would require two trips because she couldn't carry as many logs as the men. As she bent over to load her arms with wood and when she straightened up, there they were. The Indians were at the back of the house in the edge of the trees. There were at least four of them. The bright colors in their clothing stood out against the dark background of the pines. They wore red and orange feathers in the headbands that kept their black hair in tact.

B.J. was tempted to drop the logs and run as fast as her feet would carry her, but she knew she mustn't show fear. Her hand dropped to her side to her pistol and she was again tempted to take it out and shoot at them, hoping to scare them off. She thought twice about this too. What if they fired back—she was sure they were much better shots than she—so she left the pistol in it's holster and turned back towards the house as though she had not seen them. B.J. could feel their eyes in her back, watching as she walked back to the house. The Indians were watching her and the ranch trying to find out how many were on the place before they attacked.

Once inside, B.J. dumped the logs in the wood box and immediately went around and closed and latched the shutters on all the windows. She knew they would know she was afraid and she was. B.J. checked through a crack in the shutter to see if they were coming any closer. The Indians stayed right where she last saw them in the trees. B.J. got all the rifles and loaded them and put them on the kitchen table within easy reach, if needed. Her pistol was loaded and ready too. She didn't know what else to do but wait, and the waiting was making her even more nervous.

B.J. poured herself another cup of coffee and tried to think what had happened through. "The Indians came last night, but because it was dark, they couldn't tell how many were at the ranch. They left to return this morning so they could see how many they were up against. They are uncertain, that's why they are holed up in the trees." B.J. said out loud. She was trying to boost her courage, but deep inside she wished Uncle Webster, Wayne and Grady were there. Webster always managed to come up with a simple solution to each and every one of life's problems. B.J. knew she needed a plan—one that would deceive the Indians into believing she wasn't there by herself. B.J. thought for a moment and hoped she could pull it off, if she could her plan might just work.

B.J. went into Grady's room and got an old hat and one of his coats. She pulled her hair up and stuffed it into the hat and pulled up the coat collar. B.J. opened the door and started towards the barn, but halfway she stopped and yelled back to the house as though she was talking to someone inside, and then she went into the barn. B.J. waited several minutes and came out of the barn, and going back to the house she took her time like everything was normal. Maybe the Indians would think there were two now.

Why not go for three? This time B.J. took Uncle Webster's old coat and put it over Grady's—making her look fatter—and turned up the collar and started for the woodpile again. As she picked up an armful of wood she glanced towards the pines and could see the Indians talking to each other. As soon as she got into the house, she dropped the wood, pulled off all the coats and got ready for anything that might happen. B.J. checked again and the Indians sat there on their horses and talked for a while. B.J. thought she had them totally confused.

Tuffy ran up on the porch and scratched on the door. He scared B.J.

at first and then she was glad he was back home, so she opened the door and he went straight to his bowl and began eating.

"You're as predictable as Grady when it comes to eating."

Actually B.J. was relieved he was back. She would not let him out again as long as the Indians were around. B.J. went back to her window and saw the Indians riding off. Something in the back of her mind told her not to trust them; they were devious. B.J. watched till the Indians were completely out of sight, and then breathed a deep relief. B.J. felt safer and her fear had subsided—replaced with hunger—she saw it was time for supper. She fixed her a plate and took it to the fire to sit and eat. She was exhausted—the cat and mouse game she played all day with the Indians tired her physically and mentally. Tuffy came over and curled up on the bearskin rug and was snoring in a few minutes.

B.J. had to feed the stock before it got too dark. She put on her coat and hat and left, leaving Tuffy inside by the fire. Tonight she took her lighted lantern and left it hanging outside the barn. When she finished and closed and latched the barn door, she looked around real good. No signs of Indians, she guessed they had given up, at least for today. B.J. had always heard that Indians didn't bother people at night, so she went inside feeling safe till morning anyway.

Determined not to spend another night in her rocker, B.J. locked the doors and went to her bedroom. Tuffy was inside and she knew the dog would awaken her if the Indians returned. She slid under the covers and put her pistol under her pillow and hoped to get a good night's sleep.

"Lord, keep me safe until Uncle Webster, Grady and Wayne returns and thank you for watching over me today. Amen."

She lay curled in a small knot, partly because of the cold, but mostly because of fear. B.J. heard every night sound—the wind blowing through the trees, the insects, the owl when he whoed, even Tuffy moving about making his nest for the night. She turned over and stretched out her legs and vowed that she was not afraid. She had just asked the Lord to protect her and her faith told her He would. B.J. took a deep breath and the next thing she knew it was morning and the rooster was crowing.

As B.J. stretched under her warm covers, she knew she had slept peacefully, but she also knew she must still be careful of the Indians—

they might return. If the did, she had to be ready for them. B.J. got her fires going at once and put on her coffee to boil. The morning seemed a little colder, no doubt about it, they would have a bad winter and it sure was coming early. B.J. headed for the barn for her morning chores. This time out she took a rope and put it on Tuffy's collar, and he went along with her. The two of them started across the yard to the barn looking as they went for Indians. There were none to see. B.J. blew out the lantern and looked towards the woods behind the house and barn. Once inside, she tied Tuffy to a post while she fed and milked. B.J. stopped to pet Dude on his nose for a minute and marveled at how good he looked. His scars and cuts were healed and all signs of his fight with the black stallion had disappeared. Little Stormy was really growing too. Pretty soon they would have to take him away from his mother. B.J. picked up her bucket of milk and headed back to the house with Tuffy in tow. She carried the milk inside and left Tuffy and went back out to gather the eggs and feed the chickens. All this time B.J. eyes were roaming the ranch for Indians.

For some unforeseen reason B.J. was nervous this morning. She could feel the anxiety inside herself. It was probably the scare from yesterday, she silently admitted. After breakfast B.J. fed Tuffy and he went to the fire and lay down. B.J. cleaned the kitchen, made her bed and came back to her rocker to do some darning on Uncle Webster and Grady's socks. B.J. had just got her needle threaded when Tuffy raised his head and pointed his ears. B.J. watched him but didn't say anything. After a few minutes the dog lay back down and she went on with her sewing.

The quiet was deafening; all she could hear was the fire cracking and spewing. She knew it was going to be a long two weeks. She had only made it through two days and already she was running out of things to do. B.J. finished her sewing and went to put the socks in the bedroom. She looked out the bedroom window, still no sign of Indians. Now she could relax. The cause for concern was over, and she decided to take Dude for that run. Maybe some fresh air, even though cold, would clear her head. B.J. would leave Tuffy there, so she got her heaviest coat, gloves and hat and headed for the barn.

B.J. had Dude saddled and was about to mount when she heard Tuffy barking from the house. Her first thoughts were the Indians had returned.

B.J. tied Dude to the stall and eased the barn door open. She looked towards the woods, nothing, so she looked to the back of the barn; there was nothing there either. "What is that crazy dog barking about? He probably wants out."

B.J. went back to the house and as soon as she opened the door to scold Tuffy, out he shot pass her. Tuffy was gone. She closed the door and went back to get Dude. B.J. and Dude had a good run all the way to the meadow where the mares were grazing. She could see all of them and they were fine. Dude acted up when he caught the smell of the mares, but B.J. held him tightly as they circled and went back towards the ranch. One of the mares had foaled and the little foal was on its feet and sucking, so B.J. knew they both were fine.

The weather was getting too cold to stay out any longer, so she reined Dude to a stop outside the barn, dismounted and opened the door. Dude was acting strange, but B.J. though it was because he had just seen his mares. She took Dude inside and rubbed him down and brushed him and then left for the house. Half way to the house B.J. saw the Indians. They weren't in the pines at the back nor were they at the back of the barn. The Indians were riding up to the house from the West. B.J. hurried to the house, went in and locked the door. She took one of the rifles from the table. The band of Indians came right to the front door. The same group she saw in the pines yesterday. What was she to do? How long had they been watching her and did they know she was alone?

B.J. stood—rifle loaded—and waited. She watched one of them get off his horse. Up close the Indians frightened her even more. Their brown parched faces, wrinkled from days in the sun, showed no sign of emotion or feelings. B.J. found it impossible to predict their intentions. The brightly colored shirts and sashes they wore around their waist stood out in contrast to their buckskin pants and breechcloths. Their blanketed ponies stood pawing the dirt and snorting.

B.J. levered a shell into the barrel of her rifle, ready if necessary, but hoping she wouldn't have to use it on them. The Indian who dismounted stood talking to the others, and then he came up the porch steps. Before he sat foot on the porch, B.J. jerked open the door fired a round in the air over their heads, and with her rifle pointing right at him asked.

"What do you want?"

The Indians looked at the rifle for the longest and B.J. began to wonder if they understood her.

"Why are you here?" This time she hoped they didn't notice the tremor in her voice.

B.J. had closed the door not wanting them to see she was alone. She kept the rifle pointed right at the Indian and finally he pointed to the barn.

"Horses!"

"What about the horses?"

"You sell horses to us."

"No horses to sell."

The Indian walked back to the others and got a big bundle of beaver pelts and dropped them on the porch. "To pay for horses." He stooped down and untied the skins.

"No horses to sell. Come in spring we will have horses to sell then."

The Indian turned to one, who no doubt was the chief, and they talked and nodded to one another. He then tied up the pile of beaver pelts, got back on his horse, and all of them rode away. B.J. remained with rifle in hand and watched until they were out of sight. This confused her. Why would Indians offer to buy horses, when they usually took what ever they wanted? B.J. couldn't help but doubt that this was not the end of it, the Indians were simply trying to see of she was alone.

About that time Tuffy came running up and sat down at her feet. "Fine time to come home, the excitement is all over." B.J. scolded. They went back into the house, and for the rest of the day, B.J. kept Tuffy with her. About dust, B.J. had her chores to do, so she donned her coat and went to the barn. Afterwards she fixed her supper. Tomorrow would go a lot better, but just to be safe she kept Tuffy with her inside that night. B.J. would b glad when the men folks returned home. She remembered the last words Grady said to her about getting into trouble. Just wait till she told them about the visit from the Indians.

The first ten days went by slowly for B.J., and then she was surprised with a visit from the Brooks. After everyone had thawed out with a cup of hot coffee and a few welcomed words, B.J. told Ralph about what happened with the Indians and her concern of their return. Ralph and

Earline smiled and B.J. thought at first they didn't believe her, but it turned out they knew the Indians.

"It was Ole Chief Two-Toes and some of his men. They are harmless and probably wanted to barter for some of your horses. Everyone around here knows them, except you." Ralph said. "They aren't hostile, and we have accepted them as neighbors. Don't be surprised if they pay another visit in the spring."

B.J. was relieved by the news. She felt foolish, putting on a charade to make them believe she wasn't alone, but she didn't tell the Brooks about it.

"B.J. if you don't care I'll take my mare around to the breeding pen and turn Dude in with her while we're here."

"Go right ahead; you don't need me. I'll stay and visit with Earline while you and the boys take care of things."

Ralph and the boys led the mare to the pen. B.J. and Earline waited in the house. They had an opportunity to talk about Christmas. Earline helped B.J. decide on some nice gifts for the men and Grady. Earline also showed B.J. how to do needlepoint to help pass the long winter months.

"You should have had a girl in between all those boys. You have so much to pass on to a female. I wish we lived closer so we could visit more often." B.J. said.

The Brooks left for home late that night hoping their mare would be having Dude second colt. B.J. waved goodbye from the porch until they were out of sight. She went in and put several logs on the fire, warmed a cup of coffee, and then sat down to practice her needlepoint Earline had taught her. After sewing for hours, B.J. put it aside and went to bed.

When B.J. awoke the next morning she noticed how quiet it seemed. She didn't remember hearing the rooster crow. B.J. threw back the covers and got dressed as quickly as she could. The house was cold, so she went first to the stove and started the fire going there and then got the fireplace roaring in minutes. B.J. stood warming herself while her coffee boiled. The house begins to warm, so B.J. put on her coat and hat to see after the animals.

When she opened the front door, there it was; she stood frozen to the spot. It had snowed during the night and everything was covered with about two inches of solid white. The ranch was breathtakingly beautiful. Tuffy had come out the door with her and was running around the yard like something crazy. It was the dog's first snow and he was wild. B.J. knew it was the snow that had all the other animals half asleep, even the cow was quiet for a change. Looking at the sky, B.J. knew they were going to get more before the day was over. She did her chores and returned to the house to fix her some hot oats.

After setting the bucket of milk down, her thoughts went to Uncle Webster, Wayne, and Grady. Maybe they were nearly home, it had been thirteen days since they left, and even though the snow would make traveling slower, they rightfully should be home today or tomorrow.

Thirteen days was a long time to be in the saddle and on a drive, but the days flew by for all the men and Grady. They had thunderstorms to contend with and horses easily spooked from the lightening and thunder. The experience had been hard for all but Norman and he was really the only one of the four that had trail-driving knowledge, so they took all his suggestions seriously.

The thunderstorms subsided and the aftermath was mud that made it slow going with the wagon. They moved the horses at a steady pace and before long they were driving them through the gates of Fort Laramie. Once inside the troopers took charge of the horses. Grady drove the wagon to the front of the Captain's office where the young Lieutenant Jeremy Swan welcomed them.

"If ya'll will follow me, we'll get a count of the horses and then I'll give my report to the captain."

They went to the corral and the Lieutenant walked around, looking each horse over and nodding his head in approval. Webster and Wayne stood by until the Lieutenant satisfied himself and them they followed him back to the Captain's office.

They were told to enter. The Captain greeted them and offered them a chair.

"Sir, I've counted the horses, there are thirty of them. All the animals are in excellent shape and I recommend the deal be completed."

"Thank you Lieutenant that will be all. Gentlemen, I'll have your bank draft drawn up immediately."

The Captain was back in just a few minutes with the draft made out to Webster for the amount they had agreed upon. He handed it to Webster.

"Mr. Thompson looks like horse ranching has been good to you and your niece and nephew. By the way, how is the young lady thriving out here in the west? Does she like it as well as she thought she would?"

"Yes sir, we all have been blessed. These horses are part of a brood her stallion Dude managed to take from another stallion. We broke them, shod them, and now they are ready mount for your men. I hope you will let us supply ya'll with mounts in the future, because that's the business we are going to be in for a long time."

"The Army is always in need of horses, as a matter of fact, we can't exist without them. You'll be hearing from us, I'm sure. Give my regards to your niece and I hope you gentlemen will have a safe trip home."

Once outside they all smiled knowing the deal was done and the future looked good, and they were headed home.

Anticipating the men would get home early; B.J. cooked a big pot of venison stew, baked a couple of apple pies and made fresh bread. She cleaned the house and sit down with her needlepoint to wait. In just a few hours Tuffy jumped up and ran to the door. The dog whined and then barked a couple of times. B.J. could tell by the way he wagged his tail it was a friendly bark. She grabbed her coat and started out the door. Tuffy took off down the road to meet the wagon and welcome the men home. B.J. stood smiling, waiting and finally the wagon stopped in front of the house. It was loaded with supplies.

Wayne was the first one to the house and he jumped down from his horse and grabbed B.J. in his arms and swung her around like a little rag doll. Afterwards he gave her a big hug and kissed her on the lips. She stood dumbfounded. Looking up into his eyes she said, "I missed you too."

The next was Grady. He gave B.J. a big hug and she looked at him, not believing how he had grown since they left. Norman was next and he shyly gave B.J. a hug.

"Has Dad and Mom been to see you, B.J.? Were they alright?"

"They were fine, in fact, your Dad and the boys bred your mare to Dude the day they were here."

Norman smiled showing his relief from the news.

The last to come to B.J. was Uncle Webster. He took her gently in his big bear-like arms and just held her for a long time. B.J. felt so safe and secure that she hated when Webster released her.

"You have been on my mind for several days, has everything been okay here?"

"Yes sir, just lonely. It's been a long two weeks and I'm glad all of you are back safe and sound."

"Boys, we're home, but the work ain't over till we get these supplies unloaded. Let's get this stuff carried into the house and then the wagon and team taken care of. We can unload the barn stuff afterwards."

When they finished, B.J. had the table ready for them to sit down and enjoy her special cooked meal. She filled the big bowl with the hot stew and sliced the fresh bread. As each one came in knocking the snow from their boots, B.J. filled their cups with hot coffee and they sat down to enjoy a good homecoming meal. Uncle Webster said the blessing, thanking the Lord for their safe trip and good homecoming and for the food. Everyone starting eating and then the talking began. There was a lot to share.

B.J. told them about the visit from the Indians and when she mentioned Indians everyone dropped their forks and their ears perked up. When she explained what Ralph Brooks said, everyone went back to eating.

"B.J. it never fails; we leave you alone for a little while and you are knee deep in some adventure," said Webster.

Grady shared the time he spent with the pony express riders and how they showed him how they mounted their horses while running along beside for a ways. Grady was really impresses that their horses were bought for the pony express too.

"There was another colt born," B.J. announced.

"Was it a stallion or a filly?"

"I don't know. Dude was acting up and I didn't dare get off to see."

Wayne volunteered to ride out tomorrow and bring the mares in for the winter. Now they had two little one and three more to go. Their conversations went on and on, their voices breaking the silence the house held for what seemed like an eternity to B.J. Having someone to talk to was so good, especially since the snow had fallen and it was necessary to stay inside. Norman would leave for home in the morning, but for now the group just sat in front of the fire and sipped coffee till time to go to bed.

That night B.J. went to bed with a warm feeling and a light heart. No more Indian worries and her family were home safe and sound. The horses were sold and supplies bought for the winter. B.J. thanked God for all these blessings. Her heart was still throbbing from Wayne's warm kiss.

Chapter 14

The next morning Grady decided he rather stay and help Uncle Webster with one of his projects, so B.J. and Wayne rode out to see about the herd. B.J. enjoyed riding with Wayne; it was especially hard for them to be alone. Even though the sun was shining, the morning was cold and windy, so they kicked the horses to a trot and soon spotted the brood of mares in the valley. Wayne spotted the little foal and pointed in her direction. B.J. and him headed that way. The foal was staying close to her mother to stay warm and safe.

"It's a beauty. What is it?" B.J. asked as Wayne got down and eased himself up to the foal.

"She's a beautiful little lady, and a fine one at that. All the new arrivals are gonna be fine horses like the black."

The little filly stood still and Wayne picked her up. Her mother sensed that Wayne wouldn't harm her, but she followed alone anyway. Wayne handed the foal up to B.J. and she put her over her saddle.

"We'll carry her back, because she is so little, the others will follow."

The foal seemed all legs as B.J. held her in front. The filly was scared, but B.J. petted her and soothed her fears. Wayne had one foot in his stirrup when he spotted another mare down, so Wayne walked his horse to her. Wayne hoped to get close enough to see what was wrong. The mare's hind leg was cut and chewed on real bad; she had bled a lot too. Wayne eased himself up to the mare and she got to her feet. He talked gently to her and got her to be still long enough for him to take a closer look at her leg.

"I don't know what happened, but she is hurt bad. We need to get her to the barn and doctor her." Wayne took his rope and made a halter and put it over the mare's head. The injured mare's foal lay dead on the ground within feet of her. He tied the mare to his saddle horn and quickly climbed on.

"It will be slow going. The mare is hurt badly and don't need to be hurried. Her foal is dead, the wolves got to it just as she starting birthing."

B.J. nodded, and then took the lead. The herd would follow Dude and Wayne brought up the rear with the lame mare. When they got within sight of the ranch, Tuffy started barking. Uncle Webster and Grady spotted the herd and Grady tied Tuffy. Webster opened the barn door and let the poles down on the corral. Wayne led the lame mare in first and then he came back and took the little filly from B.J. The mother followed Wayne, and her baby, into a stall and Webster came over to look at her injured leg.

"Looks like a wolf might have jumped her when she was down having her foal." Wayne said. "They killed her foal, chewed up all they wanted and left its carcass."

"Were any of the other mares hurt?" Webster asked.

"Not that I could tell."

Webster got the liniment and medicine that Ralph Brooks had given them to use of Dude, and began doctoring the mare's leg. B.J. wrapped it in clean bandages and they closed the stall door and left her. The other mare and her little philly were okay. She was a beauty, strong built, and healthy. Her mother had escaped being injured, and was able to let her stallion nurse and you could tell by her size that she had been healthy from day one. Now the Rocking H Ranch had two new foals with two more to go.

Webster walked outside and inspected the other horses with a keen eye. B.J. could tell something was bothering him.

"What is wrong, Uncle Webster?"

"I don't like the idea of wolves being around; they mean trouble. If they attack once they will do it again."

"What can we do?" Asked Wayne.

"I know what I can do. I'll put out some traps and hopefully catch them. I'll bait the traps with fresh meat and maybe we can get them before any more damage is done."

All of them went back to the house to warm. Webster explained, "Wolves can't get a horse unless it's down. If there is a pack, they will seek out the weakest of the prey and attack. A healthy horse can outrun a wolf and will kick them to discourage attacking. How many more mares are ready to foal?"

"Two more are ready as far as we can tell." Said B.J.

"We better get them into the barn until this problems with wolves is solved. Grady come with me and we'll see if we can find those two and get them inside." Webster said. Grady followed him out and B.J. and Wayne were left alone in the house.

B.J. and Wayne walked over to the fireplace to warm up after being out in the cold morning. They had not been alone and close since Wayne came back from Fort Laramie. B.J. thought about the kiss Wayne gave her the morning he left and her heart started racing. Wayne stood so close their bodies touched, but he didn't say anything.

Wayne slipped his arm over her shoulder and hugged her to him. "I was proud of the way you handled that filly this morning. You were born to be a rancher's wife, B.J."

B.J. could feel the warm blush rising to her face so she kept looking into the fire. B.J. wanted to be alone with Wayne, but she felt awkward when they were. Wayne's arm felt good as he pulled her closer to him. B.J. didn't resist in fact she leaned closer to Wayne. Standing there by his side felt so right to her.

"You know B.J., I've made up my mind to claim me a section of land and try my hand at ranching."

"You're not going to leave us are you?" B.J. instantly knew she could not let this happen; she had waited so long for Wayne to get to her. "You have just got here and we've got plenty room for you."

"It will be a while yet, but I need a place to call my own." Wayne could see the disappointment on B.J.'s face; maybe it was time to tell her how he felt. That he was ready to marry and settle down on his place.

"B.J. I came out here because I love you and I want to marry you and give you a home. It turns out that you already have what you want and I'm beginning to wonder if I'm part of that future."

"Wayne, I love you too and I want to marry you, but there is no need for you to worry about claiming more land. There is plenty of land here for all of us, and we need you to help with this place, but I would understand if you did register a claim of your own."

Wayne lifted her chin and looked into her big brown eyes and said, "I'm glad to here you do love me too and that I'm needed here, but I still feel as though I need to contribute my share. This is yours, Grady's, and Uncle Webster's place. I've just moved in, after ya'll got all the work done, and enjoyed the comforts."

The touch of Wayne's hand went through her like a fire, and B.J. felt it all the way to her toes. The throbbing of desire in her heart drowned his words out. B.J. wanted Wayne to kiss her so much; she could feel his lips on hers.

"I do want you to stay and I do love you and need you, so please reconsider."

Wayne put his mouth gently on hers and kissed her. The kiss was soft to begin with but the longer their lips pressed together the harder and more passionate the kiss grew. B.J. enjoyed every moment of it and didn't try to pull back. Wayne pulled her body closer and ran his hand up and down her back, pressing against her as if to mold them into one. Wayne's body grew hard and strong, but B.J. began to weaken and go limp. She knew she had to stop this before it got out of hand, so she pushed back from him and took a long breath.

"I love you and it's harder and harder for me to be in these close surroundings and keep my hands off you. I know you're younger than I am, but I've never loved another woman. B.J. do you feel the same for me?"

Just as B.J. started to answer Wayne, the door opened and in walked Grady.

"We're back and we got the two mares in the barn and put some hay out for the others."

Neither B.J. nor Wayne said a word, but Grady sensed something had happened between them. They had a strange look about them, so Grady asked, "Have you two had a fight or something?"

"You wouldn't understand Grady, so just forget it." Wayne said as he started out the door. Grady turned to B.J. and shrugged his shoulders.

"When is lunch going to be ready?"

"All you ever think about is food."

"Wow! Why is everyone so mad; what did I do anyway?"

B.J. didn't answer; she just headed for the kitchen. Grady always showed up at the wrong time, she thought, as she got busy with lunch. B.J. was thinking about what Wayne said all the time she cooked and decided to talk to Uncle Webster. The matter had to be settled before Wayne decided to leave them and move to a place of his own.

When Uncle Webster came in for lunch he informed B.J. and Grady that Wayne had left going to town. Webster didn't say for what and they didn't ask. The day grew late and supper was ready and Wayne still was not back, so B.J. saved a plate for him. It was snowing again, falling hard and no sign of it letting up for the night.

"Wayne might not be back tonight?" Webster volunteered.

"Do you think he will be alright?" B.J. questioned.

"Wayne is a grown man and he can take care of himself." Webster smiled when he saw the concerned look on B.J.'s face.

"Well I know that, I just hate to think of him out in this weather all night."

"I doubt if he'll stay out in the weather." Webster said as he went to his easy chair by the fire.

B. J. cleaned the kitchen and settled in front of the fire to play a game of checkers with Webster. Grady and Tuffy were in a game of tug-of-war on the floor. B.J. couldn't concentrate on the checker game. She kept getting up and going to the window to see if Wayne was coming. Uncle Webster noticed how nervous B.J. was and asked.

"B.J. what is the matter with you tonight?"

"She and Wayne had a fuss this morning and now it's worrying her." Grady told Webster.

"I'm watching the snow. It's coming down harder now. By morning we'll have at least three feet." B.J. pretended, but deep inside she was worried about Wayne.

"I'm going to bed. You can stay up and watch it snow all night." Grady told her.

B.J. was glad that Grady was going to bed, now she would have the opportunity to talk to Uncle Webster alone. She took the coffee pot and filled Webster's cup. Webster touched her hand and said, "Come here and sit down, I need to talk to you."

B.J. was surprised. She was the one who needed to talk, but Uncle Webster had beaten her to it. She sat down in the chair next to him, noticing Webster had a serious look on his face. Webster took a sip of coffee and swallowed.

"B.J. ever since the first night I walked into yawl's camp, I felt a closeness to you kids. Now, I'm gonna talk to you just like your dad would if he were here."

B.J. couldn't imagine what was wrong. Suddenly Webster seemed so serious. She moved her chair closer letting him know he had her undivided attention.

"What is it Uncle Webster, are you sick or something?"

"No, I'm not sick. This has nothing to do with me."

"Have Grady or I done something wrong?"

"B.J., Wayne came to me earlier and told me what he had in mind about registering a claim of his own. I suggested if he thought he must do this to apply for land that joined this ranch and then later when you two are married it can be combined. You are planning to marry, ain't you?"

"I asked Wayne to wait. I wanted him to stay here; we have plenty of room and land."

"You mean you don't want to marry him?"

"Yes, I do, but I wanted to talk to you first—before I gave him my answer."

"B.J., if you feel about Wayne like he does about you, then why do you need to talk to me about it? I get the feeling that you doubt your love for Wayne."

"I do love him, Uncle Webster. I just don't know if my love is as real as it should be, or if it's just infatuation. When will I know? When will I know without a doubt that we were meant for each other?"

Webster saw that B.J. reply was in earnest, so he reached over and took her hand and squeezed it. "You will know when the time comes. Your heart will tell you."

Uncle Webster had set her mind at ease and she felt relief. "Why did you never marry, Uncle Webster? You would make some woman a good husband."

"I'm too old for marriage now, but I came close once. But it didn't work out, I wanted to come west and she didn't, so we parted ways. B.J. if you really love someone, you will follow him or her to the ends of the earth just to be with them. That kind of love wasn't there for me; she didn't want to follow me. I've never been able to get interested in another woman since then. Just let your heart guide you and you won't go wrong. Wayne loves you and the waiting is gonna be hard for him, so try to let him know how you feel. Wayne is a patience person; he'll wait the time needed. I'm going to bed, you sleep well and don't worry about Wayne; he'll be okay."

"Good night Uncle Webster, and thanks for the talk. I love you."

The next morning Wayne returned, but nothing was said about where he had gone or what he had done. B.J. was just relieved that he had returned and was okay. She knew until she became his wife she could not put demands on his time. The regular chores of running the ranch continued. Wood brought in and animals doctored and fed, new arrivals seen too and traps set and emptied each few days. Uncle Webster had trapped and killed several wolves and thought their problem with them was over.

The horses were turned back out into the meadow to eat all remaining grass as the snow had melted. Dude was turned out with the herd and was having himself a time as the mares came into season. B.J. wanted the word to spread about Dude stud service so other ranchers would come around with their mares. Dude looked good and B.J. tried to exercise him every day. Because Dude was kept in the barn most of the winter, he was slick and had less of a coat them the mares. His cuts and scars had healed completely and there were no signs of his fight.

Chapter 15

The first Christmas celebrated on the Rocking H Ranch was fantastic. The Brooks family joined them for dinner and there was much food and fun for all. Gifts were exchanged and all were surprised by what they got, especially the gift that Webster gave to the ranch. Webster had hand craved a wooden sign with "The Rocking H Ranch" right in the center. The sign would hand between two post they would erect coming into the ranch. B.J. and Grady were real impressed and both hugged Uncle Webster.

Now that the holidays were over the ranch settled down to the usual chores. The other two mares foaled and their arrivals were both fillies and beautiful. The black stallions bloodline really came threw in both of them. B.J. was waiting for Lady's colt to be born, Dude sired it. The New Year was off to a good start, everyone was well and healthy and all the animals were doing fine.

One cloudy, cold morning in late January, Wayne decided to go hunting. Their fresh meat supply was getting low. Wayne saddled his horse and took his rifle and rode out by himself. B.J. cautioned him to be careful because Uncle Webster thought he saw mountain lion tracks.

"I'll keep my eyes opened, don't worry."

B.J. got busy with her daily chores and soon forgot the time. When she realized how late it was, it occurred to her that Wayne had not returned.

"Uncle Webster how far would Wayne have to go to get us a deer?"

"Well, not too far."

"I'm worried about him. Shouldn't he be back by now? Maybe we need to saddle up and go search for him." B.J. remembered how Grady had stayed out all night in the cold after his misfortune while hunting the cow.

"Have a little patience, B.J.; Wayne is fully capable of taking care of himself."

B.J. tried to busy herself, but found all she could do was go from one window to another looking for Wayne to ride up. She had a deep fear inside that something was wrong. Another hour passed and there was still no sign of Wayne.

"I think we should go search for Wayne, he has never been gone this long hunting. We don't want another night like we had with Grady."

At B.J. persistence, Webster told Grady to go and saddle their horses. Webster and B.J. got on their heavy coats and met Grady outside. There really was no way of knowing what direction Wayne had gone, so Webster chose the way he usually went deer hunting. Webster led out, because he was the most familiar with the woods they hunted. B.J. and Grady followed slowly behind, trying not to disturb any signs Wayne may have left. Most of the snow had melted. What Webster. B.J. and Grady didn't know was that Wayne was tracking a deer, and a mountain lion was tracking Wayne.

Wayne couldn't see the mountain lion, it stayed in the rocks overhead. They were silent killers; a person had no way of knowing a lion was anywhere around until it picked it's spot and attacked. The attack was usually when a person was most likely unprepared.

Webster, B.J., and Grady rode on watching for prints. Webster rode a little to the left and when he did, he saw the lion tracks. Webster didn't say anything, but B.J. noticed how he stopped ever so often and looked into the trees and rocks. He slowed quite a bit too, because he was suspicious of something.

"What is it Uncle Webster? Have you seen something?" B.J. asked as she rode up next to him.

"Quiet. There are some big cat tracks going in the same direction as Wayne is going. We don't want it hearing us before we catch up with Wayne." Webster voice was calm, but B.J. could sense the anxiety there.

She noticed too that it was getting darker as they went deeper into the trees. They would soon have a problem seeing.

Suddenly the night was filled with the screaming neigh of a horse that was terrified, and then a rifle shot. All three froze, but the horses became skittish and wanted to turn and run. They held them as still and as quiet as they could. Webster held up his hand as though to quiet them, but another shot interrupted the silence.

"Was that Wayne, signaling us?" Asked B.J.

"We need to find where that shot came from in a hurry."

They kicked the horses to a trot, because under the trees it was all they could manage. Webster went in the direction the sound came from, not knowing what they would find. Webster was on the scene before he knew it and had to rein his horse to a sudden stop. There in front of him lay Wayne with the mountain lion on top of him. Webster couldn't tell if Wayne was alive or dead—blood was everywhere. The lion was bleeding and Wayne was bleeding. There were three deep slashes that ran from his cheek down his neck to his shoulder. Three slashes from the cat's paw when he jumped Wayne. The horse was the only one that escaped injury; he was standing a few feet away with the carcass of a deer hanging from him.

B.J. jumped off Dude and ran to where Wayne lay. Webster and Grady were right on her heels. The mountain lion was so big and heavy that it took all three of them to move it from Wayne, and then they could see how badly he was hurt.

Wayne was out cold. When the lion jumped him, he went backwards, hitting a rock where he fell. Webster tried reviving Wayne by putting snow on his forehead, but Wayne didn't respond. He was still bleeding and they couldn't risk him losing any more blood, so B.J. took her kerchief and began wiping away the lion's blood and trying to stop Wayne's bleeding.

"How are we going to get him out of here?" B.J. asked

Webster had been feeling Wayne's legs and arms to see if he had any broken bones. "There's nothing broken, but his back might be injured, so we better make a travois to carry him on—just to be safe."

Webster got busy finding two poles long and strong enough to carry

Wayne. He tied his bedroll to them and they lifted Wayne onto the travois. Webster and Grady threw the mountain lion over the saddle next to the deer and then climbed on his horse and led Wayne home.

The going was slow and it seemed forever before they were back at the ranch. B.J. rode by his side and kept looking down at Wayne. They wrapped him in another blanket but she noticed he had bled through her kerchief. She worried about the amount of blood he was loosing. Wayne was still unconscious. Maybe that was a blessing; at least he couldn't feel any pain. When they finally got him home it was pitch black. There were no lanterns burning so Webster went in first and lit them, and then he came back to help get Wayne inside. B.J. was standing by Wayne's side when Webster returned.

Wayne was a big man, and out cold, he was dead weight, so it took all three of them to get him inside.

"Put him in my bedroom; it is warmer than the one ya'll sleep in."

Slowly, they laid Wayne on her bed. B.J. got a pan of warm water and a clean cloth and went back to her room. Webster and Grady had Wayne undressed except for his underwear. Wayne's torn bloody clothes and boots lay on the floor by the bed. Webster helped B.J. pull the covers from under him and the two began cleaning off all the dried and wet blood. After all the blood was washed off they could see how deep the slashes in his neck were. Thank God they were not deep enough to get his jugular vein, but they were deep enough that stitches were needed.

"Grady, go pull some hair from the tail of one of the horses." Webster said.

B.J. took some alcohol and cleaned the wounds as best as she could and then she went to her sewing basket for a needle. When Grady returned she took the alcohol rag and ran it down the horsehair and threaded her needle. She dipped it in the alcohol and began stitching Wayne's wounds. Grady stood watching with a squeamish look on his face.

"It's a good thing Wayne out cold or he would be pitching a fit."

After bandaging the wounds the best she could, B.J. covered Wayne hoping he hadn't gone into shock. She picked up the pile of bloody, torn clothes and put them in a pail of water to soak. Webster left the bedroom door opened so the room would be warmer and they could hear Wayne if he came too. B.J. put on a pot of coffee and started their supper. Grady and Webster took lanterns and went to put the horses up for the night. They decided the deer could wait till morning for skinning. Webster and Grady came in ready to eat. They kept looking toward the bedroom hoping that Wayne would wake up, but he never did. B.J. cleared the table, but kept the soup on the back of the stove just in case he did.

Each time B.J. checked on Wayne, she noticed how pale he looked lying there in bed. Her heart ached seeing Wayne like this; he had always been so strong and alert. Wayne was still unconscious too.

"Uncle Webster do you think we need to go to town for a doctor."

"We'll wait till morning and see how he is. If Wayne isn't any better, I'll go get the doctor."

Grady went to bed, but made B.J. promise to wake him if she needed him during the night.

"B.J., Wayne is healthy and he'll be all right. Try not to worry. You take my bed and I will sit up with him tonight." Webster told her.

"No, you go to bed; I'll wake you if I need you. Besides if you have to ride in for the doctor, you'll need your rest."

Webster agreed and put more logs on the fire before he went in to have one last look at Wayne—still out like a light.

B.J. followed Webster and noticed the bandages were clean; at least they had managed to stop his bleeding. Webster left going to bed but B.J. stood looking down at Wayne, and then she realized how much he meant to her. She knew that she wouldn't be able to stand anything happening to Wayne. B.J.'s heart was talking to her just like Webster had said it would. Her heart was telling her that she loved Wayne much more than she had realized and she wanted him around for the rest of her life. Why had she not taken the time to let him know this? They had never finished their talk the day Grady interrupted. As soon as Wayne woke up she was going to tell him she was ready to marry him.

B.J. sat by Wayne's bed all that night, but sometime during the night she fell asleep. She woke to find Uncle Webster standing over Wayne feeling his forehead.

"What is wrong?"

"He is burning up with a fever and we need to bath him off to bring it down."

Wayne was still out and he was having problems breathing. His breath came in shallow gasp, rapid and strained. B.J. got a pan of cool water and bathed him off. She kept bathing his face and arms trying to cool Wayne fever, but it didn't seem to help him much.

Webster started breakfast and soon Grady was up. He stuck his head in and asked, "How's he doing, Sis?"

"Not too good. He is burning up with a fever." B.J. said as she continued to wipe his face, arms and chest with the cool cloth.

B.J. covered Wayne and went to get her a cup of coffee. Webster and Grady was talking.

"Maybe one of us should go for Mrs. Brooks. She could tell us if there is anything else we could do for Wayne." Webster told Grady. "I'm concerned that he hasn't gain consciousness and his breathing is becoming more difficult for him."

"I'll go get the Brooks'," Grady agreed, so he eat and saddled Lady and took off.

The house was quiet and all anyone could hear was the heavy wheezing of Wayne's breathing. B.J. was scared for Wayne, so she asked God to please help him and to help her and Webster to help Wayne. B.J. leaned close and pressed her head against Wayne's chest and heard the rattle in his lungs from congestion. She went in search of Webster.

Webster was skinning the deer but when the door opened he looked in the direction of the house. Webster wiped his hands and left the deer, "What's wrong, is Wayne worse?"

"I'm afraid Wayne has pneumonia. Come and lay your head against his chest and listen."

Webster removed his hat and leaned down to listen to Wayne's chest. He listened for a minute or two. "You're right, B.J. what we need is a hot poultice to go on his chest."

Webster went into the kitchen and began mixing mustard and herbs and spread it on a clean cloth and then he laid it on the stove to heat. When the poultice was hot through and through, Webster took it and

178

opened Wayne's underwear and laid it across his chest. Webster buttoned Wayne's underwear and pulled the covers up to his chin.

"What do we do now?" B.J. asked, feeling so helpless.

"We just wait and pray." Webster said as he left to finish the deer he was skinning.

B.J. sat down in her rocker and listened to Wayne's breathing, it seemed the poultice sure enough make a difference. Wayne was breathing near as shallow. Silently B.J. thanked God for the relief it had given Wayne.

Late that afternoon the Brooks and Grady got there. Earline went right in to see about Wayne, and Ralph followed.

"I think ya'll have done all there is to do. The stitches look clean and infection free and the poultice will definitely help his breathing. Ralph is checking Wayne now for any broken bones." Earline said to Webster and B.J…

"Get me some wide bandages and Webster I'll need your help to wrap Wayne's rib cage as tight as we can. Wayne has at least two broken ribs." Ralph told them after he finished examining Wayne.

B.J. got the bandages and Earline and her wrapped Wayne's ribs as Ralph and Webster held him upright. Afterwards, they gently laid Wayne back down. Ralph leaned over and listened to Wayne's chest.

"I don't believe he has a punctured lung, or he would be having more difficulty breathing than he is. I think it's a chest cold from lying here so long. The poultice will help that."

"His fever is down now, but it could go up later. Just keep bathing him down with cold water and the fever will stay down." Earline said.

Everyone was satisfied that all that could be done for Wayne had been done, so they went to the kitchen for a cup of coffee. B.J. poured the coffee and got a plate of sugar cookies to go with it. B.J. realized that this was all she had eaten that day, but she couldn't be satisfied staying in the kitchen, so she took her cup and cookies and went back to Wayne's bedside. B.J. sat listening to Uncle Webster telling Ralph and Earline what he thought had happened.

"I worry about Wayne being unconscious for so long." Webster said.

"Wayne suffered a concussion when he hit that rock." Ralph replied.

"That sure is a big mountain lion. Wayne's lucky he didn't get hurt worse." Grady added.

"Let's go see that thing." Ralph added.

The three men left going to the barn to see the dead mountain lion that Wayne managed to shoot. Earline stayed behind and cleared the coffee cups to begin supper for all of them, she knew that B.J. had been sitting with Wayne all day and didn't feel like cooking for them. Ralph and she came prepared to stay the night. When supper was finished the men came in to eat. Earline carried B.J. a plate to the bedroom. She could tell B.J. was worried so she patted her on the back and told her, "Wayne will be okay."

"If he would just wake up and say something."

"He'll wake up when his body has healed enough for his brain to tell him to. When you get a bad head injury like Wayne got, your body sleeps to help the healing process."

B.J. took the plate of food and thanked Earline for fixing supper for them. She tried to eat, but found her appetite was gone. B.J. hoped that Earline was right and she prayed again for Wayne to wake up and be okay."

After supper the men settled down to a game of checkers and Earline went in to relive B.J. so she could get some needed rest. B.J. stayed and the two women talked. Earline missed having another woman to talk too, and B.J. realized how badly she missed her mother.

"I can tell your concern is more than that for a friend. How long have you and Wayne been serious about each other?" Earline asked B.J.

"We met before our wagon train left St. Joseph, Missouri. He wanted to come west with us, but didn't have the money. Wayne said he would find me as soon as he saved his money up and he did. I haven't told anyone but Uncle Webster—Wayne asked me to marry him."

"Do you love him, B.J.?"

"I didn't realize how much until he got hurt and now I hurt as much as he does. I guess its love. I've never known this kind of love."

"B.J., you're still young and waiting wouldn't hurt, but it looks like you have already made up your mind."

Since Earline couldn't talk B.J. into going to bed, she left for bed with the promise that B.J. would wake her if she needed her. Webster and

Grady gave Ralph and Earline their beds and they slept on the floor in front of the fireplace. B.J. pulled her blanket up around her shoulders and sat listening to how much easier Wayne was breathing. B.J. dozed off and didn't wake until she heard Wayne coughing. She was scared at first that Wayne was worse, so she jumped up and felt Wayne's forehead to see if the fever had returned. When B.J. touched Wayne's forehead his eyes opened and he said, "Your hands are cold."

B.J. almost jumped out of her skin. "How long have you been awake?"

"I woke myself up coughing and hurting like crazy. Why am I in your bed?"

"Don't you remember what happened to you?"

"The last thing I remember was a big mountain lion jumping at me." Wayne's hand came out from under the cover and felt his neck. He felt the bandages around his ribs and moaned a little. "He fixed me up real good, didn't he?"

B.J. explained his injuries and told him to lie real still and maybe his ribs and neck wouldn't hurt so badly.

"How long have I been in your bed?"

"Since we brought you home from the woods that night. This is where you will stay until you are able to be up and about."

"Have you been in that rocker all this time?"

Before B.J. could answer the bedroom door opened and Uncle Webster stuck his head in. "What does it take for a tired ole man to get a good night's sleep around here?" He smiled. "I heard you two talking and am I glad that you decided to wake up."

"Well, two days is enough time for anyone to sleep; besides I'm hungry."

B.J. went for Wayne a cup of milk and some cookies to hold him till breakfast. Wayne tried to sit up to drink the milk, but his ribs wouldn't let him. Webster told B.J. to go get some sleep that he would keep Wayne company for the rest of the night. B.J. lay down beside Grady and slept like a baby till the aroma from breakfast woke her.

Earline had everything ready and B.J. felt guilty about letting her do the work, but she was thankful for the sleep. The breakfast was delicious—B.J's appetite was back now. She carried a tray to Wayne and sat with him while he ate it. The crisis was over and the Brooks had to go home.

"Wayne don't you rush things now. Your concussion will have you in the floor if you do. You have a good little nurse and she doesn't mind taking care of you, so let your body mend. You're lucky to have B.J. to take care of you."

Wayne thanked them both and promised he would. Everyone went back to his or her usual routine of chores, with the exception of Wayne. He had at least another three or four days to stay in bed—a feat that proved to almost kill him.

A week later Wayne was up and slowly moving about. B.J. had trouble keeping him in bed as long as she had. His concussion was healed, even though the first time up he experienced dizziness. Wayne still had soreness in his ribs and if he tried to lift anything or sit a horse, he was reminded with pain. Wayne ended up staying in with B.J. and Webster and Grady did all the outside work. This gave Wayne and B.J. the needed time to talk.

"Wayne, I was so worried about you. I guess the accident made me realize how much you really mean to me."

"I'm sorry I caused you unnecessary worry."

They kissed and made up. Their relationship had been distant since Wayne had told B.J. that he wanted a place of his own and left going to town.

"I hope your notion of getting your own place is over now." B.J. said.

"I filed on a section of land that joins the Rocking H. I have to contribute my part to this place. I couldn't have people saying I married you for your ranch."

"That's fine with me Wayne, but it wasn't necessary. If you're happy, then I'm happy too."

Wayne kissed her again as if to seal their agreement. Everything felt right between them now.

Chapter 16

Each day the weather warmed and signs of spring returning appeared. The first winter for the Rocking H had not been that bad, but it was good to see the grass greening again and Dude and the mares able to graze in the meadow. The ranch had five new colts and Dude's colt was yet to come. This was the colt that everyone waited to see. The young stallion, Stormy was growing and feeling out real good. Grady spent a lot of time working with him and Grady knew Stormy was going to make a fine horse.

Wayne was almost healed from the mountain lion attack. He and B.J. decided to ride over to the Brooks just to get Wayne out of the house for a day. It was a beautiful day for a ride, so Grady hitched up the wagon for them. Wayne still wasn't able to sit a horse without his ribs hurting him.

"Enjoy yourself and say hello for Grady and me." Uncle Webster called as they left the yard.

B.J. was driving and had not been on the main road long before they met another wagon coming in their direction. Neither recognized the folks, so they pulled over and stopped. The oncoming wagon was piled high with the people's belongings and their two children. When they got even with B.J. and Wayne, they pulled to a stop.

"Howdy, I'm Wayne Thompson and this is B.J. Hall of the Rocking H Ranch." Wayne eased himself down from their wagon and turned to help B.J. down.

"You folks new around here?" Wayne asked as he extended his hand up to the man.

"Yes we are new to this country. I'm Phillip Donilson and this is my wife Edwina and our two children, Laine and Lloyd. We've just filed a claim on a section of land west of your place."

The Donilson's climbed down from the wagon and B.J. noticed that Edwina was smoothing out the wrinkles in her dress and it revealed her pregnancy. Edwina looked embarrassed about her looks. B.J. smiled to ease her embarrassment.

"We're going visiting is why you caught us looking this good. Usually its work clothes on the ranch."

The children were real nice. The boy was a little quiet, about Grady age and Laine was just a little younger than B.J. They visited a while and B.J. and Wayne invited them to come over anytime.

"We met the Brooks a little while ago. They are real nice folks."

"Why don't ya'll come to our ranch and stay until you get your cabin built?" B.J. suggested.

"No, we couldn't do that. We're used to living in this wagon and a few more days won't hurt a bit." Edwina replied. "Thank you so much for the offer thought."

They said goodbye and went their separate ways. B.J. thought back to the day they arrived on their land and the hard work it took to get their little cabin built. Edwina was pregnant and couldn't hold out to work like B.J. had too. B.J. made up her mind that she would talk to Earline and Ralph Brooks about getting those people some neighborly help.

B.J. and Wayne pulled in the yard of the Brooks and found all of them waiting to welcome them with open arms. The subject about the new neighbors came up instantly and like B.J., Earline's heart had gone out to them. Women notice things that men never seem to, because both B.J. and Earline felt sorry for Edwina being with child and all the hard work ahead of them.

"Wonder when that baby is due?" B.J. asked.

"In about a month, is what she told me." Earline answered.

"That doesn't give them much time to get a cabin up, does it?"

"I was just thinking about sending one of the boys around to all the neighbors and getting them a house warming going real soon. Like we did for ya'll. This is a slow time for everyone anyway and most folks will want to help I'm sure."

"Well be sure to include us when you decide what day you want to work. We'll sure be there. I know what it's like being on the receiving end and now I want to know what it's like to be on the giving end." B.J. said.

They went inside to enjoy a cup of coffee and a slice of cake. Afterwards, Wayne and Ralph walked out to the barn to look at the mare they breed with Dude.

"How is Wayne doing B.J.? I noticed he was slow getting down from the wagon."

"He still sore from those broken ribs and it still hurts him to sit a horse or to lift anything. I have to stay on him constantly; you know how impatient men get."

"B.J., I can really tell how much you've matured. You've become a young woman overnight." Earline told her.

"Well, Earline I've had too, I guess. With Dad and Mom gone, I've had to take everything life offered Grady and me seriously. Uncle Webster has been a God sent, I was responsible for Grady and myself before he came alone. Responsibility makes you grow up fast whether you want to or not."

"Well, old woman, come and help me with some supper before the men come back and skin us." Earline laughed.

B.J. and Wayne stayed and visited as long as daylight allowed, and then they said their goodbyes and left. They rode in silence for a way and then Wayne reached and pulled B.J. closer to him.

"B.J., I think we're definitely meant for each other and I don't know a single other person that I enjoy being with like I do you."

"You know just how to make a girl feel wonderful."

"Thank you ma'am. I'm here to please." Wayne pulled her even closer to him and put his arm around her shoulder. "I don't want my future wife getting cold."

That was the way they rode home—happy, close, and warm.

The weeks passed fast. All the neighbors chipped in and got the Donilsons barn raised and their house finished. The new neighbors were so appreciative and it was just in the nick of time. Edwina had her baby about two weeks later. She had a boy and they named him Austin. B.J. went over every chance she had to help out, but Laine was the most help. Laine took care of most of the work around the house while Phillip and Lloyd worked outside. Someone had given the Donilson's a cow and the milk came in handy for the children.

B.J. and Wayne talked several times about their wedding, but there was always something that got in their way. Now that Wayne had added his claim there was a total of twenty five hundred and eighty-five acres of land in the Rocking H Ranch.

Dude's stud service became known and the neighbors continued wanting to breed their mares to Dude. This brought in quite a lot of money for the ranch, so they began investing in some cattle as well. Chief Two Toes and his braves came back like they said and bartered for four of their horses. The beaver furs they exchanged and the ones Webster trapped during the winter months brought in enough money for material to build a windmill to bring water from the lake to the house and barn.

Webster and Wayne's next plan was to put a bathroom inside after they figured out how to do it. The place certainly was changing. He and Webster sat down and drew plans for three more rooms to be added, making it two stories now. These were to be B.J. and Wayne's quarters when they married. Uncle Webster got busy making the furniture for them and surprised everyone with a baby carriage for one of the rooms.

"Getting the buggy before the horse, haven't you?" Wayne asked Webster.

"Nope, just doing now what I'll have to do later. You two will have children, I hope."

"Well yea. But not before we're married."

"Then you best be thinking of marrying. Neither of you are getting any younger."

"Uncle, you speak for yourself. Just because B.J. celebrated a birthday, don't mean we're over the hill."

Both men laughed as they worked. Webster was happier than he'd ever been and Wayne was too. They had a ranch that everyone envied and they had worked hard to have it. The neighbors continued to move in all around the Rocking H. Casper was filling up with people. The year 1867 looked to be another good one. B.J. couldn't believe how fast everything seemed to be moving.

The addition to the house was finally finished and the windows were the last thing installed. Wayne suggested that B.J. go into town and select some wallpaper for the rooms and told her to keep in mind that one might end up being a nursery.

"We're not even married and you and Uncle Webster are already making plans for our children." B.J. said.

"Do you think we're rushing it a little, hon?" Wayne teased her.

B.J. shook her head, knowing once Uncle Webster and Wayne made up their minds to do something, they didn't slow until they finished.

Chapter 17

Wayne contributed quite a lot of money to the ranch with a blacksmith shop he'd opened. The neighbors found out and brought all their horses to be shod and harness that needed repair. There seemed a constant flow of people coming and going from the shop he and Webster had built behind their barn. Wayne also saw to the needs of the horses on the ranch too. There was money in blacksmithing, but there also was hard work. Some days when Wayne couldn't stop even to eat; B.J. would take his lunch out to him and make him take a break. Wayne tried to get Grady interested, but Grady said it wasn't for him. Grady didn't want to be tied down. He like to saddle his horse, with her colt trailing and ride over to spend time visiting with Lloyd.

B.J. and Wayne decided to take a day off and go on a picnic. The days were still cool in the mornings but as the day wore on, it warmed. B.J. packed a lunch, and she and Wayne saddled their horses and left the house. Naturally, Grady wanted to go, but Uncle Webster knew they needed some time alone, so he found something for Grady to help him with. The two rode out to the long meadow where the black stallion was first seen. The found them a good spot near the creek that ran into the lake and spread their blanket and enjoyed their meal. Wayne and B.J. settled back, and then they heard the thunder of running horses.

"Somebody must be rounding up their horses to sell." Wayne said.

"Well, not on our property. All the horses here belong to the Rocking H." B.J. replied as she set up to look for the oncoming horses.

As the sound nearer, they could see it wasn't just somebody; it was the black stallion back again. He had another brood of mares with him, bringing them to water.

"He is a beautiful sight running with those mares. I hope none of ours are in that group." B.J. said.

Dude began neighing and pulling on his reins to get loose and go after the black again. B.J. got up to calm Dude down.

Wayne walked as close as he dared to get a better look. Wayne was downwind or the black never would have allowed him anywhere near his mares.

"We should try out luck at rounding up those horses and trying to get a rope on that stallion." Wayne told B.J.

"You would never be able to rope that stallion; he is downright mean." B.J. told Wayne about the night he came to the ranch and how he started after her. "Uncle Webster had to fire a shot at him to turn him back."

"There's not a horse alive that can't be broken by someone. I bet Norman and I could rope the black and I bet Dale could ride him. What say, B.J., let's at least think about it."

At first B.J. shook her head, "Your crazy wanting to take on that black stallion. But those horses would sell for a pretty penny and some of the mares don't look bad at all."

After eating their picnic lunch they lay back on the blanket enjoying their beautiful day together. The sky was baby blue with white puffy clouds that seemed to go on forever. Wayne reached over and kissed B.J. and asked, "When are we going to set our wedding day?"

"I'm ready if you are." They agreed on the first Sunday in June. He kissed her again and she felt warm all the way to her toes, she knew it was right when a kiss felt this that. After several kisses and some caressing that both knew was leading to something that neither could control, they decided to pack up the remains of their lunch and head back home. Neither wanted the day to end, but both knew it must. Now that the wedding date was set, they forced themselves to think only towards that day.

When they reached the ranch they told Uncle Webster and Grady about seeing the black and his herd. Wayne explained to Webster what he had in mind about the horses.

"I think it's a great idea. Norman is back from his wedding and it would give him some extra money and Dale would be glad to help."

"What about me? I can break horses too," Grady added not wanting to be left out.

"I don't want anybody hurt in this little adventure. That stallion is going to be a hand full." B.J. reminded them.

Wayne and Webster assured her that everyone would be careful, but B.J. was still bothered by the whole thing.

The next morning Wayne rode to the Brooks', and told them their plans for rounding up the new herd and taking the black too. Norman and Dale jumped at an opportunity to earn extra money.

"I'd like to help also, but forego the wages for another stud service from Dude." Ralph Brooks said.

"Well alright, welcome aboard."

It was agreed they would meet the next morning in the meadow and they would try their hand at getting the black too. If they got a rope on the black, the mares would follow him without any trouble. Wayne left satisfied with the deal and headed home as fast as he could.

Everyone had something to do before they rode out the next morning. B.J. was going along too to help bring in the horses and to cook for the men. She made fresh bread and packed preserves that would be welcomed as a mid-morning snack. B.J. packed a coffee pot, cups, cream and sugar. She knew the men had to have their morning coffee before they could even think about working.

Deep inside B.J. was thrilled as the men. They had their saddles all ready with ropes tied to them and their chaps laid out to don at daybreak. Because of the excitement it was hard for them to sleep that night. They knew when morning came the fun would began.

Dawn arrived bringing crisp cool air, but soon the day warmed and turned out to be beautiful. Jackets were soon discarded and tied behind saddles. The Brooks' reached the meadow before the Rocking H group and had a fire going and a pot of coffee brewing. The aroma could be smelled long before they got within sight of the camp. Webster had a smile across his face; with coffee waiting on him he could tackle a bear.

They enjoyed a cup while standing around talking about how they would proceed. The plan was for Wayne and Norman to rope the black first, and if they succeeded they had it made with the other horses. The waiting was the hardest. Everyone's adrenaline was pumping and it seemed an eternity before the herd came to the lake to water. First came the rumbling sound of running horses through the still of the morning. When they heard the horses, everyone moved to the cover of the trees so they couldn't be seen.

Wayne and Norman sat their horses with their rope in hand ready for the first opportunity to go after the black. They watched the black lead his herd to the water and each one dropped his or her head to sip the cool water. The mares slowed breathing and began wading into the lake to cool, so the black relaxed some too. His ears were down and Wayne and Norman saw this was their chance, so they took off after the black. The black had his back to them at first, but he was always listening for anything that might endanger his brood, so hearing the two approach, he quickly turned and looked in Wayne and Norman's direction and then neighed and ran as fast as he could in the opposite direction. Wayne and Norman stayed with him, but never got close enough for either to get a rope on him. The rest stood and watched as the black stallion led the two men on a merry chase. He was one smart stallion.

B.J. had an idea, so she motioned for Norman to come and get Dude. Norman gladly jumped on Dude and got right back in the chase with Wayne. After a while Norman was gaining on the black. Everybody was cheering Norman on and sure enough he got close enough to throw his rope over the black's head and just let him run. Wayne caught up and threw his rope over the black's head and now with two ropes on him, they begin reining the black to a stop. They got the black to the nearest tree and Wayne's horse, being a roping horse, held the black while Norman ran around the tree several times and tied him off. The black stallion was caught.

All the other caught up just as the black was rearing and trying his best to break the rope. Norman exchanged horses with B.J. "I would never have caught him without Dude."

B.J. kept Dude at a distance because she knew how the two horses had fought the first time and she didn't want to aggravate the black any worse.

The big, black pawed the air, his ears flat against his head and his eyes rolled in a wild frenzy. He flared his nostrils and curled his upper lip and screamed toward the sky, and then settled on all fours, pawing the dirt underfoot. Finally the black settled, but even standing still every muscle in his black shiny body was twitching and jerking. Norman tried walking slowly up to him and got almost within reaching distance of his head, and the black started again. The black was scared, the rope he felt around his neck was something different for him, and he wasn't going to accept it.

Regardless to who tried, none of them could get close enough to slip a halter over the black's head. Even though the black was tied, he still would kick out at each one or rear up and try to paw—there was still a lot of fight left in him. Uncle Webster was last. He began softly talking to the black before he tried to walk up to him. The others grew silent as they listened and hoped Webster succeeded. Foot by foot, Webster got closer, talking each step of the way. The black' ears were up and pointed in Webster's direction—he was listening too. Webster got closer than anyone and the black hadn't reared or kick at him. Webster stopped and let the black get use to him being that close. He was still talking as he laid his hand on the black neck and then eased it to the top of his head. The black stiffened and Webster stopped, but continued to talk softly in the black's ear. With his other hand Webster eased a rope over the black's ears and fastened it under his head. Now the halter was on and another rope was fastened to it, so Webster loosened the ropes around the black's neck. The black was still tied to the tree, but the tension on his neck was less. Webster backed away and let the black stand where he had left him.

Everyone took a break to restore his or her energy. They had a cup of coffee and fresh bread with preserves. The took all the time they wanted, their work was finished and the black needed time to settle before the trip back to the ranch. B.J. worried about taking the black home. Webster had planned to ride up to the black and untie him and lead him back to the ranch. The black let Webster approach and untie him without as much as a nicker. So far so good, the black was trailing right along beside Webster like they were life-long friends.

B.J. left ahead purposely to get Dude in the barn and out of sight of the black. She slid the corral gate poles back so the mares could head right on in. They followed after the stallion and Webster. When they had the mares in the corral, Webster brought the stallion out and tied him to a tree outside the corral. As long as he could see his herd of mares, the black was okay. The herd was larger than the one that Dude had fought for. Since the black had a history of stealing other's horses, there was no telling how many were branded and belonged to another rancher. The culling began and some were set free. They checked for branded horses, but didn't find any.

"We've got to put up another corral; this one won't hold all of these for long." Webster suggested.

The post were already cut and stacked, so all the men began digging holes to bury the poles for the second corral. Soon the rails were up and it was finished. This corral was to be used also in breaking the black stallion.

B.J. had gone inside to cook; she knew the men would need a good lunch. As soon as lunch was ready she called, and they didn't hesitate. The food was on the table in front of them and it was eat in a hurry. B.J. kept the coffee and the hot bread coming and then brought on hot cobbler for desert.

"I don't think I can ride now, I'm too full." Norman volunteered as he rubbed his stomach.

"We'll let our food settle a little before we tackle that black. He's going to be a handful." Wayne answered as he pushed his chair back and headed for the front porch. The others told B.J. they enjoyed the lunch and followed Wayne out.

B.J. hurried and clean up the lunch dishes, she didn't want to miss any of the fun. By the time she got through, Webster had led the black stallion to the new corral. As soon as the black got to the gate, he began giving Webster trouble. The black had never been confined and he didn't want to go through the gate. Wayne had to throw another rope on the black before they got him inside. Once inside the two men kept a tight rope on the black so he couldn't rear up. The black tossed his head, neighed, and pawed the ground. His ears were back and he was getting madder by the minute.

"Norman, take it easy, now. Let that stallion get use to the blanket on his back first and then throw the saddle on him." Ralph warned. Ralph remembered the promise he made to his wife to take care of their boys. The black up close was a big powerful hunk of horseflesh. Ralph was nervous for Norman.

When the black stallion saw Norman coming at him with the blanket in his hands, he began sidestepping. Wayne and Webster had to watch carefully to keep the stallion from stepping on them.

"Norman lets try putting a sack over his eyes until you get him saddled." Wayne said as he turned to Grady.

Grady knew without being told to run inside the barn for an empty feed sack. He brought it back and handed it to Norman, and then stood out of the way. Norman relieved Webster on the rope and Webster was the one who softly talked to the stallion and got close enough to put the sack between the halter and his eyes. The black didn't know what was happening then, so he settled down.

Again, Norman took the blanket and gently lay in across the black's back. The black stood still, but every muscle in his body tightened and flexed. They waited, giving the black time to get the feel of the blanket, and then Norman laid the saddle on top of it. The extra weight scared the black and he again tried to pull loose and walk around to get it off him. They waited again—and time was in their favor—the black settled down.

Since the black couldn't see, Norman reached under him and got the cinch strap and looped it tightly. Norman backed off anticipating trouble and he wasn't disappointed. This was all new to the black—it angered and scared him—the tightness around his middle was evident. The black backed off as far as the ropes allowed and shook his head, he couldn't shake the covering over his eyes, so he settled down again.

Norman eased his foot into the stirrup; this let the black feel his weight. Every muscle in the black twitched and jerked, but Norman was as determined as the black, so he pulled himself over and settled into the saddle.

"Go easy, son." His dad warned from the sideline. "Be ready for which ever way he'll buck, hold on but not so tight you can't jump off if need be."

"Dad, I'll be fine. Let me do this on my own." Norman answered aggravated with anticipation.

The black snorted and stood still. This was another first for him, something on his back. "Let him go, I'm ready as I'll ever be." Norman told Webster. Webster lifted the ropes from the black's neck and took the sack from beneath his halter. The fun began for everyone but Norman.

Wayne and Webster got out of the corral as fast as their legs would carry them. By now, the black was giving Norman a bucking ride like he'd never had before. The black turned, twisted, bucked and kicked, and then hid all these together and that was when Norman hit the ground. Even after Norman was off, the black continued to buck. Wayne got to Norman and got him out of the black's way. They waited.

Thank God, Norman wasn't hurt. He took a little time before getting back on the second time. The black stopped bucking and stood perfectly still.

"Wayne, let's get him roped while he is still." Webster said as he twirled his rope over his head. Wayne threw his rope and the two pulled the black up closer to try again at breaking him. The black stallion was mad and getting madder. He turned to bite Webster, but Webster was fast enough that he withdrew his arm and hit the black in the head with his fist. "Try that again and I'll hit you harder," Webster told the black. The black didn't try again and the sack was put back in place.

Norman climbed on the second time and when the black was turned loose the bucking started all over again, except this time Norman managed to stay on him a little longer. Norman was wearing out faster that the black. Four times Norman climbed on and rode the black; four times the black bucked Norman off.

"An ordinary horse would be worn down by now." Norman apologized. "I don't think I can break him, but I've got three bronco-busting friends I bet could. Lets call it a day and I'll get in touch with them and between the four of us, we'll get the job done."

They left that day going home and when they looked back the black was running the fences in the new corral. Grady brought the black some feed and water. They hoped he didn't end up jumping the fence and leaving.

"I know Norman is good at breaking horses and he said his friends are professional, but I wonder if they can break that black stallion." B.J. questioned.

"That horse has always been a free spirit and he will fight to remain one, no matter who is trying to tame him." Webster added. "Right now the black is content eating and talking to his mares. Tomorrow, Norman will be sore, my fist and arms hurt now from pulling on those ropes."

"Do you think he will get out tonight?"

"I don't think he'll leave those mares and since they can't get out, he'll stay."

"I hope we aren't awaken in the middle of the night with half the corral torn down and all of them gone." B.J. said as they walked towards the house.

The day started early and had been full of non-stop excitement, and everyone was tired and somewhat discussed. Their plans hadn't been fulfilled. Now they had another corral full of horses, one big black stallion, but they didn't know what tomorrow would hold for them. They were too tired to eat so a snack for supper was all anyone wanted.

"We've got one thing in our favor—winter is over and there is plenty of grass and we won't have to feed them. Maybe the Pony Express will buy them from us." Grady said unexpectingly. Grady could always come up with something to brightened their hopes.

Two days later, morning brought quite a few men to the Rocking H Ranch. Some came to try their luck at breaking the black stallion—others simple to watch—others curious. Everyone for miles around had heard about the stallion that ran with all the mares, but none of them had seen him up close. This morning the black put on a show as they gathered around the corral and watched as he pranced. The stallion knew he had a captive audience and he went all out for them. He was rested and the morning was cool and he felt good parading around, tossing his head, raring up and even pawing the air. His way of saying to the cowboys, "Come on, I'm ready for whatever you have."

The men watched in awe for the longest. There was a statement like: "He's a big S.O.B." "I don't think he'll ever be broke." "You wanta bet?" "He's the prettiest hunk of horseflesh I've ever seen." "I can see now, why he's so good at stealing mares." The black responded as though he understood everything that was said about him. He was a sight to behold and any one of them would love to own him.

The work began. The first three men tried at least three times each to break the black, but it was useless. The next two men tried several times each and the black was still going strong. The men talked among themselves trying to figure out what it was going to take to wear him down. The stallion was still giving more than he was getting.

B.J. watch but didn't understand how one horse could have such endurance. None of their horses in Kentucky had ever been this spirited. She had seen enough, so she went to Webster and Wayne.

"What the black needs is for someone to gentle him first, and then try to saddle break him. I think this is just making him meaner. Let's give him his freedom I can't stand seeing him put through this any longer. Anyway, we know where to find him and he just might keep us in mares for the future."

Webster and Wayne listened to what she had to say, and then looked at each other and nodded in agreement. They went to the corral and took off the saddle and halter, opened the rails, and set him free.

The black stallion shot out of the corral like a bullet being fired from a gun. He went so far and skidded to a stop—pawed the air, curled back his upper lip—and neighed as loudly as he could. This was his way of telling them he had won. The mares neighed back to him and every one laughed. They wondered what it would have been like to say they owned that beautiful and smart animal. Only B.J., Webster, Grady and Wayne knew, but even their ownership just lasted for a short time. The Black stallion belonged to no one, he was born free and he would remain free.

Chapter 18

The ranch was growing and prospering so that Wayne hired extra men to help break horses, keep fences up and cut hay. B.J. did some hiring herself; she hired an oriental couple, Kim and Sue Lee. Kim was to help with the yard and Sue Lee in the house. Now that Wayne and B.J. had set their wedding day, everything at the ranch was focused around getting ready for the wedding. The wedding was scheduled for the first Sunday in June. Earline Brooks was making B.J.'s dress. B.J. had been at her house all morning for the fitting.

After telling Earline and Aubrey goodbye, B.J. climbed on Dude and started for the ranch. Darkness was upon her when she got to the ranch, but the men were still working with the horses. She took Dude into the barn and brushed him and fed him. As she came out Wayne met her at the door. "I need to talk to you for a minute." Wayne seemed serious and it sort of worried B.J., her first thought was that something had happened to one of the men, but she waited for him to tell her.

The two went inside, but Wayne still had not said anything.

"What do you need to talk to me about?"

"I hired three men full time to help out. One is a real good blacksmith and can help me stay caught up and the other two can help Uncle Webster with the horses."

B.J. smiled after a little while.

"You don't care?"

"No, I don't care. How much will all this cost us?"

"The men will earn forty a month plus fond."

"I do have one question; did you stop to think where all these extra people are going to stay?"

"The bunkhouse is finished."

"Good, because I hired a housekeeper and a yardman today myself."

"I know they came earlier and ask if it was okay with Webster and me, so we told them to start to work. Webster and I will build a little cottage for the Orientals."

"Well, it looks as though we worked out all the ranch's problems."

Wayne took a deep sigh and B.J. smiled. He bent down and kissed her cheek. When they stopped and looked around they saw the kitchen was spotless and there was the biggest meal prepared. All they had to do was wash up, sit down and eat. Wayne went to the door to call in the other men. Kim was gathering chairs to go around the big table. B.J lifted the lid on a big pot of chicken and dumplings. Sue Lee stood back with her head bowed, looking down at the floor. When B.J. replaced the lid, Sue Lee asked without raising her head, "Missy, no like?"

B.J. lifted her chin and gently raised Sue Lee's head so they were looking eye to eye. "Missy like very much."

"Verily good."

Sue Lee turned out to be a fantastic cook.

They all enjoyed a fine meal and afterwards the men went back to the porch to smoke. They sat talking horses till bedtime, and then Grady showed the new men where to bunk.

B.J. started to help Sue Lee clean up the kitchen, but she shook her head. "No, Missy, me clean, you sit."

B.J told her and Kim to sit and eat their supper while she talked to them. Sue Lee cleared the table of the dirty plates and got Kim and herself a plate. While they ate they told B.J. about their pass. They left St. Joseph, Missouri about the same time as B.J.'s family, except they got stuck in the town of Medicine Bow. They worked there in a laundry for very little wages. Kim saved enough money to buy a wagon and they came on to Casper. They were told in Casper to look up the Thompson's. B.J. realized she liked both of them instantly.

Even though most of the men had left going to the bunkhouse for the night, Webster and Wayne were still sitting on the front porch, feet propped up on the porch rail, enjoying the nice evening.

"Where are Kim and Sue Lee going to sleep tonight?" B.J asked as she opened the door.

"Well, Grady said he could sleep in the bunkhouse and they could use his room." Webster answered.

Wayne followed B.J. back into the kitchen to tell them the plan. Neither of them would have it; they gathered their belongings and went to the barn to sleep in their wagon. B.J. protested, telling them it was too cold, but their only answer was, "We no stay where Master and Missy stay. We sleep in wagon, not too cold."

Wayne and B.J. realized their customs could not be changed, so they let them go to the barn for the night, but B.J. made Wayne and Webster promise that tomorrow they would get the men to work on their cabin.

After Kim and Sue Lee left for the barn, Uncle Webster went to bed too. B.J. and Wayne sat down in front of the fire talking about how the day had gone for them both. She told him about her dress fitting with Earline and Aubrey and he told her about what had been accomplished with the horses. The total count on the horses was forty, and out of those five had to be gilded. The men had broken ten today and Wayne was to shoe them next. There had been no further sign of the black stallion.

"The black doesn't like us anymore. Every time he gets himself a brood of good mares, we end up taking them from him."

They both felt good about setting him free. He needed to be free and he wouldn't wait long about collecting another herd of mares.

"I missed you today while you were gone." Wayne said.

"I don't see how, you were so busy hiring extra people." He kissed her and she knew she had missed him too. They sat for a long time just holding hands and looking into the fire.

"B.J. I hope June gets here soon; you don't want to move the date up, do you?"

"I think it's time we went to bed; morning will be here early and we both have a lot to do."

Wayne kissed her again and this time she knew they needed to go their separate ways. If this continued, she might change that date after all, so she want to her room, brushed her hair, and got in bed. B.J. laid thinking about how good the Lord had been to them. The ranch had prospered faster than any around accept the Brook's place, and they were raising cattle. The horses had been good to them, too, so she thanked God for all of it.

Chapter 19

B.J. couldn't believe the day had finally arrived and everything was ready for their wedding. Kim and Sue Lee had everything inside and outside the house immaculate. Kim had been working in the yard, planting flowerbeds and different scrubs. The Japanese really had a way with landscaping. B.J. ordered white sheeting to cover the outside tables and there was enough left for Kim and Uncle Webster to make a canopy for the wedding party to stand under. Kim had taken ivy vines and flowers and decorated every corner and it was beautiful. Sue Lei had the inside of the house clean and decorated and she would not let Wayne anywhere near B.J. Sue Lei knew of the wedding tradition of the groom not seeing the bride on the day of the wedding and she took it very serious.

The first wagon to arrive was the Brooks family. Earline came into the house with her vegetable dish and wanted to know if there was anything she could help with. Sue Lei shook her head and told her to just enjoy herself. Earline went into the bedroom where B.J. was and they heard the second wagon pulling up. It was the Donilsons, the new neighbors. Edwina came in and offered her help but was told to enjoy. Sue Lei, Kim, and Uncle Webster had been up since sunrise cooking and fixing food. Kim and Webster had a whole young calf on a spit cooking outside. There was enough food for a small army.

Edwina came into the bedroom with little Austin in her arms. She sat him in the floor to help Earline get B.J. into her dress. Later, Laine and Aubrey came in to fix B.J.'s hair up in fancy curls. B.J. was glad for all the help because she was so nervous she couldn't do anything right. She wondered if Wayne was this nervous.

Each wagon that pulled in had a full load of people. The Preacher came on horseback from a near-by town. There was no church in Casper, so when a preacher's services were needed, someone had to send for him. Some of the young men who helped with the barn raising had brought their musical instruments and were tuning up to play. When the yard began to fill with people. B.J. knew it was time to stat. She stood on s small stool and the ladies straightened out her veil, the trail was pulled out in the back and after looking in the mirror, B.J. couldn't believe how beautiful she looked. The dress fit perfectly and with her hair up and in fancy curls, she looked older. She was as ready as she could be, so Edwina handed her the bouquet that Kim had made, and then they opened the door and called for Grady. He was to give her away. Uncle Webster was to stand up with Wayne as his best man.

Grady opened the door. He looked so handsome in his new suit. He stopped and stared. "Sis, is that really you?"

B.J. smiled.

"The Preacher, Wayne, and everyone are waiting for you, so let's get this show on the road."

B.J. took Grady's arm and the ladies straightened her veil and trail as they headed for the door. Just as the front door opened, the music started and everyone turned and looked in her direction. A quiet hush fell over the crowd and all eyes were on B.J. She felt so strange being the center of attention, but after seeing their smiles, she relaxed.

Grady and she walked slowly up to the canopy, and she looked at Wayne. He was so handsome in his new suit and so was Uncle Webster. The look on Wayne's face said everything. Their eyes met and she could feel his love and admiration. His blue eyes gave his approval and the smile was one of love and pride. They joined hands and took their places in front of the Preacher. Grady stood aside and so did Uncle Webster after he gave her a big smile and a little wink. This was his way of letting B.J. know he approved. The music stopped and the Preacher began. B.J. listened to each and every word he said and took it to heart.

"In sickness, in health, for richer or poorer, till death do you part," it was then that B.J. thoughts went to her Dad and Mom. They were together till death took them and that was what she wanted for Wayne and herself. The same sweet loving marriage that her parents had and she made up her mind at that very instant that she would work hard to have the perfect marriage.

"Will you take Wayne to be your lawfully wedded husband?

"I do." B.J. replied.

"Will you take B.J. to be your lawfully wedded bride?"

"I do." Wayne replied.

"What God has joined together, let no man put asunder. I now pronounce you man and wife."

Wayne lifted her veil and looked her in the eye and said, "I love you with all my heart." Then he kissed her long and meaningful.

Everyone shouted and clapped and the music started up again and both stood as everyone filed by hugging and shaking hands and congratulating them. The day was perfect and B.J. got so many hugs and kisses, but the best came from Uncle Webster. He wanted the first dance with her and while they were dancing he reminded her of the first night he ventured into their camp and how uncertain she was of him.

"We've come a long way since that night B.J., a very long way, but love stayed with us and now who would have ever thought I would end up being your sure enough real uncle."

"I didn't that night, but now, I wouldn't have it any other way. I couldn't love you any more, that's for sure."

Wayne cut in and took B.J. from Webster. He wanted to dance with his wife too. All the neighbors ate, drank and danced until Kim and Sue Lei came out of the house carrying a beautiful triple layered white cake. Uncle Webster held up his punch cup. "To the Bride and Groom, may they always be as happy as they are right now." Again shouts and laughter started and it was about then that B.J. realized some of the men had spiked the punch with something stronger.

"This day I will never forget." Wayne pulled B.J. close to him, "Are you about ready to go?"

"I've had about all the excitement I can stand; let me change my clothes and get everything together."

Wayne & B.J. had planned to stay three nights in Casper at the hotel for their honeymoon. They had not told any of the others of their plans, so she quietly slipped into the house and changed into a dress and got the bag she had packed. Wayne brought the wagon around and they started the first day of the rest of their lives together. As they rode out of the yard they turned and tossed B.J. bouquet, Lainne caught it, and Wayne told everyone to stay, enjoy themselves and thanked them for coming. Everyone waved goodbye till they were out of sight. They headed towards town laughing and talking about the wedding. Wayne and B.J. were so happy they didn't think about the distance to town, nothing was going to ruin their day.

The main street was practically deserted when they rode into town. The town of Casper folder up at dark, but Wayne pulled up in front if the hotel and carried their bags inside and rented a room. Their room was upstairs and when they got to the door he told B.J. to wait right there. Wayne put the bags in first and then he came back and lifted B.J. into his arms and carried her through the door into their room.

"For luck." Wayne said as he sits her down on the side of the bed. "You're the most beautiful bride I've ever seen." Wayne kissed B.J. ever so gently and he could tell she was not the least bit nervous. B.J. knew that Wayne's love was genuine because he was so gentle and patient with her. Wayne let her take all the time she needed and when she was ready he made love to her. He reached for her later in the darkness of the room and she submitted to his warm loving body. Their need for each other grew, and when the time was right, she knew what real love between a man and a woman was like, and she enjoyed it as much as he did. B.J. gave him her love again and again that night. They knew in their hearts that they were meant for each other and knew they wanted to spend the rest of their lives together. Then they slept—a blissful sleep—they didn't wake till the sun was coming in their window that next day.

It was the middle of the day and B.J. awoke starved. She turned over to face Wayne and found he was laying smiling at her.

"I often wondered what it would be like to wake up in the morning and look at your beautiful face."

"Well, now you know." She said as she smiled back.

He pulled her to him and hugged her close, they kissed, "I can't think of a better way to begin every day for the rest of my life than this, B.J. I do love you." He hugged her so tight that it almost squeezed the breath from her body.

"Wayne, do you know the day is almost half over and we are still in bed?"

He smiled that devilish smile of his. "I know and I don't care as long as you're here with me." They made love again and it was perfect.

"Why did we wait so long? If I had known it was going to be this wonderful, we wouldn't have waited to get married." B.J. whispered to him.

They finally got their day started, and went down for breakfast, which turned out to be lunch. Afterwards they went to the general store and purchased some dresses for B.J. to wear around the house. Now that she was a married woman she was going to dress the part. She bought a special gift for Kim and Sue Lei's baby, who was due in a few months. Wayne picked up several items for Uncle Webster and Grady. While they were shopping a quiet sweet voice came from behind the counter. "You sure were a beautiful bride yesterday, Mrs. Thompson."

B.J. turned and there stood Stephanie, the storeowner's daughter. They had been at the wedding and had brought two beautiful lamps as a gift. "Oh, Stephanie you are so kind, thanks. Someday, you will make someone a beautiful bride too."

"Stephanie what have I told you about bothering the customers?" Her dad asked.

"She isn't bothering me, she's complimenting me."

The storeowner agreed with Stephanie about the wedding.

"I noticed that Grady was paying you special attention yesterday." B.J. whispered to Stephanie.

Stephanie blushed. "I like Grady a lot but he didn't seem too interested in me."

"With boys, it's usually a little longer for them to find out just what they want. Don't get discouraged, his attention will soon turn to you."

Wayne paid for the purchases and they started down the street to their hotel. A young boy stopped them and handed Wayne a telegram. Wayne gave him a nickel and thanked him.

"It's for you, B.J."

"Well, open it. What's mine is yours now."

Wayne tore open the telegram and read it. "It's from the U. S. Postal Service. They definitely want to purchase the horses for the Pony Express. They want as many as we can sell."

"Uncle Webster and Grady will be happy about this." B.J. remarked.

"I'm happy about it too."

They talked about it when they went back to their room and decided the two new men, Chad and Luke, could go with Webster and Grady to deliver this shipment of horses. Wayne would stay at home, and he and Charlie would get the blacksmithing caught up.

"Anyway, I don't want to leave my bride this soon."

That night that had supper at a nice restaurant and retired early since they didn't get too much sleep the night before. Once they were in their bed with the lights out, the two of them became one again. Afterwards they slept soundly in each other's arms.

The next day was spent looking over cattle to improve their herd. When the horses were sold, there would be plenty of grazing for cattle. Wayne talked to the man about bringing out 100 head to the ranch. They rented a buggy, rode down to a lake and had a picnic lunch. They lay on a blanket and enjoyed their day, knowing this was their last day away from the ranch. That night, they dressed up and went to a theater to see a play performed by live actors. This trip to Casper was one that B.J. would never forget as long as she lived.

B.J. had a list of supplies that Kim and Sue Lei had given her, plus what Uncle Webster needed. They filled the lists and loaded the things into their wagon and headed toward the ranch the next morning. The trip had been wonderful, just too short, but they both knew they couldn't stay gone any longer. On the trip home B.J and Wayne talked about their good friends and neighbors. Each had brought them a wedding gift. Each family gave as God blessed them. There were lamps, quilts, dishes, cows, and even a pig. All of this had special meaning to them.

"This is a wonderful place to make a home and we have been blessed with special neighbors." Wayne agreed and reached over and kissed her.

"The town is really growing too."

The sound of Tuffy barking reached them before they could even see the house. The dog came running down the road to greet them. By the time they got to the house, everyone was waiting for them in the front yard. After greeting, and hugging, and handing out gifts, they started taking their bags into the house. Kim took the bags from Wayne and led the way. Sue Lei had moved Wayne and B.J. belongings to the upstairs room, and Grady had been moved into B.J. old bedroom. Everyone was settled into his or her new place, and they were glad to see the couple back home.

After settling down in front of the fire, Wayne told them about the telegram from the U. S. Postal Service for the purchase of the horses. Webster and Grady became ecstatic. Wayne suggested to Uncle Webster how the delivery was to be made and he agreed with him. As soon as all the horses were broke and ready to travel, they planned to leave for Fort Laramie, the place designated for delivery.

Grady was excited the most about the trip. He was happy that he wouldn't have to drive the chuck wagon this trip. Grady had worked hard and learned all the skills and now he was a full-fledged cowboy. The other men had taught him how to rope and he even tried his hand at breaking one of the horses. They tried to make it as easy for him as they could without letting him know. The new men had turned out to be a good bunch of workers and Wayne was proud that he had hired them.

Their first night at home seemed strange, but after Wayne pulled B.J. into his arms, everything changed. They made it a nightly ritual after making love to always tell each other how much they loved each other.

"Good night, Mrs. Thompson. I love you."

"Good night, Wayne. I love you too." 'Mrs. Thompson, I sure like the sound of that'. B.J. thanked God that night for sending her Wayne to love her and want to take care of her for the rest of her life. She wondered if Wayne talked to God like she did, he never openly said anything, and she had never asked him. Maybe the right time would come for her to approach the subject of faith with him. She added that to her prayers, hoping God would let her know the right time and way to bring up the subject. She knew God would.

Chapter 20

The wagon was packed with supplies and Sue Lei had cooked extra food for the men. When the time came to leave all were anxious to get on the road. They were taking thirty-five horses this time and it was going to be slower. Webster and Wayne agreed that since the horses were broke and shod, the going price should be higher.

The men begin slowly moving the herd of horses out of the holding pens and down the road. Wayne and B.J. stood watching till they were out of sight and then went in for another cup of coffee. They sat across the table looking at each other with a thousand thoughts going through their heads. B.J. was wondering about the safety of Grady and Webster, and Wayne was thinking about all the things that could happen on the trip that could cause them to loose the herd. Neither of them mentioned their thoughts.

"What do you have planned for today?" Wayne finally broke the silence.

"There isn't much for me to do now that Kim and Sue Lei are here."

"Fine! Then why don't we take the day and go visit the Donilsons? We haven't visited them since the housewarming and I feel it's time."

"Okay! I need to give Dude a good ride. I haven't ridden him in some time and this would be my chance."

Wayne left for the barn to saddle their horses and B.J. explained to Sue Lei that they would be gone most of the day, but would be home before dark. When Wayne came back with their horses, they stepped up on them and rode off.

The Donilson farm was closer than the Brooks ranch, so it didn't take them long to get there. By mid-morning the day had warmed and turned out to be beautiful. When they rode into the yard everyone was glad to see them. Wayne took the large piece of venison that he had brought them and gave it to Edwina. Her eyes lit up and B.J. and Wayne could tell that the family was in need of fresh meat. Edwina made some coffee and the four adults sat down to bring each other up on all the latest happenings. Phillip wanted to show Wayne the last field he had prepared for planting. This was his corn crop for grain. Phillip's plan was to grow grain and mill it for the ranchers for feed; he thought it would sell good. While Wayne was there he shod two of Phillip's horses. B.J. and Edwina fixed lunch. Lainne was taking care of baby Austin so her mother could get more done. The baby was sure growing and B.J. asked if she could play with him a little while. Austin was such a happy baby that it made B.J. wish for one like him.

After a nice lunch they sat and talked while Lainne cleaned up the table. B.J. thanked Lainne for letting her take Edwina away from chores to visit. She also invited Lainne over to visit with her; there wasn't too much difference in their ages. B.J. promised to teach Lainne to needlepoint if she would visit some times. When time came to leave, B.J. hugged Edwina, little Austin, and Lainne, she would have hugged Lloyd except, like Grady, he thought he was too old for hugging. After thanking the Donilson's for the nice lunch and got on their horses and headed towards home.

The days passed slowly while the men were gone, and for some reason B.J. had a feeling of uncertainty gnawing at her. She tried to put it out of her head but it hung over her like a dark cloud. For days she felt depressed and couldn't understand why. When she mentioned this to Wayne, he shrugged his shoulders and said maybe it was something she had eaten. Somehow B.J. managed to get through each day.

At night Charlie would go to the bunkhouse and Kim and Sue Lei would go to their cabin. Wayne and B.J. were left alone in the big house. B.J. found that she loved Wayne more with each passing day. He was so thoughtful, gentle and loving to her. Once they were upstairs, they were in their own private haven where Wayne would catch up on the books for the ranch and try his best to keep a hand on all the expenses. He never discussed this with anyone but B.J. and Webster. When Wayne finished his bookwork, he would turn all his attention to B.J. There was nothing he wouldn't do for her.

One evening when they were in their bedroom, B.J. got around to asking Wayne his feelings concerning God. "Yes, I believe in God and His Son Jesus Christ." Wayne answered.

"I would like for us to have a nightly devotion. We used to do this each night before Dad and Mom died. I've missed it so much."

"B.J. I don't know much about the Bible, but if that's what you want, then we'll do it, providing you do the reading."

So beginning then, each night before they went to bed, B.J. got out her Dad's Bible and selected a portion of scripture and read it. Wayne would sometimes ask her questions afterwards, trying to get a better understanding of exactly what the verses meant. They were learning together and growing closer to the Lord in the process.

One night after their devotional time, Wayne said, "What this town needs is a church."

"I agree, and we need to talk to our neighbors and get one built. The town is growing now and we need more than just a circuit rider visiting for funerals and weddings. We need a permanent pastor."

"Yes, the town is growing. It would be good to see all our friends and neighbors each Sunday."

B.J. loved Wayne more for thinking about a church for the community. She knew in her heart that he loved the Lord by the way he responded. She vowed to herself that when Uncle Webster and Grady came back they would tell them about their plans for a church and then they would see the building built. Afterwards the town would send the word out that a preacher was needed and wait for the Lord to send them one. B.J. had no way of knowing that night, but a church would be needed sooner than they wanted.

Chapter 21

Webster, Grady, and the other men had been trailing the horses for five days and so far there hadn't been any trouble. Grady enjoyed riding herd like all the other experienced men, and not having to drive the wagon this trip. Although he felt as old and experienced as all the others, Uncle Webster still kept his eye on him most of the time. There had been times that Grady ventured off further than he needed, and Webster blamed this on him being kept so close to home for so long. Webster left Grady alone; thinking the urge to see the new open spaces would eventually wear off.

One morning Webster awoke, thinking he was the first up, but discovered that Grady had saddled up and rode out of camp without telling anyone where he was going. Webster had him a cup of coffee, waiting for Grady's return, but Grady still hadn't rode back into camp. Concern settled deep in Webster's heart, until he finally asked. "Do either of you men now where or which way Grady went?" The men just shook their heads. This prompted Webster to saddle his horse for a search of Grady. "You men stay here, keep your eyes on the horses, and I'll find Grady and bring that boy back."

Webster stepped up and settled into his saddle and rode out, not knowing if he was going in the right direction or not. He found so many hoof prints that it made it impossible to know which ones to follow. Webster rode on, hoping that eventually He would catch up with Grady.

Webster was a good four or five miles from camp when he saw something shiny in the distance. He climbed a higher knoll to get a better look and saw then that it was a tin can reflecting in the sunlight. Webster hopes left him, but he still rode on, letting his eyes take in the horizon all around him. There was nothing unusual anywhere. "Where can that boy be?" Webster asked aloud. He sat his horse thinking that maybe he should go back to camp and get one of the other men to help him. "No, I've come this far, I hate to backtrack, and so I'm going on as long as there is light to see." Webster concern had now turned to fear. Fear for Grady, fear for his inexperience in this big unfamiliar country.

Over the next ridge was a strand of trees with a little creek running through them, so Webster went in that direction for two reasons. He needed to water his horse and just maybe he could pick up fresh tracks if Grady stopped there. Webster kicked his horse to a full gallop and headed for the trees. Once there he slowed, not wanting to disturb any tracks, got down and walked his horse to the stream. As his horse drank, Webster walked around looking at the ground for any sign that maybe Grady had been here.

There were wagon wheel prints in the soft dirt next to the water's edge. Webster looked closer and then he saw two different sets of hoof prints. Probably one pulled the wagon and one was someone else's. The wagon tracks were too narrow to be drawn by two horses, so Webster figured it was a buggy instead of a wagon. After filling his canteen, Webster mounted his horse and followed the buggy's trail. It was an easier trail to follow and Webster knew he had come about three miles when the terrain changed from open range to slight hills and hollows.

Webster began to notice his surroundings more than the buggy's tracks. He saw smoke curling up out of the trees. Webster turned his horse in the direction of the smoke, not knowing what he would encounter. He unbuckled his rifle strap and slid it from its scabbard. Holding his rifle across his saddle, Webster rode in real slow. Back in the deep shadows of the trees, almost hidden to the naked eye, was a cabin, and Grady's horse was tied outside. He rode on a little further and stepped down real easy, looking around for anyone who might be outside, guarding the cabin. There was no one, so he eased himself to the door and laid his ear against it hoping to here how many were inside. The only sound he heard was the soft crying of a woman.

Webster stood back and took his foot and kicked the cabin door as hard as he could. It was unlocked and now stood opened. Holding his rifle in a firing position he slid through the open door into the dark. Once inside, Webster saw the only light was the glow from an open fireplace. His eyes adjusted to the darkness enough that he could see there wasn't much in the room except a bed, table, and a couple of chairs. He saw the floor was bare dirt and his nostrils filled with the musty smell of the wet dirt.

The sobs stopped as soon as Webster entered the room, and as his eyes adjusted, he saw a young girl sitting on the dirt floor by the side of the bed, the bed where Grady laid. Webster lowered his rifle and laid it on the table, and then went to the bed to check on Grady. The girl hurriedly slid to the corner of the cabin, where she cowed down with her head on her drawn-up knees. She never raised her head the whole time Webster stood looking down at Grady. Webster's breath caught in his chest and it seemed his lungs would explode; he fought back the tears that filled his eyes. Webster dropped to his knees and felt for Grady's pulse—there was no pulse. Grady's body was still warm, meaning he hadn't been dead long, but his face was a mass of blood and swollen bruises, and his clothes had been torn likely from a fight. Webster continued to feel his arms and legs and Grady felt more like a rag doll than a human, possible every bone in his body was broken. Webster knew Grady must have suffered terrible before death came to him.

"Why? Who did this to him?" Webster shouted as he turned to the girl. His anger getting the best of him, he reached down and grabbed the girl to a standing position. She kept her eyes lowered and let Webster snatch her off the floor. When Webster looked at her real good, he could tell she was only a kid—dirty, ragged, and thin as a rail, with hair that had not seen soap or water in some time and never a comb. Her dress was much too big for her and kept sliding off one of her shoulders, exposing the fact that she wore no undergarments.

"Who did this to him?" Webster demanded as he pointed toward Grady.

"My Uncle John!"

"John who?" Webster asked as he shook her by her shoulders.

"Uncle John Flannery. He caught him talking to me at the creek. I went there to bathe, but I never got in the water when the boy rode up. Uncle John is a mad man. He accused me of everything bad and he wouldn't listen when I tried to tell him nothing happened. The boy tried explaining, but he kept hitting him and hitting him, until he passed out. Even with him on the ground, Uncle John kept kicking him with his boots, over and over again. He wanted to leave him there to die, but after he rode off to get drunk, I loaded the boy in my buggy and brought him here, hoping to make him well enough so he could take his horse and leave. But he only lived to say a few words just before you came in." She was sobbing again.

"What words did he say?"

"Tell Uncle Webster and B.J. I'm sorry and I love them." She sobbed to Webster.

Webster turned his head so she would not see his tears. He swallowed hard and went back to the bed where Grady lay. He took Grady's limp broken body in his arms and held him as close as he could. Webster held Grady for the longest, wishing he could squeeze life back into him again. The girl moved to put wood on the fire and that was when the horses snorted, and Webster knew someone was coming to the cabin. He eased Grady back down on the bed and stood listening. Webster moved to the table to get his rifle and motioned for the girl to get behind him and to be quiet. The sound of a horse walking came closer. Whoever it was had not seen Webster's horse and didn't know he was inside the cabin.

"If you utter one sound, I'll kill you." He whispered to the girl. She shook her head and Webster pushed her on back into the corner where she had been before. The cabin was dark with the door closed, except for the light from the fire. Webster's eyes had grown accustomed to the dimmed light and he could see fine. The approaching horse stopped, and Webster heard a loud clump hit the dirt. Whoever it was had fell from his horse, and it was then that Webster realized that the drunken fool John Flannery had returned. He returned so drunk that he couldn't get off his horse, so he just fell off.

Webster stood with rifle in hand poised for whatever was to happen between them. About that time the man banged his whole body against the cabin door and shouted.

"Ellie, where are you girl? Can't you see I need your help?" Shortly after the shout, the cabin door eased open and he staggered inside. As soon as his eyes adjusted he saw Webster, grabbed his pistol from its holster, pulled the hammer back, but before he could get the trigger pulled, Webster fired his rifle right into the man's middle section. The rifle blast sent John Flannery back out the door just as he had come in. The gun smoke was stifling in the small cabin. Webster cocked his rifle again and followed Flannery outside to see if he was still alive. Never in his life had he killed another human, but for some reason he felt no remorse from this killing. A man who would beat a young boy to death, for no reason, didn't deserve to live, but Webster prayed silently that God would forgive him for what he had done. He walked over and checked Flannery's pulse—he was dead. He went back inside the cabin.

"Do you have two blankets?"

The girl just stood against the wall, scared from the shooting.

"I'm not going to kill you. I want to wrap your Uncle's body in it and take him to town to the sheriff. I also need one for Grady's body."

The girl called Ellie went to the other wall and took down two blankets from a shelf. She helped Webster wrap Grady's body and tie him on his horse. The wrapped her Uncle Flannery and put him in the buggy. Webster got his horse and told her to drive the buggy and lead the way to town.

Town was four half-built buildings. The storefronts were wood, but the back of the buildings was canvas. There were maybe eighteen or twenty people who lived in this so-called town. It had once been a gold boomtown and the gold had petered out and most had moved on with the exceptions of the few remaining. There was no sheriff and no one objected to Webster killing John Flannery because most knew him for the mean vicious person he was. Flannery was always drunk, never caring about anything or anyone including his niece, Ellie. She stayed in town and Webster left the burying of her Uncle to the townspeople; he had other important business to attend too. Business he dreaded more than anything he had ever done in his whole life.

Mounting, and leading Grady's horse with him tied to the saddle, Webster rode as hard as he could back towards their camp. His men would be worried, and Webster knew it would be nightfall before he could get Grady's body back into camp. When Webster rode in after dark he called. "Hello the camp."

"Ride in Webster; we've been worried sick about you and Grady." But then the men saw Grady wrapped in a blanket and tied to his saddle and they knew he was dead. First they helped Webster take Grady's body down and lay it in the wagon, and then they handed Webster a cup of hot coffee and told him to sit by the fire and rest while he told them what happened. Both men listened, hurting just like Webster at the loss of such a young boy, in his prime of life and one who didn't deserve to die such a brutal death. Grady was a good friend to all the men.

"Webster, you were justified and right in killing that man."

They left Webster setting by the fire, deep in thought. They knew at a time like this their words were not consoling him. Webster was a fine man and he had seen two people die this day and he dearly loved.

The next morning, Webster and the men rode on to fort Laramie, and sealed the deal on the horses for the Pony Express. Webster explained why they had to hurry to get home and the Captain expressed his condolences and gave Webster the price he asked for the horses. When the business with the horses was finished, Webster drove the wagon over to the funeral parlor and got the undertaker to fix Grady's body in a nice coffin. The coffin was put in the back of the wagon and started the long, dreaded trip home. His heart grew heavier and heavier with each mile that brought them closer to the ranch. Ordinarily Webster would be glad to be going home, but this trip made him feel differently. How was he going to explain to B.J. that he had let Grady get killed? Would she ever be able to forgive him? Could he ever forgive himself?

It took six days to reach the ranch and Webster had been awfully quiet since they started home. Now, they were close enough to hear Grady's dog barking and then they saw the dog coming down the road to meet them. The men noticed how the dog looked for Grady and then went to the back of the wagon and jumped in and sat down by the coffin. The dog stayed there, whining and scratching on the wooden box. No one scolded him because they knew he was mourning Grady.

As hard as it had been bringing Grady's body home, the men and Webster knew they just could not bury him out on the plains and leave him there. So the trip home was hard on all of them. As the house came into sight, they saw B.J., Wayne, and Charlie standing, looking down the road in their direction. Webster was out front of the wagon and they were going slow.

B.J.'s expression changed the minute she counted riders and then she saw Grady's empty horse tied to the back of the wagon. Wayne had seen it too and he moved closer to her and put his arms around her as if to steady her for whatever the news might be.

Webster stepped down from his horse, took off his hat and held it in his hand as he approached B.J. and Wayne. His head was bowed, and when he came face to face with them and looked up, there were tears streaming down his cheeks. Webster took his handkerchief from his back pocket and wiped his tears and then blew his nose. Now he was ready to face B.J. with the bad news.

"What happened, Uncle Webster?"

"Honey, I hate more than anything to be the bearer of this news. Grady is dead. I'm so sorry I had to be the one to bring him home to you in that pine box. I couldn't leave him out yonder by himself. Please forgive me, B.J. If I could, I would have taken his place gladly, but God, nor time, didn't allow it to be that way."

Before Webster finished, B.J. broke down and was crying her eyes out. Wayne kept a tight hold on her and she leaned against Wayne for support. After a few minutes, she wiped her eyes and looked up at Webster. "I don't hold you responsible. I love and appreciate you bringing him home to me. I know you are hurting as badly as I am right now and have been all the way home. But Grady wouldn't want us to be sad. He was always the one to make us laugh. I love you Uncle Webster and he did too." B.J. went to Webster and he hugged her to him and they walked on to the house to grieve together.

Wayne took charge after they left. "Take the body on to the house and unload him, and then get the supplies unloaded and take care of the horses. I know you men have had a rough trip and I appreciate you standing by Webster and Grady through all this. Later I would like to talk to you about what happened, but now I've got to see to B.J. and Uncle Webster."

"Yes sir, we'll take care of everything we can for you. When you folks decide on where Grady is to be buried, we'll be happy to dig his grave for you."

Wayne nodded his thanks to them and started to the house. His heart was heavy for B.J. and especially for Webster. Something went bad wrong and he needed to find out what. Wayne entered the house and found Webster and B.J. sitting at the kitchen table over cups of hot coffee. He started for a cup, but Sue Lei beat him to it. He pulled out his chair and listened as Webster was explaining what happened to Grady.

Webster told them everything that happened, just as it happened. "Grady was dead when I got there. Ellie, the girl said his last words were to you and me. He said 'tell B.J. and Uncle Webster I love them and I'm sorry.' While I was there, John Flannery staggered into the cabin. He was so drunk he could hardly stand on his feet. When he saw me, he pulled down on me with his pistol, but I had my rifle ready and I got off a shot before he even cocked his hammer."

Webster gave B.J. and Wayne a minute to absorb what he had said and then finished. "I brought Grady back to camp afterwards and then we took the horses on to Fort Laramie."

As B.J. listen to each word Webster used to describe how badly Grady was beaten; she gripped Wayne's hand that she was now holding onto. When Webster told about shooting the man who killed her baby brother, she dropped her head, knowing in heart that killing wouldn't bring Grady back, but she understood Uncle Webster had no choice. It was either he or Uncle Webster and she couldn't bear loosing anyone else.

Wayne had listened, and after hearing the sad story he had mixed feelings. His heart went out to Grady and how he much he had suffered. He ached for Webster, not getting there in time to help, and his heart broke for B.J., losing her only living kin. "B.J., would you like me to send word to the Brooks family and the Donilsons? When do you want to hold a proper burial for Grady?"

"Yes, we need to make arrangement soon. Have one of the men to ride to the Brooks ranch and tell them. Let's plan on tomorrow, we'll have enough time to contact the Preacher and get the grave dug. I've got to lie down for a few minutes; can you handle things for me?"

"Of course. Sue Lei will help you to your room and you take all the time you need. Uncle Webster, you go and lie down too. I know you probably haven't slept in days. I'll take care of the rest of things." Wayne reached over and hugged B.J. long and hard and kissed her as she turned to leave. Then he walked over to Uncle Webster and hugged him long and hard, patting him on the back as he did. "I love you man. You're the salt of the earth to me, now go and get you a good hot bath and rest. I don't want you to go thinking it was your fault now, cause it wasn't. The Lord's in control of our entire destiny, and I guess he just needed Grady more than we needed him here. I'm glad you're okay."

Wayne went out to send one of the men to tell their neighbors and another to fetch the Preacher. He saddled his horse and rode out to look for a proper burying place for Grady. I may as well find a place where we all can be laid to rest, Wayne though as he rode out. He came to a little knoll west of the house and rode up and looked around. There was one big cottonwood tree right on top and the land gradually sloped downward to the meadow leading to the house. "This is our family burial grounds; this is where we will bury Grady." Wayne rode back to get the men to dig Grady's grave and to tell B.J.

The next two days were different from their usual workdays. The ranch shut down in respect to B.J., Wayne, and Webster. The neighbors came as soon as they heard; bringing food and offering help if needed. Mrs. Earline and Edwina stayed upstairs with B.J., consoling her as much as possible. B.J. had kept to herself mostly and had been so quiet, so when the women came, Wayne suggested they go and keep her company.

Sue Lei helped B.J dress the next day and fixed her hair. B.J. then came down to meet all the friend and neighbors who had come for Grady's funeral. She greeted each one and thanked then for coming.

When the time came the Preacher came to her and asked if she was ready. B.J. only nodded to him. All the family, friends and neighbors would walk behind the black clad casket that lay in the back of the wagon.

The man driving took off his hat and laid it on the seat next to him. The preacher nodded to him to start the horses and everyone fell in after B.J., Wayne, and Webster. They followed the wagon carrying Grady to the little knoll. It was a beautiful day, but a sad one. The ranch hands unloaded Grady's coffin and placed it over the grave. Everyone gathered as close as they could while the Preacher read John 14:1-4. "Let not your hearts be troubled; ye believe in God, believe also in me. I go to prepare a place for you, I will come again, and receive you unto myself, that where I am, there ye may be also. And where I go ye know, and the way ye know." (KJV) The Preacher said many nice things about Grady, how he and B.J. buried their parents and came there to make a life for themselves. He also said that it was terrible that Grady, being so young, had been cut down in his prime, but that the Lord had him now and Grady was enjoying being with his parents.

This made B.J. smile; she knew he was being loved and taken care of. Webster put his arms around her and hugged her close to him. When they finished, the friends that had attended sang a hymn, Precious Memories. Wayne, B.J., and Webster walked back to the house and left the men to cover the grave. Stephanie put a bouquet of wild flowers on it afterwards.

Chapter 22

Three years since Grady's death and B.J. and Wayne's marriage just seemed to grow happier. Everything worked out so well for them. Dude's colts were showing up everywhere. Lady's colt was a stallion, and he looked more Morgan bred than Kentucky thoroughbreds. Everyone who saw the little stallion was impressed and this brought more stud service from other ranchers. It seemed that all wanted part of the Morgan bloodline now. The little stallion, named Stormy, who had been Grady's horse, had developed into a fine horse and before long he could be used for stud service too. The mares on the ranch were dropping foals each week and as soon as they were old enough, the men began working them.

The investment in cattle had paid off for them also. Now the ranch had as many head of cattle as it did horses. Wayne called it protecting them; they knew the time would soon come when the Pony Express was replaced by the railroad and the supply and demand for horses would cease. With cattle now to fall back on, the Rocking H could always sell them to the market to cover expenses. The ranch was also producing its own feed, planting some of their acreage in corn and grain, cutting their own hay. It had become a big business now and B.J. left most of the running of it to the men folks.

B.J. settled into fixing up the inside of the house, now that the money was available. She brought better furniture and curtains and she and Sue Lei busied themselves with work. One night B.J. and Wayne were just finishing their Bible study reading and she turned out the lamp and as usual Wayne reached over to kiss her goodnight. Wayne let his arm come to rest on her stomach.

"Do you know what you are feeling?"

"The one I love."

"Feel again, there is more than one there."

Wayne set straight up in bed and looked at B.J. "Did I understand you right?"

"Yes. I'm almost sure I'm pregnant. My time has passed two months. I didn't want to say anything until I visited the doctor."

Wayne laid his head on her stomach and tried to listen for the baby.

"Oh, it's too soon for that yet. In a couple more months you'll be able to."

"B.J., you've made me the happiest person in the world. I'm going to wake up Uncle Webster and tell him."

"Why don't we wait till breakfast and we'll tell him together?"

Wayne kissed her again and held her real tight for a long time.

The next morning they told Uncle Webster the good news. Sue Lei and Kim had a little girl, but Wayne and B.J. wanted a boy, but they eventually said they would take anything the Good Lord saw fit to bless them with. Uncle Webster began immediately telling B.J. things she shouldn't do. She listened and decided she would go on just like always until the doctor told her differently. She was young and healthy and there was no reason to expect trouble during this pregnancy. Now, Sue Lei and she had another bedroom to fix into a nursery. B.J. would enjoy this.

B.J.'s next visit to town, she stopped in and saw the doctor. He confirmed everything. She was now definitely going to have a baby. She felt fine until about the third month and it was then that she began experiencing some morning sickness. Sue Lei had just the remedy for this and soon B.J. appetite was back to normal. Everyone teased B.J. about how much she eats.

Sue Lei came to her defense by saying, "Missy eats for two now, she needs all the nourishment she can get."

Wayne was the only one that never said anything about her being hungry. "You get more beautiful with each day. I just wish you wouldn't ride Dude. I'm afraid you will hurt yourself."

B.J. assured Wayne she would stop riding when she got further along in her pregnancy. This satisfied him, so B.J. continued to ride every chance she could, knowing once the baby came her hands would be full and she wouldn't have the time to ride. After all Dude and she had come a long way together and they shared closeness. B.J. enjoyed her rides almost as much as her time alone with Wayne. She tried to ride him at least three times a week. The men would saddle dude for B.J. and she would ride out to the meadow where the black brought them mares. The black seemed a part of this ranch. When they turned him loose that day, it was the best investment they had ever made. B.J. regretted letting him go; he still wanted his freedom.

Each time the black stallion gathered a brood of mares he would bring them to the meadow and they would graze in the tall grass. B.J. and the others watched with each visit at how his herd grew. The men would then roundup the horses and brand them with the Rocking H brand, break them, shoe them, and sell them. The word leaked out about how the Rocking H got its start in the horse business and soon there were some who would gladly buy the mares from them. Everyone knew of the famous Black Stallion and what a good bloodline he came from, so they knew they were getting good horses, even if the Rocking H brand was on them.

The last time B.J. had ridden to the meadow, she mentioned to Wayne about how big the Black's herd had grown.

"I'll ride out with you next time and have a look. I don't want you getting too close to that black. I still don't trust that horse."

B.J. wondered if it was because they never succeeded in breaking the Black, but she didn't say anything.

B.J. continued to keep track of the Black and his herd, and she would ride to Grady's grave and put wild flowers on it. She stood over the grave and looked down on the valley and ranch below. The days were warm and beautiful. B.J. thought how fast time was moving in her life now. She wondered if her Dad and Mom and Grady would be proud of the way everything had turned out.

The months passed quickly and before B.J. knew it she could feel the baby moving inside her. The first time she let Wayne feel, it thrilled him and she could see the happiness in his eyes. The nursery was all fixed and ready for the baby's arrival and she had even made up a lot of baby clothes and blankets. It was time now to stop her riding. Everywhere she went was in a wagon with Wayne.

B.J. had gained a lot of weight and everybody who saw her said she was going to have a big, healthy baby. Uncle Webster had hand-carved a baby chest for the clothes, a cradle, and a baby bed.

Anxiously waiting the time for the baby's arrival, B.J. never once thought anything could go wrong, but something did. One day a rider came to the house and said that she was badly needed by Mr. Brooks. The message said that Mrs. Earline was sick and none of the men knew what to do for her. That particular day, all the men were gone from the Rocking H doing something.

"B.J. told the man to go into town for the doctor and she would leave immediately to do what she could for Mrs. Earline."

The man left the ranch riding hard for town and B.J. called for Kim to hitch up the horses to the wagon. She bundles up as warm as she could because the weather had turned cool and was threatening rain. B.J. was ready to head for the Brooks ranch, but Kim and Sue lei begged her not to risk going along.

"Missy, please let Kim drive you. I scare you going by yourself."

"I'll be fine Sue Lei. Kim, go find Wayne and send him over as soon as you can."

"Then let Sue Lei go with you, please."

"Sue Lei, I've wasted enough time, you got your own baby to worry about. I'll be fine."

B.J. climbed into the wagon and wrapped a warm blanket over her legs. She had a hat and coat on and felt that she would be fine. The temperature had dropped since morning and the sky; she noticed had darkened with clouds. It looked as though the first snow was on the way. B.J. silently prayed that she would get to the Brooks ranch before the weather got worse. She snapped the reins and the horses went faster. The wagon was harder to handle than she realized, so she tried to slow the horses because she feared they were going too fast. But instead of slowing, the horses got faster. Now they were running all out. B.J. thought she could control them, but ended up letting them run as fast as they could. Everything would have been fine except for a bolt of lightening. When it struck, it lit up the sky alone with a loud clap of thunder that scared the already out of control horses. B.J. pulled on the reins, sawing their mouths as hard as she tried she couldn't control the horses. The two horses fought her and got even faster.

Then it happened, the wagon got over to the side of the road and hit a big rock. When it did, the front wheels turned enough to head the wagon completely off the road and into the edge of the woods. B.J. knew she was in trouble and she pulled even harder trying to stop the team. She stood thinking she could find more strength in her arms, but had to sit back down to avoid being hit by low-hanging limbs. Pulling on the reins with all her strength; she had to stop the team. But her problem was she was too far along in her pregnancy to use the foot brake, so the team carried the wagon deeper and deeper into the woods.

B.J. kept hoping the horses would get tired and slow themselves down, but the lightening had them really spooked. Up ahead was a dead log on the ground. B.J. saw it and knew the horse would jump it, but she also knew the wagon could not. The wagon hit the log too large for it to cross and then it happened. B.J. felt the wagon turning over, but she couldn't jump. Her feet were all tangled in the blanket that had been wrapped around her legs. B.J. knew she was destined to go over with the wagon. She turned the reins loose when the wagon started over. The horses managed to pull free of the wagon, but B.J. hit the ground and hit it hard. She was having difficulty breathing, her chest hurt so bad and she felt herself drifting into a void of black nothing.

How long she lay there, she had no way of knowing. But when she gained consciousness, the pain she felt in her chest and stomach was almost more than she could bear. B. J. realized her stomach had hit the ground first. "My baby! Lord please don't let anything happen to my baby." A pain so gripping hit her again and she grabbed her stomach with both hands. The pains wouldn't stop, getting worse each time, until B.J. passed out completely.

Two days later B.J. came too. When she opened her eyes she discovered she was in her clean warm bed. Wayne was sitting beside her.

The look on his face showed concern. B.J. felt her stomach, it was flat, and her baby was not there. She sat straight up in bed and asked. "Our baby, is it okay?"

"B.J. lay back; you've had a bad lick to your head, a possible concussion."

She hurt all over, but it was her heart that ached the most. B.J. knew the baby was dead. Wayne would have told her if it hadn't been, instead he chose not to answer. She lay back on her pillow and screamed. Wayne tried to comfort her; he held her and rocked her in his arms, even crying with her for the loss of their baby. Nothing Wayne said or did helped to ease the hurt she felt at that very moment.

"I killed our child! Why wasn't it me instead?"

Wayne couldn't answer her. There were no answers in him right then. He sat down in his chair and let B.J. cry. Over and over she screamed, blaming herself for the baby's death, until finally she was exhausted and only then did sleep come.

How long B.J. slept she didn't know or care. The dark stillness that enveloped her was her choice. She didn't want to wake knowing what faced her. B.J. stayed in the soft darkness until she heard a distant voice calling to her. It was Uncle Webster calling her, but why?

"B.J., do you hear me? B.J., please answer me."

"Leave me alone, let me be!"

"B.J." Webster called again and this time she was forced to open her eyes. She blinked trying to focus on his face. Uncle Webster was sitting next to her on the bed and when he saw she responded, he smiled.

B.J. turned from him; the guilt wouldn't let her look him in the face. Webster moved to the other side of the bed and tried to talk to her. She refused to be comforted by him and started crying again. A voice inside her kept saying she should be punished, not comforted. Webster realized he was making matters worse, so he turned and left the room. B.J. closed her eyes again and drifted back into her void, away from reality.

B.J.'s withdrawal lasted seven days; she came and went, slept and cried. She was making herself sick blaming herself for the death of their baby. It was when the Preacher came that the situation changed. He made B.J. listen to what he had to say. "B.J., the Lord gives and the Lord takes. He gave you and Wayne a son, but then had a greater need for him, so He called him home to Heaven. That's where he will wait for you and Wayne. You are young and healthy and able to have more children, so you should thank God for sparing your life so you can still have a family. Don't be selfish, just lying there thinking of your own grief. Wayne has lost a son too, and he is grieving just as much as you. You could be a comfort to each other now if you would just let the Lord lead ya'll through this tragedy."

The Preacher and she prayed for a long time. He asked God to give B.J. peace of mind about loosing her baby boy and to help her and Wayne to be closer and that their marriage grows stronger. B.J. thanked him for coming and she promised the Preacher that she would work at getting her strength back. When he left, Wayne came in and reached down and kissed her.

"I love you so much, B.J. I'm so thankful you were not hurt or killed in that accident. I don't know how I could survive without you." They held each other for the longest.

B.J. knew in her heart they would have other children. The Lord would give them another one when He was ready for them to have one. "Wayne, I'm sorry for carrying on so and not thinking of you and your grief."

"Hush! We have each other and that's what counts."

"We will always have each other."

The door eased opened and the rest of the family asked if they could come in. Uncle Webster was the first to reach down and kiss her and then Kim and Sue Lei were right behind him. All of them had been worried sick about B.J.

"Can I get out of bed?" B.J. asked.

"The doctor says another week of bed rest."

"Can I have something to eat?"

Everyone smiled at her last request and Sue Lei left to prepare B.J. a tray of food. Everyone left except Wayne and he reached over and took her hand and just held it.

Several days later, Wayne broke the bad news to B.J. about Mrs. Earline. She had died from pneumonia two days after B.J's accident. The Brooks were grieving just as they were. B.J. had another onslaught of guilt to fight. She remembered she was on her way when she had the accident.

Maybe she could have made some difference, but only God knew for sure.

"How is the family?"

"They miss her. They worried about you as well."

"Wayne, take Sue Lei over to cook for them and to do their laundry and clean house, till I'm able to go myself. Assure them that I'm fine, and that I'm so sorry about their lost. Tell them the Lord has two new angels in Heaven with Him now, our son and Mrs. Earline."

Chapter 23

The next weeks passed slowly for B.J., she felt herself gaining strength each day, but her heart more than her body did. The day came when she could get out of bed. Her legs felt like rubber and without Wayne's help she never would have made it. He put his big, strong arms around her now tiny waist and half carried her down the stairs. B.J. sat down in her favorite rocker by the fire. She was exhausted. Sue Lei covered her legs with a light blanket. Sue Lei was like a mothering hen when it came to caring for her.

Little Amme, Sue's daughter came to B.J. and wanted to climb into her lap, but Sue told her no. B.J. reached down and helped the child climb up and then she held Amme for the longest, hugging her and wondering how it would have felt to be hugging her own son. Sue Lei sensed what was happening, because she took the child from B.J. and made her go into the kitchen to play.

"Missy needs rest. Amme wear Missy out climbing all over Missy."

With each passing week, B.J. grew stronger and tried to go on as though nothing had happened. Each time she passed the nursery she couldn't help but look inside. B.J would stand and look into the empty room trying to visualize how it would have been if their son had lived. The doctor told her it would take time for the nurturing part of her body to heal and he was definitely right. Her breast had milk that needed to be extracted, but no baby to do it. They hurt her, making her heart ache too for their lost son.

Finally after weeks, the milk dried up, and this helped, but the empty feeling inside took much longer. B.J. knew she needed to be busy doing something, or the feeling would never leave.

"Wayne, will you help me to walk the barn so I can see Dude and all the new foals."

"Sure, but it's cool out today, so bundle up."

B.J. made her first venture out of the house and it did seem to clear her head. Dude was sure glad to see her. After staying awhile, looking at the new foals, B.J. realized how tired she was and Wayne helped her back to the house.

The days became weeks, then months, and before she knew it, the year was almost gone. B.J. had stayed inside more than usual because she just couldn't seem to get her strength back. She had lost a lot of weight and her resistance was low. She was content just sitting in front of the fire doing needlepoint. B.J. also worked on several quilts through the winter months to help pass her time. She took Grady's clothes and cut them into quilt pattern pieces and sewed them into beautiful quilt tops. This was something to help her remember Grady by and also enjoy the warmth they provided.

All the men were busy with the new foals and the cattle, keeping the stock well fed through the winter months. Nights were the best for B.J., she and Wayne would go to their bedroom, which also had a fireplace and he would do his book work and afterwards they would sit by the fire and have their devotional and talk about the days events. As B.J. grew stronger, when they went to bed they would make love. With each passing day their love grew stronger between them.

"Wayne can we go visit the Brookes? I need to get out of this house; I've got cabin fever in the worse way."

"We'll go tomorrow, if the weather permits." So they kissed goodnight and said I love you and went to sleep.

It seemed strange pulling up in the front yard of the Brooks and not having Mrs. Earline come out to greet you. Everyone was inside trying to stay warm. Norman and Aubrey had been staying there with Ralph and the boys. Aubrey was doing most of the cooking and cleaning for them now. They were none the less glad to see B.J. and Wayne. Every one hugged her and told her how good she looked.

They sat at the table where once Mrs. Earline had filled with food and enjoyed a piece of cake and a cup of coffee. B.J. looked around half expecting Earline to appear at any time, but realized it was not going to happen. Earline's presence was sorrowfully missed, but her family seemed to be doing okay. B.J. knew that men grieved differently than women, they kept everything inside. Men kept their grief hid from one another and the world. But you could tell they had lost their beloved mother and wife.

Wayne suggested they leave early; he didn't want B.J. wearing herself out. When they got to the door, Aubrey walked up to B.J. and motioned her to come to the other room.

"I'm pregnant. Norman and I are going to have a baby in about five months." Aubrey said shyly, holding her stomach,

B.J. hugged her, "I so happy for you two. You take care of yourself now, and I'll get back over to see you long before then."

When she went back to the others, B.J. could see how happy Norman was by the smile on his face. She knew the reason Aubrey hesitated telling her, she thought it would upset her and Wayne. That family was made of sensitive people and they would never hurt any one in the world.

Wayne and B.J. left the Brooks ranch that day knowing the family had something to look forward to; a blessing that would give them years of happiness, even though they had lost their mother. B.J. felt real good on the ride home and do did Wayne.

"Wayne, it's just like the Preacher said, "The Lord gives and the Lord takes," and we need to praise His name because He does know what He is doing in people's lives, even when we don't."

Right then and there, B.J. prayed silently. "Thank you Lord for the blessing you have given the Brooks family and for mine and Wayne's happiness that You have given us today."

Uncle Webster was waiting when they pulled up in front of the house and he helped B.J. down from the wagon. Wayne drove the wagon to the barn and unhitched the team. B.J. went in with Uncle Webster and they sat down to have a cup of fresh hot coffee to help get the chill gone.

Chapter 24

The next week in bed passed slowly for B.J. She felt her strength returning with each day, but her heart ached for her baby. The day came when she could get out of bed. B.J. legs felt like rubber and without Wayne to help, she wouldn't have made it. Wayne put his arm around her now tiny waist and half carried her sown the stairs. B.J. sat down in her favorite rocker by the fire. She was exhausted. Sue Lei was like a little mother, she came with a blanket to go around her legs.

Amme, Kim and Sue's little daughter crawled over to B.J. chair and reached up for her to take her. B.J. reached down and helped the little girl climb into her lap. B.J. held Amme a long time, hugging her and wondering how it would have felt to be hugging her own son. Sue Lei saw tears in B.J.s eyes and sensed what was happening, so she took the child from B.J. and made her go into the kitchen to play. "Missy, need rest. Amme wear Missy out climbing all over her."

Each week B.J grew physically stronger, but mentally, she seemed at a standstill. She tried to act as though nothing had happened, but when she passed the nursery, she would stop and look inside and visualize how it would be if her son have lived. The doctor said it would take time for the nurturing part of her body to heal and he was definitely right. Her breasts were swollen and sore from the milk that needed to be extracted. This hurt made her heart ache too, until finally after weeks, the milk dried up. This helped, but the empty feeling inside took much longer. B.J. decided she needed to be busy doing something, or the feeling would never leave her.

"Wayne, walk me to the barn so I can see Dude and all the new foals."

"It's cold outside, do you think you should?"

"I need to get out of this house for a few minutes."

"Well, bundle up."

She made her first venture out and it did seem to clear her head. Dude was glad to see her. After staying a while looking at the new foals, she realized how tired she way and Wayne helped her back inside.

Days became weeks, then months, and before B.J. knew it the year was almost gone. She had stayed inside more than usual because she just couldn't seem to get her strength back. B.J. knew she had lost a lot of weight and this had her resistance low. She had resolved to sitting in front of the fire and doing needlepoint. B.J. worked on several quilts to help pass the winter months. She took Grady's clothes and cut them into quilt pieces and sewed several beautiful quilt tops. The quilts helped her to remember Grady and enjoy the comfort the warmth provided too.

All the men folks were busy with the new foals and the cattle, seeing that the stock had hay and water through the months of snow. The nights were the best for B.J. Wayne and she would go to their bedroom, which also had a fireplace, and he would do the bookwork and afterwards they would sit by the fire and have their devotional and talk about the day's events. Then when B.J. got her strength back, they would go to bed and make love. With each passing day, their love grew stronger. They wanted another child, but they left it in god's hands. He knew when it was best for them to have another child.

"Wayne can we go visit the Brookes? I need to get out of this house; I've got cabin fever bad."

"We'll go tomorrow if the weather permits." They kissed goodnight and went to sleep.

It seemed strange driving into the front yard of the Brooks ranch and not having Mrs. Earline come running out to greet you. The men were all inside trying to stay warm. Norman and Aubrey had been staying with Ralph and the boys since their loss. Aubrey was doing most of the cooking and cleaning for them. They were naturally grad to see Wayne and B.J. that day. They all hugged and told her how good she looked.

They sat down at the table; the one Mrs. Earline always had filled with food, and had a piece of cake and a cup of hot coffee. B.J. looked around half expecting Mrs. Earline to appear at any time, and then realize it wasn't going to happen. Mrs. Earline's presence was sorrowfully missed, but the family seemed to be doing okay. Men grieved differently from women, keeping it all inside, and hid from each other and the world. Still anyone could tell her death had taken its toll on all of them. She had loss a dear friend, but they had lost their beloved mother and wife.

Wayne cut short their visit because he didn't want B.J. wearing herself out. When they started to leave, Aubrey walked up to B.J. and motioned her to come into the other room.

"I'm pregnant. Norman and I are going to have a baby in about five months." Aubrey shyly said as she held her stomach.

B.J. hugged her. "I'm so happy for ya'll. You take care of yourself now and I'll get back over to see you long before then."

She knew Aubrey hesitated telling her, but when she saw the smile Norman was wearing, she was happy for them. Wayne and B.J. left the Brooks ranch that day knowing the family had something to look forward too. A blessing that would give them many days of happiness, even though that had lost their mother. She felt good going home and so did Wayne. They sensed a burden had been lifted from that family.

"Wayne, it's just as the Preacher said. "The Lord gives and the Lord takes." We need to praise His name because he does know what He is doing in people's lives, even when we don't."

Uncle Webster was waiting when they pulled up in front of the house. He helped B.J. down from the wagon. Wayne carried the wagon to the barn to unhitch the horses and feed them for the night. B.J. went in with Webster. They had a cup of hot coffee to rid them of the chill.

"Uncle Webster, guess what? Norman and Aubrey are gonna have a baby in five months, isn't that great? I think it's the sweetest thing that could happen to that family right now."

"You've got that right. Those folks deserve some good news and happy times."

"Well, Wayne and I ain't giving up. We're leaving it in the hands of the Lord. The nursery is ready to be occupied and when the Lord is ready, we'll be ready."

Webster smiled; it was good to know that B.J. had accepted the loss of her baby and was ready to move on with life. Webster had worried when she said she wanted to visit the Brookes that she would come home depressed, but instead she came back rejoicing for the family. B.J. had been through a lot, but her faith still remained strong.

After supper that night B.J. sat working on her quilt and Webster and Wayne were playing checkers in front of the fire.

"B.J. you'll never guess what happened today? Stormy had his first mare."

"Is he that big already?"

"Oh yea, he's been ready for some time, we just had to wait for the right mare to be in season."

"More babies being born around here. Life has a way of continuing in both humans and animals." Webster smiled as he double jumped Wayne checkers on the board. Wayne sat looking down at the board astonished at the move.

B.J. busied herself by adding new touches to the house. They had put inside plumbing, and slowly the ranch house was becoming modern. The men were busy from daylight to past sundown getting chores completed, but there was not much more inside that B.J. could do to the house. She found it hard just finding something to fill the hours of each day. It was very hard for her to sit and quilt for any length of time. The weeks passed slowly, but spring finally surfaced. The mornings still had a definite sting, but later the days warmed some.

"I do believe spring is heading our way." B.J. told Sue Lei. With all that had happened, the long winter months dragged by. Now you could see the beginning of new life everywhere you looked. The wild flowers had popped up over night and soon the trees were showing buds bursting to open into leaves. Springtime was usually a happy time for B.J. because all the depression of winter was passing and new life was in the air.

Wayne and the men were busy getting the stock to different pastures and taking the new calves from their mothers for branding. The first of the spring storms was brewing off in the distance, but inside B.J. another type of storm was brewing. She was a bit angry with Wayne, not that he had done anything to justify her anger. She couldn't understand why she felt the way she did either. Her anger turned to hurt, then to frustration, and then to bitterness. All three began to feed on her loneliness and dissatisfaction. B.J. thought with spring, things around the ranch would be different, but found she was still sitting around waiting, but for what?

Each day was the same. No one noticed, she appeared to them to be the same, but after getting her chores done, she found her days long and sat for hours in idle thoughts. The longer this continued, the more she became concerned, and once thought of talking to Wayne about it. B.J. changed her mind thinking the discontentment would pass. Why was she having these feelings? Why did she have such a sense of worthlessness? The ranch had grown beyond all expectations and was making money hand over fist for them and even with times so easy for her she still felt depressed.

It was March and B.J. got up one morning determined not to go another day feeling like she had. She made up her mind that she had been plagued long enough, so she saddled Dude and took off to town, telling no one but Sue Lei. B.J. stopped Dude in front of the doctor's office and went in. Her first thoughts were to demand that he do something to get her into a better frame of mind, but before she could go in to see him, it occurred that only she controlled her mind, not the doctor. So when the doctor called her back to the examining room, she simple told him the strange feelings she had been having for the last months or so.

"When was your last period, B.J.?

She hadn't even thought about her cycle and she had to admit that she had completely lost count.

"You get undressed and I'll examine you. Maybe afterwards, I can tell you what's going on inside that body of yours."

The doctor left the room and B.J. undressed and lay down on the examination table. The door opened and he and his nurse came in. He gave B.J. an examination and simple told her to get dressed and come to his office. So B.J. did as he said.

"Well young lady, you are going to have another baby."

"For sure! You know for sure?"

"Certainly, I know for sure and you shouldn't have a bit of trouble, providing you take care of yourself and do as I tell you."

The doctor gave her a lot of instructions and told her he wanted to see her in two months unless she needed him before then. Even though B.J. was riding Dude's back, it felt more like she was floating on a cloud, she was so happy. She could hardly wait to tell Wayne and Uncle Webster. On her way home she noticed all the anger, bitterness, frustration and disappointment that she had experienced lately was gone. In their place were love, joy, and contentment. Tears begin to form in B.J.'s eyes, but these were tears of joy and happiness, so she rode on, crying, but her heart was singing praises of thankfulness.

When she rode into the ranch yard and stopped Dude at the barn door, Wayne came out to meet her. "I was getting a little worried about you. You've been gone a long time."

B.J. stepped down from Dude, walked over to Wayne and put her arms around his neck, making him lean over because she was so much shorter. "Don't worry about me, I'm fine. I'm pregnant. I just came from the doctor's office and he confirmed it." She smiled and then kissed Wayne long and hard.

Wayne had listened but was having a hard time believing what he had heard. Nearly three years had passed since they lost their son, and he was almost ready to give up having another one. He held B.J. close and hugged her tight, running his hands up and down the small of her back. "I'm glad, so glad. Did the doctor say everything was okay?"

"I'm healthy as a horse and our baby is too."

Uncle Webster was just coming out of his shop and saw the display of affection between the two of them and caught the word "baby." "Who is having a baby now?"

Wayne and B.J. turned towards him smiling and answered. "We are." All three broke into laughter.

Chapter 25

December came and their son Dale was born. He was so tiny and red. All the babies B.J. visualized were pink and cuddly, but Sue Lei assured her he would change from red to pink shortly. Sue Lei took the baby from the doctor and bathed him off. After dressing Dale in one of the warm flannel gowns, Sue wrapped him in a blanket and carried him out for the men to see. B.J. could here all the "oh's" and "ah's" as each one of the ranch hands looked him over real good. Several of the men told Wayne that certain features were just like his and this made Wayne's head swell even bigger.

Sue Lei returned Dale to his mother and B.J.'s pride began to swell within her and she wanted nothing more than just to hold her son.

"Look Sue Lei, he's sucking his fist."

"Missy, he is hungry for his mother's milk."

Sue Lei left and B.J. let Dale nurse for the first time. B.J. was so busy making sure she did everything just right, that she didn't notice that Wayne was in the room. He walked over and sat on the bed, watching the two people he loved the most in life, B.J. and Grady Dale Thompson and was he enjoying his first meal.

After Dale finished nursing, B.J. purped him and he immediately went to sleep. She was really exhausted, so she relaxed on her pillow and dozed off too. She never knew when Wayne got up and eased out of her room. The two slept a long time and afterwards she felt wonderful. Sue Lei was a great help. She took all the fear of being a new mother from her. She had a daughter and was experienced and soon B.J.'s confidence began to grow and she soon took over all the duties of caring for her son. B.J. spent a lot of time with Dale in the beginning, but soon learned he didn't require much attention. Once he was fed, he was content to just sleep or lie in his crib and entertain himself.

Dale was a good baby, not like some that require a lot of rocking. When he was about two months old, Wayne would take him out of his crib and go downstairs so Uncle Webster could hold him and see how much he was growing. Soon Dale got to expect these visit with his dad and Uncle Webster. B.J. consented so that afterwards Dale would sleep better at night. The men would pass Dale back and forth and tire him out till B.J. would intervene and take him back to the nursery for the night.

B.J. would like nothing more than to keep Dale a baby for as long as she could, but you could see him growing right in front of your eyes. It wasn't long before Dale was turning over in his crib. They began putting him on a quilt on the floor in front of the fire and he would roll over and then came the crawling, and not long after that he was pulling himself up to the furniture. B.J had Little Amme to sit on the quilt and play or entertain Dale. The little girl was as gentle as she could be with him, for a four year old.

Amme was at the curious stage, she either wanted to why or how about everything. B.J. was changing Dale's diaper and Amme noticed he was different from her down there, so she made a point to tell B.J. B.J. was at a lost as to how to explain to Amme, so she went to Sue and told her about it.

"I will talk to her when the time is right, she will know, now, Amme just curious."

B.J. felt better, but then it occurred to her that one day Dale would be asking those same questions.

"Well, I'll just let Wayne do the explaining when he does." B.J. said to herself.

If days passed quickly before Dale was born, now they were just flying by. Taking care of the baby and doing her chores kept B.J. pretty busy. Dale was walking and into everything. He had to be watched every minute. Wayne and B.J. carried him to visit Norman and Aubrey's little girl. B.J. couldn't believe the difference in the size of the two. Even though Aubrey's little girl, Bridgette, was older, she was so tiny and delicate. Dale seemed so rough and rowdy around her, but the men had made him as tough as nails. After holding Brigette, B.J. wanted a daughter too. But right now it was out of the question, Dale was a handful and she wouldn't be able to manage another one.

When Christmas came this time, Dale was a year old and walking real good. The Christmas tree was his favorite target. Dale managed to pull it over on top of him and it scared B.J. to death, but Wayne got it off in a hurry and Dale just lay on the floor laughing. They invited the Brooks family and the Donilson family to Christmas dinner and afterwards they sat around and sang Christmas songs. They enjoyed cider punch and fruitcake that Sue Lei had made.

The children had more fun playing with the paper wrapping than their gifts. Each one had a gift. This had been a good year for Wayne and B.J. so they shared their good fortune with their neighbors. B.J.'s Dad had always said, "It is more blessed to give than receive." This year proved how true that saying was and they knew what being blessed was. Having good neighbors and friends, a happy, healthy family was the greatest blessing of all.

The holidays came and went and things got back to normal, or at least for a time. The Rocking H Ranch had existed for ten years and some had been good years, but there had also been some bad. The good outweighed the bad so far, but it was inevitable that something would change. The first change came when the Army contract for horses for the Pony Express was canceled. Progress had come west and with it came the railroad. Tracks were being laid into Casper and even further west, and the need for horses decreased with this progress. The Rocking H's income from the sale of the Black Stallion's mares was no longer needed, and this began hurting the income for Wayne and B.J and their family.

Several years ago Wayne had invested in some cattle. It looked as though they would be dealing more in cattle now than horses. There was still the income from the stud fees from Dude and Stormy, but the sale of any horses was few. Uncle Webster suggested that Wayne try the freight lines, they always needed teams to pull the big freight wagons. Wayne and he had already been breeding their draft mares, but what they needed was to purchase a draft stallion. With this scheme in mind, they began checking thing out. Most of the working on the ranch now was left to the hired men. Wayne still had his blacksmith shop and plenty of business, so he couldn't complain; the ranch was still providing them with a good living.

Uncle Webster was the one who took on less and less work. It wasn't his desire, his health was failing him and he had little choice. The cold weather was especially hard on him, so he stayed in most of the time and helped B.J. with Dale. The winter that Dale turned three was Webster's worse winter. His bones hurt and he ached worse than he ever had. On real cold mornings it was all he could do to just get out of bed. Webster never complained, but his physical condition was very noticeable. He was drawn in his shoulders and limped when he walked, and it was obvious to all that he was suffering.

Wayne stopped at the doctor's office one trip in town and got him a bottle of liniment to rub his back and shoulders each night. When the weather warmed, Webster would get to feeling better. For someone seventy-four years old he still got about pretty good. Wayne and her talked one night after Uncle Webster had gone to bed about how soon he would have to give up even more. They agreed they would be there for him when that time came. This ranch would not exist if not for Webster Thompson. He had always pulled his share of the work load and now the time had come for his life to be easier for him. B.J. knew in her heart that Wayne thought Webster would be around forever, but she knew different. But for now, B.J. would enjoy having Webster around as much as possible. On those cold mornings she deliberately found something to keep Webster inside with her and Dale.

"Uncle Webster will you keep Dale company while I sew on my quilt today?" B.J. asked. Webster would gladly sit and read Dale his little books and taught him to blow a whistle he had carved for him. Sometimes the two would fall asleep in the big stuffed chair and B. J. just simple threw a blanket over them and let them sleep. He would take Dale by the hand and the two would walk around outside when the weather warmed. Dale loved Uncle Webster and Webster loved the boy.

The year Dale turned five, the Lord blessed B.J. and Wayne with another baby, a little girl. They named her Lynn. She was beautiful, so chubby with big blue eyes and a pixie face. Lynn smiled all the time. There was one thing missing, she had very little hair. What hair she had was blond, and more like peach fuzz than hair. After being used to Dale's head full of curly hair, it seemed strange having a bald headed baby girl. But Lynn didn't remain bald long, anyway hair or no hair they thought she was the prettiest little girl in the world. Her little round mouth made Wayne nickname her "Button", and that name stuck with her for years.

Wayne and B.J. were afraid Dale would be jealous, but he was too old for that now. He loved being referred to as the "big brother." Anyway, he and Uncle Webster had got to be such good buddies, that he had no time to mess with the baby. Uncle Webster had picked Dale out a little filly and was letting him get used to the little horse. The two spent hours in the barn rubbing and grooming the little horse. Dale's next thrill came when he got to lead her around the coral on a rope. Dale wasn't afraid of horses; he loved them just like his mother had when she was little. Wayne still cautioned Dale about getting too close when he was putting shoes on them for customers.

While Uncle Webster kept up with Dale outside, B.J. had her hands full with Lynn inside. Lynn was right the opposite of Dale; she demanded B.J.'s full attention. There was nothing that satisfied her for long, she was very impatient. B.J. had to reschedule all her chores to pacificy Lynn. She only cat-napped, instead of the two or three hour naps liked Dale took. By bed time, B.J. was worn out but Lynn was still going strong. Wayne would pick her up and take her to the rocker and rock her to sleep, humming gospel songs in her ear each night.

Time stands still for no one, especially those who have growing children. Dale was outgrowing all his clothes and Lynn was trying to walk. B.J. went to Wayne one day and told him Dale had to have new clothes.

"We'll go into town tomorrow and take them and Uncle Webster with us and spend the day shopping."

B.J. was excited as the children, but Uncle Webster didn't want to go to town, he wanted to stay at home and keep Dale with him.

"Uncle Webster, we have to take Dale and fit his clothes on him. He had outgrown everything he owns. We'll have fun and you can shop too."

B.J. thought she explained going shopping in a way that Webster would want to go, but with Webster, you never knew his mood, come morning he might go and he might not. Uncle Webster fooled them and got up the next morning all dressed to go to town. Casper was more a city now than a town. The rate Casper was growing surprised B.J. each time she went into town. The train stopped now and people came from all over to settle and the streets were running over with the new motor cars that had become so popular.

Wayne mentioned buying one, but B.J. held out for horses. After all they raised horses and what would people think of them? Their buggy had two seats and Webster and Dale shared the back While Wayne, B.J. and baby Lynn sat in the front. Casper was noisy that day as Wayne pulled the team to a stop in front of the general store. He got out and carefully tied their horses to the rail, and then he came around to help B.J. down with the baby. Without thinking, Uncle Webster got out on the traffic side and just as he reached for Dale, one of the new motor cars came by honking its horn, and it frightened Uncle Webster causing him to stumble and fall. He was almost hit by the car. He got up mad and red in the face, but Wayne calmed him down. B.J. got so nervous about all that was happening that she reached for Dale and took him out of the buggy on her side. Her actions added to the already brewing anger that Webster was feeling.

All of them went in the store, but Uncle Webster had sulled up and stayed more to himself. B.J. shopped for Dale while Wayne held on to Lynn. She fought her Daddy wanting to get down and get into everything, but Wayne kept her in his arms. After fitting Dale with three outfits, blue jeans and shirts and even a pair of boots, she turned to look for her a new dress. B.J. looked around but didn't see Webster anywhere.

"Where did Uncle Webster Go?"

"He is sitting in the buggy."

B.J. knew he was angry, so she forgot about her dress and gave the list of supplies to the clerk to fill as quickly as possible. When the supplies were all loaded and tied down, the family headed for home. Uncle

Webster grumbled all the way home. Wayne noticed, but didn't remark because he was busy getting through the traffic in Casper, it was terrible. So no one said anything to Uncle Webster and he finally stopped grumbling. When Wayne pulled the horses to a stop in front of the house, B.J. handed Lynn to Sue Lei and then she turned to help Dale and Uncle Webster.

"I'm not a child; I can take care of myself. I don't need any help getting in or out of a wagon."

B.J. pulled her hand back and didn't say a word, but all the same she was hurt by his remark and confused about why Webster would react to her in that manner. After she got the supplies put up, and supper eaten, she took Dale's new clothes and the two children and got them ready for bed. Dale went back downstairs to say goodnight to his daddy and Uncle Webster. Wayne was there in front of the fire and B.J. expected to see Uncle Webster there too, but he had already retired. Dale kissed his daddy and Wayne shooed him back upstairs to B.J. and to bed.

When B.J. finally got both of them asleep, she came back down to Wayne. She was glad that Uncle Webster had gone to bed early because she wanted to talk to Wayne about his attitude that day. Wayne listened, but she could tell from the look on his face that he thought it more her imagination than it was Webster. So B.J. put it out of her mind as though nothing had happened. They both went up to bed, it had been a long, tiring day

The next morning Uncle Webster was telling Wayne at the table about overhearing two ranchers talking in town. B.J. listened, hoping to catch what had upset Uncle Webster so bad.

"Change is coming; it's getting closer to us each day. Those ranchers were talking of men who were fencing in their land with this new wire with barbs on it. Why, that stuff could cut a horse or a cow to pieces if they got caught in it. Those ranchers were talking about rustling that is taking place, and said that was why the owners went to this wire for fences."

"I'm glad we still have open range here. But you're right, change is coming. Maybe it will hold off a bit; those kinds of changes I don't like at all." Wayne answered.

B.J. just sat listening, sipping her coffee. When Webster left going outside she asked Wayne, "Was that what was bothering Uncle Webster? Is he worried about the future of our ranch?"

B.J. looked to Wayne for answers but all he did was shrug his shoulders. "When a man got Uncle Webster's age, who could tell what worried him." B.J. thought to herself.

Shortly after their trip into town and Uncle Webster overhearing the rancher's conversation, they noticed a change had come over him. Always an outside person, Webster seemed content to just sat in front of the fire more and more with each day. He never complained, so they let him alone to do as he pleased, but even Dale noticed he couldn't get Uncle Webster to come out and help brush his horse. Every now and then Webster would wander out to the blacksmith shop and sit around and talk to Wayne or Charlie's customers and then one day he just chose to sit alone in the warm sunshine, rubbing his gnarled and twisted hands together. Two or three weeks went by and the next change was his appetite. Webster had always had a good appetite, but now he wasn't eating well at all.

"Uncle Webster are you feeling alright? Has something upset your stomach?"

"I'm fine. No need to fret over me, you plenty to fret about in those two youngsters."

So again B.J. dismissed his actions and then one day he had sit by the fire all morning, B.J. noticed he had not moved a muscle. She went to him and he had this blank stare on his face, as though he was totally in another world. She called his name but nothing changed. She sent for Sue Lei and told her to get Wayne quickly, that Uncle Webster wouldn't respond to her. When Wayne came, Webster wouldn't respond to him either.

"Let's get him to bed. I'll send one of the men into town for the doctor; maybe he can tell us what is wrong with him."

They picked up Uncle Webster and carried him to his room Wayne tried talking to him, but Webster never answered or said anything to anyone.

The doctor finally arrived and went in and examined Webster with Wayne present. The door opened and both men came out.

"I didn't want to say in front of Webster because there a possibility he might understand what we're saying. He's had a stroke. He won't get any better, it'll just get worse. How long he may lie like this, there is no telling, we'll just have to wait and see. Keep trying to get him to eat and drink, but if he doesn't, don't be disappointed. About all you can do is make him as comfortable as possible."

The doctor left. B.J. sat down in her rocker, the rocker that Uncle Webster had carved, and cried. Wayne came over and put his arm around her.

"It was bound to happen. Uncle Webster is nearly eighty and he has lived a rough life."

Wayne was trying to console her, but what he said didn't make it any easier for her to accept.

"I remember the first time I laid eyes on him and how kind and good he was to me and Grady."

"I know, and he's all the family I have left, but still I knew he couldn't go on forever. B.J. you were young when you first met him, but think back he wasn't young. He had lived the best part of his life even before he walked into your camp that night. We can't hold back the years, even if we want too. Time has a way of catching up with all of us."

B.J. knew in her heart that Wayne was telling the truth, but the hurt was still in her heart. What hurt the most was to see Uncle Webster laying flat of his back and slowly fading away. They did all that anyone could do for Webster, Wayne bathed him daily and B.J. and Sue Lei fixed him meals and fed him most of the time, but with each passing day, Webster excepted less and less each time they tried to feed him. B.J. began to think that just maybe he wanted to die rather than lay like this. He always had been such a big, robust man, who could do almost anything, and she knew if it was her, she would rather be dead.

Each night she and Wayne prayed the Lord would not let Webster suffer. As near as they could tell, he wasn't in any pain, but they were hurting, seeing him like this. The doctor came each week, but he never promised anything different. One day B.J. went to feed Uncle Webster his noon meal. When she opened his door, she immediately saw he wasn't in his bed. She walked around to the other side and what she saw made her drop the tray of food and rush to him, calling his name. Sue Lei heard the tray crash and heard B.J. screaming his name and she came running. As soon as she got to the door, she went back after Wayne.

When Wayne got to the room, B.J. was sitting in the floor holding Uncle Webster's head in her lap. His eyes were looking up at her and he was actually smiling. She hugged him close and told him she loved him. Uncle Webster never spoke, he looked into B.J. eyes that one last time, smiled at her and closed his eyes, never to wake again.

"I told him I loved him but he didn't reply. He smiled at me, and then closed his eyes."

"He heard you. He knew you were there and it was his smile that was his reply." Wayne reached down and felt Webster's pulse to make sure, and then he nodded to B.J. and they knew he was gone from them. Wayne just stood by and kept quiet while B.J. had her last moments with Uncle Webster, and then he took Uncle Webster in his arms and laid him back on the bed. He took B.J. arm and lifted her to her feet. She had a peaceful look in her eyes about letting Uncle Webster go.

The door was closed so the children couldn't enter. B.J. had Dale on the porch talking to him about Uncle Webster being in heaven with God. Dale seemed to understand and he didn't cry. Wayne came out and Lynn was in his arms and was hugging him around the neck. Lynn knew her Daddy needed comforting, so she gave him a big kiss. The four sat on the porch for a long time, not saying anything.

The ranch hands knew what to do, so one went into town to the undertakers and then told all the friends and neighbors. Two of the men went to the family cemetery and began digging Webster's grave. None of them wanted Wayne or B.J. to worry about anything at a time like this.

It was hard on all of them giving up one who had been so good, worked so hard, and made life so pleasurable. Uncle Webster was a good Christian man who believed in god, and it was God that he was with now. Knowing this made it a lot easier to give him up.

The preacher was notified and the undertaker brought out his coffin. Webster was bathed and dressed in his suit and placed in it. Neighbors and friends came from miles around to pay their last respects the next day. Food was brought and friends and neighbors stayed and offered their help and sympathy.

When the time came, they followed the wagon carrying Uncle Webster's body up that little hill, with a possession of black clad mourners behind them. Everyone, it seemed, had come to pay their respects. Webster was well thought of by a lot of folks and it showed that day. The Preacher spoke highly of him, telling everyone that he had gone to be with the Lord. From the Bible he read Matthew 11:28 "Come unto me, all ye that labor and are heavy laden, and I will give you rest." (K.J.V.) Webster Thompson was now at rest with the Lord. His favorite hymn, "Amazing Grace" was sung, and then the men covered him. The family and friends went back down the hill to their home. Home without him, but with a lot of good memories he had given each and everyone of them.

The day was sad in the sense that Webster would never sit with them by the evening fire again, nor stand by the corral fence and talk to the horses. He would never chase the children around the yard, or go out and trap or kill fresh meat for their table. These were their memories and no one could take them, so they still had Uncle Webster in their hearts where he would stay until they could join him one day in heaven.

Chapter 26

As one season followed another and one year pushed the past one off the wall calendar, B.J. and Wayne saw their children grow right before their eyes. The years had flew by so fast that it didn't seem possible till Dale was about to finish high school. Dale's interest had turned to doctoring animals and one day B.J. approached Wayne on the subject of Dale's future.

"What do you think about sending Dale back east to finish his education?"

Wayne couldn't believe B.J. was suggesting their son leave home for any extended time, but Wayne like her had been thinking if Dale really wanted to become a veterinarian he would have to leave Casper to get his education. Wayne acted as though he was giving it some serious thought before he replied. "What do you have in mind?"

"Well—Dale shows signs of being a veterinarian; you have seen how he worries over sick animals all the time."

"Have you talked to him about all this?"

"No, but in a few months he will have finished all the education he can get here, and now is the time to make plans."

"I think perhaps we should talk with Dale and see what he wants to do with his life."

That is precisely what they did that very night after supper. Dale confirmed their hopes for him to be a vet. He got Wayne to help him send for information from a college in Cheyenne, hoping they could accept him that fall. But until they heard from the college, he went to work with the local vet, Doc Winston in Casper. Dale worked every day in the summer and came home each night sharing what they had treated that day. Each night it was something different and each night Dale seemed more excited. He had a love for animals, all kind and he hated seeing one sick or hurt. Dale love his work and Doc Winston hated to see him leave when fall came. The college had responded to his application and was waiting for him to enroll. The summer months had passed so quickly that no one was ready but Dale.

The final day came and he had his bags packed, his acceptance papers in his pocket and they all stood waiting for the train to slow enough for him to board. Everyone had gone with him to the train station to say goodbye, but Dale had tried his best to talk them out of it. He felt like a small school kid with all of them standing there with him. He rather tell them at the house instead of at the train station, but Wayne, nor B.J.

would have it that way, so that morning they stood waiting for the train too.

B.J. had promised Wayne and Dale that she would not cry, and she really had to swallow hard to keep from crying. The train stopped and the people on board got off, Dale hurriedly hugged both her and Lynn and shook hands with his Dad, picked up his bag and was aboard. They watched as he walked the length of the first car and followed him outside as he went into the second car. He took his seat there and turned and waved to them from the window. The train was slowly moving away and they stood watching till they could no longer see.

The trip home was quiet. Their new motor car got them home a lot faster than their buggy and horses had. B.J. didn't cherish going back to that house without her son. The tears that she had fought so hard to keep Dale from seeing surfaced, and see pretended it was dust in her eyes. She noticed Wayne was having trouble with the dust that day too.

The days after Dale left passed slowly mainly because B.J. wanted so bad to hear from him. Dale took his time writing, but a letter finally did come. B.J. hastened to open it and Lynn waited to hear each word he had written. Wayne came in as soon as she waved the letter to him and he too sit down and reread it.

Dale loved school. He did extra good in his studies, so good that he deceived not to return home after finishing his first year. He stayed on in Cheyenne in the summer months to work for a vet there. The family was disappointed and even made a trip to Cheyenne to visit one summer. Wayne and B.J. saw how Dale had matured, he wasn't a boy any more, and he was now a full grown man. They couldn't tell him what to do now. Four years at college and working in the summers for Dale had gone by slowly for them, but fast for Dale.

Dale wrote he had met a girl and told them that it was serious between them. Wayne and B.J. wondered if they would soon have another member to their family. If so, it would be fine with them. They wanted their children to find a mate and be as happily married as they had been all these years. It was a surprise though when Dale finished his four years and they went to his graduation ceremony to here his plans now was to stay on permanently in Cheyenne and buy into the practice with Dr. Smith. They had hoped he would come back to Casper and work with Doc Winston. Dale had his life to live, so they went along with his plans. Dale never returned to Casper to the Rocking H Ranch except to bring his pretty little future bride to meet his family.

Dianne was a sweet girl, so thoughtful of Dale and everything he wanted to do. B.H. wondered if she had ever been that thoughtful to Wayne. Dale and Dianne was married in her community church in Cheyenne. Wayne, B.J., and Lynn made the trip for their wedding. There were so many people; the little church couldn't accommodate them. So the Pastor opened the windows for all to hear the ceremony. After the ceremony and the reception and getting acquainted with Dianne's family, Wayne and B.J. and Lynn caught the train back to Casper. Dale and Dianne took a brief honeymoon.

They had been so focused on Dale and all the changes in his life, and all the time right under their noses Lynn was developing into a young lady. B.J. still considered Lynn her baby, forgetting that there was only five years difference in the two children. Before she realized it Lynn was graduating from high school and no thought had been given to her future.

When Lynn was asked her plans for the future, she would just shrug and reply, "I donno yet. I'm still thinking about it."

Some teased Wayne and B.J. telling them to be prepared to have Lynn around for a long time, that maybe by the time she was forty she would have decided. Wayne and B.J. knew different, she was a beautiful young lady and when the right man came alone, she would know it. B.J. was relieved that Lynn waited as long as she did. Lynn loved the ranch and loved the horses like B.J. when she was young. Lynn would ride out to the meadow to see the black stallion and his mares several times a week. The Rocking H was her home and she never gave any thought about leaving.

After a couple of years, when they would get letters from Dale and Dianne, Lynn always wanted to see them and read them herself. Her excuse was to keep abreast of the big city life they lived. In one of Dale's letters, he encouraged Lynn to come for a visit, so after much though Lynn asked if she could go visit and stay for a couple of weeks. Wayne and B.J. both agreed it would do her good to get away from the ranch and to be with others her age for awhile.

The trip was planned and Lynn packed her bags, but when the time came to leave she almost changed her mind. Wayne and B.J. encouraged her to go and even gave her some extra money to shop for new clothes from the big city, so she went. They drove her to the train and hugged her before she climbed on board. Lynn promised to write her Mom and Dad every day, but somehow they knew not to expect the letters. Once Lynn got with adults her age she would forget the writing.

When the train pulled away from the station, B.J. sensed an empty feeling deep in the pit of her stomach, but she kept it to herself. On their ride home she noticed how quiet Wayne had become too. Lynn was on her way to the big city and both of them wanted her to enjoy herself, even though they would be miserable while she was gone. Strange how you get used to your children being home, and when the youngest one "leaves the nest," you feel lost and empty inside.

A week passed and the first letter arrived. B.J. could hardly wait to open the first one and read all about Lynn's excitement. It was as though she was right there with her daughter. Dale and Dianne had planned so many things for her and she was enjoying each and every minute of her stay. In a couple of days the second letter came, it was less exciting and a lot more on the serious side. Immediately after reading the letter B.J. went to the blacksmith shop to show Wayne.

"Is anything wrong?" Wayne asked as he took the letter from B.J.'s hand.

"You read it, and then tell me."

"All it says is she had met a young man and really does like him." Wayne was smiling.

"Can't you read between the lines, she's in love with this man and she barely knows him? I think we need to go bring Lynn home before she does something foolish."

"Hold on! B.J. you're acting like a typical mother hen hovering over her baby that has wandered from the nest. Now Lynn has a good head on her shoulders and she won't do anything foolish, so forget about going after her."

Wayne handed the letter back to B.J. and went back to his customer and she turned and went back to the empty house.

Lynn's two week stay passed, and nothing was said about her returning home to them. B.J. was about to erupt, but promised herself that she would not say anything else to Wayne. She didn't want to be called a Mother Hen again, but she noticed that Lynn's letters grew fewer and fewer. If Wayne noticed, he kept it to himself. Finally, after four weeks, he asked one night at the supper table.

"Have you heard from Lynn lately?"

B.J. just shook her head. Sue Lei knew how bad B.J. felt, but she never got into the family's conversation,

"Why do you suppose she stopped writing?"

"All I can figure is she is too busy going out with her friend Carl and doesn't have time for us."

"Well, I think it's time we made a trip to Cheyenne to meet this Carl fellow and find out what is going on." Wayne pushed his chair back and started pacing the floor.

"Why don't we telephone Dale before we make the trip, maybe he can shed some light on things?"

Wayne nodded and went straight to the wall where the new telephone hung. The phone was seldom used, but to satisfy their son, they had one installed. Wayne dialed Dale's number and waited for someone to answer in the other end. Dale answered.

"Hello."

"Dale, this is your Dad. How is everybody? We haven't heard from Lynn in several a couple of weeks and thought we would check on ya'll."

"Hi Dad, good to hear from you. We're all fine. You say Lynn hasn't written you? She hasn't told you and Mom about her new plans?"

When Wayne heard the word "plans", his heart missed a beat. Was what B.J. said about Lynn being in love true? Was she going to marry this guy they had never met?

"Dad, you still there?"

"Yes, yes, I'm here. What were you saying about Lynn's plans son? I didn't hear all of it."

"Well Dad, maybe Lynn should be the one to break the news to you and Mom. Here, I'll put Lynn on the phone."

Dale handed the phone to Lynn and Wayne motioned for B.J. to share the earpiece with him. This way both could hear at the same time.

"Daddy, you there?"

"Yes Lynn, we're both here. Your Mom is listening too. What plans do you want to share with us?"

There was a few moments of silence and then Lynn begin.

"Daddy, Mom, I've decided to stay in Cheyenne and enroll in school. Is it okay with you two? I know it is sudden, but I've met several college students since I've been here and they have encouraged me to enroll."

"Would one in particular be Carl?"

"Yes Dad, him also, but I've talked it over with Dale and Dianne and they say I can stay right here with them and go to school every day and it won't cost as much. Can I, please?"

"Sure you can, but we insist on sending money to pay board to Dale and Dianne for your stay. Won't you need to come home and get the rest of your clothes?"

"I've got enough to last till cold weather and we thought you and Mom would come up for Christmas and bring the others. See, Dad, Mom, I've already enrolled and started classes. I just haven't took the time to tell you—sorry."

Well there was no sense in trying to talk her out of what she already had going, so the three talked others matters for a short time and in the end it was confirmed that they would come for Christmas that year, and would bring Lynn her winter clothes. After hanging up, Wayne smiled at B.J.

"See, I told you she had a good head on her shoulders and she proved it to us today. Don't you feel better?"

Lynn went off to the city for a visit and discovered she wanted to continue her education. It turned out that all the office courses got her was a young professor, Carl Richer. After a year they read her letter together telling them about her new plans again. Wayne and B.J. had met Carl the first Christmas at Dale's and liked him. They both thought he was a special young man and Lynn had made a good choice. Dale and he were real good friends too and that made it easier to except him.

Lynn's new plan was to inform them about their wedding. The two were to be married in Cheyenne where all their new found friends were, so B.J. and Wayne made another trip to Cheyenne for another wedding. B.J. had so hoped that Lynn would be married at home in Casper, but they were grown and she had to respect their choices. Carl was a good Christian and they knew their daughter would be happy with him. The wedding was planned mostly by Dianne because B.J. was too far away, but it turned out beautiful.

B.J. thought back on the day she and Wayne got married and recalled their trip to Casper for their honeymoon. This was one of her most treasured memories. She thought she had herself prepared knowing that Lynn was no longer a child, and that she was a grown woman and B.J. wanted Lynn to have the happiness she and Wayne had enjoyed all their married life, but on the way home from the wedding, deep in her heart she already missed her baby girl. To her, this was who Lynn would always be—her baby. The tears were hard to control when they left her.

"It's going to be so different, knowing she won't be coming back home to us." She mused to Wayne.

Wayne never answered; he too had a lump in his throat that wouldn't let him talk, so they sat on the train in silence. When Wayne finally did speak, his words startled her.

"Both of them are good kids. I did so want one of them to think seriously about the ranch, but if it's not meant to be, it's not. I don't guess our kids love ranching as much as we do, B.J."

"No, I don't guess they do, but there is still time, who knows what tomorrow holds for any of us, except our Lord."

The big house seemed so big and empty when they returned. Sue Lei and Kim were experiencing the same thing with their daughter, Amme. She too had left home to go to school and never returned to stay.

B.J. received frequent letters from Lynn indicating she was happy with Carl and their new home. As the months faded into years, B.J. realized the letters had taken a new turn. Her eyes filled with tears of happiness when she read of Lynn being pregnant. B.J. rushed to share the news with Wayne. He beamed with joy too. Grandparents! They were going to be grandparents before Christmas. The baby was born right before Christmas. Instead of it being one baby, it turned out to be twins, two boys, so they were twice as proud.

Once the babies started coming, they seemed to come in bunches. Dale and Dianne had waited for so long, and then like overnight, they had a beautiful baby girl, and one year later, a boy. Then a letter came saying Lynn and Carl were expecting again, hoping this time it would only be one, but again two showed up, more boys. B.J. wrote Lynn and told her four boys were enough, that if she wanted another to pray hard for it to be a girl and then stop. Five children were enough for anyone. But before Lynn and Carl could have another, Dale and Dianne beat them to it, and they now had them a boy.

All total Wayne and B.J had seven grandchildren. When they all came to visit the children had a ball on the big ranch, especially the boys. Wayne had each one of them a horse and as soon as they stepped down from their car, they were off to the barn, looking for Papaw and wanting to ride. Dale and Lynn may not have been interested in the ranch, but all the grandchildren were.

When everyone left the ranch was again big and empty and quiet, but B.J. and Wayne loved it that way. With age, came the desire for peace and quiet, and now they both had settled into the routine of being alone and doing whatever they wanted to do.

If years seemed to pass fast with their own children, it passed even faster in the lives of their grandchildren. With each year they grew like weeds. The boys loved the ranch more with each visit and soon they wanted to stay all summer with their grandparents. This was something that Wayne and B.J. looked forward too. Each year when school let out the boys would pack their bags and ride the train out to stay the summer. Wayne and B.J. promised them that as soon as they got their education they could come and stay as long as they wanted.

Dale and Dianne's son Matthew was the only one, after graduating from school, that really showed he loved the Rocking H Ranch. He actually got Dale to say it was okay for him to move in with B.J. and Wayne. Dale and Lynn were glad because they worried about their parents being so far from them and getting on in age.

The big house took on some life after Matt moved in and they both enjoyed him being there. B.J was especially thankful for Matt. One day ole Charlie came running to tell her to come to the blacksmith shop, Wayne was ailing. B.J. ran out of the house as fast as her skinny old legs would carry her. For someone nearing seventy, she still moved pretty well. When she got to the shop, Wayne lay on the ground, his head in Matt's arms. Wayne just felt faint and went to the ground. Matt was the first to reach him and sent Charlie to find his grandmother.

"What happened Wayne?" B.J asked as she bent over him. She took his head from Matt and started wiping the dirt from the side of his face with her apron. Wayne looked into her eyes and smiled.

"You fret too much, B.J., I'm okay, just a little overheated and it made me lightheaded. I'll be fine after I've rested a little."

"I've told you that you work too hard. We'll get you inside in the cool and Matt can go for the Doctor. Charlie, you and Matt lift him. I don't want him walking till the doctor checks him out."

"That's nonsense, I can walk by myself. There is no need for all this fuss. Charlie, Matt, put me down now."

"Can't go against the bosses orders, Mr. Wayne, she said lift you and lift you we are, so just quit fighting us and we will have you in the house in jest a few seconds."

Charlie and Matt had Wayne up in their arms and half way across the yard before he could say another word. B.J. stood on the porch with the door open and waiting for them. They carried Wayne to their bedroom and B.J. told him to lie there till she came back. She closed the door when she came out and told Matt to take the pickup and go for the doctor as fast as he could. Then she went back in the bedroom to find Wayne lying right where they had put him.

"Now, let me get those dirty clothes off you and bathe you off a little. That way the doctor want know you're such a crud." B.J. started with Wayne's boots, and then she unbuttoned his shirt and pants and took them off. Wayne let her fuss over him, he knew once she had her mind made up, there was no need trying to buck her.

"You sure are brave, undressing me like this and me already in the bed." Wayne tried to make a joke to hide how bad he was feeling, but B.J. could tell that he was extra tired for this time of day, and it worried her the anguished look she saw ever so often on his face.

"You don't know how brave I am? If that doctor tells me you're faking this just to get extra attention, I'll show you how brave I really am." B.J smiled at him, trying not to let on how worried she really was and trying to pass time till the doctor got there. She walked to the window and opened it to let in the cool summer breeze, but also to look for the doctor. There was no sign of the car. She prayed silently, "Lord, please let Wayne be okay till the doctor gets here."

"Wayne, I've been thinking, you need to retire and let Charlie and Matt run things now. We need to spend more time together, just doing what we want to do."

"We do all we want to do, and I don't have that much business anymore. Matt has just about taken over running the place. He does what has to be done without even being told. All that's left is the books and it wouldn't hurt to show him about them. B.J. I would go bunkers if I didn't have something to keep me busy. If it will make you feel better, I'll promise to slow down a little."

She reached over and kissed him on the mouth and that same feeling came to her, the feeling she had when she first kissed him over fifty-two years ago. It thrilled her now just as it did then. Wayne was her life. Sure she had her children, her grandchildren, but he was her life. He was her mate, her lover, and her best friend all these years and she wasn't ready to live without him. "Lord, please don't let anything happen to him. Take me first; I don't think I can stand being left without him."

About that time B.J. hard the car and pickup pull up. She went to the top of the stairs to meet the doctor and tell him about Wayne. Matt had already told the doctor what had happened so he brushed her aside and went right to the bed to Wayne.

"Well, let's listen to you for a minute. Just take a few deep breaths for me. Okay, do you hurt anywhere?' The doctor was holding Wayne's wrist and looking at his watch counting his pulse at the same time. When he finished, he looked back to Wayne. "What did you feel just before you got weak and fell to the ground?"

"My arm hurt and sorta up the side of my neck, doc."

"Did your chest feel tight and heavy, like someone squeezing the breath out of you?"

"Yea, sorta. It only lasted a few minutes, but it sure sapped me of my energy."

"Well, I can say without a doubt that you just experienced a mild heart attack."

The doctor motioned for B.J to come to the bedside. "Now, Wayne was lucky this time. He might not be the next time, so you have got to keep him in bed for a couple of weeks. This might be the end of your heavy lifting and smitty work for awhile. I'm gonna give B.J some medicine for you to take and you do just as she tells you for two weeks. I'll be back to see you in a couple of days."

"Thank you, doctor." Wayne said as he laid back on his pillow.

B.J. and the doctor left the room and went downstairs where Matt and Charlie, along with Sue Lei and Kim stood waiting for the news. The doctor repeated what he had told B.J. and Wayne upstairs and told the two men not to let Wayne lift anything for at least a month. He took two bottles of pills from his bag and gave them to B.J.

"These will relax him so he won't fight you about staying in bed and the other one is to thin his blood and hopefully keep him from having another heart attack. Make sure he takes both each day. I'll stop by in a couple of days, but if you need me before then, send for me."

"Thank you, doctor." B.J walked the doctor to the door and when she returned she could see the worried look on Matt and Charlie's faces. "He's gonna be fine. It was just a mild one and we found him in time, so don't worry, he'll be up and about in no time."

"Memaw, do we need to call Dad and Aunt Lynn?' Matt asked.

"No, let's not worry them just now. Tomorrow may look a lot brighter for Papaw and all of us, if not, and then we'll call." B.J. looked to Sue Lei who already had a glass of cool water for Wayne to take his pills with. B.J took it form her and started back up the stairs to him.

When She opened the door, Wayne lay there with his eyes closed. Her heart all but stopped. She hurried to the bedside and when she brushed the bed, he opened his eyes and smiled at her.

"Scared you a bit, didn't I? Sorry, hon. Are those the pills I'm supposed to take?' Wayne held out his hand and took both of them with a long drink of the water.

"Wayne, you're gonna be fine if you do like the doctor says. I'm gonna see to it that you do. We were lucky this time, God had given you another chance and we're gonna thank Him for it for a long time." B.J. fluffed his pillow and straightened his sheet.

"B.J. quit fussing over me. I'm tired and of you will go downstairs, I'll catch me a nap, then tonight, after I've rested, we'll see who is the bravest."

She reached down and kissed him, and told him to call if he needed anything.

B.J left Wayne and went out on the porch to sit in the cool afternoon breeze. She sat looking out across the green pastures and thinking back on the years that had passed since she first set foot on this piece of land. The years had been hard in the beginning, but they had been happy ones. Grady, Uncle Webster, and she had ridden onto this special piece of land purposely to plant their roots, and they had. She was the only one left of the three, but there were strong memories of them in her mind. The Lord had blessed this land and He continues to bless us daily. She knew from what had just happened to Wayne today. She thanked the Lord again for His blessings.

Chapter 27

Wayne's days of recovering were over. Today was his first day out of bed, and he was eager to get going. B.J. and Matt helped him dress and get his boots on, and then Matt made Wayne take his arm and slowly stand up by the side of the bed till he lost the rubbery feeling in his legs. Wayne was anxious to go downstairs, but in his heart he knew it would be an effort to accomplish. Two weeks he had laid in the bed and it had taken a lot out of him. He took advantage of Matt's strong arms and slowly made his way down each step.

Once at the bottom, Wayne had to stop and rest a bit. B.J. brought him a chair and Wayne sat down for a few minutes, and then he was up and at it again. It was as though he had to prove, not only to B.J. and Matt, but to himself, that he could do this. They made it to the front porch and he rested again in the rocker. Matt stayed with Wayne each step of the way. This experience had brought the two real close. The past few weeks they were almost inseparable.

Matt had asked B.J. several times about calling his Dad, but she held him off. B.J. didn't want to worry her son unnecessarily.

"Matt, I'm ready for the barn if you are."

"Don't you think the porch is enough for today Papaw?"

"Oh, I'm fine. I've got to get my strength back, and the only way I'm gonna do it is to move about more."

B.J. stood up, making sure Wayne got her message real good. "Wayne, maybe Matt is right, maybe you've done enough for today. Let's take it one day at a time, tomorrow you can try for the barn."

Wayne nodded, he knew she was right, so he sat back down in his rocker and told them okay. He was tired to his bones, but he never let them know it. He leaned back in his rocker and just sat enjoying the breeze from the cottonwood trees.

"B.J., this place has been good to us. How long has it been since you and Uncle Webster and Grady settled this place?"

"Well, let me think, it's been fifty-four years since we first rode on this land. Don't seem like it, but yet it does. I hope it stays in the family that much longer. We've put in a lot of hard work during those years. Remember the first herd of mares that Dude, God rest his soul, brought to our door. That's what got us started, and that and you being smart enough to invest in cattle. Matt, you should have been with us back then; we had a time around here. Why with the bears, Indians, mountain lions, and the wild stallion, and God only knows what else, I wonder sometimes how er ever made it."

"I would have loved being here Memaw. I love hearing you and papaw talk about the old days."

"You're the only one of our grandchildren that loves this place like we do. I guess it will be your some day. We've put aside money for the other grandchildren, but this ranch will be yours and I hope you will see to it that it stays in the family from now on. Course, that means you'll have to find you a wife and the two of you will have to have children to pass it on too."

"Memaw, I'm gonna find a wife when the times comes, but right now, I'm just trying to learn all I can about this place and how to make it even better."

B.J never realized she and Matt had been talking so long until she looked at Wayne. First she thought he was asleep. His head was resting on the back of the rocker and his eyes were closed.

"Wayne, you want to go back to bed?"

Wayne didn't respond. Matt straightened in his chair and leaned over to his Papaw and shook him by the arm. Wayne still didn't respond. Matt jumped up, about the same time B.J. did and they both felt for a pulse. There was none. Wayne was gone.

B.J. screamed Wayne's name as she grabbed him to herself and hugged him close. Why had she sat there talking like a fool and not checking on him? Lord forgive me, I thought he was napping and all the time he left me to be with You. She could hear Matt scrambling to the phone, calling the doctor, telling him to come at once, but she knew that it would not make any difference now.

Matt returned to the porch to find Luke and Charlie there with B.J. They had her scream and stood looking on, feeling so helpless. Their hearts went out to B.J., and as she straightened up, she told the men to lift Wayne and take him to his bed. B.J. followed. Sue Lei stood with Kim in the hallway as the men passed carrying Wayne, and both were crying.

The doctor came as fast as he could. He offered his condolences to B.J. and Matt and said. "Wayne's heart just quit on him. He didn't suffer, he was with the two he loved the most and he was where he wanted to be. It was bound to happen again, no matter how careful he was, his heart was just worn out. I don't want either of you blaming yourselves. B.J., you gonna be okay? Matt you call your folks and do whatever needs to be done for her; I'll take care of things in town."

The undertaker came that evening with the Preacher. The doctor had stopped and told each of them. Charlie and Luke let the rest of the neighbors know and then they went to the little cemetery to take care of Wayne's final resting place.

B.J. went to the bedroom where Wayne lay and sat by his bedside. She reached over and straightened his wavy hair. Her Wayne, yes he was her Wayne, but now he was gone and she was left behind, without even a chance to say goodbye. It was then her tears came. She wept long and hard, her sobs racked her small body. She remembered other times that she had cried this hard, over her parents, over the loss of Grady, and Uncle Webster and their unborn baby. B.J. laid her head against Wayne's now silent heart, the heart that had beat for her once, but never again. She wept more tears.

The children and grandchildren came home for the funeral. There was a quiet group this time. Then all the neighbors, the Brooks, The Donilsons, and all the people that Wayne had ever done business with or helped in any way, showed up to pay their respects. They came and went, the hours turned to days and then the final day arrived. The little church would not hold all of them, so the service was held outdoors. Again and again, B.J. hears the words: "I'm so sorry. He was such a good man." Yes, her Wayne was a good Christian man but B.J. hated the past tense, for her he would always be her good man, and she carried that in her heart from then on.

Afterwards the children took B.J. home and made her eat something. Sue Lei brought her a cup of hot tea. The children fussed and pampered over her. It wasn't that B.J. wasn't grateful, but none of it helped. She felt empty. She wasn't sure if anyone understood how much she had lost. She had just buried a big part of herself.

Dale was the first to approach her with a question that caught B.J. totally off guard. "What are you gonna do now, Mom?"

"Whatever do you mean?"

"Are you gonna stay here?"

"Certainly, I've been here most of my life. Why wouldn't I stay here?"

"But you're on your on, now. Don't you want to come and live with Dianne and me in Cheyenne?"

"Matt is here with me, there's Kim and Sue Lei, Charlie and the other men, why do you say I'm on my own? Dale, I know you mean well, but this is the only home I've known, and I'm not about to leave it now. Your Dad would not want me leaving him here alone, so this is where I'll be until you put me next to him on that hill up there."

Her family knew that her mind was made up and there was no need to mention the subject again. Matt would be there for her and he would let them know if they were needed, so each of them began making plans to go back to their respected homes the next morning.

B.J. knew it was going to be lonely in the big house, but she also knew this was where she was the happiest. After watching the last carload drive away, Matt hugged her close and asked if she was okay. B.J. nodded, knowing she couldn't speak for fear of crying. Matt then walked out to the barn where he would grieve in private the death of his grandfather. B.J. went inside and sat down in her rocker in front of the fire and she cried for the longest. She felt totally drained. She couldn't help but wonder if she would ever feel alive again.

B.J. made herself go to their bedroom. How empty it seemed without Wayne's big form being there with her. His bright eyes, his smile and his strong arms that she felt each night were gone from her forever. She recalled their nightly devotion and went to the table where their Bible lay. B.J. picked it up and without even turning a page it automatically opened to Romans 8:28, "And we know that all things work together for good to them that love God, to them who are called according to His purpose." (KJV)

B.J. wasn't sure how or when it happened, but somehow, slowly the days slipped by with the routine of living and she triumphed over her loss. Life had to go on for the living and God had given her peace in her heart about this. She lived to bury a lot of loved ones on this land, but there was still a lot of love left here to share with others, so with that in mind, she resolved to take each day the Lord saw fit to give her and live it to its fullest.

One day Matt came to her wanting her to come to the barn to see something special. She slowly followed him. He was running the ranch totally now and doing a good job of it. They entered the big, cool barn that B.J. always liked, smelling of hay and feed and the best smell in the world to her was the smell of horses. Matt took her by the hand and led her to one of the stalls. He didn't say a word, just pointed and when B.J. looked in that direction, she smiled for the first time in months.

There in front of them stood a miniature Dude. He was just like his father, his color, statue, built and all just in miniature size. The little stallion had just been born, still moist from his mother licking him clean. B.J. felt pride well up inside her and she fought to keep her tears of joy hid from Matt. They stood silent and watched as the colt wobbled over to get his first meal.

"Matt, he is special. He takes after Dude. Almost the spitting image of him. He is yours. You deserve him and he deserves you because the two of you will keep this ranch going from now on. I loved Dude; it was him that helped us build this ranch into what it is today."

"What should I name him?"

"That's up to you, but to me he'll always be Little Dude."

"Then that's what he will be called, "Little Dude", if it's okay with you?"

"Okay. It's perfect. This is exactually what this place needs, new life, and the two of you will be supplying it."

B.J and her grandson Matt stood watching the little reincarnation of the original Dude suck his mama. B.J. reached over and patted Matt's hand and he put his strong arm around her thin frail shoulder, and they walked back to the house together. Now she could feel assured the Rocking H Ranch was in capable hands that would see to its future. B.J. knew the Rocking H had triumphed.